PRAISE FOR BAI

THE GODDESSES OF ~~.....~~ *AVENUE*

"[O'Neal's] characters are warmly drawn and sympathetic, their problems real and believable."

—*Publishers Weekly*

THIS PLACE OF WONDER

"*This Place of Wonder* is a wonderfully moving tale about four women whose journeys are all connected by one shared love: some are romantic, some are familial, but all are deeply complicated. Dealing with loss, love, hidden secrets, and second chances, this stirring tale is utterly engaging and ultimately hopeful. Set along the rugged California coastline, *This Place of Wonder* will sweep you away with the intoxicating scents, bold flavors, and sweeping views of the region and transport you to a world you won't be in any hurry to leave."

—Colleen Hoover, #1 *New York Times* bestselling author

"Kristin Hannah readers will thoroughly enjoy the family dynamic, especially the mother-daughter relationships."

—*Booklist* (starred review)

"Barbara O'Neal's latest novel is simply delicious. Engrossing, empathetic, and profoundly moving, I savored every sentence of this story of several very different women who find solace and second chances in each other after tragedy (though not before facing some hard truths and, yes, a few rock bottoms). *This Place of Wonder* is one of the best books I've read in a long time."

—Camille Pagán, bestselling author of *Everything Must Go*

"I have never much moved in the elevated circles of California farm-to-table cuisine, but O'Neal makes me feel like I'm there. Rather than simply skewering the pretensions, *This Place of Wonder* pinpoints the passions. Some of these characters have been elevated to celebrity, some are newcomers to the scene, but all are drawn together by the sensuality, the excitement, and ultimately the care that food brings them. Elegiac but also forward-looking, this is a book about eating, but more than that, it's a book about hurt and healing and women finding their way together. I loved every moment of it."

—Julie Powell, author of *Julie & Julia* and *Cleaving*

WRITE MY NAME ACROSS THE SKY

"Barbara O'Neal weaves an irresistible tale of creativity, forgery, family, and the FBI in *Write My Name Across the Sky*. Willow and Sam are fascinating, and their aunt Gloria is my dream of an incorrigible, glamorous older woman."

—Nancy Thayer, bestselling author of *Family Reunion*

"*Write My Name Across the Sky* is an exquisitely crafted novel of three remarkable women from two generations grappling with decisions of the past and the consequences of where those young, impetuous choices have led. A heartfelt story of passion, devotion, and family told as only Barbara O'Neal can."

—Suzanne Redfearn, #1 Amazon bestselling author of *In an Instant*

"With its themes of creativity and art, *Write My Name Across the Sky* is itself like a masterfully executed painting. Using refined brushstrokes, O'Neal builds her vivid, complex characters: three independent women in one family who can't quite come to terms with their fierce feelings of love for one another. O'Neal deftly switches between three points of view, adding layers of family history into this intimate and satisfying study of how women make tough choices between love and creativity and family and freedom."

—Glendy Vanderah, *Washington Post* bestselling author of
Where the Forest Meets the Stars

THE LOST GIRLS OF DEVON

One of *Travel + Leisure*'s most anticipated books of summer 2020

"A woman's strange disappearance brings together four strong women who struggle with their relationships, despite their need for one another. Fans of Sarah Addison Allen will appreciate the emphasis on nature and these women's unique gifts in this latest by the author of *When We Believed in Mermaids*."

—*Library Journal* (starred review)

"*The Lost Girls of Devon* draws us into the lives of four generations of women as they come to terms with their relationships and a mysterious tragedy that brings them together. Written in exquisite prose with the added bonus of the small Devon village as a setting, Barbara O'Neal's book will ensnare the reader from the first page, taking us on an emotional journey of love, loss, and betrayal."

—Rhys Bowen, *New York Times* and #1 Kindle bestselling author of
The Tuscan Child, In Farleigh Field, and the Royal Spyness series

"*The Lost Girls of Devon* is one of those novels that grabs you at the beginning with its imagery and rich language and won't let you go. Four generations of women deal with the pain and betrayal of the past, and Barbara O'Neal skillfully leads us to understand all of their deepest needs and fears. To read a Barbara O'Neal novel is to fall into a different world—a world of beauty and suspense, of tragedy and redemption. This one, like her others, is spellbinding."

—Maddie Dawson, bestselling author of *A Happy Catastrophe*

WHEN WE BELIEVED IN MERMAIDS

"An emotional story about the relationship between two sisters and the difficulty of facing the truth head-on."

—*Today*

"There's a reason Barbara O'Neal is one of the most decorated authors in fiction. With her trademark lyrical style, she's written a page-turner of the first order. From the very first page, I was drawn into the drama and irresistibly teased along as layers of a family's complicated past were artfully peeled away. Don't miss this masterfully told story of sisters and secrets, damage and redemption, hope and healing."

—Susan Wiggs, #1 *New York Times* bestselling author

"More than a mystery, Barbara O'Neal's *When We Believed in Mermaids* is a story of childhood—and innocence—lost, and the long-hidden secrets, lies, and betrayals two sisters must face in order to make themselves whole as adults. Plunge in and enjoy the intriguing depths of this passionate, lustrous novel, and you just might find yourself believing in mermaids."

—Juliet Blackwell, *New York Times* bestselling author of *The Lost Carousel of Provence*, *Letters from Paris*, and *The Paris Key*

"In *When We Believed in Mermaids*, Barbara O'Neal draws us into the story with her crisp prose, well-drawn settings, and compelling characters, in whom we invest our hearts as we experience the full range of human emotion and, ultimately, celebrate their triumph over the past."

—Grace Greene, author of *The Memory of Butterflies* and the
Wildflower House series

"*When We Believed in Mermaids* is a deftly woven tale of two sisters, separated by tragedy and reunited by fate, discovering that the past isn't always what it seems. By turns shattering and life affirming, as luminous and mesmerizing as the sea by which it unfolds, this is a book club essential—definitely one for the shelf!"

—Kerry Anne King, bestselling author of *Whisper Me This*

THE ART OF INHERITING SECRETS

"Great writing, terrific characters, food elements, romance, a touch of intrigue, and more than a few surprises to keep readers guessing."

—*Kirkus Reviews*

"Settle in with tea and biscuits for a charming adventure about inheriting an English manor and the means to restore it. Vivid descriptions and characters that read like best friends will stay with you long after this delightful story has ended."

—Cynthia Ellingsen, bestselling author of *The Lighthouse Keeper*

"*The Art of Inheriting Secrets* is the story of one woman's journey to uncovering her family's hidden past. Set against the backdrop of a sprawling English manor, this book is ripe with mystery. It will have you guessing until the end!"

—Nicole Meier, author of *The House of Bradbury* and
The Girl Made of Clay

"O'Neal's clever title begins an intriguing journey for readers that unfolds layer by surprising layer. Her respected masterful storytelling blends mystery, art, romance, and mayhem in a quaint English village and breathtaking countryside. Brilliant!"

—Patricia Sands, bestselling author of the Love in Provence series

The Goddesses of Kitchen Avenue

The Goddesses of Kitchen Avenue

a novel

BARBARA O'NEAL

LAKE UNION

PUBLISHING

Text copyright © 2004, 2014, 2024 by Barbara Samuel
All rights reserved.

Published by Lake Union Publishing, Seattle

www.apub.com

Amazon, the Amazon logo, and Lake Union Publishing are trademarks of Amazon.com, Inc., or its affiliates.

ISBN-13: 9781662521324 (paperback)
ISBN-13: 9781662521331 (digital)

Cover design by Shasti O'Leary Soudant
Cover images: © Alina Hvostikova / Stocksy; © sinoptic / Shutterstock; © Hannah Robinson Photos / Shutterstock

Printed in the United States of America

For my brother and his wife, Jim and Michelle Hair. Thanks for making room for me, taking care of me, making me laugh, giving me things to do and a place to hide. Thanks for the beers and the good company and the quiet acceptance. Thanks for April and thanks for Jack, the two best dogs in the universe.
And a special kiss to Jessie. It's so nice to finally have you here on earth.

JULY

Kali

Kali is depicted with black skin. She wears a necklace of skulls, carries a knife to cut through illusion, a mirror of reflection and drinks from a skull cup of blood. She stands above her disemboweled lover, phallus erect, his blood feeding the earth. Her visage is terrifying. She is loved and feared for her destructive powers, for she is both womb and tomb simultaneously.

—www.goddess.com.au

PROLOGUE

Trudy

The first time I see Lucille again, I am lying in my bed. Alone. My newly broken arm is propped on a pillow. It's very late, close to dawn. My face is hot from crying and loss and Vicodin, which they gave me at the emergency room. The drugs are not appreciably helping stop the pain in my right arm, which is imprisoned in a cast to my elbow. It's red. The cast, that is. Probably the arm, too, which feels like coyotes are chewing on it. And the world seems red, too, all around the edges.

When I open my eyes, Lucille is sitting in the chair where Rick always throws his clothes. She looks exactly the same, which should tip me off that something is slightly wrong, but in my current state, nothing seems real, so I just blink at her for a long minute.

It's been twenty-five years since I've seen her. She's wearing a shawl that a matador gave her, red with black silk fringes she plays with. There are heavy silver bracelets on her tanned arms, and she's drinking a cocktail. It's funny enough that I smile. Lucille always did believe in cocktails. My mother said she was a drunk, but she wasn't. I knew even then that my mother was just afraid of Lucille. Afraid of her sexuality, afraid of her courage, afraid of her version of womanhood. Afraid it would leak out of her house somehow, like bad water, to poison the whole neighborhood. My mother and her friends, all the ladies on the block, said terrible things about Lucille's clothes—gossamer blouses that showed her low-cut bras, the sleek way she wore her hair and let all of her back show, nape to waist, on summer days. She told me it was a woman's secret power, her back. It didn't age the way other parts might.

Men found reasons to stop by her yard when she was working with her flowers, the flowers she nudged like magic daughters from the hard ground in the desert. Poppies as big as sombreros, waving long, black, inviting stamens from their silky hearts, and roses in impossible colors, and cosmos by the thousands.

The men stopped to admire her back. And her strong brown arms, and the glimpse of her lacy bras.

But mostly they stopped to hear that wild, bold poppy laugh come out of her throat. Stopped to have her admire them. Stopped to be watered by her joy.

She was sixty-six years old when she moved into our neighborhood.

Now it has been twenty-five years and she's at the foot of my bed, not in some ghostly form, but as solid as the cat purring on my hip. When she doesn't say anything, I swallow the rawness in my throat and croak, "What are you doing here?"

"Time to take it back, kiddo."

"What?"

"Your life."

OCTOBER

Hecate

Hecate completes the goddess triad of the Maiden (Persephone), the Mother (Demeter) and the Wise Woman (Hecate). She walks between the seen and unseen world but resides in neither, carrying a flaming torch so she can see where others can't—into the human psyche. She is accompanied by her dog (or horse), her sacred animals, and offers her magical protection in times of danger.

If you have that sense of foreboding sitting in your solar plexus, it may be that you are standing at a crossroad, and are unsure about where you need to go next. Rest assured that Hecate is walking alongside you, carrying her torch with which to guide you.

—www.goddess.com.au

1

Roberta

Sunday, October 25, 20—

Dear Harriet,
My hands are shaky as the leaves on the trees today.
Hope you can read this all right. I hate seeing that
I've got old lady handwriting. But then, it stands to
reason, doesn't it? How'd we get so old?

It's Sunday and I ain't been to church. Been sitting
here all morning by my Edgar, trying to get enough
courage up to let him go. I sent everybody away—all
the parishioners who been bringing greens and pots of
stew and washing up my dishes while I sit with him.
Sent even the children away. They can all come back
later, when I've gone and done what I need to do.

Sister, I been here all morning and can't open up
my mouth to say it. *Go on, Edgar. I'll be all right.* He's
just waiting for that, because when he fell into this
coma, I grabbed his old hand and begged him not to
leave me.

And he's such a good man, he's holding on. There,
now I'm crying again.

I been holding his hand for sixty-two years. This morning, I was holding it and remembering that morning he first came to our back door, asking for a drink of water. Remember? He'd been down on his luck, but he was so proud. He looked so good in the sunshine with his pretty head and that strong old nose. My heart flipped clean over and I wasn't but fifteen. I've had no use for any other man since that day.

I been remembering all of it this morning. Wondering how it would of been if we'd stayed back there in Mississippi with all y'all. Wondering what it was he saw in Italy that made him never talk about it his whole life long. Wondering if we'd of had as good a life if we hadn't come west to Pueblo, where we've been so peaceful. Home of the Heroes. Did you know they call it that nowdays? Fitting. Edgar put away all his medals, but he was sure proud when the Medal of Honor winners all came here. He put on his best suit that morning, and went down to listen to them, all four old men like him. I went along with him, of course, but I didn't hear what he did. I asked him one time if it was so bad as all that, and he just bowed his head and said, *Worse.*

So I just let it be.

And he's not a perfect man, not by any means. He was too stern with the children, fussy about things as he got old, wanting every little thing his way. We've had our share of dark times, too, times when I wanted to take a meat cleaver to his stubborn old head. Once or twice, he hurt my heart, but he never did it on purpose.

It's not those times I'm thinking of now, though. I'm remembering how hard we could laugh, so much that Edgar would get to wheezing. I'm thinking about waking up morning after morning after morning with him lying beside me. Listening to him, whistling as he fiddled with a television dead but for the magic he gave it with his clever mind.

Lord, give me strength. I have got to let him go. He's withering away right in front of my eyes. But I'm telling you the truth, sister, I'm going, too. I asked the Lord to take me. Y'all know I love you, but you, sister, know my life won't be nothing without him.

Your sister,

Berta

2

Trudy

When Edgar dies, I am next door in my house, reading Lorca with my hands over my ears so I don't have to hear the wind. It's only because I have to take them down to turn the page that I hear Roberta's cry, that piercing wail that can only be called keening.

It's been a long day, waiting for this. Because I wanted to be here when the moment arrived, I didn't go to the movies or out to the mall to distract myself from my own troubles. Roberta's granddaughter, Jade, is on her way to Pueblo from California, but she isn't here yet, and Roberta sent everybody else away. When the moment comes, she'll need someone. So I've waited. Trying to keep warm—I'm wearing a T-shirt, a cotton sweater and a wool one, two pairs of socks, and jeans—and I'm still cold. It's like Rick was my furnace, and without him, I'm turning into an icicle.

And the wind is driving me crazy.

People often tell me how much they love the wind. I've sat, with my mouth open, while friends from elsewhere—they are always from somewhere else—rhapsodize about the winds they know, and I can tell that they're thinking of an entirely different entity—a green goddess, trailing her veils over the beach or through the forest. They love a wind that comes with moisture and beauty.

In Pueblo, our winds are of the Inquisition variety, winds that know that the secret of torture is to begin and end, to be inconstant and constant at once, to bellow and to whisper. Endlessly.

This year, it's been even worse than usual. Every morning, it gathers, gusting and stopping. Blasting and quitting. All day, it bangs on the windows and blusters around the car and buffets the trees and tears at the shrubs. Boxes blown from who knows where skitter down the street. There is no surface without grit. Static electricity can knock you down. I play music, loudly, to drown it out, put a pillow over my head at night.

But not today. I have to listen for Roberta.

For lunch, I pour some condensed chicken and stars soup into a pot and put the kettle on for tea, huddling next to the burners with my hands tucked under my armpits. The tea is indifferent, the soup the last can on the shelf. I was lucky to find that much worth consuming, really, since I keep forgetting to go to the grocery store. Right now, when I'm hungry for something better than the cupboards have to offer, I look around for my list so I can write good tea bags on there, but it's gone missing. Again. I can't keep track of anything lately.

I used to spend at least two hours a week planning menus and shopping for my crew of five. Now it's only me and my seventeen-year-old, Annie, but more often than not she eats at school or at her restaurant job or with her boyfriend, Travis. As long as I keep milk and cereal and frozen pizzas around, she's covered.

I keep forgetting that it might be good for me to cook for myself. Nobody ever liked the same foods I do—my roasted veggie dishes and exotic soups. Time to indulge. On my new list, I write, garlic, marinated pepper strips, lemon juice, whole pepper. Frozen quiches. Cheddar (the good one), Triscuits.

I won't forget the single-serving cans of tuna, which have been the mainstay of my diet lately. It's easy, and at least the cats get enthusiastic when they hear me pop the lid. I always pour the water off into a bowl for them. They are immensely grateful and I can glow over it for a good five minutes, standing at the counter eating out of the can.

I know, I know. Cats, tuna—this has all the earmarks of a Bad End.

The kettle whistles and I pour water into my cup, think maybe I'm just getting old. Bones thinning along with my skin, muscles withering away to nothing. I think of my granny, wizened down to broomstick size, and pull my sweater tighter around my torso.

Not old, not old, not old. Not at forty-six. Forty-six is young these days, or at least just beyond the cusp of middle age.

Wind blusters against the windows, and I hear the sound of the chimes my new neighbor hung on his porch. His things appeared abruptly overnight three days ago, like the plumage of some exotic bird—a trio of chimes strung across the porch, a cluster of sticks and painted canvas in the side yard that promised quiet and other things, a foreign car I thought might be an English Mini, strange and small and orange. A *ristra*, cheery, bright-red chiles in a string, hung by the door, nothing strange by itself. But it almost seemed that there was a new scent in the air, spice and chocolate and the promise of fresh yeast. Shannelle, the young mother across the street, said she'd glimpsed him, and widened her eyes to illustrate her amazement.

I move to the window to peer out. My breath makes a thick circle of condensation on the glass. At first I can only see the car, a blurry round like a giant pumpkin, so I wipe away the fog and cover my mouth with my fingers. As if called by my curiosity, he comes out on the porch.

Oh.

Despite the cold, he wears no shoes, and only some Ecuadorean-style pajama bottoms riding low on hips the color of a sticky bun. Hair runs in a fine line up the center of his belly like a stripe of cinnamon. Heavy silver bracelets cuff his dark wrists. A necklace of claws, something made in a jungle, hangs around his neck.

He stretches, showing the tufts of hair beneath his arms. I find myself holding my breath with him, letting it out again only when he lowers his chin and, in an insouciant gesture, tosses back his hair to show his face. It looks good from this distance, a high brow and wide mouth. Hair, thick and wavy, pours down to his shoulders in a tangle of honey and butter.

I half expect him to look my way, feel my gaze like some magic being, but he only bends over to pick up a newspaper and goes back inside.

Lazy thing, I think, *sleeping until past noon.*

I carry my tea and soup into the dining room, put down a place mat on the table even though there's no strict need for it. It's not as if the table needs protecting—it's ancient and beautiful, if scarred from twenty-some years of family dinners—but I like the homey look of the floral pattern against the wood. I think it might be for show, in case any-one happens by, a way to demonstrate that I'm doing just fine, but that's okay, too. I get a matching napkin out of the drawer and center every-thing on the mat, look for a magazine to read, trying to recapture the sense of well-being such old rituals used to give me when Rick went off riding with his buddy Joe Zamora, and the kids were at friends' houses or skating or whatever. In those days, time alone was a luxury—I'd put on some music no one else liked and fix some soup only I would eat, like my very special corn chowder, and read in the blissful aloneness.

But the evening looms. The house thunders with emptiness. How could my old life be over so suddenly that after years and years of never having a minute to draw my breath now I have so much time that I feel myself sinking into it like quicksand, drowning in it?

A mother finished. A wife dismissed.

Cliché-city.

"God, Trudy," I say to myself aloud, since there's no one else to say it to. "You are boring me to death now. Do something."

So I find the collection of Lorca's poems, which I've been reading in an attempt to renew my acquaintance with Spanish—a passion I left behind somewhere. His work is appropriate to accompany the sound of Roberta's singing that comes to me between bursts of wind. The houses are not that far apart and she's got one of those big gospel kinds of voices, like Aretha Franklin, though she pooh-poohs that comparison.

I knew when I heard her that she was singing her husband Edgar's favorites for him.

One last time.

Letting him go at last. He's been in a diabetic coma for two weeks, since just after supper one Friday night. I was sitting with her when it happened—he'd been sick for a while, pieces of his body just eaten away by the disease—and she grabbed his hand, and cried out, "Edgar, don't you leave me!" in such a heartbroken voice that I had to go home and cry about it later.

The hospice workers and the nurse who came in every day kept saying they didn't know what in the world was keeping him alive. But I knew. So did Roberta.

The cry comes again, a wild piercing wail, the sound of her soul tearing in half. I put down my book, put my hand to my chest, and let it move through me. In a minute, I will stand up and go to her.

In a minute.

In between, I let it swell in me, the freshened sorrow that her grief brings. My husband is not dead, just in love with somebody else, but I'm mourning him all the same, and my heart joins in Roberta's howl, as if we're a pair of coyotes. My wrist, out of the cast now for a couple of weeks, starts throbbing, and I put my other hand around it protectively.

Roberta. I put on my shoes and coat and hurry over to her house.

3

Shannelle

TO: Hopefuls@yahoogroups.com

FROM: chanelpacheco@hotmail.com

SUBJECT: How I find time

On October 11, 20—, Joanne Reed wrote:

>>>how do you guys find time to DO the writing????
I'm having such a hard time lately!<<<

Joanne—I love football season! My husband's buddies think he's the luckiest guy in the world because I make him go watch the games somewhere else. Every Sunday afternoon and most Monday nights, he puts on his Bronco coat and his Bronco jersey and goes out to his brother's house or to the Riverside so I can get my work done. I love it! This weekend, I have written nearly twenty pages on a new story!!

Shannelle

~

TO: naomiredding@rtsv.org

FROM: chanelpacheco@hotmail.com

SUBJECT: More on recent inspiration

Hi, Naomi! I don't mind the lowercase at all—carpal tunnel seems to be the worst thing of all. I'm glad you're getting the surgery.

Yeah, my tooth still hurts, but I have had many toothaches and have learned to manage them. I can't afford to waste the time Tony is at the games. He's so jealous of the writing, as if it is a lover who will steal me away, a seductive Other who has some mysterious claim on me. In a way, I suppose it's true—writing satisfies me on some level that nothing else can. I am lonely when I have no time for it, lonely for the sounds of words rolling through my mind, lonely for the sights only I can see, lonely for the people I meet on the page. When I tried to explain it to him, he was worried that I might be mentally ill! He asked me how it is different to hear voices as a schizophrenic (he works at State Hospital) than as a writer. I did not have a good answer for him.

Anyway, it spares me anxiety to simply do the writing when he is not around. I do sneak in here now and then when he's asleep, but not too often. It would be nice if I could quit the bowling alley, but then I couldn't pay for day care, and I'm getting quite a bit done on Tues and Thurs, when my youngest is at the babysitter's.

Got a new rejection on the ghost story last Friday. (I can't tell you how I've learned to hate seeing my own handwriting on an envelope!) It was a good one, a personal note from the editor, but she said many of the same things I have heard before—much praise on voice and tone, but too "different." She did not know how she would publish it, as young adult or mainstream or horror, said that it did not quite fit the constructs of any of them.

I felt so frustrated that I used your advice—I ran a huge tub of water and poured in some bubbles (all I had was Mr. Bubble, but it created quite an exuberant tub of foam!) and had a good cry. It helped. I had hoped that I might have been on track a little more with this one, but I guess it's just not time yet. I've written quite a bit on the new one—another ghost story! I don't know why I always want to write ghosts!—and I like it, so that's good. How many rejections did you say you had before you sold something? Like 43 or something, right? I only have collected 16 and a half (since one was a half yes). Miles to go.

I've been rambling on and on here. Sorry. Gotta get to work now. Talk to you soon!

Love,
Shannelle, your ever-grateful fan and friend

~

TO: chanelpacheco@hotmail.com

FROM: naomiredding@rtsv.org

SUBJECT: tooth and men and other troubles

hugs on the rejection. just remember you have loads of talent and more gumption than 99% of all the people i've ever met and i know you're going to make it in this game if you just hang in there. the piece on your neighbor was one of the most gorgeous things you've done and i want you to keep going. he's a terrific ghost—and i lol'd at his banter. you've turned pain into humor, and that's the best kind. it doesn't matter that there are ghosts in everything—you have good reasons for that, babe, and we all get stuck with certain things—you're writing a very intelligent, comic novel and it's original and it's real and it's yours. i still have faith #3 will sell. send it out to the next one on your list.

more hugs on tony's resistance to your writing. i've heard other writers talk about a spouse's jealousy of the writing. i met lyle long after i'd established myself, so it hasn't been an issue between us. we have other issues, tho—animal issues!!

things here are so chaotic. the new puppy now weighs 48 pounds and has yet to see his 6-month birthday. my dh, who thought it would be so lovely to have this darling little pup (is that dear or damned husband today? i have no idea!!), has taken his stallion to a neighboring ranch to service the mares, so i am left to mediate fights between the puppy and the tabby, who isn't quite sure if she wants to be loved so madly; make sure the old dog isn't tearing off a puppy ear; and supply peanut butter sandwiches to the real-life children. why am I having another child, again? two children, one husband, a dog, a puppy, a cat, three horses, five goats, and six sheep were not enough to keep me amused? (at least the morning sickness is gone—thanx so much for the raspberry leaf tea idea.)

ah, but what would I write about without them?

i'm sending along an application for a writer's retreat. they have full-ride scholarships and i think you'd get in with no trouble, so as your teacher, i'm ordering you to at least apply. consider it your homework for the day.

go to the dentist!!!

love,
naomi

4

Trudy

Shannelle, the new girl—well, woman, I guess, since she has two kids and a husband—showed up at Roberta's door within minutes of my arrival. The ambulance came and went, taking Edgar's withered body to the morgue. I made phone calls to break the news gently to a list Roberta had prepared ahead of time. Now I sit with the old woman on her couch, the clock ticking loudly on the wall, as gloomy a sound as I've ever heard.

Roberta has been my next-door neighbor for sixteen years, since Rick and I moved in. She welcomed our young family with a pot roast and all the trimmings and a lemon cake that is still Rick's favorite in all the world. I'd been so tired from moving boxes and trying to keep track of the children and trying to get everything at least settled enough that we could sleep that I'd wanted to throw my arms around her and cry.

And now I sit with her for the same reason—just to be a presence when she needs one. She loved Edgar more than God, though she'd never admit it. They'd been married sixty-two years last month, and if ever there was a man worth loving, he'd been it. A true Christian, loving and real, practicing his faith in everyday ways, all the time. I think about him as I sit with Roberta, knowing she must be thinking of him, too.

No, thinking is too small a word. I'm sure her entire body is filled with him just now, every cell sliced wide open.

The clock ticks in the quiet.

It's a bright room, with big, clean mirrors and a well-dusted piano against the wall. The colors are the sunny greens and yellows of a summer afternoon, the furniture as comfortable as hammocks. She uses lemon oil to clean the wood, and Pine-Sol on the floors, a trick she swears is her secret for keeping water bugs at bay. The water table is high in the neighborhood, and the nasty, giant-size cockroaches are an eternal problem, at least for everyone except Roberta.

Roberta herself is neatly dressed, as plump and kindly looking as an old-fashioned kindergarten teacher. Her skin is smooth, thanks to the care she takes to wear a hat outdoors, and there are small pearl earrings in her lobes, and the remains of a good lipstick she put on this morning. She's tearing a tissue to tiny threads, the lint falling unnoticed to the floor. I touch her upper back gently, rub it the slightest bit.

Shannelle, perky and blonde and impossibly young, is making coffee, cutting a freshly baked coffee cake into squares for us and anyone else who might be arriving. She's humming softly under her breath as she bustles around, finding a tablecloth in one of the drawers that she shakes out and spreads on the broad dining room table, then puts out a stack of napkins, forks, spoons, cups. There's a ham in the fridge and she brings it out, unwraps it, opens a can of pineapple chunks, comes into the living room. "Roberta, where would I find the brown sugar?"

Roberta surfaces for a moment. "It's in blue Tupperware, sweetie, lower left-hand counter. You puttin' that ham in?"

"Yeah," Shannelle says. "Seemed like a good thing, with everybody comin'."

"You're a good girl." Roberta's hands still for a minute. "Will you look for me, and see if there's some greens in the freezer? Church has been bringing so much around, and I think there were greens."

"I'll look." The sound of her digging, moving, talking to herself. "Found some!" she cries. "Mustard greens, right?"

We hear a car outside, a slamming door. "See who that is, Trudy, will you? I don't want nobody from the church right this minute. They can come tomorrow."

I look through the small window cut into the door. "It's Jade." Roberta's granddaughter.

Jade lived with Roberta all through college, and I knew her well, but it's been seven or eight years since I've seen her. Back then, she was a skinny thing, bouncy and full of a sweet idealism that always touched me. She was always extraordinarily beautiful, as luminous as twilight.

That was then.

The woman rounding the car wears black boots with tall, square heels and a tailored jacket of buttery black leather. She's better than six feet tall, and strides up the walk with a no-nonsense, touch-me-not aura that is more than a little intimidating.

She is still beautiful, with those high cheekbones and elegantly cut mouth and wide-set, enormous green eyes. But she's let her hair grow and it tumbles around her shoulders in wild curls, streaked with red and gold amid the darker strands. I have great hair, don't get me wrong—it's my one wealth and I'm vain about it—but for an instant, I feel a flash of envy for such untamed extravagance. "Jade!"

She grins and rushes up the steps to throw her arms around me. "Trudy! It's so good to see you! God, you don't look a single day older, I can't believe it!"

She doesn't know, of course. How could she? She's been on the road since yesterday morning. I hug her, keep my hand on her arm as I draw her inside. "I'm afraid there's some bad news, honey."

She sees her grandmother sitting with the piles of shredded Kleenex in little tufts of snow around her feet. "Oh, Grandma!" Jade says, flowing over to Roberta. "I'm so sorry, but I'm here now."

As if she'd been waiting for this anchor, Roberta crumples over and begins to weep. Shannelle and I can go now, but I'll wait for her to finish putting the greens in the pot. Jade fetches a Librium for her grandmother and I help Shannelle—we make a pitcher of sweet tea, fill the sugar and creamer containers Roberta likes, crystal and silver. I carry in a cup of hot chocolate to Roberta. It's her favorite and she thinks it sinful to drink so much. "You need a little something," I say gently.

"Thank you, darlin'."

"I'm just gonna get my things in, Gram. Be right back." Jade looks at me. There are no tears on her face, only that mask of toughness that startles me a second time—whatever has happened in her life has been hard on her. "Would you mind helping me bring in a couple of boxes before you go? I don't want to leave them out there all night."

I nod and follow her out. A gust of wind, carrying the bone-deep chill of winter arriving, sweeps over us, blowing our hair into tangles. Jade unlocks the car and reaches into the back seat. "There isn't much. I put most of it in storage." She hands me a box that looks hurriedly packed, things just thrown in without much regard for order. "I guess you heard I'm divorced."

"I did. I'm sorry."

A shiver of almost grief crosses her face and she turns back to the car, hauls out a suitcase and a cosmetic bag. "Well, yeah, what're you gonna do? Least I got out of there." She pauses, looks at me. "You, too, huh?"

I swallow. We just filed the papers. "It'll be final the end of February."

"I'm sorry."

The wind is rustling through the box, and I put a hand over the photos about to fly away. "Yikes! Hold on or the wind will take everything."

"They're all like that." For a minute she looks flummoxed.

"It's all right. We'll just make a couple more trips."

We get the boxes and bags into her old college room, a place that must look exactly as it did when she left, degree in hand. It's cluttered with the detritus of a young woman's hopes—flowers, music posters, frills, and lace. Jade tosses off her jacket, showing arms roped with hard muscle, and with a noise of disgust, reaches for a poster of a kitten and tears it violently off the wall. I smile.

"What?"

"It helps to say fuck a lot."

She laughs. "Yeah? I'll try that."

On top of one of the boxes is a photograph of a man. "This him?" I point and wait for permission to pick it up.

Jade nods. "Dante." She sighs.

He's not particularly beautiful, a dark-skinned Black man with eyes just slightly tilted upward at the corner, but there's something about his expression, a glint, a charisma that's palpable in two dimensions. My fingertips feel it. "Whew."

"Yeah." Jade takes the picture and with another brittle move, tears it in half. "Fuck you."

I laugh and give her a short hug. "If you need anything, you know where to find me."

"Thanks. And thanks for sitting with Roberta. This is gonna be so hard for her."

I only nod.

Shannelle dashes across the street to her lamp-lit house. I move more slowly toward mine. It'll be empty still, since my daughter, Annie, won't get home from work for a couple of hours. In the air is a smell of cooking mixed with the autumn-leaf cold and it makes me lonely. I'm also hungry. I wonder if it's worth the trouble to go to the grocery store.

It isn't until I start to turn into my place that I see him, the new neighbor, coming toward me, his long hair lifting and blowing.

"Hello," he says, extending a hand. "I was getting something out of my car and saw you. It seemed a good time to introduce myself."

It's dark now, but the streetlights offer plenty of illumination for me to see his face is like something out of a dream, cat-shaped with a wide, high brow and flying eyebrows and a narrower chin. His eyes are almond-shaped and alertly lazy. It's hard to tell the color in the dark, but they're light, blue or green.

He's taking my hand, which I'm not aware of stretching out. His fingers are long, graceful. "I am Angel Santiago," he says. I can't quite place the accent—it's more fluid than the Spanish that I hear in the voices of Mexican immigrants. Maybe he's from farther south, Peru or Chile.

"Trudy Marino," I say, aware as he holds my hand loosely that I am a woman, that I have breasts beneath my four layers of clothing, and hips beneath my jeans. "I live . . . here."

"I know." He's used to his effect on women, I'm sure, and I feel stupid because he's a good fifteen years my junior. Jade will like him. Jade must have him. "I saw you earlier." He lets my hand go. "Someone died?" he asks with a soft lift of his chin toward Roberta's house.

"Yes. Edgar Williams." Suddenly, my throat is full of tears because it hits me that he's really gone, and I blink hard. "He was a very good man."

"He leaves a widow?"

"Yes. Roberta. And her granddaughter, Jade." I smile. "She's very beautiful."

"I saw her, too." He gives me a slight smile that's somehow intimate, like I will understand something. I don't.

A gust of wind rains leaves down on our heads and I shiver. "It was nice to meet you, Angel."

He reaches toward me unexpectedly, taking a leaf out of my hair. He presents it to me like a gift. "Good night, Trudy," he says, and melts away into the darkness.

~

It's really too early to go to bed, only seven o'clock. The house echoes around me as if to exaggerate the loneliness. In the kitchen, I find some stale crackers and a butt of cheese that's perfectly edible once I trim off the dried-up edges.

Really have got to get to the grocery store.

I look for a magazine to read, turn on the stereo to the PBS station, which is playing agreeable and upbeat Celtic music.

I could read more Lorca. But he's reminding me of my lost dreams and I'm not in the mood.

There's always email. I hope for a note from my middle child, Colin, away at Berkeley, but there's nothing. Until three months ago, I carried on a lively correspondence with a group of natural healers and massage therapists I met in Boulder two years ago, but I haven't been participating, out of shame. There are two women who still send me emails, and there's been one waiting for me to answer for more than a week. I don't know what to say. Life sucks seems unnecessarily bleak, especially since I've always been the original positive-thinking guru.

Lotta good it did me.

I open a new window and type:

TO: jennyg@wild.com

FROM: excalibur@earthlink.net

SUBJECT: Alive and Hairy

Hey, Jen. Don't worry, I'm much better today. I should know better than to leave hysterical phone messages. It's only bad once in a while, honestly. Annie is working all the time she isn't out with her friends or in school, and that's the way it should be. She's furious at both of us, anyway, so it doesn't really matter. It's easier to have her busy.

It's just boring, really. I used to complain that I never had any time for myself, and I didn't, but I didn't expect it to end all at once. No more dinners or breakfasts to fix, nobody to hustle from place to place. No lessons. No noise making the rafters shake. Even the house stays clean since there's nobody here to mess it up.

It's boring. I'm bored out of my mind. Bored with myself. Bored with this house. Bored, bored, bored. Bored enough that I've actually had clean-shaven legs every day for a week. And my eyebrows are perfect. Just finished plucking them, as a matter of fact (and the chin hairs and the chest hairs—why didn't anyone ever tell us about the hair angles of middle age? If I ever land in the hospital for more than a week, you have to promise to bring me Nair, or I'll come out looking like something that belongs in the circus).

As for the rest, Rick's still living in his tawdry little apartment across town and everybody keeps telling me I should be glad he didn't move in with *her*, but I don't know what difference it makes, since he's not living with me. Actually, it's not a tawdry apartment at all. It's a charming Victorian place and he's made it all homey with pictures and I really wish he were suffering in a poverty of homemaking, but he's always been pretty good at that. There are pictures on the walls and plants at the windows and he makes his bed and keeps the place vacuumed. He keeps talking about getting a kitten, but he hasn't done it yet.

And you want to know how I know what the apartment looks like since

I lift my head at the sound of a motorcycle on the street, trying to resist the swift pose of waiting that straightens my body. But my head tilts of its own accord toward the sound, listening for the differences that will tell me if it is the bike I want it to be—an engine so carefully tended that even though it's more than thirty years old, it sounds like the luxurious purr of a tiger.

It stops in the driveway and I close the email, fast, click open the word processing program, and pick a document at random. I'm hurrying, feeling the long seconds of the opening of each window like an ice age, and while the document is groaning its way to open, I reach behind me for the stack of research papers I've collected on Lorca, flip one open on the keyboard. I even remember to slap my glasses on my nose before he rings the bell. Twice in quick succession, our signal.

"It's open!"

No matter how I brace myself, no matter how often I tell myself it's time to get over this, the look of my husband catches me right below the breastbone. A pain.

"Hey," I say in the direction of the computer, and pretend to save a file. He doesn't know the difference, really, but it makes me feel better. I stretch, as if I've been sitting there a long time. "What's up?"

Rick stomps his feet. "Gawd, it's getting cold out there." Unbuttoning his parka, he tosses back the hood, showing thick black hair that looks all the darker for the streaks of silver showing in it. Black licorice hair. His goatee, which he's worn since we met twenty-five years ago, is showing the same frost. It only adds to the devilish aspect that's always appealed to me so damned much. He's wearing my favorite shirt, a vivid blue corduroy that makes his eyes look like chips of turquoise.

I flip the pages on the Lorca paper closed. Wait. It seems very quiet all of a sudden. I can hear his breathing, the ring of wind chimes from next door. Rick tosses desultorily through the mail I leave for him on the table by the door, leftover stuff that doesn't go to his house. Bills. Credit-card offers. "I came by to see if Annie wants to go get something to eat with me," he says, finally.

Annie, our youngest. "She's working tonight, Rick." Just as she has every Sunday night for the past six months, though I don't add this. He'll remember as soon as I say it out loud.

"Oh. Right." He smooths his mustache. Nods. "Well, then, how 'bout you? You want to grab a quick bite somewhere?"

Very carefully, I say, "No, thank you. I just had some soup."

"Oh, boy!" It's kindly mocking. "Made from scratch?"

"Just some chicken and stars."

He inclines his head, looks me over. "You're getting pretty skinny, kid. C'mon—a nice T-bone, a baked potato, all the trimmings? I won a little Lotto last night. Wanted to spread the joy."

The question is too unbelievably obvious, and would sound catty anyway: Why not take Carolyn? "I'm kind of in the middle of something. Thanks for the offer, though."

A shrug. He looks away, drops the mail on the table. "No big deal. I guess I'll . . . uh . . . take off, then."

"Do you want me to have Annie call you when she gets in?"

"Yeah, that'd be good." He turns toward the door, putting his hands in his pockets. "Ah! I almost forgot." He carries over a handful of highlighter pens in pastel shades—green, yellow, pink, blue—at least a dozen. "They had these on special at Walmart and I know you never go in there. Thought you could use them. You know, for your research and all."

There's a cut on one of his knuckles that I haven't seen, one that hadn't been properly tended, by the angry look of it. I want to touch it, offer medicinal advice, and force myself not to. Up close, he smells of himself, a scent I've been trying to wash out of the pillows for three months now. I can't look at him as I accept the pens, feel his index finger brush over my palm. "Thanks."

"You all right?"

"Could you just go now, please?"

He backs away. "Sure." Another step, a pause. I wait, gritting my teeth. "Sure," he says again. "Sorry. I'll talk to you tomorrow or something."

I sit there frozen and staring at the highlighters, hearing the Indian's engine fire up and roar away, fade into the distance. I'm holding the pens so tightly that my wrist starts to ache. "No crying," I say aloud firmly, opening a drawer and dumping the pens inside. "No more fucking crying."

5

Jade

By ten, two of my aunts have arrived. Grandmama's sleeping, so I duck
out to get some gas for my car. I got into town on fumes. Tomorrow,
there'll be a lot to do.

That's my excuse, anyway. What I really want is a couple of drinks.
To get to the liquor store, I gotta have the gas.

There is a pack of men at the station. I reconsider going in, just to
avoid the hassle. Think again of that drink and pull in anyway. Most of
the guys are young. Doesn't matter much. Older men aren't as mouthy
as young, but they have ways of making their feelings known. I'm not
in the mood for old or young.

Pulling my hood over my hair, I get out. The wind hits my thighs
and I shiver, wishing for gloves as I fit the nozzle in the tank. Gonna be
hard to get used to the cold after eight years in California.

I punch the button for midgrade unleaded. Nothing. I look over
my shoulder, see that the fluorescent-lit convenience store is crowded
and the two clerks have probably not heard the pump click on. I jab
it again, harder. As if more force will make the bell ding more loudly
behind the counter.

Still nothing. My thighs are starting to freeze. With a sigh, I leave
it and head inside.

I see right away why the line is all male. The girls behind the counter are supple as new rubber. Their uniforms don't do anything to hide their shapes. Smart move. Hard to go wrong catering to man's lowest common denominator.

My back is hurting from the long drive from California. My eyes are stinging. I have to be very careful not to think of my grandpa. Shifting from foot to foot, I try to warm up. One girl giggles when the dog at the front of the line holds on to his money so she has to tug on it.

Good God.

I knock back my hood and lift my chin, turn sideways to push through the knot of men. "Excuse me." The waters part with little murmurs. Sure thing. Anytime. One brushes my breast with his arm. I flick a withering glance down his body, shove him with my elbow the smallest bit. To the girls I say, "Could you turn on that pump out there?"

"I'll pump it for you, baby," says someone behind me.

I turn. In my boots, I'm six foot one. Taller than most of them, which gives me the advantage of looking down my nose. I give them the same once-over they gave me. Shake my head. They part to let me through, one letting go of a low rolling trill, very soft. I don't bother to turn around again. Men.

Outside, I jam my credit card back in the slot. Blink hard in the cold. Aside from my grandpa, men are dogs. Pigs. I don't know why I keep hoping to find out something different.

I drive a mile up the road to a liquor store and buy a bottle of Rémy Martin, small enough to tuck in my pocket. It makes me feel guilty— my grandmama doesn't tolerate alcohol—but I'm thirty years old. Hot milk ain't gonna do the trick.

I avoid the cousins and aunties in the living room. Hide in my room behind the closed door, pour a hefty measure of cognac in a juice glass, put on Alicia Keys.

My girl. Her first CD is just about the only thing that's gotten me through the past eighteen months. "Fallin'" took on some deep meaning when Dante went to jail, mainly because of the video. Which, if you haven't seen it, shows a woman going to see her man in prison.

I'm wishing my mama were in the other room, but she called and said she'd be on down in the morning. One of her kids is in a little trouble. Not a child of her body, you understand, a child of her heart. She has dozens. Mostly I love her for it.

From the trash, I pull out the picture of Dante that I tore in half, fit together the two sides of his face. My chest feels like somebody's jumping up and down on it. Just because a man turns out to be a snake doesn't mean you stop loving him.

In the desk is some yellowed tape. It still sticks, and I use it to patch the picture together from the back, taking care to match the edges exactly.

I take a long swallow of Rémy. It doesn't burn away my self-hatred any.

~

The relatives start pouring in the next morning. Most of them get on my last nerve before an hour has passed. They fill my grandmama's house like a flock of ravens, all noise and shine.

Some of them are all right. Aunt Ti-ti, with her elegant head and smooth voice, Uncle Jerome with his big old laugh. Others—well. Loudmouth Tyrell, my cousin Jo Ester's husband, with his gold tooth and constant smell of alcohol; Alberta, my grandmother's sister, who wants to boss everybody around and takes charge of the kitchen with her hefty self; the low-life second cousins who are all about their fashion show and bad manners and sulky selves. I push them up off the chairs when adults come in. "Find some way to make yourselves useful."

"Like what?" says Malik. He's the leader of the second cousins, seventeen, and already six foot three. He wears a sparkling-clean jersey, jeans so big you could fit three people inside them, his boxers carefully hanging out. He stands up to intimidate me, show me how big he is. "We're guests here."

"Boy, please." I roll my eyes. "You're not guests, you're children, and you're here to show your grandmother some respect, so start showing it.

Get your butts up and go help Aunt Alberta with whatever she needs. You give her any lip, I'll tell all your girlfriends about changing your nasty drawers when you were two. Hear me?"

His eyes slide away. He mutters. The others almost snicker.

"Excuse me? I didn't quite hear you."

He's a big bad boy, but not stupid. "Yes, ma'am," he says in my general direction.

"That's what I thought."

My mama touches my arm, bends in to talk to the boys. "How you doin'?" she cries, and hugs each one in turn. Real hugs. They can't help but respond. She says each of their names, touches their heads and arms. "Why don't you boys come with me and we'll see about getting the beds made in the basement for some more folks?"

Her way is better than mine. My tolerance for bad children stops at about age nine. Hers continues well into the early twenties. In some circles, including my world of social services, we'd call her codependent.

She sweeps them away. Like my grandmother, she's getting hippier and hippier as the years go by, but she's vain about her figure and works hard to keep what she can. Today she's wearing light blue slacks and a blouse with a peacock-feather design. Her natural hair is cut short and slicked back at the sides, which shows off her Choctaw cheekbones and long eyes. Maybe she feels my gaze, because she winks over her shoulder, making us coconspirators.

She's not codependent. That's what I'd tell my work circle. It might look like it sometimes, but my mama just makes a place for people to be themselves, figure it out. One of these boys will likely land in her apartment before he's through, trading cooking and cleaning for a room while he gets on his feet.

The funeral is in two more days. Two more days of all this noise and nonsense, and I'm going to be ready for a shotgun and a big bottle of Rémy Martin. When the phone rings, I'm not expecting anything. I grab it to stop any more noise from polluting this world.

"Hello." I bark it, the way I would at work on a busy day.

"Collect call from Dante Kingman. Will you accept the charges?"

No, says the sensible part of my brain.

"Yes," says my speaking voice.

Dante comes on the line. "Hey, baby." His voice is a weapon, a blanket of dangerous velvet. It invites me to set down my burdens, let myself be wrapped up in it.

Which is why I moved a thousand miles away from him.

I have made ten thousand resolves not to let him get to me. He is twelve hundred miles away. We are divorced. He has turned out to be what everybody always said, a two-bit hustler who has a way with women.

And still I say, "Hey, Dante."

"God, girl, it's good to hear your voice. I was hoping I'd get you."

I'm already walking across the room, carrying the remote with me into my bedroom, and closing the door. "How are you?"

"I'm all right, but I'm calling to see how you are, baby. You holdin' up okay?"

In my mind, I see my grandfather's face. His wild salt-and-pepper eyebrows, his patient eyes. The way he worked his mouth when he had a tool in his hand. I make a little sound. "I missed him by maybe an hour."

"Oh, baby, I'm so sorry."

I cry a little bit. Dante is so patient, just makes comforting noises over the line. I imagine my head is tucked into the place between his neck and shoulder, where he smells like starch and a hot iron and Dial soap. His hand is rubbing up and down my spine, his lips on the top of my head. The vision is so real, I stay with it longer than I should.

After a minute, I take a breath. "Sorry. Thanks for listening." Wipe tears off my face with the flat of my hand. "How are you doing, Dante? Have everything you need?" I make a small joke. "Plenty of stamps?" Since cigarettes aren't allowed anymore, stamps are the money of the penal system.

His low, wicked laughter comes through the line. "I'm all right for now. I'm taking some classes, in accounting, so maybe I can do something constructive when I get outta here." He pauses. His voice deepens, softens. "I know you don't believe me, Jade, but I'm gonna do right this time. Goddamn, baby, I miss you."

I speak the truth in a whisper. "I miss you, too, Dante. So much."

"Don't stay gone too long, all right?"

"We'll see. My grandma needs me right now."

"I know. Don't forget your man needs you, too. I am your man, baby. Maybe you're not my woman anymore, but that don't change my heart any."

In front of my eyes, I see his throat, think of it against my lips. "Somebody wants the phone here, Dante. I have to go. Take care, okay?"

"Baby, write me a letter, will you? Please?"

"I can do that. Tonight."

"I love you," he says.

I can't think what to say back. "Bye, Dante." Gently, I hang up.

Maybe I was wrong to leave California. He sounds so sad and lonely out there. The truth is, there was a lot wrong, but none of it had to do with me doubting how much he loves me. He does.

Dante. Ribbons of my insides fall in bloody pieces on the floor. I have to sit down on the bed and put my face in my hands, put a pillow over my mouth. I want to tell him to stop calling. I want to forget all of it, get rid of my memories, go on to the next part of my life.

Instead, I'll write him a letter.

It doesn't make any sense, this passion I feel for Dante Kingman. From the outside, I know what it looks like. One of those twisted, lust-based sexual connections in which a smart woman makes a big mistake. And maybe that's what it is, but how could I be that stupid?

One of the cousins bangs on the door. "Yo, Jade. You done wit' that phone yet?"

"I'll bring it out in a second." But I can't bear to stay in the house. Trudy is going to be sick of me before we're through, but just this minute I don't have any other escape. I throw on my coat. On the way to the door, I dump the phone in Malik's lap.

6

Trudy

Monday mornings used to be a nightmare—kids running helter-skelter, tossing through book bags for missing homework assignments, lost mittens, a shoe finally discovered behind a bathroom door, and me trying to make sure everyone had at least a few bites of breakfast, a glass of milk, some protein and carbs to see them through their days. We went through it every Monday, as if we were surprised, over and over, at the stunning return to routine.

My fault, I'm sure. I was never able to be one of those mothers who had all important appointments written in ink on a big main calendar. In fact, I'm pretty sure they invented those reminder calls from dentists and doctors just for me.

Now I welcome Mondays with the glee reserved for special occasions, since going to work offers relief from the endless, lonely weekends. And this Monday is a beauty. Minute ice crystals give the air a diamond-like brilliance, catching and exaggerating the long strokes of gold sunlight coming over the world. Barren treetops poke witch fingers into the Crayola blue of the sky.

I yank the drapes open to let it all fall into the house. Dust motes dance quietly across the living room, and I realize that I'm humming under my breath, a wordless tune I remember from childhood, light and happy. A good sign. I choose a turquoise skirt with folk embroidery from the closet, and a peasant blouse with a neckline that makes me look slightly daring, put on my makeup—not that much of it, admittedly, some blush and mascara and a see-through brownish lipstick. Big hoop earrings make me feel exotic and youngish.

I can do this. Be single. Even a single mother. I roust a groggy Annie from bed. She complains, as all my teenagers have done, and I think again that the high schools would have much better luck if they'd change their schedule to accommodate this teenage need to sleep till at least ten. It would make so much more sense for school to run from noon to seven p.m.

In the kitchen, I discover we are down to the last packet of Instant Breakfast—the only thing Annie can tolerate first thing in the morning. The Nutri-Grain breakfast bars box, though it is sitting promisingly on the shelf in its usual place, is empty. A deeper search produces one dried-up grapefruit, twelve raisins in the bottom of a box, about twenty grains of whole oats. Resigning myself to a pot of coffee and some milk, I discover there are only enough grounds left in the can for a three-cup pot.

I'll stop at Mo's on the way to work—get a muffin and a latte. Which leaves me time to water the plants in the greenhouse.

The greenhouse. I fell in love with the house for a lot of reasons— it's an Arts and Crafts bungalow with all the attendant features—stained glass on either side of the fireplace, smooth woodwork and wainscoting through the main rooms, built-in cupboards with glass fronts. It was, admittedly, a jewel in disguise when we bought it sixteen years ago. Very deeply disguised, since it had been a rental for a decade.

But once I saw the greenhouse, no other house would do. I could not sleep at night, thinking someone else might get it. For three days, I fretted and worried and paced. Rick pointed out that it wasn't really large enough for us, that we needed four bedrooms rather than three and a greenhouse. The garage was separate and unheated. That's what he says now, anyway. Said it a lot more when the boys were killing each other sharing a room, hanging curtains, and laying duct tape across the carpet to divide it up. I told him they wouldn't die from sharing a room, and they didn't.

Poor dears. I never felt sorry for them. Never bought the American commandment that All Children Shalt Occupy Rooms of Their Own. I shared a room just slightly larger than a queen-size bed with my sister. Bunk beds freed exactly enough space for two dressers. We did our homework at the dining room table, just as all of our other friends did. I knew girls who had to share a room with two or three sisters.

Anyway, Rick wanted a room for each child, and I agreed, at least in theory. But I fell in love with the greenhouse. And for all that he claims he tried to talk me out of the house, he wanted it, too. He was crazy for the huge garage, where he could putter and take engines apart and put them back together. We both got what we wanted.

This sunny Monday morning, I open the antique wrought-iron and glass door from the kitchen to the greenhouse, and carry my coffee into the moist green world, pausing to let Zorro the cat run in on his black-and-white pantaloon legs. The door closes behind us, shutting out the sudden din of Annie's techno music.

Click. Gone.

Oasis.

Zorro leaps happily onto the wide table attached to the glass and iron, and winds through the pots, rubbing his nose hard on the jade tree. We agree, Zorro and I, that this is the best place in the house.

It smells of humus and damp earth and the breath of leaves. I almost hear a stir of welcome, the flowers and leaves turning toward me. The angel-wing begonia is blooming, a heavy cluster of deep-pink blossoms beneath green-and-white spotted leaves. It is taller than I am, the stalks as thick as half my wrist, and I cup the flowers in my palm in greeting. In return, I fancy I hear a trill as light as fairy laughter. I move on to the others, touching a leaf, a flower, a stalk. Put my fingers in the soil of one pot, check the humidity levels there, open the vent for air circulation later in the day.

It's not large—long and crowded with nothing more exotic than African violets and a few orchids and geraniums. Seedlings and cuttings sprout hither and yon. Beneath the long, waist-high shelf are empty pots and all my tools. I like it to be slightly untidy in here, so I feel like I'm entering a jungle in the wild. I'd like to have canaries or parakeets flying around loose, but Zorro would probably like it, too.

In the farthest corner is a white wicker chair and a small table where I set up my goddess altars. They are hidden here because Rick was so acutely uncomfortable with them, but I don't really mind. Once a month, on the full moon, I change them.

This month it is Hecate, one that Rick especially disliked, or perhaps was afraid of. It's a dark statue of a crone with flying gray hair and a dog at her side. The altar cloth is a black scarf printed with silvery stars, and her incense is myrrh. I light a stick of it, then pick up an egg-shaped tourmaline.

Rick is not alone in not understanding this practice of mine. My children, too, find it odd and even threatening. We were all more or less Catholic, though I have been lapsed for a long time. A couple of years ago, I really needed to find the female in God, and I found Her everywhere, in Hecate and Spider Woman and Mary, all of them. It gives me pleasure to have my altars, and it gives me pleasure that they are, in a way, my secret, that they live here in my private sanctuary.

Holding the stone in my hand, I sit in the chair, feeling the breath of plants on my flesh. Zorro leaps up into my lap, purring, and I stroke his fur, looking out the window. It has a view of the neighbor's house, a rental we've all complained about for years, the house Angel Santiago now occupies. On a clothesline in the backyard, I can see he's hung a few clothes. The pajama bottoms he was wearing yesterday morning, a poet's shirt with full white sleeves, a pair of jeans.

In the kitchen, I hear Annie clattering and muttering. She's never really mastered Mondays, and now she bellows, "Mom! I can't find my purple socks. Did you wash them again?"

Zorro looks at me, his full soft tail twitching, and licks his lips. "God, imagine that," I say to him. "Me washing something."

"Mom!" Annie yanks open the door. "Did you hear me?"

Break time over. But I rise with a sense of purpose, needed for something anyway. "Yes, I washed them. Check the dryer."

"I keep telling you not to wash my stuff!"

"They were standing up by themselves, Annie." I fetch the socks, folded together and smelling of fabric softener instead of dead toes.

She flings her red hair out of her face, darker than mine, but the same wavy, thick texture. This morning, she's wearing a long-sleeve T-shirt printed with a Celtic design. She's very Celtic everything these days; she wanted to know recently whether she could adopt my maiden name, O'Neal, instead of Marino.

I told her to give it some more thought.

The shirt shows a slice of lower tummy above the hip-huggers and thick belt. A river of bracelets pours down her arms as she yanks on her socks. Her hair is like mine, but the face belongs to her father—big eyes and full lips, his beautiful nose. It makes me want to touch her, but I wisely do not. "Did you call your dad last night?"

She looks away. "No, I forgot."

"He misses you, Annie."

"He should have thought about that before."

"It's not about you, sweetie," I say gently.

She gives her shoelace a final tug and stomps her foot down. "Don't patronize me, Mother. It's just as much about me as it is you. He left all of us."

Technically, he didn't leave—I kicked him out. This seems like the wrong time to say that. "He loves you, Annie. And you know that when you're not being so unforgiving."

"Whatever."

"Give me a call after school."

"I will. Don't I always?" She grabs her backpack, shoves her arms into her jacket, rushes out when her boyfriend honks. They've been going together now for more than eight months and I'm pretty sure they're sleeping together, probably in the back of his car and other such comfortable places. There are birth control pills in her sock drawer, which is why I've been warned off washing and putting away her clothes. We need to talk about it, and I make a mental note to do so. I'm proud of her for being smart about preventing pregnancy, but there's more to sex than mechanics.

In the meantime, I have to get moving if I'm going to have time to stop at Mo's. My stomach is growling, and I can't remember what I had for supper, then realize that's because I didn't.

Mo's neighborhood grocery isn't far away. It's an old-fashioned place, with time-darkened wooden floors and wooden shelves, a cooler in the back filled with beer and soda and bottled water. It's a convenience store in better packaging, with lottery tickets and cigarettes behind the counter and a couple of gas pumps outside. I grab a muffin from the bakery case and pour an extra-large coffee into a paper cup and carry them up to the counter, where the owner is waiting. "How you doing today?" he says. Tall and handsome, in his late forties, Mo is originally from Iran. He's been running the grocery for almost a decade now.

"Good, Mo. How are you?"

"Good, good." His voice drops respectfully. "Edgar die last night, huh?"

Some of the sheen rubs off the day. "Yes. Roberta's granddaughter, Jade, came in last night, though, so she has somebody with her." I couldn't remember if he'd been here before Jade left. "Do you remember Jade? Beautiful girl."

"Mmm. That's good, a good granddaughter to take care of her grandmother." Abrupt change of subject: "Where's Rick been?" He smiles, but there's worry in his dark eyes. He gestures at the counter, where the lottery tickets are held beneath glass. "I not seeing him too much."

It's not the first time he's asked. "Um, he's just been . . . busy, I guess."

"Yeah?" He waits for more, ringing up my purchases slowly. The bell rings over the door behind me.

I don't know why I can't just say it: We're separated. I can hear the words in my head, but somehow they don't seem to make it to my lips. Picking up my muffin and coffee, I hold out my hand for my change. Reluctantly he puts it in my palm, his heavy brows beetling the slightest bit.

"You tell him for me that he needs to buy more lottery tickets from me. Sales are down."

"I will." Rushing to get away, I nearly slam into the person who has come in behind me. A hand comes out to steady me as I try to avoid dropping my coffee or spilling any through the little hole on top. "Sorry."

"No problem." The accent is like chocolate.

I look up into the beautiful face of Angel Santiago. "Oh! Um. Hi."

"Good morning." Is it my imagination or is he admiring my clothes? He smiles, slow and lazy as a cat, knowledge in his eyes, and I think of him raising his arms on his porch. Vividly, suddenly, I imagine putting my face there, smelling him close up.

It shocks me. "Running late. Gotta go. See ya, Mo!"

"Bye-bye now. Tell your husband what I said."

It makes me chuckle and I wave on my way out. In the car, I start the engine and sit for a minute, aware that I'm not laughing only at Mo's comment, but at myself. I'm as giddy as a sixth grader, my limbs filled with sunshine. I take one moment to enjoy it, admiring the sky and sipping my coffee, then shake my head and pull out into traffic.

He smells so good. So good. The man must be loaded with pheromones.

～

Work is just . . . work. I'm a secretary for the music department at the local university, a sprawl of white quartz buildings on a hill above

Pueblo. A friend from out of town saw it once for the first time and said, "Whoa. Looks like it was built all at once in a really bad decade." Which is almost painfully true, though the buildings are beautiful when the sun shines on all that glittery quartz.

It's not the job I thought I'd end up with, and in fact, until I broke my arm in July, I had been building a pretty decent massage practice after taking a nine-month holistic healing class on the weekends in Boulder. For two years, the client list had built steadily and satisfyingly, but that ended when my arm was in a cast for three months. Thinking of it, I rub the wrist. It doesn't hurt anymore. I don't know why I haven't called my clients to let them know I'm back in business.

At any rate, the music department is a relatively interesting place, and I can have access to the university library and research materials. It's harder than you'd think to keep things going for a bunch of busy, artistically inclined professors and their equally busy, scattered students. At least once a day, I get to be a hero by rescuing some lost information or tracking down a vital bit of data required for graduation or financial aid or any number of other things. Lately, too, I've been thankful for the fact that it's enough to support me after the divorce, and that I have excellent benefits.

I can also take one class per semester for free, not that I've done it most years.

This sunny cold Monday, however, I'm bored all day. I hit one like that every so often. I'm irked when the professors treat me like an invisible servant. I'm annoyed that the students do not respect my intelligence. It's all busywork—repetitive and boring.

On the way home, I do remember to stop at the grocery store, which feels like a victory. I fill the basket with all the things on my mental list, hoping I'm not forgetting anything. It isn't until I'm putting the groceries on the conveyor belt that I realize how obvious it is that I'm a woman cooking for herself only. The baby cans of tuna and frozen individual quiches and fussy things like goat cheese and roasted pepper strips and a bag of spinach pasta. I look behind me to the young mother trying to control her toddler. Her basket is filled with lunch meat and cookies and a litany of WIC items—apple juice and cheese and Kix cereal. There are also packages of meat. Mostly hamburger, but some chicken and a promising roast. A man lives in her house.

I don't know why this embarrasses me so much, but I look away, feeling ashamed, and my gaze falls on the couple at the next checkout. She is quite, quite ordinary. Plump. Not tall. Not particularly well dressed. Her hair is that desultory not-blonde, not-brown, and she wears an unappealing pair of glasses. But her husband, a plain but not awful man, touches her shoulder lightly, slides his hand around to the back of her neck. His gold band glints on his finger, and she turns to look up at him, tell him something. He kisses her.

And I think it isn't fair that she gets to keep the love of her husband when I worked so hard at my marriage and lost anyway. She's not worrying every second about her hair or keeping herself perfect, as I have been doing these past months, looking for some flaw that might have led to this breakdown. My wrinkles, I think, some days. My chipped fingernails that I've never painted. The fact that I forget my lipstick most of the time, don't even own a plunging neckline. My sagging rear end. My skin, the color of egg whites.

Something. It had to be something.

But here in front of me is the truth. She's lumpy and ordinary and plainly loved. It sends up a little roar in my head, and I only see the lips of the cashier move at first. I blink. "Sorry, Ken. What?"

He grins, kindly, a man who has been waiting on us at this Safeway for a dozen years or more. "How's that ornery husband of yours? I've been wanting to make a bet on Sunday's game, but he hasn't been around much."

"Oh, uh, he's been busy." I watch him scan the items, and think I should have bought a steak for show. Is it possible that they haven't figured out by now that we're not living together, that he's doing his shopping in another store, closer to his apartment? Or do they know? Is that sad sympathy I see in his eyes?

A face-saving joke appears in my mind: "He's probably avoiding you—doesn't want to lose."

He laughs politely, bags my female groceries, gives me my change. As I head out to the car, the young woman and her adoring husband are right in front of me. I see that she's pregnant, and he's leaning into her tenderly, touching her belly. I'm fine until I put the key in my ignition and the radio plays a snippet of a Pink Floyd song, "So, so you think you can tell heaven from hell . . ."

I look at my white, freckled, ringless hands on the steering wheel and listen to the car engine rumble quietly.

I thought I could. Tell, I mean. Heaven from hell.

Jade materializes as I'm taking the groceries out of the trunk. She has circles under her eyes and there are lines around her mouth that I didn't notice last night. I break out of my self-pity with relief and put my hand on her shoulder. "How you doing, honey?"

"I'm fine." She grabs two bags of groceries in one hand.

"Roberta?"

She shakes her head. "She's been in bed all day. Not crying, but not doing anything, either." She waits as I unlock the door, and we go inside. "That's why I'm here, really. I'm hoping you can help me with figuring out some details for the funeral."

"Absolutely. Come on in, let's have some coffee or something, and tell me what you need."

"Oh, girl!" Jade stops in the middle of the living room. "This looks great!"

"I guess it's been a while since you've seen it." I pause to look through her eyes. Afternoon sunlight is pouring through the green-and-fiery-coral stained-glass windows on either side of the fireplace. Dragonflies, period pieces I found on eBay. The light melts over the smooth wood wainscoting, the Arts and Crafts mantel we found in a house about to be torn down. It's a beautiful room and I've worked very hard to make it so. Lately, I'm a little tired of the muted colors of the period and have been looking for models of brighter styles. I wonder if all the muting might be because the samples we have to look at are old and faded.

"Come on in the kitchen. Coffee okay?"

"Love it." She puts the bags down on the counter and sheds her jacket. Beneath, she's wearing a silky T-shirt that shows off her body. When she crosses her arms, her biceps show, and her belly is as hard as a frying pan.

"Jeez, Jade. You're all muscle—are you working out?"

She grins, and for the first time, I see the girl she used to be. She raises an arm and flexes. "Nice, huh?" She laughs, almost a giggle. "You would not believe how strong I am."

I rinse the coffeemaker and open the can of coffee, almost swooning at the smell, and I remember that I didn't get much this morning.

"Weights?"

"Well, I've added weights, but I started with kickboxing. When Dante went to jail—" At my raised eyebrows, she adds, "Yeah, jail. Burglary." She shakes her head. "When he went, I was just crazy, waiting for the trial, and a friend of mine took me to kickboxing. It's a great way to get rid of your aggressions, trust me." She jabs the air at an imaginary opponent. "Pop, pop, pop." Even the air punches make a sweep of sound, and I think I would not like having that fist connect with my face.

"Probably even better than saying fuck a lot." I grin. "Maybe I should try it."

"That's one of the first things I have to do, find a class in town. I'll go crazy if I can't work out. You should come when I find one. Check it out."

"Maybe." It's plain she needs this quiet pool of normal conversation. "I don't know if I'm in good enough shape."

"Oh, it's not like aerobics, where you have to learn a bunch of fancy footsteps. You'd be surprised."

"Maybe."

I open a bag of cookies, a Pepperidge Farm collection that are my weakness. They're a fussy woman kind of grocery, too, but I don't care now. It's women who are going to be eating them. "Have some." I settle into a chair at the table, put out napkins for us. Jade flows into the chair opposite, and there's a relief in it.

She picks out a Milano, examines it, takes a healthy bite. Closes her eyes for one second. "God, that's good." Leans earnestly toward me, her voice lowered. "What I really want to do? Get in the ring."

"Like real boxing?"

"Yeah."

I'm not quite sure what to say. Her green-gold eyes are glowing with the idea, and for that reason alone, it's worth encouraging her. "You know Shannelle, the girl who was there with me last night?"

"Yeah, she's been over a couple of times today. Sweet."

"Her husband's brother is a boxer. Maybe he'd know something."

She clutches my arm, just above the wrist. "Really?"

"He's pretty well known around town, kind of a local hero in boxing circles. He has to train somewhere, right?"

Jade juts out her jaw, leans back, eats the rest of the cookie. There is a flow to her movements, an easy glide and comfort that I envy. "My mama's going to have a heart attack, but she's got to get over it. It's what I need to do."

A face floats in front of my eyes, blonde hair, brown eyes. Carolyn, the woman who has given me so much trouble, so many nightmares. The woman who has torn my life to ribbons. It isn't her fault, exactly. I know that. A man has to participate or a woman can't get anywhere. He's as responsible for the destruction as she is, maybe more.

But I have a hard time actively hating Rick and I need to hate someone. It flows up through my body in a deceptively silver flow, filling my veins with cold power, and like mercury, it breaks apart and floods my lungs and heart, my stomach. I imagine getting into a boxing ring with her, smashing her face with my big gloves, knocking her down. I stand over her, breathing hard with triumph, see Rick out of the corner of my eye looking at me with new respect and awe.

Jade must be even angrier than I am. I pick out a raspberry tart and incline my head. "I'd love to see you fight, as long as you don't get yourself killed. That would be kind of a waste."

She gives me a little smile. "I see that glint in your eye, girl. It feels good to think about it, doesn't it?"

"Maybe," I admit. "Who are you punching?"

She looks toward the windows, a flash of pain on her face. "I don't know. Men, maybe."

"All of them?"

"Yeah," she says more definitely. "Every last one of them. How 'bout you?"

As if it holds the memories of my Great Breach, my wrist begins to ache. I shake it out, and stand up to pour our coffee. "Let's drink this and figure out the best plan for the funeral, then I think we need to get Roberta up and moving, at least for a little while. What d'you say?"

7

Roberta

Dear Lord,
A few prayers for the folks this morning. I've done lost my list, but I reckon I can remember most of them anyway. Bless Sister Pierce, Lord, give her relief from the pain of her arthritis in this cold weather. Look after my sister Harriet's grandbaby. Keep him out of harm's way. Bless Trudy and her broken heart, Lord. Shannelle, who has such trouble with her teeth, poor child. Lighten Jade's heart, Lord, and cut the ties between her and that man who has cast such a spell over her. Bless him, too, Dante Kingman. Bring him those who will show him Truth.

Take this cup from me. I can't stand another minute of this pain, you know I can't. I been a devoted woman all my life, sweet Jesus, and I don't aim to hurt myself in no way, so I'm asking, just you take me away. Let me go on to heaven with my Edgar. Just take me, Lord.

In Jesus' name, Amen.

8

Jade

October 27, 20—

Dear Dante,

It's been crazy here, getting things ready for the funeral, and I just haven't had a minute. The house is full from morning till night, streaming with all the folks who loved my grandfather, and all those who want to take care of Roberta. There are enough casseroles in the freezer to last a year, and I've started taking the overflow across the street to a young family who will make good use of lasagnas and pasta salads.

I don't have your last letter with me, but I do remember it sounded hopeful regarding your chances for early release. It sounds like the lawyer—What was her name? Janice, maybe?—is a good advocate, and she's right that you need to keep trying to better yourself. You're a smart man, Dante, and have too many gifts to throw them away like this. I hope you've learned your lesson and can start dealing with the world as it is, rather than constantly running a game. You have a lot to offer the world. Never forget that.

I know you like to hear what I'm doing, but there hasn't been much since I left Sacramento. Just the long, lonely drive across the country and now my grandmother and her grief and all these people. I sent an application to Social Services and to several other private facilities that deal with children and am hoping to get a job from one of them soon. There is a boarding home facility on the south side, almost an old-fashioned orphanage, which appeals to me. I'll get busy following up on those résumés next week sometime.

I'm sorry, babe, to be so depressive. I know you like upbeat letters. I'll do better next time. Take care of yourself, all right? Don't get into any power struggles with anyone, and keep up with your studies, and listen to the advice of your lawyer. I've enclosed a few things—a small care package. Hope you enjoy it.

Love,

Jade

9

Trudy

Here is one thing that is good about being forty-six: I have a grand-daughter. Minna is her name. And I know this is as clichéd as every-thing else in my life at the moment, but she is truly the apple of my eye.

When Joanna, my eldest son Richard's wife, drops her by, Minna comes in wearing a fluffy pink coat trimmed with fur around the hood. "Hey, there's my girl!" I grab her and pretend to chomp on all of her fingers. She grabs my necklace and puts the heart in my mouth, which I then spit out with a great deal of noise. It's our standard greeting.

"I really appreciate this, Trudy," Joanna says, dropping the diaper bag in the chair and bending over to kiss her daughter's rosy cheek. "They're desperate for help on the ward tonight and my mother was not at all interested."

A tiny prick of jealousy touches me, even though I know it's natural for a daughter to be closer to her mother than her mother-in-law. Jo is quite close to hers—Linda, whom I like very much. They're very alike, mother and daughter, and I see a lot of them in Minna. They must love having three generations of girls in a row like that, and I'm determined not to be the Evil Mother-in-Law. I let Minna yank my bracelets off my wrist. "You know I adore her. Anytime."

When Jo has left, I take off Minna's jacket, chattering back and forth with her. She claims my bracelets and has learned how to hold her arm, the tiny hand cocked upward to keep them on. I bought her some glittery ones of her own, and Jo told me they were a big hit.

Minna also likes my purse, because it's small, and she snatches it off the couch to put over her head. Fully adorned, she fixes her bright-blue eyes on me and says, "Plants?" It's really something like "Plantus," but I know what she means.

"Let's do it, girl." I hold out my hand for us to walk, but she rushes my knees instead and makes a grunting noise, so I pick her up and carry her to the greenhouse. Zorro rushes in around my ankles and Minna tucks her head around my shoulder. "Hi, kiii." She sends him a kiss.

We go through the plants. She can say flower and leaf and pot, a word she adores. "Pot pot pot," she says, throwing her head back to laugh gaily. Lately, we've been working on actual names. Geranium is "ranium," and begonia is "gona," and no one believes me, but she does know the difference.

Her favorite part is the potting area. It sits at the far end, and it's always a little cool down there. I have my spades and little rakes hung on hooks above the table. To one side is a wooden box, lined with heavy black plastic to keep the black widows at bay, where I keep soil. I lift the lid, releasing the smell of earth and moisture, and we both inhale and say together, "Mmm."

The doorbell rings and Minna makes an exaggerated *oooh!* sound. My heart jumps without my permission, because I think it's probably Rick and it would be very nice to see him while Minna is here. She's hoping, too. "Popo?" she says, kicking her legs to move me toward the door.

"I don't know. Let's go see."

It's not Rick, but Jade. She has tear-swollen eyes and that downcast look that says it's been a rough day. "Hi," she says. "Is this a bad time?"

"No. It's great. Come in and meet my girl. This is Minna, my granddaughter. Can you say hi to Jade?"

Not just now. She stares at Jade with the wariness of eighteen months, and looks at me with a scowl. "Popo?"

"He's not here, sweetie."

She reaches up and grabs her hair with one fist and makes a furious noise.

"Ow," I say, and take her hand down. "Don't do that!"

She also smashes her head against the ground or a wall or cabinet when she's displeased. The sign of mightiness, I say. Jo worried a lot about it until I told her Annie used to do the same thing.

I close the door behind Jade and gesture for her to sit. I put Minna down, rescue my bracelets from the floor, and say, "Go get your toys, sweetie."

"Toys," she agrees, and heads off to the corner cabinet where I keep them.

To Jade, I say, "Rough day?"

She rubs her hands together, looks at the palms. "Dante called me."

"You don't want to talk to him?"

"No. And yes."

I think of my hope that it would be Rick at the door just now. "I know how that goes."

"So you miss Rick?"

"Understatement of the century."

Her eyes light on my face. "What in the world happened, Trudy? I always told people that I never saw a man so in love with his wife as Rick was with you. He was almost silly about it."

Her words bring a picture of Rick, or rather, dozens of them, bringing me an offering. Or coming in late with one too many beers in his belly, to throw his arms around me and kiss my neck and tell me what a great wife I was, how lucky he was to find me. I straighten against the pain under my left breast. "I don't know," I say. "I guess he fell in love with someone else. It happens."

"Do you see him?"

"Sure. All the time."

"And doesn't it kill you? That's why I left. I couldn't stop going to see Dante in jail. We were already divorced, he's proven he's a shit, and I still kept hanging on. I still am, in a way."

I nod. Lift my shoulders. "I know. Me, too."

She bends her head into her hands, rubs her face hard. "I just want to go on to the next thing, whatever it is. Feel normal again."

"You will, Jade. It takes a while, but you'll feel right again, I promise."

"Do you?"

I lower my eyes, shake my head. "It hasn't been that long. We were together over twenty years, and it's only been three months since I found out about it."

Minna brings me a ball and a book and puts them in my hands. "Thank you." She toddles back to the box, squats, digs busily through again. Athena, my fat, asthmatic gray tabby, flops down next to her and starts to purr. Even when Minna is a little too rough, Athena never minds.

Jade says, "Yeah, that makes it harder. Have you seen a counselor?"

I nod. "You?"

"Sure. I'm a social worker, right? Mental health is my middle name." She rolls her eyes. "I've read every self-help book out there, too." She starts ticking them off on her fingers. "*The Secret of Letting Go, Help for Emotional Betrayal, How to Get on with Your Life*—"

I'm laughing, and bend over to open a drawer in the table next to the couch, pulling out a stack of trade-size paperbacks. I read the titles, *The Art of Forgiveness, How Could You Do That to Me, Living the Life You Were Meant to Live.*

Jade is starting to smile. *How to Love a Black Man.*

The Lord Ain't Done with Me Yet.

The Ways Couples Grow Apart.

How to solve every problem you ever had through pop psychology.

How to live your life perfectly so nothing bad ever happens to you.

"Freakin' bullshit, all of it," Jade says. "Why do we read it?"

I put the books back in the drawer, close it harder than I have to. "I kept thinking there was something I could do to fix it. If I just had a little more information, maybe it would all make sense."

She sags, leans back in the chair. "Yeah. I wanted to love him till he was healed, and I know that's impossible. You can't fix anybody." She steeples her fingers. "Except yourself, I guess."

"And that," I say with some feeling, "pisses me off."

"Me, too, girl." She inclines her head. "You have any more of those cookies?"

Minna stops in her tracks. "Cookie?"

We both laugh. "Yeah, sweetie. Let's get cookies."

In the kitchen, I put on a pot for tea and dig out the bag of Milanos. Also some cheese, the good kind, and Triscuits, which I love. I think about apples, but they're still too hard for Minna to eat, and I open a can of sliced peaches instead. In her high chair, Minna starts humming as she picks apart her cookie, savoring every little bit of it like it's heaven.

"Mmm!" she says loudly, smelling it. She offers some to Jade, who thinks nothing of the baby slobber on it, and bends to accept the bite. "Ooooh, that's yummy. Thank you."

Minna points to Jade's cookie. "Thank you?"

Jade holds it out and Minna takes a bite, staring in the impolite way of children. Jade says, "You probably don't see too many folks like me, huh, girl?"

"Berta?" she says.

"Yeah, Roberta is my grandmama."

Minna kicks her feet, evidently satisfied. Points to me. "G'ma?"

"That's right." I nibble her fingers.

"I love babies," Jade says. "One thing about Dante was that he has the most wonderful children. I'm going to really miss them." She runs a finger playfully down Minna's arm, and she giggles.

"How many children does he have?" I take cups out, pull out the tray of teas, put everything on the table while the water is boiling.

"Four." She says it with a lift of her eyebrows, as if she knows it's shocking. "Two different women. I know it sounds terrible, but that's how I met him, at Social Services. He was strapped because he was paying so much child support and wanted to see if there was anything he qualified for. None of the babies were on any programs—the mamas were both smart women with decent jobs—but Dante qualified for food stamps because he was paying so much out."

"Really," I say, a trick I learned from listening to teens who need to get a story out. "How old are the kids?"

She takes a breath. "Let's see—Portia's two are eleven and ten. That's Jacob and Danielle. Eileen's two—Keisha and Tyrone—are eight and six. Tyrone was just a baby when I met Dante, but Eileen had tossed him out." She accepts another bite of cookie from Minna, who laughs happily. "I know how it sounds. I should have known better."

I put spoons on the table. "Maybe. Maybe not. Obviously he has a talent with women."

"I knew better. I saw my grandfather and my stepfather. Saw how they did things."

The teakettle whistles and I take it off the burner, glancing out the window, as is my habit, to see the lights burning next door. "Have you seen the guy next door yet?"

"Should I?"

"Oh, yeah." I raise my brows and can't think of any words to do him justice. "Trust me."

She brushes her palms together. "I'm not interested in any man. A year. I have to be celibate for a year, and then I can think about men again."

"That's sensible."

"But?"

"Nothing. I wish I could get my head together that much." I sit down, stir sugar into the tea. "And, too, maybe the easiest way over one man is to fall in love with another one."

"Maybe."

A knock sounds at the back door, and we startle, both of us looking at the door like it's marauders about to slam inside. I stand up and hurry over, hoping it might be Angel to tempt Jade away from her vow. All it will take is five minutes in his company.

But it's Rick. The yellow porch light skates over his hair, touches his nose. His mouth. "Hey," I say, and it's surprising how natural I sound. I'm proud of myself for leaving the door open, walking away casually, like it's all no big deal for me. "Your granddaughter is here."

"Minna-girl?" he says.

Minna shrieks, "Popo!" and starts trying to scramble out of her chair. I lift her out, give her to her grandpa so he can make noises on her tummy and tickle her and lift her high over his head. Vigorous, that's the word for Rick and babies. Hands-on and vigorous, and I've never met one yet who didn't absolutely adore him.

"You remember Jade," I say, gesturing toward her like a game show host. "Roberta's granddaughter?"

"Sure. How are ya, kiddo?"

Jade is aloof. "All right."

"Roberta doing okay?"

"As well as can be expected." She takes another cookie out of the box, doesn't look at him.

I say, "The funeral is Wednesday at two o'clock at the church, if you're interested."

He looks away. Nods. He won't go, because he's ashamed to face everyone we'll see there, but he says, "We'll see." He pats Minna's legs. "I just came by to get a couple of tools out of the garage. Got a restoration going tomorrow."

I notice his jaw has the painful newness of a fresh shave, and under his coat, he's wearing a red shirt I've never seen. He smells of cologne, and I look at the clock, wondering if he's going out to dinner, or maybe out to hear some music. Taking a breath suddenly feels as if I have shards of glass in my lungs.

"Come here, Minna," I say, holding out my arms to her. "Grandpa's got things to do."

She turns away fiercely, putting her head on his chest. "Popo."

"I'll take her out with me, bring her back in a minute."

"Bye?" she asks hopefully. "See ya?"

He cocks his head, looks right into her eyes. Winks. "Let's go out to Grandpa's workshop. I'll let you put an eye out with a screwdriver."

She nods, jerks her body like someone on the back of a horse. "Le'ss go."

~

As they walk out, I notice his pants are bagging around his butt a little, and his cologne lingers in the air like a ghost. For a minute, I'm just lost in it, in a thousand days when this never even figured into anything I could ever have conceived.

Jade is looking at me, and I say, "Where were we?"

"Men are assholes."

"Oh, yeah," I say. But for one long, hot minute, I am afraid I'm going to cry if I say anything else.

She raises her fists in front of her and feints punches, right, left, right. Her breath comes out in hard whooshes with each one, whoo whoo whoo. Then she wiggles one great, arched eyebrow.

It's enough to make me move past the dangerous moment, grin wryly. "I'm glad you're here, Jade."

"Me, too."

10

Shannelle

TO: naomiredding@rtsv.org

FROM: chanelpacheco@hotmail.com

SUBJECT: sneaking in late at night

It's 3:34 a.m. on a Tuesday morning. I have to get up at six to get my eldest ready for school, and I have to work at the bowling alley tomorrow night, and I'll be feeling the fact that I've only slept two hours by then. The next day is the funeral. My tooth hurts. I'm cross-eyed with exhaustion.

But I don't care. Oh, what a great night!

I went to bed with Tony at ten thirty and we had a cuddle, then he fell asleep. I just laid there in the dark, seeing scenes and hearing dialogue, as if I were a director sitting in a theater and the actors were trying out their parts. It upsets Tony when I do this, so I tried to resist, but in the end, I couldn't sleep at all and I got up very quietly. I started writing at a quarter to twelve, and have written thirteen pages. Good pages, I think.

The reason is, of course, that it's quiet. No distractions. No phone ringing. No one coming to the door. No requests for macaroni and cheese, or fights to mediate. No comments from Tony about the television program he is watching (one thing I dream of is a real study, a place where I can shut the door and not be in the middle of all the chaos). I can play my earphones and write with everyone around, but it's often in fits and starts and I can't get the flow going the way I did tonight.

Tony will be annoyed with me in the morning, and maybe with some justification. I'll end up making Hamburger Helper for dinner because I'm tired, and he doesn't much like it, and I'll want to fall asleep when I get home from work and not want to sit and chat with him. But I don't do it that often—only when I can't stand not to. I wish he'd make an effort to understand that.

Sorry. No whining. I really just came in to tell you how excited I am about getting thirteen pages done tonight!!

Love,
Shannelle

~

TO: chanelpacheco@hotmail.com

FROM: naomiredding@rtsv.org

SUBJECT: re: sneaking in late at night

shhh! that's the sound of two children asleep. it's five a.m. and i got up to write and just sneaked in here to find your note. great minds. i'm so close to the end of this book and really want it finished before the end-of-pregnancy brain drain arrives. do you have time to do a quick read of a chapter that's bugging me?

love,
naomi

11

Trudy

Bedtime is the worst. For the first month, I drank a lot of wine every night just to be able to face it, but since I don't seem to have any natural tendencies toward true self-destruction, I got tired of the hangovers and decided to white-knuckle my way through the nights in a bed that smells of him still, no matter how I try to wash the scent of him out of the pillows. They smell of laundry soap and fabric softener for the first few days, but the minute I accidentally spend a night hugging one to my chest, my body heat sets it free again. You might ask why I don't just put them away in a closet or something.

Good question.

I have developed some new rituals. I used to take quick showers before bed, wanting to hurry in and lie down before Rick fell asleep so we could have a few minutes of conversation with my head tucked into the hollow of his shoulder. We touched bases about little things going on in our lives then, shared concerns about the children, or laughed about something one of them had done, or reminded each other about little things that needed doing. All the while, our bodies close together on the queen-size bed, because I never wanted a king, his hand on my back, mine on his bare tummy. One of those ordinary rituals of a long marriage.

One that never changed, by the way. You'd think an infidelity might put a wedge in moments like that, even if only one person knows about it, but it didn't. The night before I found out, actually, we'd laughed hysterically over a major scene with our middle child, Colin, who thought himself completely grown and declared, "I am almost twenty and I know what I'm talking about." Then, after the laughing, we made love. There weren't any major rockets going off or anything—just ordinary, warm, pleasing.

I really didn't appreciate it enough.

Now I take baths instead of showers. Attempting to treat myself, luxuriate in the bathroom I adore so much. It's Arts and Crafts all the way, with built-in cabinets tiled in an intricate pattern, and a huge, old tub. A big window lets in plenty of north light for the orchids, which love the humidity. There's one blooming now, a cattelya in purple and white, and as I wait for the water to get hot, I notice another one, a lady's slipper, is about to bloom again, too.

Pouring lavender oil into the tub to relax, I pin up my long hair and take off my clothes, avoiding my reflection in the mirror, and light the candles I've been collecting lately. They smell of patchouli, a fragrance that makes me think of a stronger version of myself, the one who lived in a wonderful old apartment close to downtown. I had a view of the city from the top of my hill, and quirky black-and-white prints of faraway places on the walls, and I was sure I would end up as a professor, cheerfully eccentric and alone, taking lovers when I wished, traveling through the summers granted by academia.

I turn off the lights, sink into the hot, scented water, and reach for my mug of Sleepytime tea. I have put quiet Spanish guitar on the CD player, and pick up the paperback edition of Lorca's selected poems. It's a soft practice, this one, reading aloud in the Spanish I have largely forgotten. Sunk to my shoulders in the hot, scented water, I open the book at random and read aloud. By luck, it's one of my favorites. In English, it's beautiful:

And at the fall of night,
The night benighted by nightfall.

But you don't even have to speak Spanish to hear the difference in syllabic roll in the Spanish version:

Cuando llegaba la noche,
Noche que noche nochera.

Lorca and Spanish distract me from Rick. I sink low in the water and keep time with the music by running my toes back and forth beneath the slight drip of the faucet. I read another poem aloud, taking pleasure in my own voice echoing around the tiles in the room, bouncing off the water, in a language I fell in love with at three and have not spoken in at least fifteen years.

Reclining in the water, seeing the whiteness of my breasts, the green of the orchids reflected mistily in the mirror, the young woman in me turns around for the first time.

You let us down, she says.

I close my eyes against her.

The CD ends and the water is cold, so I dry off with the big towels I treated myself to when I sent all the old, yucky, threadbare ones with Rick. A small revenge that I'm sure he noticed. To be honest, in the second round of boxes, I did stick in his favorites—a beach towel my mother sent him once, and a fluffy green one he loves. It surprised me to discover that my capacity for meanness, even when he deserves it, is so small.

But really, how can you be cruel to someone you've been focused on taking care of for twenty-four years?

I blow out the candles, put on my flannel nightgown because the house is really not easy to heat, and to save money we've always turned off the furnace at night. On the landing outside the bathroom, I pause to listen for Annie, but the house is silent and I have nothing left to do but go in my room, crawl into bed, push my pillows to the middle in an attempt to be luxurious instead of lonely, and read. Late, because he didn't like it when I left the light on, hated the rustling of pages. I read a thriller until it falls on my face, and hope that when I roll over, I can stay asleep.

Tonight, I manage to last until two thirty before I wake up in the utter silence of no one breathing beside me. Somehow, though I always put my pillows in the middle of the bed, I always end up on the far right side. Leaving Rick's place open for him.

There are no defenses available in the middle of the night. I roll over, dislodging the cats, who meow at me with annoyance, then settle back in on various parts of my body. Athena, all twenty pounds of her, collapses on my stomach and starts to purr. Zorro stands up, circles, bumps against my ankle.

At least the cats are happy.

If I close my eyes, I can pretend he's there, sleeping on his stomach, naked beneath the covers. The ghost of his shape settles with a sigh in the darkness, and I can almost smell his skin, think of his thick, coarse hair scattered over the pillow, hear the sound of his breathing. The tension in my chest eases away and I even imagine I reach over and put my hand on the small of his back, where it stays so hot. It's real enough to get me through the night.

～

I've been to a lot of funerals in the last few years, starting with Rick's mother in August three years ago. She died of breast cancer after a decade of ups and downs, and there really wasn't much relief even then. We all wanted her to live longer, me and the kids, and mostly Rick, who still misses her painfully. They were close—he was the son she counted on, the one who ran errands for her, stopped by every day to see how she was doing.

And I must be the only woman in the world who doesn't have some awful mother-in-law story to tell. She was good to me. Accepted me into her heart the first time we met, and did everything she could to make me feel good about my marriage, my mothering, myself. I miss her. She was a lot warmer—and closer—than my own mother, who still lives in Clovis, New Mexico, with my father, the machinist. My mother spends her time complaining about their lot in life. My father spends all his time fishing or bowling. We check in once a month. The last time I saw them was three years ago, and no one seems in any hurry to schedule a new date.

There have been other funerals, too. They're in my mind as I dress this bright cold Wednesday morning. A thin black sweater, a black skirt, a black suit coat—my funeral clothes. And as I put them on, I think about buying them. Not for Rick's mother. For his best friend, Joe Zamora, who died as he lived, driving too fast on his Harley on a hot summer night a little over two years ago. Smashed into a guardrail on the bad turns on the highway through town, and ended up thirty feet below in a junkyard.

Zipping up my skirt, I can see his swarthy, bearded face as clearly as if he is standing beside me. In my vision, he's lifting a beer with one beefy arm, tattoos blueing his skin all the way to the shoulder and beyond. In his other hand is a pool cue, and he's grinning as he says, "One for the ditch?"

I twist my too-bright hair into a knot and think that the sudden deaths are a lot harder than the ones you expect. Joe was one of those wild, bigger-than-life guys—robust and hearty, a cheerful renegade who never married and never intended to. He was Rick's best friend from the time they were six, living next door to each other just a few streets away from here.

I miss him, too, but for Rick, the wound is still so raw that he'll choke on it sometimes when Santana comes on the radio, and he still can't talk about him much, though I noticed a lot of pictures are coming out of the trunk, going up on the bare walls at his apartment.

Joe's funeral was a biker bash, so big that they had to move it to Sacred Heart Cathedral. The line of bikers in their fringes and chrome and cherry paint jobs snaked all the way through town, soberly shining in the hot August day to the graveyard on the south side of town, where Joe was laid to rest with his family. The wake afterward lasted well into the night.

Edgar's funeral is huge, too. It's held at Bethlehem Baptist, the biggest Black church in town, and the pews are overflowing. Shannelle and I have arrived together, and she sticks to my side as we navigate the roomful of dark faces. No one glares at us or anything, but we do stand out, the tall redhead and the lush little blonde. Shannelle is wearing a flowered dress that looks like she might have bought it for a high school dance. It's about ten years out of date, with some lace around the collar. Her high-heeled sandals are a tawdry brown plastic that have seen better days, and my heart aches a little for her, because she is quite aware of how it all looks. Her nails are freshly manicured with a tasteful nude polish, and she's tucked her thick blonde hair into a knot, and she smells—very delicately—of her sacred Chanel No. 5. I wish I could have loaned her something without hurting her pride.

Because she is proud, and has reason to be. She is from a challenging background for sure. Her father is a fat drunk who collects disability checks for his bad back. Her mother, who seems nice enough, is a waitress at a diner. I've never seen her when she didn't look as worn as an ancient dishrag. Her brother is a petty criminal who's in and out of jail for a series of pathetic crimes. They live in a trailer park.

There used to be a sister, a year older than Shannelle, but she died—I've gathered it was suicide—and Shannelle doesn't talk about her much.

But the other side of Shannelle is the part that intrigues me. She graduated from high school with a straight-A average. She dated her husband Tony from the ninth grade on, and they married the summer after graduation, and she found in his large, loving Hispanic family all the things she'd missed. Her home is like something out of *Better Homes and Gardens*—cheerful and sweet and warm. Her children are always scrubbed and ready for school on time, and she haunts computer shops for used programs for them.

And she wants to be a writer. Barely twenty-four, and fierce, with all this baggage, and she's very devoted to the idea. I privately think she's going to get her heart broken, but that's life, isn't it?

Today, she's looking around curiously, and leans over to whisper, "I've never been in an all-Black church before. It's kinda cool, isn't it?"

I nod.

"Why are so many of the women wearing white?"

"I don't know. We can ask Jade later."

The preacher comes to the pulpit, and the service begins.

It's not a funeral, he tells us. It's a home-going, for a man who deserved the mighty reward he's earned in this life of toil and trouble. A home-going. Edgar going to be crowned in heaven, welcomed by the armies of angels he served.

I'm choked up in five minutes, and trying hard not to weep copiously, because the spirit of joy in that church is so palpable and huge and shimmering that it would be insulting to weep.

Next to me, Shannelle is awash. She doesn't try to hide it, or try to be anyone she isn't. She truly loved Edgar, even though she didn't know him very long. She sat with him, listened to his stories, brought him homemade sugarless brownies and fresh beans from the farmer's market. She looked up to him, like everyone did.

I think now that he was something of a fill-in for her own worthless father.

The preacher goes on, his mighty voice filling the room, and the music swells, and Roberta gets up to put a rose on Edgar's chest. She does it so gently, with so much love, that I can't hold back my tears anymore. Shannelle wordlessly hands me a tissue when I soak the few I brought with me.

And I am an awful person, because the reason I'm crying is not for Edgar, or even Roberta. The tears should be green acid, because that's how they feel spilling over my cheeks, too hot and bitter. They are tears of savage jealousy, an emotion so raw and ugly that I hate myself for it, for feeling something so shallow and selfish at such a moment. Edgar is dead. Roberta will never, ever hold his hand again. I can see her now, hollowed out the way she's been the past few days, like he took a big chunk of her with him, and I can see him being laid in the ground, but none of that makes any difference. My heart still boils up those ugly bitter tears.

Edgar loved her until he died.

~

By the time we get to the basement of the church—Shannelle and I skip the burial to get everything ready, along with several of the sisters of the church—I'm under control again, but breathless with shame.

I used to think I was a pretty nice person, and not fakey nice, either. Genuinely and honestly kind, with the best interests of the world in my heart. Giving and faithful and all those other things, a spiritually grounded person. I practiced holistic teachings, and spoke to my goddesses every morning, and Rick had given me stability. Not that I was perfect or anything. Who is?

But here is what I've learned: It's easy to be nice when everything is fine. Take a few body blows, and the character shows up in a hurry. I am as evil as anyone I've ever met. No, not evil—that has levels of interesting that are too flattering. I am petty. Shallow. Jealousy is such a self-centered emotion, and I have taken it to some ugly places. This upsets me, but since I can't stand meditating right now, it's going to be a while before I can fix it.

Shannelle looks pale and keeps rubbing her cheekbone. "Are you all right, honey?" I ask as I hold a bowl for her and she pours in gallons of potato salad.

"It's just a toothache. They're going to pull it tomorrow."

"Ow! Can't they do a root canal or something instead?"

Her eyes are way too old for her face when she looks at me. "Do you know how much a root canal costs?"

"You have insurance, don't you?" Her husband works for the state.

"Yeah. My portion of the root canal would be four hundred and seventy dollars. The crown is another three hundred." She scrapes the jug carefully with a spatula. "It's fifty dollars to have it pulled." She puts the jug down, picks up another one. "I'm only worried because it's the third one I've lost this year, and pretty soon I'll be a toothless old hag." She smiles to lighten the comment.

See? Some people have real problems. I run my tongue over my whole teeth, all thirty-two of them, and feel even smaller than I did at the funeral. "That sucks, Shannelle."

Her smile is more genuine this time. "Yeah, it does. But hey"—she shrugs—"there are worse things than losing teeth, right? I mean, what are dentures for?"

"Oh, don't even say that, honey!"

She puts her hands on the sink. "I never went to a dentist until I was married to Tony. Not even once. That one tried to fix some things, but you go that long without anybody lookin' in your mouth, and it's not pretty. I just want to hang on to the front ones, because you can always tell when somebody's had a cap, and I don't know how we'd afford one anyway."

A woman in her fifties, dressed in a beautiful rayon dress, hands Shannelle a glass with about an inch of something clear in the bottom. "Try this, sugar. Hydrogen peroxide. Swish it around that tooth real good, and then spit it out." At Shannelle's dubious expression, she smiles. "Good black medicine."

Shannelle winces at the taste, but does as she's told, spits it out in the sink. "Hmmm," she says, and more eagerly tries it the second time. "How long does it last?"

"Not that long, but you can do it as often as you want."

"Cool. Thank you."

The woman winks. Looking at her teeth, it's hard to imagine she ever had trouble like this, and she says, "One of my boys had a terrible time with his teeth. Just rotten from the day he was born, I swear. What you want to do, if they keep blowing up on you, is keep some antibiotics around to tide you over till the dentist can get you in. That's what makes it hurt, the infection." She pats Shannelle's arm encouragingly.

"I'd rather have ten babies than one toothache," chimes in an old woman. Her name is Sister Eleanor. I know her from her visits to Roberta while Edgar was sick. "Rather lose a toe."

Shannelle grins. "Amen."

"Come on, girls, let's get cracking," says the first woman. "We got a lot to do before they get back here."

We carry out the food to tables set along the wall. So much food—steaming bowls of baked beans, green beans, butter beans, bean salad; potato casseroles and potato salad and potato chips; fruit salad with marshmallows and Jell-O salad with coconut; fried chicken wings and barbecue brisket and piles of fluffy white rolls; some of the most beautiful cakes I have ever seen. It's something I miss about traditional religion.

The mourners file in, their mood subdued at first. But as the room starts to fill up, the murmurs rise, and after a while, there is much talk. Laughter, which surprises me the first time, but it's right.

Roberta sits in one place, and people swirl around her, touching her shoulder, offering condolences. She can't quite sit up straight, this proper old woman, with her matching shoes and purse and hat, her delicate hankie clutched in her hand. She looks bewildered. Her lipstick has worn off.

I go to the table and fill a plate with her favorite things—the baked beans, some brisket, a piece of the lemon cake, and carry it over to her. Her children are swollen-eyed and overwhelmed, too, and I see Jade, who looks almost as bad as Roberta, sitting with her mother.

A pocket clears around Roberta, and I sit down with her, rubbing her back lightly. "I brought you some food."

"That was sweet, baby, but I'm not hungry."

"A few bites," I say, and smile gently because it's what she said to Edgar.

Her eyes fill with tears and I start to say, "Oh, I'm sorry, that was the wrong thing—"

"No, it was just right." She pulls the paper plate closer, picks up the fork. Stares at it as if it's a mountain she has to climb.

"Start with the cake, maybe. It's so good I had two pieces, but don't tell anyone."

"Sister High makes this cake." She lifts a little to her lips, puts it in her mouth. "Mmm. Not better than mine."

"No. And Rick would shoot anybody who said so."

"How is that husband of yours?"

I want to correct her, but the timing is wrong. "Fine."

"Jade said he came by when she was there."

"He comes by all the time."

She takes a big forkful of the cake and levels her gaze at me. "Why do you reckon that is?"

Why are we talking about this now? I'm embarrassed, but she is eating. "I don't know," I say. "Habit, I guess."

"Maybe he doesn't really want that other woman, child. You ever think about that?"

I blink. Quickly. "Oh, I'd say he does."

"'Let no man put asunder what God hath joined together,'" she quotes.

"Roberta, I didn't leave him. He left me."

She digs into the beans, the cake now a faint smear of frosting left in the corner. "You threw him out."

For ages, she's been wanting to lecture me like this, but I wouldn't let her. I walked away. I blocked her. Changed the subject. And my pettiness rises up again, screaming like a four-year-old having a tantrum: It's not fair!

"What else was I supposed to do? He's been sleeping with her for a year." A year. God. It echoes around inside of me. "What kind of man does that to two women?"

"One who's lost."

I am spared the need to answer by a big, heavyset man in an oily-looking suit who lowers his girth and takes Roberta's hand. I take the chance to flee. Which is just more evidence of my small-minded selfishness—I can't even sit still for a lecture from a brand-new widow who obviously needs to deliver it.

But her words sliced my soul to the quick, and I'm pretty sure I'm going to bleed to death if the pain is any way to judge. I duck into the bathroom and slam the door closed and sit on the toilet, breathing, until it gets better.

It takes a while.

The bathroom has been redone with cheap wood-look paneling, and someone keeps it very, very clean. It smells like disinfectant. The toilet is low and my knees are jutting up from the high heels, and I'm clutching my ringless fingers together so tightly that you can't even see the freckles anymore, trying not to cry because it'll ruin my makeup. I'm freezing, even in my jacket.

I hate this. I miss my husband so much I can't even breathe, and all I'm supposed to do is just get on with things, be a grown-up. I don't want to. I want to stand up on top of a building and scream about it. I want to slice my body, chop off all my hair, something to show how much it hurts.

I put my head in my hands, press on the bridge of my nose. I'm so sick of living in this cold, gray place, numb or in pain, bewildered and furious and lost. It's been almost four months and I don't want to live here anymore.

Stop resisting. The thought steals in, quiet and reasonable. *Stop resisting. Feel it. Embrace it.*

A polite knock sounds on the door. "One minute," I call, and flush the toilet I didn't use, wash my hands by rote. Something in me eases. I raise my head, look at myself in the mirror, at the blue shadows that have lived beneath my eyes for months now, at the too-high ridge of collarbone that shows how little I've been eating.

Maybe what I need to do is have a funeral for my marriage. A funeral and a wake. Annie isn't home tonight, and my emotions are in an uproar anyway. For the first time all day, I can take a breath without wanting to scream.

I open the door, apologize softly, go back into the main room. For a minute, I stand there, looking around. Jade and Shannelle and Shannelle's husband, Tony, are in a corner, talking. I hope it's about boxing. Roberta is covered with a trio of sisters. I pause by each of them, offer my condolences one more time, head out.

12

Trudy

It's cold and getting dark by the time I get home, carrying a large chilled bottle of pinot grigio under my arm. In the kitchen, I put it on the counter, kick off my shoes, check the voice mail. There are seven messages. A lot for me these days.

The first is from Annie. "Hi, Mom. Hope you're not feeling too sad after the funeral, and I'm thinking about you, okay? The weather is not great up in Denver, and we almost didn't go to the concert, but Travis's dad said he'd pay for a hotel room if that's okay with you. I have my cell phone with me, but I won't be able to hear it inside, so, like, you can call and leave a message if you want and I will call and leave a message when we get out, so you know I'm safe. I hope this is okay. You always say you want me to be safe first, and I had no way to ask you ahead of time." I'm grinning to myself before it's finished, knowing she's nervous and sweating her brazenness. "Oh," she adds after a pause. "I really hope you're not too sad tonight. Maybe we can go out to dinner someplace cool later this week. My treat."

I'm chuckling when I push the number seven to erase the message. I do intend to take her up on that dinner out.

The next message is from my job—there was a plumbing disaster and I don't have to come in on Thursday or Friday while they clean up the mess.

Number three is from Rick, midafternoon. "Hey, kid. Just calling to see how the funeral was, how you're doing. Call me."

Number four is from my son Colin, the one in school at Berkeley.

Now, mothers don't have favorites, and that's absolutely true, but this middle boy has always been the most like me, and I miss him terribly. He's in his junior year of college—majoring in literature and Romance languages. Rick doesn't get it—he figures any kid with such a brain oughta be studying engineering or something practical like that—but I know I infected him with poetry when he was tiny so I'd have someone to talk to, and it's worked out very well.

Until he grew up, the rat. Last summer, he spent six weeks in Italy—something I ached for painfully when I was a starving student. Few things in my life have made me as happy as writing the check for that trip for him. It came out of a fund I've kept for twenty-some years, supposedly for my own travel.

Everyone told me I'd miss him less as time went by, but it doesn't seem to be true. Probably just more evidence of my neurotic resistance to change, like being unable to let go of my marriage—hell, I even hated when the longtime neighbors moved—but the truth is, there isn't anyone else like him. I've already started counting the days until Christmas break—six weeks away.

"Hey, Mom," he says in his rich, deep voice. Rick's father's voice. "I saw a movie with some friends that I think you'd like a lot—*Quills*. It's just your kind of tragedy, and it blew me away. I'll write you an email, or you can call me tomorrow. I don't have class until noon. Love ya."

The next one is from Rick. "Yeah, it's me. Guess you're still with Roberta."

And Rick again: "Hey, kid. Hope you're doing okay after the funeral. Call me if you want to talk. I'll be here. Damn, he was a great old man."

Number seven, too, is from Rick. No wonder I can't get over him. "Last time, I promise. I was just thinking about Ed some more, kind of have been all day. I was thinking about all the times we went fishing with the boys and how he said you could hear God in the wind on the water, and how great he cooked catfish. Give me a call if you want."

I hang up the phone and eye the bottle of wine. Condensation makes it look like a television commercial. If I call him now, I can set up my boundaries a little, so I can get safely drunk and grieve the end of this relationship all by myself.

Or I can take the phone off the hook and do it without talking to him at all. Yeah. That's the ticket. I go upstairs to change into some sweats and socks and a heavy sweater a friend brought me from Ireland. On the way back down the stairs it occurs to me that he might very well come by if I don't call him, so I punch in the numbers. He answers on the second ring. "Hello?"

"Hey, Rick," I say, sticking the corkscrew into the top of the wine. "Got your messages."

"How's Roberta?"

"She's all right. I worry that she might be one of those old people who dies in six months, though."

"Yeah, me, too. Are you okay?"

"Tired. Sad. But I'm okay. You?"

"I didn't expect it to hit me so hard." His voice scratches a little, and in my mind's eye, I can see the wiggling of his mustache that goes along with that need to repress his strong emotions. "But I've been thinking about him all day."

"You probably should have gone to the funeral."

"I know." The words are heavy with regret. "I just"—he clears his throat—"had a hard time thinking about another one, you know?"

"I figured that might be it. I'm sorry, Rick. You've lost a lot of important people the past couple of years."

"Yeah."

"I was thinking about Joe today. About his funeral and the bikes all shining in the sun." Tears are lurking in my throat, but I swallow a sip of wine and they recede.

"Me, too. Not about the bikes. About him."

I'm quiet, giving him space to say more, but he doesn't. He doesn't seem in a big hurry to get off the phone, either. "Are you okay?" I ask softly.

"I don't know. I guess we're just getting old now, huh? People dying on us like this."

"I guess so."

He clears his throat. "Sorry. Didn't mean to get all choked up on you."

"That's okay. I really just called to tell you that I'm home and I'm going to take a nice hot bath and go to bed early."

"All right. Call me if you need me."

Oh, Irony, thy name is husband.

Or maybe that should be Idiocy. "I will."

I never planned to get married. Back in my hometown of Clovis, New Mexico, the girls got married young and beautiful, had a couple of babies, got fat and put on spectacles, and lived the rest of their lives in a gray between-place that seemed as barren to me as the dry desert that swept away, vast and empty, from the edges of town.

Even before I met Lucille, I knew I didn't want a life made up of Tupperware parties and the slightly wild desperation I saw in those women's eyes. I would sometimes lie in my bed, sweating in terror and the heat, trying to imagine where I could go, what I could do. How I could escape. People like us didn't really go to college. Nobody in my family ever had, and they were suspicious of the dream.

Then Lucille blew into my neighborhood, fresh from Peru. Her health was failing after fifty years of traveling the globe as an archaeologist, and she landed in Clovis because she had a brother there and he convinced her the weather would be good for her. It was. She moved into a house on the route to the grocery store, and I saw her the first day she moved in, a hot July Saturday.

I was on my way to the store to buy a red cream soda. Sun was beating down out of the sky, mercilessly sucking what little green might be left in the plants and grass, making my scalp sweat so much, rivulets were running down my neck.

And suddenly, right in front of me, was Lucille, a tall woman draped in thin white cotton that showed her bra and underwear. Her feet were bare, with red toenails, and when she stepped I glimpsed a bracelet of bells around her ankle. She had thick strands of exotic beads around her neck, and at least a dozen bracelets on her sun-darkened arm. She was carrying a drum. A giant drum made of skins and wood, painted with primary colors in some tribal design.

I didn't mean to stare, but I had never seen anyone like her in my life. I fell instantly in love. In love with that wild, long gray hair tied in a braid, her eyes bright and clear when they lit on me, a face as wise and lined as a river goddess.

"Hello," she said to me. "I'm Lucille. I'm new here."

I blinked, clutched my sweaty, folded bill more firmly. "I'm Gertrude, but everybody calls me Trudy." I pointed back. "I live over there, in the blue house."

She looked, nodded. Inclined her head. "I'd pay you to help me bring these things inside. Then perhaps we could have a cup of tea."

"You don't have to pay me."

"Oh, never turn down an offer of payment. Women need money to maintain their independence."

Oh.

Over the next three years, Lucille became my friend and my mentor and the single most influential person I'd met before or since. I adored everything about her—the exotic clothes she wore, things she bought all over the world. Comfortable things that sometimes showed parts of her body that women in my world did not ever show once they passed the age of twenty-five—her long, freckled back with the slight rolls on either side, a snippet of belly, ample and tanned. Thighs like crumpled paper sticking out of her bathing suit.

She had never married. But she kept a wooden box with the pictures of men with whom she'd had great love affairs—the matador with his fierce nose, the Black African attaché with his wide mouth and kind eyes, the wiry German archaeologist—and she was bold about the details of their seductions and the grand times they had here or there. I asked her once if she minded that one didn't stay, and she laughed and laughed. They all wanted to stay. She wouldn't let them. Life was short and she didn't intend to tether herself to any one part of it.

She taught me to dream, Lucille. Prodded me to imagine the life I most wanted. I started dressing like her, draping myself in light India cottons and peasant blouses. I grew out my hair, which my mother had always kept short because it was wavy, "uncontrollable." Lucille helped me figure out the bewildering steps it took to get into college—taking the SAT and the ACT, the scholarship and financial aid papers, the application fees. I wanted to study Spanish and travel the world as a teacher. The first place I would go was Seville, to learn to dance the flamenco, for Lucille, who died two days before my college graduation, leaving me a considerable sum, along with a letter that said, "Use this to see the world, child. Dream big!"

It still sits in an annuity, gathering interest. I've dipped into it twice. The first time was to pay for the natural healing school in Boulder two years ago. The second was to pay for Colin's trip to Italy. I haven't touched it for anything else. I was waiting for the kids to grow up, so Rick and I could go together.

Sitting now in my living room, sorting through the CDs, I pause over a Gipsy Kings collection of love songs that I bought because the music reminded me of her. But tonight, I'm not grieving Lucille. I'm letting go of Rick and my marriage. That requires a different soundtrack.

I pull out all the CDs I've been avoiding the past few months, the Allman Brothers and Jimmy Buffett and Lucinda Williams, which I put aside to listen to last.

First the Allman Brothers, because that's what was playing the night I met him. I pop it in the CD player, pour some wine, get comfortable on the floor. Let myself flow into the music, let it pluck the pains I've been hiding and ignoring.

"Whipping Post" fills the room, the excellent guitar and fine voice of Greg Allman. It was this song that was playing when I met Rick at a party for someone's thirtieth birthday.

Here's the truth: He was not my type. I had just graduated from college with my Spanish degree, and I thought very well of myself, thank you very much. In the fall, I would be moving to Boulder to study for a master's degree, and in the meantime, I was dating intense, scholarly types who liked to talk poetry over too much Guinness in dark clubs. Or well, one club, anyway, the Irish Pub, which was agreeably atmospheric and reliably hip. I liked men who wrote and played their folk or blues songs, who wore wire-rimmed glasses, and had clean hands. Men who, like me, were headed for academia someday. A world that kept you alive and young, I thought. Away from things like Tupperware parties.

My hipness did not end there, though, I must tell you. I was a vegetarian and eschewed cigarettes long before it was popular, and did yoga three times a week in a tiny studio over on Union Avenue. My apartment had nothing of Clovis in it. The entire second floor of a slightly seedy Victorian in Mesa Junction, it had bare wood floors I painted red. There were no curtains and at least twelve dozen candles. I'd taped go-get-'em mottoes up over the kitchen counters and in the bathroom, the Marilyn Monroe one about having too many fantasies to be a housewife, bits of wisdom from all kinds of women who'd done things. I thought at the time it was wonderfully quirky of me.

Brave, I think now. Brave to believe in that vision of myself.

The walls of that apartment were hung with black-and-white photographs of the places I wanted to visit and had not yet managed to go, thanks to the struggle of putting myself through college.

I was even proud of that, fiercely proud of my poverty and the reason for it—I made it through the bachelor's degree, sometimes making fifteen dollars stretch for an entire week of groceries. I worked in a restaurant in order to guarantee myself a solid meal five days a week, and at least a little bit of free alcohol.

I really did think I was so mighty. So immune to falling into the ordinary life of a woman, a wife, a mother.

Sipping my wine, I look at my feet. Feet I thought would carry me to Seville and carried me only over here to the north side of Pueblo. One night that summer, I went with a friend to that party for someone's thirtieth birthday. It was noisy and full of students, not all of a traditional age, since the University of Colorado Pueblo has always catered to a larger population than that—something I liked about it. So much diversity gave it an interesting energy.

Thus, it wasn't odd to see this slightly older guy there—he wasn't quite thirty—but he was oddly misfit in other ways. Working class, in a black leather motorcycle jacket, jeans, an ordinary Budweiser in his hands. He looked at me boldly when I dug in the cooler, looking for a Heineken, which was slightly less smart than a Guinness, but only a little. "Hey, darlin'," he said, "don't you know Heinekens are made of skunk piss?"

Well, with an opening like that, how could he lose? I looked up with my most withering gaze. "And Budweiser is made of what? Buffalo piss?"

He laughed.

It sounds so small now, to say it like that. But it was robust. Rich. In the sound, I heard children screeching on a playground in glee, and the pulse of an orgasm, and lemonade pouring into a glass. It caught me, made me look at him. And he was looking back with eyes as blue as morning, lively as his laugh. In that first minute, I didn't notice that he had hands as elegant as a painter's, or the depth of his lostness. I was mesmerized by the way he was looking at me. Boldly. With amusement. As if he saw right through me to the girl who used to blow soap bubbles on the back porch.

I ran. Hid in the sharp barbs and tough intellectualism in the other rooms, places where one had to stay on one's toes to keep ahead of the verbal banter; ducked when I saw the softness of his wink. I could hear him, talking and laughing, turning aside the sly questions about his bike, his leathers, his work as a mechanic. His voice was deep and warm, like a thick mattress.

He captured me outside on the porch, where I'd retreated to breathe in the starry night. He carried a Heineken and a Budweiser. Pointed to the spot next to me on the step and said, "Mind?"

I shook my head, accepted the beer. He settled, and I noticed his long legs, next to mine. His hair was too long, looked as if it had been cut with a dull ax, but it was a rich, thick black, and he smelled of afternoon. It was like meeting Lucille for the first time. Like I already knew him and had just been waiting for him to show up. All the words that tripped off my tongue so easily, all the time, the bright, funny, brittle words I used to hide behind so no one would see the girl from Clovis, dried up, and I looked at the sky.

He pointed. "That's Orion."

"Yeah?" I pretended I knew what he meant. But I didn't know the stars.

"Look for the three stars. That's his belt. See it?"

I did, suddenly. Winking in a row. I sipped my beer, felt my skin shifting, like it had grown too tight. I thought about his shins, his ankles. If they would be that dead white of unseen skin, or if he sometimes went out in shorts. I glanced at him. No. He wouldn't wear shorts.

He pointed out some more of the stars. His arm brushed mine. He leaned in, shoulder to shoulder. "It's a lot easier to see them from the prairie. Want to go for a ride?"

The first time he kissed me was out there under those stars, under a sky so wide and dark and filled with so many millions of blinking stars that we lay down on our backs and admired them for an hour. Maybe two. Maybe ten. I don't know. By the end of the night, I knew he was in love with me, and that hadn't ever happened before, that someone fell so deep and hard. Not for me.

But I knew it. When he kissed me, I tasted it on his wide mouth. Focus. Recognition. His body fit me as he leaned in. He knew exactly how to open my blouse, let the wind press over my breasts, his fingers skilled, his kisses rich. It was so easy to make love to him out there in the prairie, the first night we met, and I never did that. Never slept with a guy on the first date. He just made it seem reasonable.

And it was so amazingly good. I wasn't in love with him yet, but one taste of his body, his mouth, his hands was absolutely not enough. I needed more and more and more.

All summer, that's what we did. Made love and rode his motorcycle and ate and drank. We camped nearly every weekend, finding hot springs to swim in naked, and making love by campfires, and getting drunk on Budweiser, which always gave me a headache the next morning. He cooked for me, finding a dozen fresh ways to make vegetarian delights.

For me, it was a way to pass the summer. I enjoyed him, sometimes even felt a piercing sense of recognition, but I was going to Boulder in the fall and he wasn't going to follow me, and that was that. It gave the fleeting weeks a gilded sense of magic. I knew I'd remember it forever, but I truly didn't think he was The One.

Rick pretended to go along with that, but he was in love. In Love. I have never known why. God, I was obnoxious in those days. Skinny and intense and full of myself, covering a vast sense of insecurity with bravado and snobbishness. I was quite clear about my plans, about my feelings for him, never promised him anything at all. I have never understood what Rick Marino saw in me to love—which of course makes it all the harder to figure out why he fell out so suddenly and with no warning.

Anyway.

In August, I packed up my apartment and Rick helped me mop the floors and clean it up. I had the blues. The apartment had been my first home, and I'd been there three years. I hated leaving it.

And Rick, too, seemed suddenly precious. I couldn't stop watching him as he taped up boxes and hauled them down to the truck I'd rented.

I saw a million things I would miss—the way light, even the brightest August sunlight, was sucked into the depths of his thick long hair, the way his arms corded with so much power, the crinkle of his eyes when he teased me. I ended up jumping him in the empty living room, and we made love in a pool of sunlight.

Afterward, curled against his chest, I said, "I am really going to miss you."

"I know," he said, and kissed my forehead. "It'll be all right. We can get together on the weekends."

My chest felt hollow and I closed my eyes, smelling him, rubbing my fingers across the hair on his chest, my foot across his very white ankle. How could I have missed the fact that I'd fallen in love with him? And what in the world could I do about it now? "I wish you'd move to Boulder."

"Too many granola-heads."

"I'm a granola-head."

He chuckled, rubbed his hand through my hair. "Yeah, but I've got you trained to drink Bud now."

"You know I'll revert the minute you're away."

"But I'll know you're wishing for a Bud in your heart."

Very quietly, I said, "This summer has been the best time of my life."

"Mine, too, kid."

"Maybe," I said earnestly, lifting up on one elbow, "I should just stay. I could transfer to UCCS in the Springs, just commute."

He shook his head. "That's not what you want."

That was the thing about him. He supported even my most grandiose plans for the future, believed in my abilities even more than I did. He was extremely proud of my fierce journey to this point, of my need to escape the small world of Clovis and find a bigger, more challenging life for myself. Tears stinging my eyes, I bent down and kissed him hard. "I love you, Rick." It was the first time I said it, the first time I knew it.

"You can't help it," he said.

13

TO: naomiredding@rtvs.com

FROM: chanelpacheco@hotmail.com

SUBJECT: filling the well

The funeral was today and I can't tell anyone else this—it was so artistically thrilling! I will miss Edgar—he was a very kind old man and he told wonderful stories of his life and his childhood in segregated Mississippi and his passing will leave a gap.

But his funeral—oh, my God!—what an experience! It wasn't a funeral, first of all: It was a home-going. And the ladies in the church were not dressed in funereal black, but in shining white to celebrate a saint going home. (I think that might be one of the most beautiful things I've ever heard.) I was so moved by the ceremony—by the big voices, singing so boldly and in such celebration, by the granddaughter who could not help but weep in her grief, by the nurse in her uniform who was there in case anyone fainted in sorrow. It was strangely heady to be one of only a handful of white faces in a church packed with Black people. It made me think about what it must be like to be Black most of the time, an interesting turn-around. Not that anyone was even the slightest bit unkind—quite the opposite—but it was an interesting thing to notice.

The person who was falling apart the most was my neighbor. Not Roberta, Edgar's wife, but the woman across the street who is getting divorced and is still so painfully in love with her husband that she shimmers with longing when he rides up on his motorcy-cle. She looked like a walking skeleton in her black suit and red hair, like a Day of the Dead figure, her cheeks and eyes hollow, her hands shaking. I felt sorry for her, but when I went to find her later, she was gone.

I see the dentist tomorrow, finally!

DO NOT REPLY.

Love,
Shannelle

14

Trudy

The Allman Brothers CD is over and the next one spins into place. I pour a third glass of wine. Still no tears, just a hard knot of undissolved emotion in my throat. My stomach is not feeling all that thrilled at the gulped wine, and I get up to get some cookies. The last of the Pepperidge Farm. While I'm in there, I make a plate of cheese and fruit, too, and carry it all back in with me. If I'm going to wallow, I may as well cover all the bases.

I settle the plate on the coffee table and hear a step outside on the porch. Shit. If it's Rick, I'm in trouble. But the bell rings, and when I open the door, it's Jade. There's weariness on her cheeks, in her eyes. "Hi," she says, holding up a bottle of wine. "I brought spirits. Am I interrupting anything?"

I let go of a short laugh, swing my arm around to the wine and cookies. "I was having a wake for my marriage. You're welcome to join, but I'm warning you now, I'm in a very maudlin mood."

"That makes two of us."

"Did Dante call again?"

She nods miserably.

"Sit." I take her coat. With my toe, I kick the CD case over to her. "Pick something that makes you the most maudlin of all. I'll get you some wine."

She lifts her head, smiles bitterly. Nods to herself. "I'll be right back."

I tuck her bottle of wine into the fridge, get out another wineglass, which I have to wash because it's so dusty. I only ever use one.

Jade comes back in, waves a CD at me. "Alicia Keys. You heard her?"

I shake my head.

"Oh, girl." She bends, all long limbs and power, and puts it in the CD player. She takes the glass of wine I've filled and we sit down. "Listen."

A woman's soft voice, surrounded with poignant piano, fills the room. At the sound of a second voice, rising behind the main, tears spring to my eyes. I look at Jade, blinking. She nods. "Just wait."

We settle on the floor, and both of us let the music just slide around and into us. The sound is pure sorrow, mixed with resolution. Mightiness. "I don't know how many nights this song got me through," Jade says. "It's like she's singing my life story."

"Her voice is fabulous."

"And she's young, not even twenty-five. This is her first album—it won about five Grammys."

The song ends, and she picks up the remote control that I'd left on the table. "This is the song, though. It was song of the year."

A song comes on that I know, vaguely. I've heard it on the radio, but not like this, not at this level. Jade turns it up, so the sound of that rich, soul voice and delicate piano fills the room, the hollow of my chest. Jade sings along and I close my eyes, feeling the real tears coming on now. They stream down my face in a hot wash, and I just let them, because I sense that Jade is doing the same thing, letting it go. The song ends and she plays it again, and then another time, lowering the volume.

I can't speak for a moment, and hide my face. My shoulders are shaking with the violence of the sorrow in me. Choking, I say, "I don't know how . . . I'm going to do . . . this. Go on . . . without him. I . . . don't . . . want to."

Jade reaches over, and she's got tears in her eyes, too. "I know."

"It's not . . . fair. I don't know what . . . I . . . did. Or . . . didn't . . . do. I don't understand any of it, and I don't know how to do this, and it just hurts so much."

She turns the music down a little more and lifts her glass, sniffing. "It does," she says, toasting me.

I click my glass to hers, wipe a gathered collection of tears from below my chin. "How do we go on, Jade?"

"Not there yet," she says. "I want to tell somebody why I loved him first. And then you can tell me."

I laugh a little. "Group therapy?"

"You better believe it." She takes a breath. "Dante called tonight supposedly to check on me, but he was asking for money, you know? And I was disappointed all over again for falling in love with such a player."

I nod.

"It's just that . . . he's not a bad man in his heart. He learned to hustle young and he doesn't know another way, and even in the middle of all his hustles, I know he loved me." She stops, looks at the ceiling, narrows her eyes. "Or loved me as much as he could, I guess. That's what's hard. That I was out there, so earnestly believing all of it, and he's just not capable of really loving anybody." Her face crumples. In the background, Alicia sings about a woman's worth. "But that doesn't change how much I loved him."

"I know," I say. But I'm thinking that Rick really is a good man, and he's capable of great love. I've felt it. My stomach is feeling better and it crosses my mind that it was held-in tears making it hurt. I meet Jade's eyes. "I had a really good marriage. That's what I don't understand. I mean, not just okay. But real. Peaceful and full of love and conversation and sex and everything." I shake my head. "What I can't understand is where was that moment? You know, that moment when it could have

91

been changed, when I could have done something. When there was a chance."

"It's not about you, Trudy."

"It has to be! I mean, a happy man doesn't do that—have an affair. How could I not have seen that he was so unhappy?"

"Why couldn't he just come to you and say that he was unhappy?"

I look at her. "That would have been a lot easier."

We listen to music quietly for a while, drink some more wine. Weep a little more. In an hour, we're both getting drunk, and it's better. The wounds are open and bleeding, making a big pool of gore on the floor between us. But we dip our fingers into it and write on the air. I'm leaning against the couch, my feet sprawled out in front of me. "I wasn't going to marry Rick. I was getting my master's and I thought eventually we'd just drift apart. But he came up to see me about two weekends a month, and on the ones he stayed in Pueblo all I could do was think about who he might have met, and I'd drive myself insane with jealousy." I purse my lips. "Then I got pregnant, and the rest of it all seemed so small in comparison."

"I never knew that, that you got married because you were pregnant."

"Yeah. Everybody thought I was crazy. He was too blue collar, drank too much beer, blah blah blah, but I knew it was the right thing to do."

She turns her head. "Knowing everything you know now, would you still do it that way?"

The answer is very simple. "Yes."

"Then that's all you need to know." She pushes away from the couch. "I guess I should go. The masses are going to be gone tomorrow. Need to get some sleep."

I stand up and hug her. "Thanks, Jade."

At the door, she stops. "I'm going to the boxing gym with Tony next week. Maybe find a trainer."

"That's great!"

"Yeah. I'm excited."

She zips her coat.

"Knowing everything you know, Jade," I say, "would you do it again?"

She ducks her head. Studies the floor. Nods. "How could I be where I am if not for that?"

"There you go."

As I close the door, I think I should go to bed, and I'm honestly headed that way, but the CD player moves to the next CD in the lineup and it's Lucinda Williams. Bonnie Raitt meets Keb' Mo', stirred with J. D., as Dr. Anthony, the professor who recommended her, said. I've been listening to her a lot, and now I pour the last of the wine into my glass—might as well finish it up—and settle back down on the floor.

And I think about Rick. Not then, not long ago. Now. I think of the threads of silver in his hair, each thread appearing before my eyes. I think of the way he makes love, with such easy abandon, forgetting everything and making me forget about my flat chest and my freckles and everything else.

Oh, God! I miss him so much. Everything about him. The smell of his skin, the way his mouth looks when he's sleeping, the sight of him sprawled on the couch, his long legs out in front of him ending in gray socks. I miss him coming into the kitchen with a greasy rag and greasy hands and a sparkling, unrecognizable motorcycle part to say, "Look at that!" in awe and happiness. I miss my big, hearty, man's man biker getting tears in his eyes over something and trying to hide it. I love that no one knows this about him, that he has to duck his head at the end of movies or when the music is great.

"Admit it, Trudy," I say. "Say it out loud: *He left me for another woman. Get over it.*" I shake my head, hearing the words everyone keeps saying to me: *Get over it, life goes on, not everyone has it this easy, take this chance to build yourself a new life.*

And it's true, all of it. I know that. I have some comfort, will not want for money. Rick will never be one of those disappearing fathers.

It's a good chance for me to assess my dreams and see what else I want of life. My kids are practically grown, even. I'm free.

Lucinda is singing about a man who once loved a woman, and I sing along, loudly, letting more tears come. I think, a little blearily, that this might be the best heartbreak CD ever in the history of the world. I rock and sing, sip the wine to make it last through the album.

Then she gets to the one that pierces me. It says everything. *The days go by, but they don't seem the same . . . Still I long for your kiss.*

And I realize with a sudden, dead-on clarity that I didn't get drunk tonight to grieve. I got drunk so I would have the courage to:

Pick up the phone. Punch in the numbers to Rick's cell phone. Wait for him to answer.

Which he does, sleepy and worried. "Trudy?"

I take a deep breath and say, "I miss you. I hate this. I wanted you to bury me or me to bury you and it doesn't seem fair and I don't know how to make it right." And now my tears are as hot and real as they ever have been in my life, and I know I'm going to hate myself in the morning, but I have to just say it this time, out loud. "I hate this, Rick."

He's stricken. "Trudy, are you okay?"

"No, no, no," I say. "I'm not okay. Can I just tell you, on the basis of the fact that we are best friends, that I would trade everything, Rick—not the kids, but everything else, to make this right? I'd be fat. I'd be ugly. I'd cut my hair and go to a Southern Baptist church and bake brownies."

On the other end of the phone, he laughs, very gently. "I don't think anyone would want to eat them."

"You are totally ruining my complete humiliation of myself, you know it?"

"Well, if you really want to, I'll let you."

And suddenly, I can see him, shirtless, his hair messed up from sleeping, and my grief swells up like a monster and swallows me. For a long time, I just weep on the phone, deep, heartfelt sobs that I haven't shared with him.

He doesn't hang up.

Finally, I whisper, "I'm sorry," and break the connection.

When the phone rings a minute later, I don't answer. Instead, I click off the CD player, take the glasses into the kitchen, turn off the lights. The phone rings a second time, and I leave it, going upstairs to wash my face.

That was productive, I say to my reflection in the bathroom mirror. My eyes are red and my nose is sloppy and there are blotchy marks all over my chest. Gorgeous.

I shake my head. Time to move on. As I crawl into bed, I realize I'm warm for the first time in days. Must be the wine.

I am dreaming that I've found an entire shopping mall between the dining room and the kitchen. I often dream I find extra rooms—probably an offshoot of the space problems we had all those years—but the mall is a first. It's elegant, hung with crystal chandeliers, the floors lined with marble. There are jewelry stores everywhere, and for some reason, I have a platinum card, because, after all, it is my house. In my dream, I'm standing by a fountain, trying to decide between the possibilities, when Rick pops in. He's wearing his turquoise shirt.

"Trudy," he says, and there's a sound of laughter in it. I shake my head, go back to contemplating the rich jewels awaiting. "Trudy." Then again, singsong, "Truuuu-dddeeee."

I jerk away to find him standing, flesh and blood, at the foot of the bed. He has a large latte in his hand. "Good morning."

The light, yellow and cheery, stabs into my right eye and I close it hastily. "You're not supposed to be in my bedroom," I say, and pull the pillow over my head. My humiliating phone call comes back to me, and through the feathers, I say, "And I really don't want to talk about it, okay? G'way."

He pulls the covers down, and I'm wearing a very ratty old nightgown, so I leave the pillow and grab the covers and glare at him. "I know the latte's mine, and I do deserve it, so hand it over and then let yourself out."

Chuckling, he sits on the bed, on his side. I notice it's undisturbed. I wonder if he does. "I just wanted to be sure you were okay," he says, handing the coffee over.

"I'm fine." The coffee is perfect. Three sugars and whole milk. "Mmm. Thank you."

He inclines his head, smooths his hand over the covers. "So, I saw Mo, obviously."

"Yeah?"

"He was in rare form."

I raise my eyes.

"He says to me, 'You've been a bad boy, eh?'" Rick imitates Mo's accent perfectly.

"Really." This is an interesting development.

Rick touches his mustache with one finger, smoothing away a grin, and keeps going in Mo's voice, "You know what you do with a wife? She say it's morning, and it's midnight, you say, 'Oh, yes, dear! It's very bright this morning.'"

I laugh, and Rick joins me.

"It's midnight," I say.

"So it is," he says, looking at me. "Look at that moon." There is something I don't quite understand in his eyes, a pleading or an apology. After a minute, he looks away, hops off the bed. "I've gotta get to work. So do you."

"Canceled. Some kind of plumbing disaster. I don't work until Monday."

He nods, walks to the door. "Talk at you later."

"Thanks for the coffee."

At the door, he pauses, that long hand resting against the threshold. "Whatever you think, Trudy, it's never had anything to do with you. Or us. Or anything like that."

I want to protest. How could it not? But I take it in the spirit he intends it—he's trying to make me feel better. I just nod.

15

Jade

On Friday afternoon, I put on my gym clothes. A pair of black sweats that have seen better days, a heavy-duty sports bra, an old T-shirt of Dante's that has a cigar logo from New Orleans on it. The sleeves are ripped off. I put my hair in a scrunchie and wash off my makeup and put on my oldest workout shoes. A female in a gym has to look serious. No cute little spandex, no tight T-shirts, no perfect eyeliner. Leave it at home, baby.

I cross the street to Shannelle's house. There are paper ghosts taped to the window, and a string of pumpkin lights around the window. On cue, a silky black cat rubs against my ankles. "Hey, you." I bend down and rub him. Soft as a cloud.

Shannelle opens the door. She looks about a million times better. The swelling from her extraction is gone, and the faint gray of pain has evaporated, revealing skin as clear as a milkmaid's. "Hi!" she says. "Come on in. Tony's just putting on his shoes. We've been kind of lazy around here this morning, so excuse the mess."

The "mess" is a scattering of newspapers on the couch. There is a toy truck under the table. The boys peek around the corner, giggle, pull back. I shoot a grin toward their mother. These two boys have been flirting with me all week long. I tiptoe to the doorway and scrunch down. When they peek out again, I roar and grab them both, tickling them, loving their shrieks.

"Mom! Save us, save us!"

Tony shakes his pant leg down and stands up. "You sure you're feeling okay, baby?" he asks Shannelle. He's a tall, good-looking man. His children are his spitting image. I like the way he puts his hand on the back of Shannelle's neck.

"I'm fine," she says with an edge of exasperation. "It's been days."

"All right, then. Sure you don't want to come with us?"

"No, sweetie." She waves at the computer. "I told you I want to spend some time writing today. Okay?"

He's scared of me. Of the way I look. Of what he might think about my body when he's sitting next to me in a car. Maybe that sounds vain, but I don't mean it that way. He's one of the good guys. He doesn't ogle and wants not to think about anybody but his wife.

Or maybe he's not that kind of guy, and he's worried about what people will think of him escorting me.

I say, "Shannelle, I forgot—do you have a ring of some kind, something that maybe looks a little like a wedding ring?" I lift a shoulder. "Keeps the bullshit down."

"Oh, pretty smart. Sure." She comes back with a silver ring, carved and set with turquoise. I put it on and it fits perfectly. She winks when Tony's not looking.

I'm nervous on the way down there. So is Tony. It's weirdly quiet. It only takes about ten minutes before we're pulling up in front of a block of storefronts on Northern. There's a Mexican bodega with pink and green goods in the window and the signs all in Spanish. Tony pulls open a door next to it and gestures for me to go in first. We climb a narrow set of stairs to the second floor. It's dark and smells of sweat. At the top of the stairs, I have to pause a minute to get my bearings.

By then, our entry has been noticed. I'm suddenly thinking I'm an idiot to want this. These are tough guys here, most of them Black or Mexican, dressed in the same kind of uniform I'm wearing. At least I got that right. Sun is coming in from a wall of windows toward the back. It's not terribly crowded. Some young guys on the speed bags, a sparring match in the ring, some guys jumping rope and taping their hands and doing push-ups and crunches. I'm the only woman. They notice.

But after that first minute, I just don't care. The sound of hands slamming bags, the smell of chalk and dust and bodies, the sharp scent of competition jazzes me up. I can do this. I know I can. I just need some help.

"Yo, Tony!" A man with Tony's face, shorter and stockier, dances over, eyes bright with curiosity. There's approval on his face when he sticks out his hand. "You're Jade, huh?"

I take the hand, nodding.

"I'm Gabe."

"Nice to meet you."

"So, Tony says you want to train." He crosses his arms on his chest. "How come?"

I lift a shoulder. "Why does anybody?"

"Lotta guys think it makes 'em tough. They just wanna swagger around and brag about being boxers. Lotta women have something to prove."

I meet his eyes dead-on. "I have a right cross that knocked a man clean out with one shot. I want to see what else."

"No kiddin'." He inclines his head, tips it toward the other side of the room. Slapping his brother on the arm, he says, "Bro, go have a soda or something." To me he says, "Come on." I follow him, trying not to be self-conscious, but I feel eyes measuring me. "My trainer doesn't want to deal with women, but I've found somebody who's willing to talk to you. Hey, Rueben. This is her."

From the shadows peels away another shadow, as big as Darth Vader. As he comes into the light, I blink. Because this is one beautiful man. A dark, angular face, the biggest, softest dark brown eyes I've ever seen, a great mouth. His skin has the sleek shine of a seal and his arms are gigantic. I can tell by the way he walks that he's in prime condition.

He holds out his hand, his eyes evaluating me in a way that doesn't feel threatening. "How you doin'," he says in a low, blurred voice. Texas, I know, in that second. My grandfather spoke just like this. "I'm Rueben."

"Jade." His hand engulfs mine. The palm is sturdy and dry. "Nice to meet you."

Gabe motions toward the ring. "You two cool?"

Rueben nods. "So, you want to box?"

I look at a youth punching a heavy bag. Hunger rises up in me. "Yeah. I started training out in Sacramento, but my grandfather got sick and I came home to take care of my grandmother." I blink. "Sorry," I say, clearing my throat. "He just died a few days ago. It's still pretty raw."

"Don't be sorry. Speaks well of you that you're there for the folks. Not everybody cares like that these days."

"Yeah, well, they're good people."

He nods, those empathetic eyes on my face, his hands braced on his waist. "I'll want to see what you've got, but I'm looking at you thinking you're in good condition. Started with kickboxing?"

"How did you know?"

"Lucky guess." His grin is filled with big, very white teeth. I both relax and feel a zing in my chest. More seriously, he says, "Why not compete there? Or take up martial arts?"

"Because I want to get in the ring. The boxing ring."

"Why?"

I get tired of this question. "Because I do, that's all." I glare at him. "Because I want to see if I have what it takes. Maybe win."

"People get killed boxing."

"They get killed riding buses."

"You might end up not so pretty."

"Well, let me tell you, pretty has never gotten me one damned thing."

He laughs. Out loud. "Sister, that's a lie." He winks, punches my arm. "Ask a plain woman what your fine self has been getting you."

I think of the men at the gas station, but I also think of the boy at the grocery store who gave me an extra quarter pound of roast beef from the deli. "I'm willing to risk it." I pause and add, "I want to be strong. As strong as I can be. I want to see what I can do with this. It's not any deeper than that. I just want to."

"Good answer," he says. "I've got an appointment in a little while, but why don't we get together next week and we'll see what you've got."

"Really?"

"Yeah. How's Thursday? Say six thirty?"

"Excellent." A surge of excitement makes me reach out and take his hand. "Thank you, Rueben. I mean it."

"No promises, now."

"I understand."

He turns my hand over. "Your husband cool with this?"

"I'm divorced." There is more bitterness in the words than I would have liked. Rueben only nods.

Tony sees me crossing the gym and I manage to maintain all the way down the stairs and out to the street. There I stop and do a little quick dance and a couple of air-punches. "Whoo!" I say to him. He's laughing.

When I get home, there's a message for me from Social Services. They must need somebody right now, because the woman asks me to call this evening about the résumé I'd sent them. They need a foster care liaison, which is what I'd worked in before I left.

Yeah. Life is looking up.

16

Trudy

This weekend I'm not going to brood. On Friday night, I make a plan, a list of things I can do to keep myself busy. I won't sit by the phone and wish for better days. I won't beat myself up about anything. I'm just going to live in the moment—even if I need to have an action plan to make it work.

The list says:

1. Take a nice long walk in the morning. Bring the camera and enjoy it
2. Check in on Roberta
3. Go to the Lowe's to look at paint
4. Buy some if there's anything good
5. Paint the living room
6. Get ready for trick-or-treaters. Make something special for Shannelle's boys.

Sunday

1. Go to the movies. NO romantic comedies. Thriller?
2. Fix a nice supper for Annie. Make her call her father

3. If I get restless, call a friend and talk about something else
4. Spend an hour with Roberta.

Just having the list makes me feel more in control, and I wake up to discover it's one of those brilliant fall days again. Bright, sunny, even warm. Which, frankly, bodes ill for the trick-or-treaters who will be running around in their goblin and princess and firefighter uniforms tonight. I don't know why it always snows on Halloween around here, but I remember countless nights I shivered around with my three, coming home apple-cheeked and frozen and wet.

First, I spend some time in the greenhouse, tending my plants and humming under my breath. I sit with Spider Woman for a while, trying to quiet my restless spirit, but when I start getting flashes of Rick's other woman, my wrist starts to ache, and I quit.

After breakfast, I set out for a walk. The wind is calm for once, exhilarating. I bring my camera with me, and shoot little things along the way—a cat in a window, a beer can sitting on a fence post, frosted over and glittering in the morning, the Vietnam memorial in the island on Elizabeth.

I walk to Mineral Palace Park. It's quiet and I can walk in grass there, as many miles as I like. It used to be two or three miles, two or three times a week, a habit I started because I get backaches from sitting at the computer all day at work. Walking helps. Since Rick moved out, there are days I've lost track of how many times I've paced around that park and gone home exhausted, but in a good way. A way that gets rid of all that pain in my chest.

This morning, I'm not particularly in pain, which is a surprising and pleasant feeling. I've been feeling a lot better since the night I got drunk, for reasons that are not clear. But I'm also tired of introspection and brooding and thinking only of my relationship on every bloody possible level. There's more to life.

Like walking through the mini-neighborhoods on the way to the park. The first is a four-block square filled with neat ranch houses built in the fifties by a man named Bonforte, who had a thing for crab apple trees. He built the houses and lined the streets of his developments with crab apple trees. They are a wonder in the spring. This pocket neighborhood is extraordinarily well tended, the lawns clear of dandelions, their hoses rolled up on reels, the pristine driveways filled with silver Buicks and Lincolns and the odd Camry.

It abuts one of the oldest spots in town—a pioneer cemetery through which I sometimes wander, counting my blessings that children don't fall to so many things these days, and wondering about the humans attached to the sinking tombstones.

Today, I veer in another direction, so that I can admire the mansions along Greenwood and Elizabeth, and to a lesser degree, Grand, which has not yet been claimed entirely by the upwardly mobile. The homes are enormous Victorians on generous lots, with old, tall trees and mature lilac bushes. I get my best ideas for perennial plantings from these yards.

This morning, they're preparing for the Halloween onslaught. People come from all over town to bring their children trick-or-treating on these streets, and the owners are good-natured about it, even generous. There are cardboard coffins in the grass and sheet ghosts hanging from trees, and special sound effects playing from enough houses that the whole area echoes with goblinesque noises. It is in this neighborhood that children gleefully scream over surprise mummies popping up from behind a bush.

On a wide porch, a man and his daughter are hanging twisting orange crepe paper. The little girl, about seven, has whiskers and a cat nose drawn on her face in black, and she's wearing pink cat slippers. She's twirling and twirling and I raise my camera to capture her. She sees me and waves. "Hey, did you know it's Halloween today?"

Her father lifts his chin in greeting, smiling wryly.

"I did. What are you going to be?"

"A cat! Meow, meow!"

"Have a good time," I say, waving. Maybe I'll put on a nice warm coat and come out here tonight to wander with the hordes of children. I don't have many trick-or-treaters anymore, but I do so love the excitement and seeing all the little costumes, from the toddlers to the teenagers pretending they're dressed up, in trench coats and rock 'n' roll faces. Boys. Girls don't seem to hang on to the habit as long as boys. I've had many a sixteen-year-old boy come to my door on Halloween.

And that reminds me—what will Rick do tonight? He adores Halloween. Loves to answer the door and pass out candy and act scared over the monsters. He's the one who buys all the decorations for Halloween and Christmas. Sometimes he even dresses up as a vampire, complete with bloody teeth.

I have to admit it's a good way to get me in bed. I love it when he comes after me with those teeth.

Or I mean loved it.

Snakelike slithers of memory like that are hard to ignore. I decide to just let them be. Those days did happen. They're still mine. I don't know what will happen tonight, and it's not my problem. I have to worry only about me today. Do I wish he was going to be there dressed up as a vampire and making love to me afterward? Yes. Can I live without it?

It's beginning to look that way.

The park is one of the jewels of the city, an oasis of greenery and tall trees just north of downtown. Once upon a time, there was a building that housed King Coal and Queen Silver, statues carved out of their respective minerals. But someone stole them and the building fell into disrepair and was eventually torn down. I'm not even sure where it once stood.

These days, there's a swimming pool for the kids, rose gardens, and herb gardens, and my favorite thing—a lovely pond with an island in the middle of it. An old stone bridge arches over the water, and it's this picture that's been in my mind on the way here.

To my delight, a thin crust of bluish ice covers the pond, all except for a perfect circle where a fountain has melted it. Ducks are skating and waddling over the ice, and paddling happily in the melted bit. The colors are extraordinary, a vivid sky with pipe-smoke puffs of cloud, the blue of the ice, the arches of the bridge echoing the circle of melted ice. I photograph it from the south end from several perspectives, even kneeling in the damp grass to shoot the scene through the old wrought-iron fence around it. I love the camera for the same reason I love plants—the shapes and colors and quiet make me feel calm.

Thinking of shooting the same scene from the opposite angle, I wander north and spy a man on the bridge. He's bending over the edge to scatter bread to the ducks below, and there's a great symmetry to the echo of his arm and an old gaslight fixture to one side, and I raise the camera, shooting far, then zooming in a little at a time.

He raises his head to look in the middle distance and I realize with a little shock that it's my new neighbor, Angel. Since he doesn't see me, I zoom in close, closer, admiring his elegantly carved face, the way the light breaks down his straight, strong nose. They say a language shapes a person's mouth, and I wonder if Spanish somehow makes for generosity of lips.

At that moment, I realize he's turned toward me and is looking directly into the camera. As if he's used to being photographed, he smiles very slightly and inclines his head. I shoot the picture and lower the camera, smiling.

He ambles my way, loose as a cat. "Good morning! Do you remember? We met last week?"

I laugh, pulling hair away from my face. "Of course I remember. You're Angel."

"And you are Trudy." His tongue softens the hard consonants of my name.

"Do you mind that I took your picture?"

"No." He smiles, gives me a charming shrug, then gestures toward the landscape around us. "Beautiful, eh?"

I nod. From this angle, sunlight glitters and dances in places where the ice is melting. "I walk here a lot."

"This is the first time I have come here. Happy chance you are here, too."

God, I love his accent, the phrasings. It makes me want to be serious about my Spanish again. "Where are you from, Angel?"

"*Andalucía*—the city of Sevilla. Do you know it?"

It's a magic word to me. "Oh! Flamenco." I put my hand on my heart. "I have always wanted to go there. Always."

There's a sudden openness in his eyes, which in the sunlight are the color of a hawk's. "It is a wonderful city."

The day is bright yellow around us, a backdrop of leaves turning colors contrasting with the wavy darkness of his hair, the symmetry of his face. I don't want to go anywhere. I want to stand here talking to him. "I was going to go to Spain to study when I graduated with my master's, but I didn't."

"Why not?"

I lift my shoulders. "A baby came instead."

"Ah." He looks at me, and I can see him in that old Spanish city, walking the streets easily. "What were you going to study?"

"Lorca."

Angel's face brightens. "Federico García Lorca?"

"Yes."

He smiles, closes his eyes, and shakes his head very slowly. Then very quietly, he quotes, "*Me he perdido muchas veces por el mar; con el oído lleno de flores recién cortadas.*"

As he speaks in his honeyed voice, my skin breaks out in gooseflesh. It takes me a minute to find the best English translation I remember. My voice is huskier than normal when I say in return, "'I have lost myself in the sea many times, with my ear full of freshly cut flowers.'"

His smile is slow and luscious. "*Con la lengua llena de amor y de agonía.*"

"'With my tongue full of love and agony.'"

"*Muchas veces me he perdido por el mar,*" he quotes, his eyes on my face. "*Como me pierdo en el corazón de algunos niños.*"

"'I have lost myself in the sea many times, as I lose myself in the heart of certain children.'"

I have impressed him. He laughs, reaches out, and touches my hand, quickly lets it go. "I see you are intelligent as well as beautiful." He gestures toward the sidewalk in front of us. "Are you walking back? May I walk with you?"

"Of course."

We walk side by side, hands swinging next to us. After a moment, he says, "You should go to Andalucía now that your children are old enough."

I nod.

He smiles. "You don't believe me. Do you want me to tell you why?"

It is impossible not to smile up at him in return. "All right."

"For one thing, it is very beautiful. And old. And the people are friendly."

"Good reasons."

"But there is more. Flamenco, of course. Bullfighting." He pauses with a little frown. "Do you want to see the bullfights?"

I wince. "No."

"It is too cruel for me." He slides a coy glance my way. "Do you now think me . . ." He tsks, throws out a hand, finds the word. ". . . too girly?"

Raising my head, I meet his gaze. "No."

"Good." We pause at the corner to let a car pass. "Sevilla smells of flowers." With an extravagant gesture, he opens his arms and smells the memory. "Orange blossoms and jasmine and roses. So many flowers, pouring through little cracks in the walls, and tumbling over the balconies." He tsks again, gives a little cock of the head. "It is beautiful."

Reaction is rushing down my spine. He is a poem come to life—as if the goddesses gathered together to think up someone to send to me. I can see them, Gaia and Spider Woman and Brigid—and probably

Lucille—sitting together over cocktails, a bawdy bunch of seasoned women. I lift an eyebrow at them privately.

Angel catches it. "That's a wicked thought. Will you share it?"

How long since anyone saw me this way? "Not today," I tell him with a secret smile I know he will like. And something about the quirk of his lips then makes me notice how young he is. That's the only part the goddesses got wrong.

In my imagination, Lucille snorts. I ignore her. "How old are you, Angel?"

"Thirty-three," he says, and smiles, showing his big shiny teeth. "Not so young, huh?"

When I was graduating from high school, he was headed into what, third grade? I take a breath, focus my gaze on the sidewalk rolling out before us beneath shedding trees. Our feet crunch through piles of crisp leaves. "You're lucky to be able to travel. I've never had much of a chance."

"Americans always say that."

"Maybe it's easier when the countries are close together."

He lifts a shoulder. "Australians travel. To Europe, to America."

"True."

"So why don't Americans do it so much?"

I think of my own reasons. "It's expensive, I guess, but that's not really it. It costs a lot more to buy an expensive vehicle, like an SUV or something."

"And you like your cars, very much." He points to the shiny black Suburban parked in front of a small bungalow.

I laugh softly. "Oh, yes. I think travel seems more expensive because it's not something you have to do. It's a luxury."

He looks at me. "Is it?"

"Is it necessary?"

"For the mind," he says, nodding, and touches the center of his chest. "For the soul. To see what else lies around the world, to see how people do things, to share your own ways."

I walk beside him quietly for a moment. He's wearing sturdy Teva sandals, and his feet are long and tanned, with long toes. Graceful feet. Feet that have carried him around the world. "I suppose if more Americans traveled with honest intentions, there would be less hatred of us, wouldn't there?"

"*Sí.*" He smiles at me gently, as if he is the instructor and I the student. "Now, how did you come to love Lorca, Trudy?"

There's genuine interest in his voice, so I allow myself to tell him about Lucille, and the winding path to discovering Lorca one dusty winter day in my sophomore year. Angel feeds me questions to keep me talking, and before I know it we are turning up our street, and stand in front of my house for a moment in the lovely bright morning, talking a little longer.

And for the first time since I met Rick Marino twenty-some years before, I realize I am flirting with someone. I forgot how it felt. There I am one moment, and then something in me turns, and I remember how to incline my head, how to look at him sideways. Something in me is devouring details—his cheekbones, his throat. His skin is so smooth, I want to pet it, rub it.

Now he says to me, "I have music from Spain. Flamenco, too." His eyes are steady on mine. Open. "I would love to play some for you"— he lifts a shoulder—"some evening. I will cook. Feed your dreams of Spain, eh?"

"I would love that."

"Good. And perhaps you will do the same for me. Show me your music, your special dishes."

I laugh, and the sound surprises me. It's big and green. Genuine. "I'm not much of a cook."

"I do not think that is true. You are a sensual woman, no? Cooking is a sensual thing."

It startles me, this sudden richness in his voice, and as if to underscore it, he blinks, slowly, and smiles. If he were my contemporary, if it were any other situation, I would think he wanted me. "Thank you for a good conversation, Trudy."

"Anytime."

As he walks away, I find I'm remembering Lucille. Angel reminds me of her—she used to say the same things about travel. A wisp of the girl I was stands to one side, an eyebrow lifted as she reminds me I used to know it myself.

She shimmers a moment in the light, smelling of patchouli and dreams.

～

The local Lowe's is crowded to the rafters. I have come here to buy paint, and there are magazine photos in my hands. It's wicked to pick out paint for the living room without consulting anyone, but it's my house and I'm thinking of something vivid for one wall, something I wouldn't be able to do if Rick were there. Red. Or rather, a red orange, burnt orange almost, to match the gown in an Edwardian painting I have hanging on one wall.

I love hardware superstores. The smell of fresh wood, the rows and rows and rows of possibilities in every aisle. Border paper and hammers and chains; tiles and carpets and lighting fixtures. I never miss a chance to admire the kitchen and bath possibilities. It's a serene activity, and it adds a lot to my sense of well-being this afternoon. There is a gorgeous Arts and Crafts lighting fixture with stained glass that would be beautiful in my kitchen, and as I turn down the tiling aisle to admire the ceramics, I'm wondering if it would be extravagant to do something like that.

And my soap bubble of peacefulness, so fragile to start with, explodes, because there at the end of the aisle is Rick.

With Carolyn.

It's the first time I've seen her in several months, and I see again with bewilderment that she is ordinary. Even plain. I mean, if you put us side by side and said, "Which is the mistress and which is the wife?" you'd pick me as the mistress every single time.

She isn't tall; she isn't short. She's not fat. She's not thin. She's not blonde or redheaded or brunette, just that bland color in between all of them. She's older than me, and it shows that she's smoked her whole life, in the little lines on her top lip and through her cheeks. Her eyes are good, I have to admit. Susan Sarandon eyes. In fact, she reminds me a bit of Sarandon, enough that I can't stand the actress anymore, and I loved her a lot once.

The difference is that Carolyn has no sheen. Not even Glamour Shots could make her look good.

Okay, I take it back. She has good breasts. It's hard not to admire the pear-shaped weight of them beneath her blue sweater. And I think she must be one of those women who tan to a rosy gold. Probably her hair gets streaks in the summer, too. A sun goddess in a bikini.

Still. She isn't smart, she isn't accomplished, she's a failure at marriage, and her kids are running wild all over town, and as I'm standing there frozen, my heart pounding so hard I think it might be possible I will have a heart attack right there, they turn around and see me.

I can't move. All I can think is that I hope my hands aren't shaking as visibly as it feels like they are.

Carolyn sees me first and dives behind Rick, her hands on his shoulders, like I'm going to come after her. I roll my eyes. I mean, yeah, she might have reason to be afraid, but really.

"Oh, please," I say to her. "If I was going to kick your ass, I would have already done it."

Rick's face has the expression that reminds me of our sons' when they were busted doing something they knew they shouldn't be doing, but they were going to brazen it out in hopes of a lesser punishment. I meet his eyes. Toss my hair out of my face. Pass by close so I can say quietly to his ear, "I hope she likes your vampire teeth."

Adrenaline carries me around the corner. I head blindly for the paint samples. By the time I reach the display, I'm panting and my hands are shaking so hard that I have to tuck them under my armpits. I practice yoga breathing, and after a minute it helps.

He was holding her hand. He's always claimed that he thought that was smarmy. And I agreed with him.

Things change, I guess.

"Something I can help you with, ma'am?" a thirtyish boy asks me. Ma'am. Why not just say old lady? "Maybe in a minute."

How do people get through this? How can they stand the buffets of humiliation, over and over again? It's like the endless winds, stopping and starting. Stopping and starting. I want to bow my head and howl, but I just keep doing the breathing. There are millions and millions of divorced women in the world. Some of them have to be happy.

Finally, I can at least look at the samples. I choose a poppy shade in a semigloss, the highest quality, and have the boy mix it up for me. It seems like a victory.

On the way home, I realize I have no candy for the trick-or-treaters, and stop in Mo's grocery. When I carry up the bags of tiny chocolate bars, he says, "So, how's that husband of yours? I see him yesterday." He gives me a big smile. "He been bad, huh?"

"Yeah," I bite out.

"It happens, no? Marriage, she goes up and down."

I glare at him. "I guess."

"A little work, you'll be happy again."

"We're divorcing, Mo." I hand him a ten. "He's not living with me, okay?"

"You make a place for him, he'll come home," he says, and puts the change gently in my hand. "You'll see."

"Whatever."

In my car, I can't help but sigh. Mo's KwickWay and Marriage Fix-It Shoppe. Right in your very own neighborhood.

17

Trudy

Annie has awakened and flown the coop by the time I get back. There's a note on the table from her: no work tonight. She'll be home early—just went to the movies with her friends. It cheers me marginally. I'll have some supper ready, in case she wants to eat.

Still determined not to brood, no matter what, I visit Roberta for a little while. Jade has gone to Denver to visit her mother, and Roberta is sorting through old books and papers, separating them into boxes. Her spirits seem subdued, but good. What she seems is a little winded, like it's all too much. "Maybe," I say, "you need to just rest a little bit, Roberta. Why don't we have a cup of tea?"

"Well," she says, and frowns in a befuddled way at the circle of boxes around her. "I guess that would be all right. Would you put on the water, honey?"

"Sure thing." I return in a minute and sink down on the floor. "What is all this?"

"Pictures," she says. "Letters. Can you believe it? I got letters in here back as far as 1935."

"Is there some way I can help you?"

She blinks as if this possibility has never occurred to her. "Why, I reckon you could." She points at the boxes. "They're all labeled, one for each of my children. I'm trying to be fair, so each of them has a piece of the history. I don't expect Earl to give a hoot one way or t'other, but his wife's a good woman. She'll take care of it for the grandchildren. I'll give Earl something nice of his daddy's—maybe the watches. Edgar collected them, you know."

"Yes."

She pauses with a stack of letters in her hand. "These are some Edgar wrote me in the war. He wasn't much of a speller, but I got the idea." The papers start to tremble, and she raises her kind brown eyes. "You know," she says in her sweet voice, "I just don't know how I'm goin' to do this, Trudy. Live without him."

I reach for her hand, and hold it. "Did he write you love letters?"

She looks down at the letters in her hand. "He did."

"Would you like to read me one of them?"

Her face crumples, and I'm afraid I've said the wrong thing. "Oh, I know it's silly, that all I want to do is talk about him. I know everybody's goin' to get tired of it."

"I won't. Why don't you read me one?"

"All right." She lets go of my hand to slip out one thin sheet from a yellowed envelope. There are holes cut in it. "See those? That's from the censors."

I smile.

Roberta begins to read.

"'Dear Berta. Hope this letter finds you fine as you always are. When I get home, I want you to wear that red dress, the one with buttons all up the front. Can you guess what I'm gonna do with them buttons?

"'It ain't like home here, Berta. Folks take us in just the same as the white soldiers. They's just as happy to see us. Been a long war for some of 'em. Give your mama my love. Know that I'm thinking about you all the time, sugar-girl. No woman for me but you. (I know how you worry!) Your man for now and for always, Edgar.'"

She's smiling as she folds the letter up again. "I didn't worry, you know. He was the one that was always worrying."

I laugh with her, and the teakettle whistles. "Why don't we have that tea and you can read me some more?"

"All right," she says in her sweet voice, and she sounds better.

Maybe, I think, all she wants is to live there where Edgar is still alive. I can listen.

~

Back in my own kitchen, I feel a creeping sense of depression that I'm determined will not control my evening. Not control one more second of my life. I defrost a package of chicken breasts and put them in a lime-and-tequila marinade, then sign on to the internet, answer a little bit of email, and then, thinking of Lucille and her travels, and Angel and his encouragement, I go online to look at websites of Spain.

My mood immediately lifts, and I play Enya—she of all possibilities—to keep me company. I look at hotels. One is a tenth-century Moorish estate on a hilltop, but it's fifteen kilometers out of town. Another is in the Old Quarter of the city, but it's a new high-rise, and if I'm going to visit an ancient city, I'm sure as hell not staying in a room that could be interchanged with any other room in any other city. I need something that speaks to me of Seville and all that it suggests.

I find one, finally, that seems as if it would be just right, in the Old Jewish Quarter. The price is modest, and the pictures show a yellow building with wrought iron overlooking a patio. I bookmark it, and take a break to put the chicken in the oven.

As I'm bending over the stove, I see a flash of Rick and Carolyn at the store. It carries a blade of pain with it, but I straighten with determination and go back to the computer.

Flights. How much would it cost to fly to Spain?

The airline searches require me to look up dates. If I went, when could I actually do it? During my spring break? Not too hot, not too far away, not too close. End of March. I feed in the dates. It asks how many passengers, and thinking defiantly of Lucille, I click one.

The price surprises me. Less than eight hundred dollars, which would probably go down some if I waited until a sixty-day outing to purchase it. It's a very long flight, however. Denver to London, London to Madrid, then Madrid to Seville. Fifteen hours flying. There's another option—Denver to New York to Madrid to Seville, but I'd rather fly to London. Just because.

Eight hundred dollars for the plane. Six hundred for the hotel.

Hmmm.

It's an exercise in forgetting, that's all, a way to keep my mind occupied. I know I'll never do it, not alone. What life has taught me is that I wanted to be Lucille, but I lacked her courage.

And as if to chide me, she's suddenly sitting on the living room couch. She flips the fringes on her shawl. "Oh, I remember some great times in Seville." She looks at me and lowers her voice. "I slept with a flamenco dancer. Dashing thing. Couldn't speak a word of English. He's the one who gave me this shawl, you know."

For a minute, I blink at her. "Are you real?"

She waves a long hand. "What's real, girl?"

The first time, I was on Vicodin. This time, I haven't even had a glass of wine. I close my eyes, and when I open them the apparition or figment of my imagination or hallucination is gone.

I'm disappointed.

Once I had asked her, "Don't you miss having a husband and children?"

She put her feet on a table. "Sometimes. But how could I trade what I did have for something I don't know anything about?"

She was so brave, Lucille, and in my recent victimhood, I've let her down.

Impulsively, I search for a tours option. The idea of a group frightens me less, but there isn't much. There are shorter tours, and those that cover all of Andalusia, but that's not really what I'm thinking of. I want Seville. Immersion.

Defiantly, I send for brochures of the city and turn off the computer, humming under my breath, and fix the rest of the meal. Annie hasn't arrived by the time it's ready, so I set the table for myself, with place mat and candles and the good silverware. I turn the radio to the classical station, and although I'm tempted to find a book or magazine to read in order to keep myself company, I resist. I eat the meal I've prepared so beautifully for myself, by myself.

The phone has not rung. How pathetic that I expected it to, somehow, that I've been half waiting for Rick's call since I came home. But the sun is setting and the hours have gone and he has not called. I stand at my front window and watch the lights come on, thinking of a dozen Halloweens—

A white car drives up and Annie tumbles out, her hair flying in the increasing wind. She waves and runs up the walk, and I smile as she comes in. "Hi. Did you have a good time?"

"Sure." She picks up the mail. "Any calls for me?"

"Nope." I perch on the edge of my chair. "How was it?"

She's reading a piece of mail. "Hmmm?"

"How was the movie? What did you see?"

"I'm sorry. What?"

"Never mind. Are you hungry? I made some dinner for once. Tequila-lime chicken. It was pretty good."

"Nah, Travis is picking me up in a little while. Didn't I tell you? We're going to a party at Kim's house."

Oh. "Who's going to be there?"

She shrugs, sitting down on the couch, and pulls off her shoes. "The usuals, I guess. Everybody from work and some of their boyfriends and girlfriends."

"Any adults?"

"Mom. Kim is twenty."

Right. I knew that. "Have you called your dad this week?"

"No, I just haven't had time."

"Annie. We have an agreement. He gets to see you three nights a week."

Her mouth is hard and she strips off thick woolen socks. "Well, I'm sorry, but my schedule isn't all that flexible, and if you think I'm going to go spend the night at that crummy little apartment where there isn't even a decent stereo, you can think again." She stands up. "I'm going to take a shower."

"Did you eat anything today at all?"

"I had a hot dog at the movie."

"Great nutrition there. Why don't you let me fix you a plate, warm it up, and you can eat when you get out of the shower?"

"Mom!" She spins around. "Would you stop hovering? God! You're driving me crazy. Why don't you get a life?"

I'm stung too deeply to be able to hide it. The whole day comes crashing back on me and I have to blink hard to avoid letting any tears fall. Which makes me even more pathetic and victimish and I stand up and go to the kitchen. "Fine."

"Mom," she says behind me, but I keep walking. Yank open the greenhouse door, head for the back corner, fling open the lid over the potting soil, and stick my hands into the black earth. It's cool and smells of possibilities. I stand there, smarting, letting the heat drain through my hands.

She follows me, puts her arms around me from behind, her head on my neck. "I'm sorry," she says, and I can hear tears in her voice. "That was just evil. I know you're sad, and I'm sorry and I can't fix it and I'm just too mad at Dad to be able to deal with him right now, okay?"

"I know." I stare at the black dirt beneath my hands, smell the rich, damp humusy scent. Annie smells of herbal shampoo and popcorn, and her slim body, her hair on my cheek, eases some deep tension in me.

Quietly, I say, "I miss you."

"I'm growing up. I'm sorry. It just happens."

"I'm not sorry you're growing up, but you are going to be leaving home for school next year and then things will really be different for both of us. Let's make a deal, all right? I would really like to have one sit-down meal every week with you. I'd like to just have this last bit of time when you're still a kid in my house, all right?"

She squeezes me. "Okay. And I owe you a dinner, too, for not getting mad at me over the Denver thing."

"Yes, you do."

"How about tomorrow night? The Black-Eyed Pea?"

I chuckle. "Where grown-ups go for dinner?"

"Yeah. So you can have something wicked. And I can have some banana pudding."

"It's a deal."

She lets me go and I turn around to face her. She's so beautiful, my little girl, with her clear skin and clear eyes and soft rose of a mouth. "Sorry I keep hovering," I say. "I'll put the chicken in the fridge and you can have some later if you're hungry."

"I just might."

When she goes up to shower, I decide I might as well be productive. No one will be here to complain if I play classical music—loudly—on the living room stereo, if I pull out the couches and tables and cover them with black trash bags torn open along the seam. I carry in a big pile of newspapers, arrange the furniture, set the bowl of chocolate bars in front of the door, and put on some old, ugly clothes for painting. I'll be a bag lady for the trick-or-treaters.

And paint the wall. To the sound of the Gipsy Kings. I'll dream of Seville. And maybe even allow a little fantasy of Angel Santiago's smooth skin.

As I'm putting the newspapers down, the phone rings. Hope sails up through me, light and clear, into my throat, and I'm reaching for it in relief before I remember. He was standing there, holding hands with a woman who is . . . whatever. Not me. I look at the caller ID and it's Rick, so I let it ring. When it quits, I check for a message, but he hasn't left one.

"Time to move on, Trudy, my dear," I say aloud, and spread the newspapers.

18

Shannelle

TO: naomiredding@rtsv.org

FROM: chanelpacheco@hotmail.com

SUBJECT: frustrated!!!

Hi, Naomi. It's past eleven and I really should go to bed, but I'm just so mad at my husband that I'm absolutely not going to do it. This is a whiny post, so you can skip it and read it later if you want, but I just need to vent to someone.

It's Halloween, right? I am really a freak about holidays, because my mother just never did that much. (It's not her fault—she worked all the time because of my dad's bad back—she just didn't have any energy left over. My dad, sad to say, is the loser, not my mom.) Anyway, I made the boys each a costume, and we had a party this afternoon with their friends and some of Tony's nieces and nephews. I baked a cake with gummy worms crawling out of a dirt graveyard with little tombstones and everything. (It was SO cute! You make the dirt with crushed Oreos.) I cooked a big supper for everybody, and then we went out trick-or-treating, and Tony helped me clean up the kitchen, and then he wanted to have sex (and it's not like I mind that—LOL!) so I did and then I wanted to get up and come in here and write for a while. I mean, I was dying for it. I saw Angel and Trudy talking outside today, and it gave me so many ideas for the book that I just wanted to come in here and write.

And Tony got mad at me. He's so jealous of the writing, and I just don't get it! He keeps saying we have so much, that it's selfish of me to want more. He says I'm just going to get my heart broken. He says if I loved him, I wouldn't want to get up and write all night long, but that I'd want to lie there with him.

ARRGGGH! It's not fair, and usually I give in because he's right—we do have a great life, and I'm really lucky to have such a steady, loving husband who is so good to his kids and takes care of business. But I just feel like if I give so much to them, it doesn't hurt anything for me to have something that's mine. I didn't do all that stuff for Halloween to earn my time at the computer or anything like that. I love doing it. It makes me happy to make a homey world for my kids and for me. I'm good at it.

But now it's nearly midnight and if I want to write for an hour or two, what does it hurt? So what if I get my heart broken? It's my heart and I can do whatever I want with it. Maybe he's right and people like us don't do things like publish books, and no matter how hard I try I'll never make it. I know the odds are against me.

I have to try anyway. I have to give it everything I have so that when I'm eighty and sitting in my back-yard, thinking about what I did and why, I can say I did my best.

Thanks for listening. I'm NOT going to bed now. I'm going to write some pages. I have 63 already!! My neighbor loaned me a CD of an eighteenth-century composer after I heard a little bit of it yesterday, and the soundtrack is perfect.

Shannelle, putting on headphones

~

TO: chanelpacheco@hotmail.com

FROM: naomiredding@rtsv.org

SUBJECT: re: frustrated!!

did you fill out the form for the writer's retreat? it's a miracle you write as much as you do, and i think you might be amazed what'd come out of you if you had time on your own. just a little bit. it's not that much to ask of your family.

keep fighting for your right to do the work. you deserve it.

love,
naomi

THANKSGIVING

Kuan Yin

Kuan Yin, Mother of Compassion in ancient Chinese culture, blows gently into your life, and should be welcomed as an eternal source of comfort and peace. Kuan Yin's values are about co-operation, sharing, balance, harmony and partnership; she is highly sensitive and aware.

Kuan Yin is light and weightless—the qualities that result from highly tuned vales of tolerance and acceptance.

—www.goddess.com.au

19

Jade

Sunday, I go to church with Grandmama. She was going to stay in bed, but I made her get up and put on her clothes, protesting all the way. It does her some good to be there. Her hands are still shaky, and she makes me take her right back home after to avoid the well-meaning press of folks coming to surround her. In the car, she pats my hand. "Thank you, baby. I just can't tolerate another minute of noise."

After lunch of some ham and beans, which she picks at, she puts on her slacks, and a kerchief over her head, rolls up her sleeves. She's working on some boxes she had me carry up out of the basement. Pictures, baby clothes, old books. Everything you can think of. I sit with her for a while before my appointment with Rueben, just looking through all of the stuff. "You think your mama would want this?" Roberta asks, holding up a fifties-style apron. "Or should it go to Goodwill?"

"Goodwill. Why in the world would you store something like that, Grandmama?"

She grunts, bending over the box again. "Waste not, want not."

There are hundreds of photographs. She instructs me to sort them according to the family involved. Those of her and Grandpa and either of their families or when the children were younger go into one box. Individual shots of particular children and their spouses and kids go into another. I'm doing okay until I come across one of me and Mama and my daddy. My real daddy.

"Lord, they're young," I say.

"Mmm-hmmm. We all were, child."

Mama is about twenty-two, slim and beautiful and mocha-skinned, her good hair falling in loose curls to her shoulders. Next to her, my daddy is as tall and slim as a pine. His shoulders are still hanger-like over his skinny chest. He's handsome, with long blond hair and wire-frame glasses. He's got one arm around my mama, and me on his hip. I'm still a baby, fat and laughing, with a bunch of barrettes in my braided hair.

He lives in Seattle now. I saw him last year for about two hours, when he came to Sacramento for a conference. We had dinner, he and I alone since Dante begged off. He's still skinny and still wears a form of the wire-frame glasses, but the hair is going fast. He's quite well-to-do, a fact that showed in a million casual details. His expensive shoes, worn with jeans. The cut of his shirt. The painful cleanliness of his hands.

I toss the picture in the box for my mother. I must have made some sound, because Grandmama says, "Why you still mad at him all these years later, girl? People can't be forgiven?"

"I'm not mad at him. I just don't care."

"Is that right?"

I shrug, look at the clock. "I've gotta get to the gym."

"You got enough to be mad about without putting your daddy in the mix, Jade Kingman." Her grief-worn face turns toward me. God, she's aged a decade in the past week. "Life is long. You might as well learn now to put down whatever doesn't do you any good."

"I'm not mad at him, Grandmama," I say, leaning over to kiss her head. "Just seems to me that there aren't a whole lot of good men in the world."

"You'll find one, baby. I promise."

"I'm not looking."

"Mmm-hmmm," she says, like she knows everything.

There's no answer to that sound. "Why don't you take a little nap, and we'll do some more of this when I get back?"

The way she sighs tells me everything. "Maybe I just will. Help me up."

I haul her to her feet. "You know, I'm not sure why you're tackling this big project right now. Why don't you give yourself a little time?"

She looks at the boxes. "No, I got to get it done."

And for a minute, I'm scared. Scared that she's going to go too fast, wanting to follow my grandpa to the grave. "All right," I say gently. "But at least get some rest right now. I'll take you out to supper later, how's that? Country Kitchen?" She likes the country-style food there, and a young blonde waitress named Shelly.

"We'll see." She pats my arm. "You go on, now. No sense wasting your youth on an old woman."

The gym is crowded. I'm pleased to see a few other women there. A teenager who is with what looks to be her older brother, a tough, wiry-looking blonde who lifts her chin in greeting, and a Spanish or maybe Indian girl with a tattoo on her arm who only watches me cross the gym with flat, cold eyes. I meet her gaze straight: You don't scare me.

She punches her gloves together. Sneers. "Pretty girl."

I raise a brow. I seriously doubt we'd be in the same weight class, though it's hard to judge. She has one of those low, square torsos. Sweats too baggy to make out if she has the sturdy legs that often go with it, but I'm betting she does.

"Jade." Rueben is in the same dark corner he was in before. I cross over to him, ignoring the woman, though when I pull off my sweatshirt, I hope she's seeing the hard muscles in my shoulders and arms.

I'm shy, suddenly, with Rueben. He's not unfriendly, just matter-of-fact as he puts me through some tests and paces, asks me to show him my jabs and punches. I can see they're not great, and ask him to let me do it again. "I'm a little tense."

He steadies the bag and nods. I take a breath, try to forget about the rest of the room, find my center, that middle place where the power comes from, and swing. The sound of glove to bag is loud enough that the guy next to us turns to look. "Good," Rueben says. "Again."

I think of my father. Hard hook. Bam. Another, and a combination. Bam, bam.

A ripple goes through my shoulders, slides down my spine. My hips loosen, and all of a sudden it's not about anything but this. Just the thrill of hitting so hard, the way it makes my body feel. The energy wells like a ball of blue-white electricity. I can almost see it rolling from my hips, through my torso, into my arms. I swing my left cross.

Bam!

Rueben stumbles as the force of it hits the bag and knocks him sideways. As I gather the energy for another one, he holds up his hand, a quirky little smile on his mouth. "Damn," he says, raising his eyebrows.

I drop my arms. Lick some sweat off my upper lip. Wait.

"Shee, sister," says the guy next to us. "I'd hate to be your old man." He means it as a compliment. I acknowledge it with a glance.

Rueben still has said nothing. He's got the bag against his body, and his eyes are narrowed. The angle of his arm shows one bicep as big as my thigh. "Where'd you learn to hit like that?"

"I told you, I started with kickboxing and just liked how it felt, so I started some training in Sacramento." A loose piece of hair falls in my eye and I toss it out. Tell the truth. "I didn't know I could hit like that until somebody attacked me one night. He grabbed me and I hit him and I knocked him out."

"Is that who you're mad at?"

"I'm mad at a lot of people. But I'm not thinking of them when I swing a punch. It makes me hold back."

He likes this answer. "What are you thinking?"

I shrug. Around us is the sound of someone jumping rope, the staccato slap of the speed bag, a coach hoarsely haranguing a boxer sparring. "Nothing. Just feeling it." I'm almost holding my breath, I want him to train me so badly.

"All right." He lets the bag go and gestures for me to follow him. We go down a narrow hallway. He fills the passage almost completely. I try not to notice his body, but it's been so long since I had sex that for one second, my evil imagination gives me a clear image of that long back and fine ass completely naked. I squeeze my eyes shut to block it. Inappropriate.

We turn into a small office, with lots of sunlight streaming in from the south. There are a couple of green metal desks, pictures of boxers on the walls. He opens a cabinet and takes out a key attached to a ring with a number on it—14. "This is your locker key. Women's locker room is to the left as you come in. It's small, but there's showers and lockers. Enough."

I nod, clutch the key in my palm.

He sprawls in an old-style office chair, his long legs out in front of him, his big hands crossed on his rock-hard belly. I do not allow the vision of nakedness to rise.

So to speak.

He's dead serious when he says, "You got some talent, Jade. Haven't seen a woman hit that hard, not ever. You can train and you can get in the ring, but I need to be sure you know what you're doing."

"I—"

He stops me with an upheld hand. "Let me finish. You're a beautiful woman, which isn't a come-on. It's a fact. You could get that nose broken, those cheekbones smashed." He cocks a thumb toward the gym. "Chantall, the woman in there baiting you, would consider it her duty, and she's not alone."

Not sure where this is going, I nod.

"At some point, you're gonna feel the choice in you: pretty or strong. I want you to know they're both cool with me. I'll train you and I can make a boxer out of you, but you're gonna have to work your ass off, and you're gonna hate me some days."

"That's okay! I—"

That hand again. This time, it comes with a smile that is both sexy and kind. "Baby, I know it all, okay? Just want you to know there's no shame, ever, in deciding this isn't what you really want. Capisce?"

Something about his words makes me feel emotional. I lower my head, pull my upper lip between my teeth.

He gets to his feet. "All right, let's get to work, then."

And this time, I smile, showing that I'm thrilled. "Thank you," I say fiercely, and shake his hand. "I will work hard. You won't believe how hard."

"I believe you." He pulls his hand away. "Let's go."

20

Trudy

The deep coral wall startles me the next morning. I stand and admire it, surprised and pleased at my bravery, thinking that I might get some India cotton pillows—with tiny mirrors—to go with it.

Emboldened, I put on some music and turn it up so that I can hear it in the kitchen, not caring if I awaken my slugabed child. The rule is, you can sleep as late as you like, but I don't have to change what I'd be doing during normal hours. The CD is a Paul Simon collection I've had for years, one that never fails to lift my spirits. Once Richard, my eldest, came by and I was playing it, and he said, "This CD always makes me think of my childhood. We always used to catch you dancing all wild in the kitchen."

Darling boy.

This morning, I'm barefoot beneath my loose pajamas with their drawstring waist. The small weight of my breasts bobble around unfettered, and it makes me feel young. Like I might have a life ahead of me still. Singing along to "Me and Julio Down by the Schoolyard," I pull out a heavy ceramic bowl one of the students in the art department made for me years ago, and check the fridge for the ingredients for blintzes. There are some blackberries in the freezer, some cottage cheese

I bought the other day, and although there's no sour cream, there is applesauce.

Blintzes are also one of my few kitchen specialties. I burn waffles every single time, and it irks me to have to keep a waffle iron clean, and I don't seem to have the knack of keeping biscuits soft enough, but my blintzes are excellent. If I'm making breakfast for me, I might as well do what I like. Singing aloud, I put cottage cheese, cream cheese, eggs, and butter into the blender, whirl it all together, and set it aside. After "Me and Julio" are a couple of songs I don't like, and I hit the CD player to skip to "Rock of Ages." Measure flour, milk, eggs, and oil into a bowl and stir it smooth, singing, "Ooh, my mama loves me." I do love my children. This song used to make them happy when I'd grab them and rock them back and forth. I'm glad one of them remembers.

I don't have a crêpe pan, but the biggest cast-iron skillet works very well, and I set it to heating while I open the berries and put them in the microwave.

And bopping in my kitchen, in my bare feet, I suddenly feel so excited. God, I can do anything! Go anywhere, be anybody! I'm healthy. I have resources. My kids are practically grown. Beneath my old pajamas is skin that could still be touched by someone in love. Or passion.

Skip cut seven. Also eight, which is "50 Ways to Leave Your Lover." Also nine, which is a sort of hymn-like thing I'm not in the mood for right now. Which takes us to ten, "Late in the Evening," and I take the pan off the burner just so I can give it my full attention.

This is the song the kids used to try to sneak up on me on. The Latin rhythms, the slightly Cuban sound just stirs me up, and although I'm not much of an elegant dancer, I do love to get down, especially in my own kitchen, all alone, where it doesn't matter if my shimmy is lousy (which it is). This morning, it's a joy because I can throw up my hands and dance like I'm really good at it, because there's no one to see me.

And there I am, a gorgeous young woman, Spanish maybe, with breasts spilling lusciously out of a tight blouse, and I have on high heels, and my arms are above my head, bracelets skittering down in a feminine wash. My hair swishes over my shoulders, breasts, arms, and I'm singing, too.

God, it's so much fun. I think of Lucille, and Angel, who probably knows how to dance really well, and my red wall, and I'm alive for the first time in months. I'm warm. Hot, even. I want to drink and dance and have wild sex.

Rick Marino is an idiot. How could he ever want anyone besides me? The thought comes to me as I get to the end of the song, and it makes me laugh.

I open my eyes.

And scream before I can register it's only Rick standing there. He's leaning against the back door, his eyes smiling, his tongue tucked under his lip in the way I know so well. He looks awful. Haggard and pale, like he hasn't slept, but I don't care this time. My cheeks flush with humiliation and before I know it, I've hit him, hard, in the arm. "That's not fair!"

He laughs. "What? I've seen you do that a million times."

I slam the pan down on the burner. "I don't care!" I whirl around. "You have no right to just keep coming in here like this without any warning."

"I knocked—you didn't hear me, but I could hear the music. I didn't think you'd mind."

"Well, I do! This is my house. I don't just come into your house. I don't even go to your house."

"You could, if you wanted to."

"Well, I don't." Humiliation, full-throated as a scream, pulses through me, and I put my hands over my face. "God, Rick, I was having so much fun, and you took it all away by spying on me!"

He casts his eyes downward. "Sorry. I just stopped by to bring you some things." He lifts a plastic shopping bag. From Lowe's, I notice, and heat fills my belly. One by one, he puts the goods on the counter. Lightbulbs, both sixty watt and one hundred. "I noticed the porch light was out the other day." Dish soap for the dishwasher. A hammer, because I complained that I didn't have one when he took his tools with him. "Check this out. It should be a nice size for you."

"It's good. Thanks."

His nose twitches. He doesn't look at me. "Making blintzes?"

"Yeah. Figure I might as well make my favorite things since I'm the only one eating around here."

He nods. "Well, sorry I bothered you. Put your song back on and dance all you want."

"Rick," I say to stop him as he's turning. He stops, hope in his face. Hope of what, I wonder? "We can't just keep living in the middle like this. I need to go on. It's too hard to have you just coming and going. You have to call me first."

"That's fair."

Why do I feel so lousy about this? I'm not the sinner here. He is. Still, I can't leave it at that. "Annie is off work tomorrow night."

"Yeah. Lotta good it'll do me. She hasn't returned one of my phone calls in a week."

"She's been pretty busy."

"Right." He swallows. It makes me notice his throat, how thin his neck looks.

"Can I offer a suggestion?"

"Sure."

"Just show up, Rick. Be there when she gets off work tonight. Usually she gets off around ten, but sometimes they go a little later."

"I didn't want to make her madder."

"I'm not saying it will work for sure, but it's worth a try."

He nods.

Some demon, the old wife-person I was for so long, says, "I know they aren't your favorites, but if you want some blintzes, I have plenty."

"Thanks, but I made some bacon and eggs already."

"Okay." I smile. "Have a good day."

For a minute, he stands by the door, his arms limp at his sides, and just looks around the kitchen. "You, too," he says, and goes.

~

Annie says, about the new wall, "I hate it."

Jade says, "Wow. Fantastic!"

Shannelle suggests that a few lemon-colored accents might be really great, and she's right. I buy pillows in pale orange and lemon yellow.

Rick has been scarce, mainly because I check the caller ID every time the phone rings and I answer it only when I'm feeling calm and strong. Today, he's stopped by to bring me some tamales from a customer's wife. He stands in the middle of the living room and stares at the wall, saying nothing until he notices the television is gone. Wide-eyed, he says, "What'd you do with it?"

"I put it upstairs. I never watch it."

"Yes, you do. What about *The Sopranos*?"

I shrug. "It's not the same. I canceled HBO anyway. Seemed stupid to pay sixty dollars a month for something I never use."

"You canceled cable?"

The tamale I've heated in the microwave is absolutely perfect. I stand in the kitchen barefooted, eating it at the counter. "God, this is good."

"Trudy. Why did you cancel cable?" He swings a hand at the wall. "And how could you do something like this without talking to me?"

I laugh. It's somewhere between bitter and sad. "You don't live here anymore, Rick."

"Yeah, but—"

I raise my eyebrows. "A mechanic also fixed the brakes on my car."

Hands on his hips, he says, "Well, that was brilliant. Why didn't you just ask me?"

"It's time I learned to do things on my own." My voice is very calm. My heart isn't pounding. "I mean, I don't know what you're planning on, exactly, but I told you two weeks ago that I'm tired of living in the middle. You're obviously really in love with Carolyn, and it's time I accepted that and moved on."

"It's not like that."

"Whatever it is." I shrug, stick another tamale in the microwave. "We can be friends because I have a hard time imagining a life without you in it and our kids need you, no matter what they think right now. I also think you need them."

"Of course I do." His brow is beetling, drawing that dark look into his eyes. Boiling in the blue. "Is this what you want?"

"Rick, I have things to do and I don't want to get into a big fight. Maybe this isn't the best time to talk."

He looks back at the red wall. Nods. "When is Colin going to be home for Thanksgiving?"

A pain hits my solar plexus. "He's not. He's going to a friend's instead. He'll be home at Christmas." The microwave dings and I take out the tamale, wrap it in a napkin, give it to Rick. "Have you talked to him?"

He sits heavily at the table, unwraps the corn husk, salts it. "If you want to call it that. He's polite and answers my questions, but then there's always some reason to get off the phone."

I pour him a glass of milk, sit with him at the table. "He'll come around."

He says nothing.

Suddenly, I am aware of his mouth, his hands. His hair, shining. The silence of a childless house all around us, the luxury of a couple of free hours. I think of our bed—my bed—how good it would be to lie down in it with him, have his hands on me. I eye the line of his throat and imagine kissing it, and my nipples pearl under my blouse.

He notices, raises his eyes. There's surprise there, but something else, too. A taut sense of anticipation, green with possibility, and blue around the edges with memory, grows, fills the kitchen like some wild jungle plant.

I turn away, stand up, move a spoon from the counter to the sink, focus on breathing evenly. It's been months since I had sex, and I feel every long minute of deprivation now, feel it on the nape of my neck and the soles of my feet, every single inch of my body so starved for touch that a single brush of his finger on my shoulder would probably make me shake from head to toe.

"That shirt's new, isn't it?" he says.

It's an airy green peasant blouse, a little too thin for the current weather, but it's warm inside. "Yeah," I say. "I'm turning back into a hippie, I guess."

"It's a good look for you."

It might be safe to turn around, and I do, but he looks at my flushed face and his eyes glitter. "You should probably go," I say, putting my hands on the counter behind me. Both defiant and relaxed. I don't need you.

But his blue, blue eyes have been looking at me for years, and he knows exactly what's in my mind just this minute. "We could fool around," he says, lightly. "Friends do that for each other once in a while, right?"

And God, I am tempted. It dries my throat, and makes me shake, I want it so much. But if I do, if I let myself take this beautiful, sexy man upstairs to my room, I will be right back to square one, and I've made a lot of progress the past few weeks.

I close my eyes. "Can't do it."

"All right." He's so lighthearted that I realize I was hoping for a little coercion, which only sends flames of anger into my body to mix with the flames of hunger, and I'm ready to have a mad orgasm, or chop all my furniture to bits, and it requires everything I have to turn away, put my hands in my pockets so I won't hit him or reach for him or whatever it is that is roaring through me. "You change your mind, you know where to find me."

I toss my hair out of my face. Glare at him. For a single, heart-wrenching second, I see past the glitter he's trying so hard to put on for my sake, down to the bottom of his empty, empty world.

Then he's gone, and I'm calling, "Thanks for the tamales!"

~

By evening, my mood is no better. It's a week to Thanksgiving, and I'm trying not to think about what it's going to be like to have all those missing plates around the table. Richard, Jo, and Minna are coming, and I'll coax a sullen Annie to the table, but it's not going to be easy.

I call Jade, who is not home, go out for a walk, and come home even more restless. Contemplate a movie. I need a life, is what I need. I spend an hour on the computer looking up courses I could take in January. Spanish meets five days a week, but I think I might do it anyway.

Finally, I do what I've been thinking about for hours: I put on my makeup, very subtly so it won't show, bundle up the tamales, and carry them next door. It's just dusk, and the wind chimes are ringing in the wind that's blowing my hair as Angel answers the door.

"Hi," I say, grabbing a hank of hair out of my face so I can see him. He's wearing jeans and a simple white shirt, and looks like something you'd want to take a really long time to eat. "I won't bother you, but I thought you might like some tamales. My hus—my soon-to-be ex-husband, that is, brought them over and I can't eat all of them."

"Come in." He smiles and steps back, bowing in a courtly way to gesture me in.

"That's okay. I just wanted you to try them. They're made by a woman in town who—"

Gently, he reaches for my hand and pulls me over the threshold. "It is too cold to talk on the porch."

"I just didn't want to interrupt anything."

"No," he says, spreading his hands, "as you see, I am doing nothing at all and am glad to have a visitor. Would you like some coffee?"

I hesitate, wonder what I'm doing. "I'd rather have something stronger."

His smile is brilliant, shiny white and knowing. "Wine, then. I prefer it myself." He points to a sofa. "Sit. I will be right back."

I perch on the very edge of the couch, and don't take off my coat. It's a small place, just four rooms in a box, but I am pleased by the small touches of home he's given it. There is a serape over a chair, purple and green, and some velvet throw pillows around the room. No television, I notice, but it might be in the bedroom. A collection of black-and-white photos adorns one wall, and I get up to look at them. "Are these your work?" I call.

He brings big goblets of red wine. "Yes. Do you like them?"

Like is an understatement. They are all of women, some beautiful, some not. Their bodies are all sorts of shapes, slim and long, round and squat, some nude, some just ordinary sittings—a peasant Native woman, an old white woman at a fair, balloons around her head. In every one, he has caught something extraordinary, and I'm struggling with what it is. "They're luminous." My finger hovers over the curve of a pale nude's back, the skin glowing as if lit from within, and I point to the cheekbones of another. "You have a wonderful eye."

"Thank you."

I turn. "Are you a professional?"

He lifts a shoulder, meets my eyes. "*Sí*. It is how I travel. The travel gives me subjects, and the subjects give me money to keep seeing new things."

"Why did you stop in Pueblo?" I sip the wine. It's a light-bodied crisp thing, like a harvest night. "It seems an unlikely spot."

He looks over my shoulder to the photos. "Not really." He sits and gestures for me to do the same, and he's so comfortable in his own skin and with me there that I start to relax. He flips through a stack of CDs on the floor, picks one out, sticks it in. Spanish guitar fills the room, and he smiles. "Will this do?"

"Perfect."

Sitting cross-legged with his back against a chair, he sips the wine. "A friend told me that Colorado Springs was beautiful, and there were things I should see there, but I did not like it." He shook his head. "There is a coldness in the air. No warmth in the faces. So I was going to drive to New Mexico, but first I have a relative here and I stopped to see him, my uncle."

"Oh, really? Where does he live?"

He points over his shoulder. "One block away. That night, the light came down the street, and it looked as if there would be fairies coming out of the shrubs. So I stayed to see if I could find them." He smiles. "Are you afraid of me now?"

I laugh. "No. Not at all. I know just what you mean." The guitar is throaty and full of sex, and yet I feel no urgency, just sitting here. He's too young, too beautiful, too everything for me, but it does my wounded soul some good to have him being kind this way. I don't feel like a hag sitting in Angel's house. "Now I feel a little silly that I was taking your picture in the park, like I knew what I was doing."

"No, no! How did it turn out?"

"I haven't developed them yet."

"You should. Then show me. I will teach you, if you like."

"All right. Sure. I was thinking today I'm ready to learn some new things."

"In return," he said, inclining his head, making his thick, wavy hair fall over one shoulder, "I would like to take your photo."

I raise my eyebrows. "How?"

"However you like. However you are comfortable." He grins, and there is a devastating dimple in one cheek. "I swear I will not ask you to take off your clothes."

"Oh." I'm disappointed, and embarrassed when I realize it. I gulp some wine, feeling like every cliché in the known universe, and, flustered, I stand up. "That would be fine. I mean, the photos, not the—"

I stop, and for some reason, I'm laughing. At myself, at the situation, at everything that is so wrong and stupid about my life right this minute. My hair falls forward, covering my face, and I swing it back, over my shoulder, a defense, because I know people look at that hair instead of me. "Sorry," I say. "I guess I got a little flustered."

"Forgive me." He stands, too, puts down his wine. "I did not mean to embarrass you. But . . ." Earnestly, he puts his hands in his back pockets and I see in the gesture his youth. "Let me tell you a little truth. I am here in this neighborhood because when I came looking for a house to rent, I saw a very beautiful woman standing in that beautiful light, and I wanted to take her picture very, very much. So I must seem young and foolish to you, but I am sincere."

"Who did you see?"

He takes out one hand and touches a length of my hair, as if it is something rare and precious. "You," he says, as if it is obvious.

He is, without a doubt, the most beautiful man I have ever seen in my life. It's like he's not even real. Those cheekbones and hair and smooth skin, the Continental way he has about him—

"If I let you take my picture," I say, "will you let me take yours?"

A quirk of a grin, tilting one side of his mouth. "How?" he says, echoing my question.

"However you like."

"Even nude?" His nostrils flare at this boldness.

"Especially."

He laughs, and takes my hand, pulling me down to the wine we've left sitting on a low table. "Time enough for photos. Tonight, let's play chess and tell stories, hmm?"

"Maybe I could practice my rusty Spanish."

"*Sin disputa,*" he says. *Without question.*

By the time I go home, three hours later, I'm flushed and hot with wine, with the dashing Angel's flirtatious ways. We played chess and talked of his travels and my new-old desire to study Spanish. I'm humming Spanish guitar as I open the front door.

Annie is on the couch. "Where have you been?"

"Hi!" I drift over and kiss her head. "I didn't know you'd be home so early or I would have left a note."

"The car was here," she persists. "You couldn't have gone too far. Jade said she hadn't seen you."

I peel off my coat and drape it over the back of a chair. "Did I worry you? I'm sorry."

"Mom." She stands up and her arms are crossed hard on her chest. "Dad called three times. I didn't know what to tell him."

I strip off my shoes, pleased that I wasn't home for once. "Did he say what he wanted?"

"No, just that he wanted to talk."

"I'll call him tomorrow, then." Yawning, I ask, "Did you talk to him?"

"Mom."

"Yes, my dear?"

"Where were you?"

"Next door."

Her breath huffs out of her throat. "That's what I thought. That's disgusting, Mother! He's too young for you." She covers her face. "Oh, my God! Next you'll be wanting to meet my friends from school."

I laugh. "Well, now that you mention it, Nathan is a very sexy boy. He's nineteen, right?"

"Mom, that is not funny!"

The lovely red glow of the evening is a bubble around me. "You need to lighten up, Annie."

She makes a noise halfway between a scream and groan. "This is what kids do not want, okay? To think about their parents and sex. I mean, Dad forced me to, but I don't want to see this with you. It's gross."

Recklessly, I say, "You can look away, then, because I'm not putting myself on a shelf to make you comfortable. You are one part of my life, and the most important, but I have a right to live as a woman, too."

"Even if the whole neighborhood is laughing at you for having an affair with a sleazy Spanish gigolo? It's pathetic!"

Heat creeps up my face, and I know she can see it under my egg-white skin. "First of all, it's none of your business. Second, I'm not having an affair, but it may surprise you to discover that not everyone thinks your mother is over the hill. Third—" I can't think of a third. "I really don't understand why you're so angry."

"Because Dad called and called. I think he really wanted to talk to you! And what if this was the one chance to get it all back again, and now it's all ruined?" She bursts into tears.

"Oh, Annie." I put my arms around her, cradle her to me. She's still so much smaller than me. Like my mother, she's short and sturdy. She flings her arms around me and sobs into my shoulder and I stroke her hair and whisper soft things. When she slows down, I take her to the kitchen for a cup of tea. She slumps at the table and I busy myself with the pot and measuring leaves.

"When I'm keeping Minna," I say quietly, "the thing I always think about is how easy it is to keep her safe at this age. Put the poisons up high, cover the electrical outlets, keep breakables out of reach." I sigh and turn. "I wish I could keep you safe from all the things that are going to hurt you the rest of your life, and I can't."

"I just wish you guys could fix this."

"I know. But I don't know that it's fixable." Tears spring to my eyes and I blink. "Maybe you're going to have to love your dad as he is, and let me find out what my new life looks like."

"Maybe you should just call him and find out what he wanted?"

Gently, I say, "Not tonight, honey. I promise I'll call him tomorrow." The kettle whistles. "Now, let's have some tea and forget all this, huh? Want to play some spades?"

Her mouth is sad, but she nods. "Might as well."

∼

Upstairs, alone in my bed later, I touch my ribs, feel the skin over them. Pull back the curtain protecting my daughter from her mother's sensuality and remember the evening. My body sings with an agitation I have not felt in a long, long time. A sense of possibility. We only played chess and drank wine and listened to the Spanish music he played. That was all. But my mind is alive now with shimmery moments out of it, and I replay some of them over and over. His head ducked the slightest bit, so he had to cut a glance upward at me, his irises golden and full of mischief. A moment when I leaned forward a little and knew he was admiring the shape of my profile. That last minute before I put on my coat, when he moved a little too close and smiled down at me, thanking me for coming. I hugged him impulsively and it went on too long and I suspect if I had not turned my head at just the right instant, he would have kissed me.

The ache of it burns against my ribs now, down in my liver, in my kidneys.

I will never sleep tonight.

He is too young for me. I am probably imagining that he is attracted to me. But it doesn't matter. I love this feeling in my limbs, in my organs, in my throat, this sense of wanting someone else, even for a little while. It gives me relief from wanting the one I cannot have anymore.

I live the moments again. One more time. His hand on my neck. Mine on his hard arm.

Sleep sneaks in, unnoticed, and carries me away where the moments can become dreams.

21

Trudy

Saturday morning, Angel shows up at my door before I've put on my normal clothes. He has his worn rucksack over his shoulder and a very sexy leather bomber jacket that doesn't look sleazy, just European, and his camera bag.

I open the door, trying to face the fact that I'm much too old for him and he needs to see me as I am, in my old sweats and the T-shirt I slept in, without a scrap of makeup on my ghost face. "Hi, Angel." I push open the screen. "Come in."

"No, no. I am unable—I have a paying job this morning, but I brought you something." He gives me a box of film—three rolls. "Shoot them, then bring me the pictures, huh?"

"Let me give you some money!"

He smiles, waves a hand. "Just enjoy it."

"Okay."

Unfortunately, it's what I think of as a "Carolyn Day," which means I can't stop thinking about this woman who somehow landed my husband when I wasn't looking. Everywhere I go, I see women who look like her, who make me do a double-take. Women who have her hair, who move like her, who wear the same kind of clothes. It's exhausting, not to mention my neck hurts from whipping around so often.

I take their pictures, wondering how long it will take me to get over all of this. The rest of my bloody life?

In the evening, I have a date with Jade. She talked me into it two days ago. I'm nervous, haunted by the Carolyn images—which I cannot explain. Why today, when I'm feeling so much more positive?—and it's good to be getting ready, even if I am worried about having that hard, just-divorced-pissed-and-ready-for-revenge look. My hair, so long and unstyled, suddenly seems in that category, but it's not like I can chop it all off for a night on the town, although I'm nearly sick enough with nerves to do it. I pick out the new green India cotton blouse and a pair of jeans, a simple leather jacket to go over it. Looking in the mirror, I think I look okay. Not young anymore, but everybody gets older, right? So do men. A man my age might think I look good.

Annie is not thrilled that I'm going out, so I'm not going to ask her advice. She'll like my outfit only if it covers me from neck to ankles. Loosely.

The doorbell rings and I rush to answer it, thinking it's Jade. Instead, it's Rick. "Hi," he says. "I forgot to call first. Is this a bad time?"

Attaching an earring, I back away from the door, letting him come in, then sit on the couch to put on my boots. I'm careful not to look at him too closely, see the weary lines around his mouth that make me want to hug him, rub his back for a minute.

"What's up?" I ask, tugging on the new ankle-high brown boots that match my coat. The heels make me even taller, but I'm going out with Jade, so who cares? Probably, I think to myself with a quick frown, all my trouble is for nothing, since no man will see me while I'm standing next to the Stun Gun.

"You going out or something?" Rick asks.

"Yeah, me and Jade." I lift an eyebrow, half smile. "Should be interesting."

He nods. "Guess my timing is pretty bad, then. Maybe I can catch you tomorrow."

"For?"

"Nothing. Just talk or something. Something normal, maybe?" He sighs. "I don't know, Trudy."

I put my hands in my lap, look at him. "You look so tired. Are you taking your vitamins?"

"Yeah." He leans on the wall, hands in his coat pockets. Athena comes out of the kitchen and trips over to him, rubbing his ankles. "Hey, you," he says, picking her up to scrub her ears. "I was thinking about getting a kitty."

"Really?" We often had discussions on too many cats. I'm a sucker for all the lost felines of the world, I have to admit, and sometimes the numbers have crept up to three—or, for a small stretch once, four—but I've been good about it lately. Two, but no more.

"You don't realize how nice it is to have a cat in your lap until you don't have one anymore."

"I think you should, then. Lots of homeless cats all the time."

He rubs Athena's ear. "Where you guys going? The Pub?"

"No. Not her style. Some new place downtown. She's gone there a couple of times with friends from work."

"I know which one. Secretary place, full of ferns and stuff."

I don't ask how he knows about it. Carolyn is a bartender around the corner. She probably has aspirations to be a secretary. Like me.

Probably not.

Suddenly, my gut is on fire with a certain brand of anxiety or anticipation that got me into a fair bit of trouble through the first part of all this. It makes me want to storm into her workplace and make a fool of her, as she has made a fool of me. To paper the walls and windows around the bar with her racy, detailed email letters to my husband, which he read in my own bedroom.

Jade saves me from starting a fight by popping in the front door. "Hey!" she says cheerfully, bringing a scent of exotic perfume with her. She's simply dressed, in a red silk T-shirt with a neckline that shows off her beautiful, young cleavage, black jeans, black boots. That hair is a wild, luscious tangle on her shoulders. "You ready?"

I stand, grab my purse. Rick walks out with us. "Have a good time."

"Oh, yeah!" Jade laces her arm through mine. "We're gonna raise some hell." She wiggles the fingers on her free hand over my shoulder. "Have a good night!"

And it's stupid, but I feel guilty and sad that he's standing on the porch, watching us go, his hands loose at his sides, like he's winded.

I look back. "If you want, I'll help you pick out a cat tomorrow."

He nods, once.

"Girl," Jade says close to my neck, her arm still firmly looped in mine, "don't you dare start feeling bad. He deserves it. Don't forget that."

"You're right."

The nightclub is not terribly crowded so early, and we find a decent table a little bit away from the bar. There are a lot of young professional types drinking wine and margaritas and cherry-colored martinis. Jade orders one, calling it a Jolly Rancher. I order Chardonnay, but she insists I taste the martini. "It does taste just like candy," I say, "but that's not what martinis are supposed to be about."

She grins. "Loosen up, Grandma. This is a new century. Out with the old, in with the new."

Trouble is, I am a grandmother, and I know the answer to what a martini is—dry and perfect for sipping. They are James Bond and Las Vegas, circa 1963, and a lost world of diamonds and elegance and things I never believed in, but some people did. Making them cherry seems somehow disrespectful.

There is no one my age in the place. I find myself thinking of Carolyn too much, wanting to slip out and go sit in the dark, old place where she works, with its bluesy jukebox and pool tables. A lot more likely to connect with somebody there than here. Except that I'd have to deal with Carolyn herself, probably, and that would be a drag.

Maybe it's because I'm thinking about her so hard, but there is a woman who walks in just then who reminds me of her. Same long, straw-like hair, same kind of clothes, same slightly defensive body language.

I sip my wine with narrowed eyes. "That's kind of what Rick's new girlfriend looks like," I say.

She's satisfyingly shocked. "Gross! What is he thinking?"

"Who knows?"

"You want to talk about it?" Jade says. "It's obviously getting to you right now."

"What is there to say?"

She leans in over her drink. "How did it happen? Did he just come to you one day and say he was in love with somebody else and he was leaving?"

"Not exactly." I give a short, humorless laugh. "He'd just been acting weird for a couple of months. I wasn't sure what was going on, but I thought it was connected to grief issues—you know his best friend, Joe, died, right?"

"The motorcycle guy? Oh, no."

"Yeah, that's him. It's been two years now, and his mother died, too. So it was a lot, you know? I was trying to follow his lead, let him work through it all." I sigh. "Not the best course of action, as it turns out."

"Oh, you don't know that, Trudy." She touches my hand. "It doesn't have anything to do with you."

"Maybe not."

"Anyway . . ."

"Anyway, I kept getting hang-up phone calls. A couple of times, he acted really weird when he came home from being out with the guys. Honestly, I didn't even suspect another woman." Suddenly my wrist aches with a violent pain and I shake my arm. A steel wall comes sliding down over my heart with a clunk. I shake my head, squeeze my eyes tight. "It was ugly. I don't want to talk about it. Another time, okay?"

"All right. We're here to have a good time."

She raises her glass and I toast it. We drink.

~

Hours later, long after I switched to club soda with lime so I could drive us home, we leave the nightclub. It's been heady for Jade. Her cheeks are flushed with the power of it, all the men talking and talking and talking to her all night.

I, on the other hand, have left whatever self-esteem I might have owned back there in a melted puddle on the table. I was invisible, not just because I was next to Jade, but because I was way too old for that crowd. It was humiliating after a while, the way their eyes would skitter over mine, carefully look away, as if I might leap up with my crone-like hands and snatch one of their young bodies home to devour in my bed.

We emerge into the windy night, and on impulse, I drag on Jade's coat sleeve. "Let's take a little detour."

She gives me a look. "Am I gonna like this?"

"Sure. Why not?" My heart is suddenly pounding in an exalted sort of rhythm. Adrenaline. Better than nothing. Sure better than sorrow.

The street is dark between the bars, and the wind is kicking leaves and cigarette butts and an empty Subway cup over the sidewalk. We pass a hole-in-the-wall bar with ancient doors that have round windows set into them, and Jade says, "Huh. It looks like a saloon, doesn't it?"

I nod. Keep walking. Stop three doors down in front of a plate glass window, hiding myself in the shadows by the street, away from the low light coming out of the bar. Jade follows me and whispers, "What are we looking for? Rick?"

"No. I mean, he might be here, because this is one of his favorites, but actually, I hope we don't see him." Now my heart is really racing, because I hadn't really thought of that angle, and it would be painful.

The window is painted red to halfway up, with gold lettering in Old West script reading, MAGGIE'S PLACE. Inside, it's comfortably dark except around the bar and over the pool table in the back, which you can't really see that well from this angle. Soft purple neon runs in thin tubes up around the antique bar, and a mirror reflects the dozens and dozens of bottles on the counter. Around the bar, on red Naugahyde stools, are a collection of patrons—a handful of the usual suspects, men in baseball hats with construction and tool logos on them, Anglo and Spanish, their hands rough with their work. They're drinking beers, for the most part. A pair of women are hunched close together at one end, body language shutting the men out. Some Bob Seger can be heard. No Rick, thank God.

But, "There she is."

"Who?"

"Carolyn."

She's standing behind the bar, one hip jutted out, a bar rag in the hand propped on her hip. The violet neon makes her hair look soft, and light from some other source pours over the generous amount of cleavage showing over her low-cut blouse. It's not trashy. Her clothes are tight, maybe too tight for a woman of her age, but I'm not judging her. That's what a bartender has to do. She has kids to support, not a lot of education. What're you going to do? It's an honest living.

My heart is sinking as I stare through the gilt framing the window and her. The low light covers her wrinkles; it's obvious she's comfortable with her body. Maybe, I think for the first time, she only hunches her shoulders when I'm around. I mean, I sure wouldn't hunch my shoulders if I had a chest like that. And really, knowing my husband as I do, he wasn't likely to pick some scared, sexless person. She probably does things like buys black lace garter belts and massage oil.

I want to throw up. Or throw a rock through the window at her head. "Let's go."

Jade grabs my arm. "Let's go in, instead."

"No."

"You have a right to go anywhere you want. Maybe we just wandered over this way and thought it looked like a nice place to be."

I give her a look.

She shrugs. "Maybe I'll come back some other day."

"Rick comes here all the time. He'll know what you're doing."

"Don't you think he deserves to suffer?"

He is suffering, but I don't say that. I stare at Carolyn through the windows, thinking she really does look like Susan Sarandon and I can understand how Rick fell under her spell.

Except: "I was a good wife."

Jade says, "Me, too."

"Maybe that's not what they want from us." I nestle my hands more deeply in my pockets, watch Carolyn laugh at somebody's joke as she pours a draw beer. Perfectly. Her fingers loop the dollar bills like a paper chain around her knuckles. She's nodding politely. God, what a hard job!

"Good cleavage," Jade says.

I snort, halfway between laughter and a moan. "Jade! Thanks a lot!"

"Well, you don't have much chest, but that's the only damned thing she's got over you, Trudy. I'm serious as a heart attack. I mean, look at her. You look at least ten years younger! Didn't you tell me she has a couple of wild kids?"

I nod.

"So, you gave this man a family and a home and tried to keep everything together for him, and he comes out and finds some bar wench with big tits and personal problems and then you're out?"

"Never looked at it like that."

"Yeah, well, maybe you should." She looks at me. "And when you think about it, ask yourself what kind of man would leave his wife and family like this, and ask yourself if maybe you were mistaken in believing what you have about him all these years."

My ears start ringing, resistance or agreement or both, and suddenly I'm crossing the sidewalk, chest tight, and flinging open the door. The men at the bar turn around and look, then see Jade behind me and straighten, smooth the front of their shirts.

Carolyn doesn't look up right away. It takes a minute, and then we're staring at each other over a cold, open space covered in brown and white linoleum tiles. Bob Seger is singing about growing older, and there's a clop of pool balls falling, and she still just stands there, looking sad, the dollar bills looping through her fingers over and over and over. I hate that I can see beauty in her suddenly, in the light where Rick found her. I wonder what she's thinking of me, flushed and dressed up to cause a stir, and in fact, a man from a booth sees me and comes over and says, "Babe. Why don't you two come on over?"

I shake my head. I don't know why I came inside. Maybe because I'm tired of seeing her and her never seeing me. It feels like I stand there a long, long time, Jade at my back, ready to go forward or pull me back, whatever is required.

But it just strikes me that we've traded places, Carolyn and I. For so long, she knew I was there and suffered eating crumbs from my feast. Now it's the other way around. I know she's there, too. I can't read her expression, but she's seeing me for real, and it's suddenly enough.

I turn and Jade follows me out. We don't say anything on the way home.

22

Roberta

November 12, 20—

Dear Harriet,

I got your letter last week, and haven't had a minute to answer till this evening. It was a fine card and letter and I know how hard it is to find the right card for times like this. It brought me comfort, sister, it truly did.

Don't go worrying too much about me, now. That was just grief talking. I'm going through my things, it's true, but this old body ain't going nowhere yet. Doctor gave me the once-over just Monday and said I'm fit as a fiddle. I gone to see him on account of my heart racing, but he said it's just sorrow and will heal. I got Jade here now, and she's real good to me, making sure I eat regular and get my orange juice and has me eating wheat bread instead of the white I like, but I let her take charge in some ways so she feels useful.

I also have two neighbor women, Trudy and Shannelle, stopping in day after day. Like they afraid I'll put my head in the oven or something. Trudy's good about listening to all my old stories.

To tell the truth, there is not a single minute when I don't think of my Edgar. I think of him in the mornings, at breakfast, and can't hardly stand to eat sausage, which was always his favorite. Middle of the day, I think about the sound of lawn mowers. Dinner, it's the news. I don't turn it on no more. Every time I hear that music, I'm thinking I'll come around the corner and see him sitting in his chair. 'Bout kills me every time.

Nighttimes, I just pray until it stops hurting long enough for me to go to sleep, then the next morning it starts all over again.

Well, listen to me run on about me. What have the grandchildren been up to? Greg pull up those grades? What did your doctor say? And how is Elmus?

Don't you be calling me every week, neither, Harriet! I know you can't afford all that long-distance. Save a call and go have you a banana split with that ornery husband of yours and just send me a letter next time, why don't you?

I'm doing just fine. I always have the Lord to lean on.

Love, your sister,
Berta

23

Jade

Sunday morning, I take Grandma to church. She's wearing a black dress with a black hat, and dresses it up just a little with strings of beads. But she doesn't say much. She's so quiet all the time lately, I don't know what to think.

"I love you, Grandma," I say, pulling into the parking lot of the Church of God.

"You're a good girl, Jade." Her fingers fiddle over to mine, give them a squeeze. But she's not really in it. She's somewhere else all the time. Vague with me. With her friends, who have been calling trying to get her to go do something, get her out of the house. It's been nearly a month since Gramps died, and she hasn't left the house once except for church. Only then because I make her go. Our ritual is the same: I settle her with her friends, then go down to the nursery to hang out with the babies.

Babies are my weakness. All babies, of every race in the world, but especially laughing Black babies with their curly heads and big old eyes and smooth skin and fat little toes. They make me mushy. I love to smell their lotioned selves, admire the little girls in their teeny patent leather shoes and frilly socks. The boys have their baseball hats and tennis shoes.

We tumble and cuddle. I play blocks with them, read them picture books, and generally make a fool of myself.

It's also a relief to go to church, where the mothers and daddies are loving their babies, taking good care of them, doting on them as parents ought to do. A contrast to the babies I see at work.

Not a lot of happy babies in my job as a foster care liaison. Sometimes I can find ways to make their lives better. Sometimes it doesn't work out. Everyone tells me that eventually I'm going to burn out on the losses. What I tell them is that I can't imagine doing anything more important than this, that every time it does work out, I know exactly why I'm on the planet.

This thought, sneaking over my brain as I wash the face of Johniqua Parker, one of the sweetest babies I've ever seen in my life, gives me some insight into my grandmother's current state of mind. What does she have to live for these days? What purpose?

Hmmm. I have noticed that Shannelle comes over every day or two to get Roberta's advice on some little household thing—the best way to wash the windows or clean an oven. She asks what to do about one of her boys. How to get along better with her husband, Tony, who doesn't want Shannelle to write novels. He wants her to go to work as a waitress so they can get some new furniture.

In fact, Shannelle shows up just after we get home from church. She looks very bad. Usually she's so tidy about her appearance that it's alarming. Roberta is instantly on Grandmother alert. "Sit down, child," she says. Her gnarled hands brush over Shannelle's hair. "What's wrong?"

"I have another toothache," she says, pressing her hand to her mouth. "Not even the peroxide treatment is helping. What else can I do?"

"Oh, baby!"

"It's just"—tears start to leak out of her china-blue eyes—"this one is in the front, and I'm going to have to let them pull it and then I'm going to look like an old hag and . . ." She bends over to put her head in her lap. "God, it hurts. Like someone is hammering on my face."

I meet Roberta's eyes. "Shannelle, maybe I can find some help for you. Don't get the tooth pulled. Let me make some calls in the morning. In the meantime, I have some good painkillers. Let me get them for you."

She shakes her head. The circles under her eyes are like lakes. "I have to watch the boys this afternoon. I can't get too messed up."

"Bring them over here," Roberta says. "Jade's got to go to her boxing lesson, but I'd love a chance to spoil those babies a little bit. You take the medicine and go sleep, and let Jade see what she can do."

Her agony is so perfect, she just nods. Her eyes fill with tears again. "Thank you."

I fetch a couple of Vicodin for her. They're left over from a bad sprain I had last spring. She takes one and puts the other in her pocket. In a few minutes, she brings the boys over and goes home to sleep. Roberta, for the first time in weeks, seems genuinely happy when she hustles the boys into the kitchen to make chocolate chip cookies.

Which makes it a lot easier for me to leave for my training session. I've been looking forward to it all week. As I put on my workout clothes, I'm feeling a little jittery. Nothing fancy, of course, but I do pick the coppery tank that makes the best of my skin, and put on some shorts beneath my sweats.

I tell myself I'm excited because I get to box this afternoon. I really am learning something, getting stronger, figuring it all out. But my closed-off heart opens up as I walk into the gym and see Rueben jumping rope.

He winks as I come up. "How you doin' today, Jade?"

"Very well, thank you. Went to church with my grandmother"—I tie up my hair in a scrunchie—"and she's happy now with some little boys to babysit."

He nods, an alert interest in his face. "Where do you go to church?"

"Church of God, over on Elm."

"I miss church lately."

I smile. "You're welcome to come with us anytime. And," the idea is brilliant, "what you should do is come and have breakfast with us first, let my grandmother spoil a Texas boy. She's Texan, you know. It'd thrill her to pieces to cook you some biscuits."

"I might just do that." For a second, it seems like there's something in his face; then he says, "Let's get you warmed up."

Over the past few weeks, I've learned very, very little about Rueben Perry. He works for Boys Ranch. It's a tough group of children. He's from east of Dallas somewhere. He's divorced, but doesn't talk about her. No children.

It's the things he doesn't say that intrigue me. There are scars on his arms where tattoos have been removed. I wonder what they used to say, how they got there. What made him take them off. How did he get from Dallas to Pueblo? He doesn't drink or smoke. There's no woman in his life. I asked Shannelle's husband.

He's also a hard taskmaster. I'm working harder than I ever have in my life. Running five miles every morning, working with weights three times a week after work, a hundred crunches every night before bed. These sessions twice a week. He's teaching me my footwork and punches, and he's not exactly easy to please. Not that he yells or anything. Just gets that slightly disappointed wrinkle in his forehead when I'm not getting it. When I do get something, he's pleasant but curt.

"Good," is what he says.

This afternoon, the gym is nearly empty. Nearly everyone else went to see the local hero box in Denver tonight. I'm conscious of it. It feels like Rueben is being hard on me. He snaps at one point. "Get your fists up, Jade! I just broke your nose."

He's right. I try it again. "How long until I can spar with someone for real?"

"A while." There's boredom in the words.

I drop my arms. "All right, what is it? What's going on here?"

"What do you mean?"

"I mean, you act like I'm being clueless, and if I am, I don't know what I'm doing wrong."

He inclines his head, those big soft eyes looking right through me. "You partied hard last night, huh?"

"Yeah, so?" I shrug. Bang my gloved hands together.

"Then went to church this morning with your grandma and came here to work out?"

I scowl. "So?" I say again, harder this time.

"And there you are, all dressed up to kill, even in your gym clothes. Makeup on, hair all falling down, the shorts to show off your legs."

It makes me angry because it's so on target. How can he see through me like that? But what I say is, "I put on makeup for church and didn't think I had to wash it off to come to the gym. I like my legs and if I want to show them off, that's my business. And so what if I partied? I'm thirty years old, have a hole in my chest the size of the Eisenhower Tunnel, and it makes me feel good to go somewhere and be admired for five minutes." He sure as hell isn't admiring me. I hate that it makes me feel so cheap to have him look at me that way.

"You're better than that, Jade. Somewhere, somebody made you think the only thing you had is the way you look, and it's not true."

"You don't know me!"

He nods. "You're right."

For a minute, I glare at him. He reflects it right back to me. What I hate is how much I like looking at his face, how right it seems. Almost familiar.

Which is just bullshit. I look away.

"C'mon. Let's get to work. Do me a favor and don't party before we work out. It slows you down."

I nod.

I work harder. He's a little kinder. By the time the sun sets, I'm wiped out, gin-scented sweat coating my flesh. My legs and arms are like rubber. I sink down to a chair, pull off the gloves, take a long, long pull of water. He comes up behind me and drops his hands on my shoulders. I start, but then he uses his thumbs on the tight places in my lower neck, across my shoulder blades. It feels so good, I groan aloud.

"'Bout dead now, aren't you?" he says. It sounds almost gentle.

"Yeah. You're right about the partying. Sorry. I won't do it again before our sessions."

"Drinking's just a way to hide from the pain, baby. Better to just go through it, feel it. Someday, it'll feel better."

That almost brings tears to my eyes. I duck away to pick up my towel. "Yeah, well, I'll believe it when I see it."

We're alone in there, just me and Rueben. I'm wishing, as I turn around, that he seemed even a little bit interested in me. It's hard not to look at his mouth. Hard not to want to kiss him, not because he's so gorgeous, but because he's so real. He makes me feel like I could let down my guard, sink into his big embrace. Just be . . . safe, finally.

I bite the inside of my cheek. "You don't like me very much, do you?"

For a minute, he doesn't say anything at all. I stand there waiting, heat in my face.

"Invite me again to your grandma's house, Jade."

"You mean now?"

He nods.

"You want to come to breakfast next week, go to church with us?"

"Yes, ma'am," he says. "I'd like that a lot." He cocks his head toward the locker room. "Go on and get your shower. I'll wait and walk you out to your car."

24

Trudy

Thanksgiving morning, I'm awake at five a.m. I set the alarm for five thirty so I can get the turkey in, but depression drags me awake before that. I lie in my bed and have a hollow chest, remembering how it used to be. The house filled with good smells. By now, Rick would have been baking his pecan pies, so they would be finished before I put the turkey in the oven. This morning, the air just smells damp.

"Okay, get to it," I say aloud. I take a shower and get dressed in some jeans and a warm sweater, put on my heavy wool socks, and pad downstairs. It's snowing, which accounts for the damp smell, and it's so beautiful—big fat flakes—that I put on my boots and go for a walk.

It's still dark, and not terribly cold, and very, very still. Not a single whisper of wind. The flakes are the size of teacups, tumbling down through yellow tents of streetlights, lighting on my nose and mittens. My feet make a slight squeaking noise on the accumulation.

I don't realize until that minute, feeling the dampness in my lungs and on my face, how devastating the winds have been this fall. They've stolen all the moisture from the world, sucked the trees to brittle twigs, sucked the prairies to clinging tufts of yellow grass. Even the cacti are beginning to look withered.

I pass the paperboy. We don't speak, just nod to each other. I walk on.

And the cool stillness somehow gives me a clarity of my own, as if moisture is feeding my dried-up brain tissues, opens eyes that have been squinched tight against the brutal onslaught of winds. I smell hope in the dampness, hear possibility in the stillness. In the distance, I see a quivering mirage of adventure.

It's scary to be alone, to start over, but maybe there is something wonderful waiting. Maybe today, instead of mourning everything that isn't, I'll just focus on celebrating what is. Be thankful, create new routines and traditions.

Yeah.

To that end, I head back home and find Rick's recipe for pecan pie and bake two of them. My crust is lumpier than his, which has always been as flaky and light as a Betty Crocker illustration. As I do it, I play Cat Stevens's *Teaser and the Firecat*, very quietly. I do it even though Rick has always sort of reminded me of Cat, do it because it's one of the lightest, sweetest, most peaceful bits of music ever recorded. The sun comes up behind the clouds and I can turn off the overhead light. I get the turkey out and prepare the stuffing, put the bird in the oven to roast.

I scrub celery and cut it into perfectly even pieces of three inches, then prepare my grandmother's filling—mainly grated cheddar with a little onion, celery salt, and Miracle Whip. (Don't ask me why, but we never ate real mayo and it tastes weird to me even now.) It is one of my favorite things on the planet, and there's a lot of pleasure in singing along with "Who'll be my love?" as I dip another fresh piece of celery into the mix and munch on it. Maybe Thanksgiving will give me back a pound or two.

Suddenly I notice the lightness in my chest and recognize it as happiness. I'm happy. Happy to be cooking for my family, doing things I love to do, the same way I've always done them. I love the house filling up with the right smells, love the snow, love that I get to play with Minna all afternoon, that I am lucky enough to be healthy and alive, with so much human wealth in my life.

Wow.

When I finish the preparations, I sit at the table and start looking around the kitchen. It seems to me that I spend my whole life in this room. Everything that happens happens here. I've made love to Rick on this very table. I've scrubbed faces, served thousands of snacks and quick meals, had a million Important Discussions. Sitting there by myself, I realize I'm kind of tired of it, of the way it looks. The cupboards are painted a cream color that's not anywhere close to fresh anymore, and on top of them is a clutter of little-used appliances. The border paper is a pattern of grapes that I once liked and seems now a little too homey.

Maybe I should paint in here, too. Something bold. Maybe get a couple of glass-fronted cupboard doors to show off my collection of goblets, get rid of the scarred, rickety table and find something else. There was a pretty little breakfast bar at Sears the other day—it required assembly, which freaked me out, but I bet I can do it. The table. A couple of little stools.

I'm nodding to myself when Rick bursts in through the back door, carrying pie. He stops when he sees me. "Good morning." There is snow in his hair, big tufts of white against the glossy black. Dots of melted snow dampen his face. "I thought you'd still be asleep."

"Had to cook," I say, gesturing.

"Smells good."

"Thanks." I don't want him to ruin my fragile sense of well-being, so I don't get up.

"Well," he says, after a minute, "I just brought you a pie. Thought the kids might like it."

I gesture toward the counter. "Thanks, but as you see, I already made two. I don't think we can eat three."

He looks from the cooling pies on the counter to the one in his hands. "Oh." Crushed. And by the color creeping up his face, he's embarrassed.

As he turns to leave, I'm filled with remorse. He's always taken a lot of pleasure in holidays, and this one is going to be rough on him, without his kids, no Joe to make him feel better, his mom gone. I don't want to ask him to come here because it will raise expectations in the kids, and I also don't want to think about Carolyn, in some other house, cooking a turkey her way for him to eat.

But I can't ignore his embarrassment, and I jump up, tug his sleeve. "Hey," I say. "Leave it. Yours is bound to be better than mine." I take the pie out of his hands, put it down on the counter. "That was bitchy. I'm sorry." I meet his eyes.

His eyes are so sad that I just reach over to give him a hug. And his arms go around me hard.

He feels so right. Just the right height, his body so intimately familiar to me, his hair touching my nose. I close my eyes and absorb some sense of strength or comfort or maybe just rest. He smells like himself, the smell I can't get out of my pillows, and I inhale it deeply, closing my eyes. It makes me wish to go back in time, scrub away whatever it was that happened to us. He's holding me so tight that I can feel his sorrow thrumming through every cell in his body. It's going to be an awful day for him.

Before I can get maudlin, I pull away, patting his arm. "Thanks, honey. That was sweet of you."

Annie comes around the corner then, her face so falsely bright that I know she's seen us embracing. "Hi, Dad! Are you staying to eat with us?"

He clears his throat. "No, I just brought the pie. You want to come over later, watch some TV with me?"

Her face goes hard. "I have plans," she says, and exits.

And here is the miracle: It's a beautiful day. I spread a bright batik cloth over the table and instead of the usual family china, I take down all that old beautiful glass I've been collecting—one-of-a-kind things, like the black china dinner plate painted with fuchsias, and the paper-thin rose one, and the goblets of carnival glass. None of it is particularly valuable, but I love the way it looks on the table. Rick always wants everything to match. He pretends he doesn't, but that's how it was done in his world, and that's how he's comfortable. In some ways, he's aggravatingly traditional.

I gather up all the cloth napkins, too, and put down a different one at each place. It still lacks something. Candles and flowers. The candles, smelling of patchouli, I find in the bathroom. The flowers—oh, why have I never done this before?—are orchids from my greenhouse. They look so beautiful that I move a bunch of potted begonias into the room, too.

Annie comes in and stops. Her mouth opens, and I brace myself for her to dislike it. Instead, she raises eyes that are shining. "Mom, this is so beautiful!" She laughs. "I always knew you were a hippie at heart."

"Thank you." I incline my head. "Listen, Annie, I don't want to upset you, so this one time, I'm asking your opinion. I would like to invite our neighbor Angel over to eat with us." I think about adding more, a disclaimer, but the truth is, I am attracted to him and that's why I'm going to ask him, and I don't want to start any falseness.

She lowers her eyes, reaches out with one hand to caress the waxy petal of a bright-pink cattleya. "I guess I don't mind."

"He might not come."

She straightens, takes a breath. "Well, I hope he does. You aren't the only one who thinks he's gorgeous, okay?"

I laugh, and the sound comes from deep in my chest. "Another flower for the table?"

"Why not?"

"Everybody will be here in just a little bit, so I'm going to nip out and ask him right now." Before I can chicken out. It's only neighborly, after all. And he probably already has plans.

Angel opens the door and I smell something hot and spicy on the air that escapes from his rooms. "Hello!" he says, and there is just the right amount of happy surprise in his voice. "Come in!"

"No, I can't—I have people coming any minute, but I wanted to let you know that if you don't have any plans, we'd love to have you come over and eat with us. You know, for Thanksgiving. If you're not doing anything." I cross my arms. "If you want."

His mouth is curving upward in a smile, making those golden eyes twinkle, and everything about his physical person makes me want to jump him. No promises to keep, none to offer.

He puts his hand to his chest, sighs in regret. "To my sorrow, Roberta already invited me and I said yes."

I step back. "That's great. I just wanted to make sure you had a good American Thanksgiving."

"Wait." He captures my hand, pulls me over the threshold, where the smell of chocolate and spices makes me want to lick the air. "Come in," he says, "*un momento*. I have something I need for you to taste for me."

In the kitchen, the smell is even more concentrated, and something about it makes me light-headed, as if he's cooked some dangerous spell. I wonder wildly if he's even real, or if I made him up because I need something wicked and magical in my life. He dips a spoon into a beef mixture in a rich, dark brown sauce and holds it up for me to taste. I have to lean forward to do it, open my mouth, let him pour it in.

It hits my tongue, spicy and hot. "Oh!"

"Good?" he says, cocking one brow. "Or too much for Americans?"

I touch my fingers to my mouth. "It's wonderful."

He blinks, and there is something swirling around us, heat and the smell of cinnamon and something more nourishing, and he lifts one hand to my cheek. "Such skin," he nearly whispers, his fingers light as butterfly wings. "Like milk. Like the moon."

If he kisses me, I will dissolve, melt like brown sugar on the floor, and nothing will put me back together again, but I'm looking at his mouth, almost shivering with the want of it. I imagine it will taste the way the air smells, that his tongue will glide into my mouth and deliver the moisture I've been dying for. My breath comes a little fast as I wait, but he only strokes my cheek a little more, then with the very tip of his index finger traces the lower edge of my mouth. He drops his hand, and the smile he gives me is not what I would have expected. A little unsure, maybe. He dips his head away, stirs the sauce.

I stand with my hands loose at my sides. "I have to get back. It's very good, the food. Enjoy your afternoon."

"Trudy," he says, following me, stopping me in the middle of the room. The word is different on his tongue, Truuddeee. Softer. "Will you let me take your photograph, just once right now?"

"Um." I fling up my arms, drop them. "Okay."

He lifts a finger, ducks into his bedroom, comes back with a sturdy and much-used 35 mm Minolta, then takes my hand and brings me back into the kitchen. "Stand here." He puts me back where I was a moment ago, and I realize the light coming in through the north window must be very good. I look toward it, through it, and see that my bedroom window is just visible. Has he ever seen my shadow there?

"Look at me," he says, his voice thick with something, and I turn toward the camera, seeing his succulent mouth below it. I wish he would ask me to take off my blouse, because I would do it, stand there bare-breasted in all my milk-whiteness for his camera. He shoots a frame, and then another, and I'm imagining how it would feel to have that camera on my nakedness.

As if that is somehow translated, his nostrils flare and he lowers the camera. Swallows. "Gracias," he says, and the word is quite soft.

On the street is the sound of a big truck, and I'm startled back to reality. "Oh! That's my son!" I pull at the neckline of my blouse, as if I've actually taken it off, and whirl around. "I have to go!"

"Thank you," he calls behind me.

"No problem!" I dash out into the day, the cold air popping and sizzling against my skin.

~

We're all sitting around eating pie when the ruckus across the street starts. Richard has taken his dad's spot at the table, and it's nice to see him carving the turkey, being a dad to his daughter. My oldest son is dark like the Marinos, with his grandmother's smooth velvet-brown eyes and a wickedly droll sense of humor. He was my football player, with his burly shoulders and immovability on a field. Now he's making piles of money in computer networking, consulting. He's young to have moved so fast, but he was always one to make up his mind to do something, then just get it done.

I have no idea where he came by this quality. Certainly it is not a hallmark of either of his parents. My astrologer friend would say it's the double Taurus, sun and moon, and who knows, maybe she's right. Today, his presence is jovial and warm, and I hold his daughter in my lap more often than I let her sit in the chair, because she makes me happy.

The trouble starts just as we're deciding whether to have pie now or wait. The first thing we hear is a loud engine, and a clatter like a bunch of tools in the bed of a truck. In spite of myself, I think of Rick, wonder if he'd dare just show up. But there's the slam of a door, and a shout. Then another, and another, a squall out in the street. I glance at Annie, and we both jump up. Annie grabs the phone, just in case, and we cross to the window to see what's going on.

In front of Shannelle's neat little house is a truck parked at a crooked angle on the grass. Once it might have been gold, but is now faded to a patchy dull brown. A man I know to be Shannelle's father, a balding, potbellied caricature of a disability bum, is standing on the grass, swaying and yelling. Tony comes out, neatly dressed up for the day in a white button-up shirt and a clean pair of jeans and cowboy boots. He looks like a caballero, and he's heroic as he tries to calm the man down, putting a hand on his arm, talking quietly.

But the old drunk isn't having it. "Patty, you bitch, get yer ass out here and come fix my dinner."

Shannelle comes out on the porch. She's wearing a dress and sandals, neither warm enough for the day. Her hair is curled around her shoulders. She says something to her father, pointing away from the house.

But he's not having it. He throws a sloppy punch at Tony, and there's more shouting, and then Shannelle's mother comes out, a woman so colorless from her defeats that she looks like a sepia photo. She starts to walk toward her husband, talking to Shannelle, who pulls her back and lifts a phone to her ear.

Good for her. "Let's give her a little privacy," I say, touching Annie's arm. "I'm sure she doesn't want all the neighbors staring at her drunken father."

But then a car comes racing down the street, a muscle car I know belongs to Shannelle's brother, and he screeches to a stop and gets out and starts yelling, though it's unclear whether it's at Shannelle or at his father or at his mother. Obviously father and son are cut from the same cloth—but the son is younger, and he throws a punch at Tony, knocking him down, hard. "Rich, maybe you need to get out there."

My sturdy son is on his feet, but Jo isn't happy with it. "What if they have a gun or something? I don't want you to get hurt."

He stands there, torn, between his mother and his wife, and I relent. "Maybe she's right. Let the police handle it."

"Jade's coming," Annie says.

I open the front door to let Jade know I'm there if she needs me, step out onto the porch. Annie hands me the phone.

Jade is running. "Shannelle, go inside, right now!" She kneels beside Tony, who is getting to his feet with a bloody lip, and he's mad as hell, struggling against Jade's admonishments—and her strength. She has a grip on his arm, which he keeps trying to loosen, and she's not budging. There is a fierce discussion between them, Tony shouting, Jade shaking her head.

"Patty! Get your ass out here!" the drunken father yells, and the brother is on his way to the door, maybe to physically drag the mother out. Jade is on her feet and tackles him before he can get there, but to do it, she's got to let go of Tony, who is on the father in an instant, and there are punches flying in two fights.

Sirens thankfully roar down the street, a quick response. Everybody halts immediately.

"Let's get back to dinner," I say. Close the door. But my heart is thrilled by Jade's strength. Her visible power. What would that be like? To be so strong you could tackle two men?

25

Trudy

Once the dishes are done, Jo and Rich take Minna over to Jo's mom's for pie and coffee. Before they leave, I pause and give my big son a giant hug. "Thanks, kiddo. I know you were taking care of me."

He pats my shoulder. "I hope you and Dad work it out, Mom."

I'm not sure what to say to that, so I turn to Jo and hug her, too. In her ear, quietly, I say, "You're an angel, sweetheart. Thanks for bringing your darlin' girl over."

"Oh, Trudy, you are so welcome." Her hug is tight and sincere, and I think all at once that I am truly blessed.

Annie helps me carry all the pots back into the greenhouse, then wiggles around so much I know what she wants. "Travis's coming, isn't he?"

"Do you mind? I don't want to leave you alone if you're feeling sad."

I laugh softly, brush her hair over her shoulder. "Did you guys plan this out? How to keep Mom busy all day so she won't brood?"

"Yeah, kinda. Do you mind? Colin's going to call in a little while, too. He promised."

"I don't mind. It's sweet."

It's quiet enough after she leaves, though, that in spite of my upbeat resolve, a stealthy sense of sadness steals through the house. Me. The radio is background noise, echoey against the emptiness of the house.

It's not so much the big things that get me, I'm discovering. It's all the little tiny threads that make up a whole life.

It's been a good day. I finish straightening, trying not to think of the way things used to be. Not think of the way Rick used to settle in after the feast, kick his feet up on a recliner, turn on the television after everyone had gone, and sigh. Not think, as I put away the last platter of turkey, that turkey sandwiches are his favorite, made with lots of mayo and plenty of salt. He won't be eating any of these leftovers.

I want to sit down in his chair and put my nose in it and see if I can smell him still, but as I move toward it, I have a sudden vision of where he might be right now. Sitting in Carolyn's house with her rotten children, drinking beer she bought for him, his feet kicked up on her footstool. I can see him, clearly, as she brings him a turkey sandwich, reaching out to put his hand around her knee, and I halt in my tracks. Jealousy pours like acid through me, and I know I have to do something, break the pattern. What do unmarried people do on holiday evenings?

Go to the movies, maybe? Go to the store?

Go anywhere.

I grab my coat and my keys and slam the door behind me, so anxious to not be here that it's not until I'm driving down Twenty-Ninth Street toward Pueblo Boulevard that I realize what I'm really doing.

Again. It's like having a bad pair of great-looking shoes. I know they're going to give me raw blisters, but I still keep putting them on.

In the first month of our breakup, I did this so often that I can do it on autopilot now. It's dead quiet. I loop through a run-down little neighborhood to the west, and see through the windows the bright happy families within, kids and grandmas and dads and moms. The blister pops and starts to burn. I head down the boulevard, trying to tell myself there's still time to turn back, that I do not have to do this, that it will only make me feel worse.

I keep driving, and as I get closer to the golf course, an anxious burn starts in my belly, and I wrestle my hands tighter on the wheel because they're sweating. The radio is on, playing Fleetwood Mac, and

I sing along with "The Chain," and even I can tell it's bravado, and it embarrasses me enough that I stop singing.

But I don't turn back. I glance in the rearview mirror like anyone else, anyone not on an insane mission to see how raw she can rub those blisters, but maybe someone on the way home from a great Thanksgiving meal, and I turn on my signal, turn left on Abriendo. Now my heart really starts to pound, because if Rick sees me I'll have no excuse. I just want his truck to be there, parked in front of his apartment, and then I'll know he's home, watching television by himself. Maybe missing us.

I slow as I pass the intersection and peer down the street, but of course the truck is gone. I loop around the block, decide to be bold, and turn on the street, just to be sure. There are no lights on.

My heart is pounding so hard, I can't really hear the radio, and there's a strange, strangled sense of something behind my eyes, and I think I'm an idiot, but I have to just see, so I head back down Fourth Street and drive all the way to the east side, and turn north on Monument, and cruise very, very slowly past Seventh Street. But I don't have to go that slow. The truck is obvious. Parked boldly right in front, like it belongs there.

The wounds on my heart are screaming now, pouring bloody pus into my chest cavity, making it hard to breathe. My hands are trembling and there's an almost vicious cackling in my ear. But do I heed the warning?

No. I turn down the narrow little street, a deep fear in me not of what I will see, but that I might be seen doing this. I have to do it anyway. Go see.

As if to facilitate my self-immolation, the curtains on Carolyn's picture window are open and I can see inside. I can't see her, but I see Rick, sitting on the couch without his shoes, drinking a beer. He's watching television under the glow of a lamp, and a young woman is beside him. Not his daughter. Hers. His daughter is out with her boyfriend, her heart shattered.

The tears are dripping off my chin before I realize I'm even crying, and I've driven down the short block and around the corner, where I pull over in a dark spot. I put my head down on the steering wheel and let them come, the tears. In great washes, soaking my hands, my face, the wheel.

I'm crying because it hurts and I did it to myself. But I didn't, did I? He did it to me, and I should hate him for it. Hate him for being so threatened by my quest to find out who I might be for the rest of my life that he had to run into the arms of a nice, nonthreatening bartender who never went to college, either. I should hate him for all the pain he's caused my family, and hate him for the betrayals he's heaped upon my head. Hate him for lying, hate him for his idiocy. Hate him for—

But the truth is, what I realize I'm thinking is that I wish he had glimpsed my car through the window and had suddenly come after me, that he turned this way and saw my car and came to the driver's side and peered in and said, "Trudy? Are you okay?"

Seeing this particular fantasy unfolding in my mind, the tears slow, the ache eases a bit, and I raise my head. The neighborhood around me is utterly still with postholiday satiety. A whip-lean dog trots down the middle of the street, cheerfully stopping to sniff a pile of leaves at the gutter. Wind is softly tossing tree branches overhead. I wipe the itchy tears off my face. Why would I want him to come find me demolished and spying on him?

And the answer is pathetic: because it would prove I mean more to him than she does.

My nose is disgusting, and I can find only a tiny scrap of tissue in my purse, and I am forced to drive back home marveling at how unbelievably ridiculous the whole thing was. It always is. It's like some other woman takes charge of my body, turns me into one of those awful women you see on daytime talk shows.

As I pull up in front of my house, I realize that the pressure that had been so agonizing is gone, as if those blisters on my heart were boils, and they've drained now. I think about the crying jag I had after Edgar died, the night I got drunk and humiliated myself by calling Rick and pouring my heart out to him. I cried like I would die that night, too, and woke up feeling a hundred times better.

There are lights on at Roberta's and I suddenly do not want to be alone anymore, not in my head, not in the house I used to love and sometimes now hate. In this very moment, I hate it so much that I pick up a pinecone and throw it, hard, at the side, then rub tear tracks off my face with my sleeve and head next door. Jade and I can talk about crying, and I can eat some of Roberta's pie. The night, I notice, is crisp and cool, very refreshing. It feels great on my hot face.

I knock and Jade answers, swinging the door wide in pleasure when she sees me standing there. "Hi," I say brightly. "Are you guys done in yet?"

"Not at all! Come in!" There's a shimmer or something around her, and I'm wondering, too late, because I'm already inside, if Angel might be there. I also notice a twinge of jealousy over the idea that he's put this light on her face. Jade steps sideways and I see that not only is Angel there, grinning around a straw at a hand of cards, but so is Roberta, and another man, as big as a football player, dressed neatly in a button-up shirt. He looks very clean somehow.

He's the first to look up, and gives me a nod of greeting, and I suddenly grab Jade's arm. In her ear, I say urgently, "Take me to wash my face."

"What?" She looks at me. "Come on. We'll be right back."

And I will love her forever for blocking me as we move toward the bathroom. When we are safely behind the door, she touches my cheek. "What happened?"

I bend over the sink and splash cold water over my hot eyes, rub away the tear tracks, raise my head to see how bad it is, and splash some more. "I did a stupid thing, Jade. But I think I learned something, and we can talk about it tomorrow or something." I look again, and at least it's clean. "I need Visine. And maybe a little lipstick or something?"

"You're gorgeous, Trudy." She hands me the Visine, then digs in a drawer. "Most of these are way too dark. Try this one."

It's dead black when I open it. "This?"

"Trust me."

I try it, and it goes on with a liquid smoothness, a clear plum that is surprisingly flattering. "Not bad."

Her arms are folded as she inclines her head. The coppery streaks in her curls glint, bringing out the green in her eyes. "You have a crush on him, don't you?"

"Who?" I blot my lips without looking at her.

She smiles softly. "He sure has one on you."

I meet her eyes in the mirror, raise my eyebrows. A zing of something like excitement zips through my body—there and gone so fast, I barely notice it.

"Hmmm," is all I can think of to say. "You ready?"

She leans down to see herself in the mirror, adjusts her shirt so a little more cleavage shows. "Sure."

When we enter the other room, my attention zooms right onto Angel, sitting with his back to the window. He's been running his hands through his hair, and it stands up a little at the back. If I didn't know that Roberta wouldn't allow it, I would think he had been drinking—there is that shiny look to his eyes, a flush high on those angles of cheekbone. An intensity to his gaze, which he fixes on me. "Hello, Trudy," he says, shuffling cards. "Are you going to play?"

"What's the game?" I bend down to hug Roberta. "How are you, honey?"

She squeezes my hand. "I'm fine, darlin'. You know me."

"Rummy," Angel says. In the way he's holding his straw between his teeth, I can see him in some tropical place with a little cigar, his shirt open to show his sweaty chest, a fan beating the air, very slowly, over his head. "Roberta"—it rolls over his tongue—"would not allow gambling."

"Trudy," Jade says, "this is Rueben, my boxing coach, from the gym, who came by and we snared him. Grandma's been feeding him since he got here an hour ago."

It's a long speech for Jade, and I suddenly realize that he, not Angel, is the source of that glow. And I can see why. "How do you do?" he says, standing to shake my hand. There is such a courtliness to the gesture, and such a roundness to his speaking voice, such a genuineness about his eyes, that I'm instantly trusting.

"Very well, thank you," I say, and sit down in the chair that he pulls over to the table for me.

It might be only rummy, but it's rousing. Angel is on high stun—verbal and funny, and runs a commentary on the proceedings as if we are playing high-stakes games in some exotic casino. He flirts outrageously with Roberta, making her laugh, and he defers to Jade's size and strength, which makes her laugh. I do not think Rueben is as charmed as the rest of us, but he isn't doing a big-dog bristle, either.

I tell myself that Angel is flirting with everyone, and he is, but he's also specifically, pointedly flirting with me, in a charming, courtly way that makes me breathless and giddy by the end of the evening, when Angel has amassed about twenty times as many points as the rest of us put together.

Roberta protests as we start to collect the empty glasses and saucers that litter the table. "Y'all just leave all that, now. I'm not crippled."

Jade gives me a nod. There's something hopeful in it. I push in my chair and kiss Roberta's cheek. "Thanks, sweetie," I say so only she can hear. "I was feeling blue when I got here, but this was great."

"You don't go lettin' nobody turn your head now, you hear me?" Her fingers tighten on mine. "Remember what's important."

"Mmm." My recent humiliation, self-inflicted though it was, is still fresh enough that I feel a throb in my wrist. "I'll see you tomorrow."

Angel walks with me as if it's the obvious conclusion, and out in the night, he takes a big deep breath. "I like your Thanksgiving, very much."

"I bet you're something to see at a poker table."

He winks. He's still playing with the straw. It moves back and forth, making me think of his tongue, and I wonder if it's deliberate. "Dangerous," he agrees.

I stop in front of my house. "You're pretty dangerous all the way around."

He faces me, comes a little closer. "Am I?" He looks at my mouth, takes the straw out of his own.

Time halts. We stand just outside the pool of the streetlight, in the shadows. The same soft wind from earlier brushes our hair around a little. Some of his touches his cheek and I am mesmerized by it, not even realizing that I'm swaying closer, that we are suddenly only breaths apart. He touches my hand, weaves his fingers through mine, and I wonder what he's waiting for, if he wants some signal from me, but I don't know what it should be.

The heat from earlier comes back, starts to burn in that small hot space between us, and it seems incredible that there should be so much electricity in just standing here, anticipating.

Anticipating.

He's shifting a little, but I'm so dizzy I don't know what or how until his hand curls around my neck, and his thumb tilts up my chin, and he kisses it. My chin. Then my cheek, then my eye, and I'm swaying with it, putting my hands up to his hair, which I've been wanting to touch for weeks, and it's as silky as it looks, deep and wild, and so much of it. Our bodies touch lightly down the front.

And then there are car lights coming down the street, blasting across the thinness of my closed eyelids, and I'm jolted back to the mundane. I pull away, worried it might be my daughter, who would then see her mother kissing someone. "I'm sorry," I whisper, and he touches my hand, once lightly, before he melts into the darkness like a cat.

It is my daughter, getting out of the car, and she slams the door, then startles when she sees me on the sidewalk. "What are you doing out here?"

"Just came from Roberta's," I say, and it sounds perfectly legitimate. It's not, I realize, a lie, but my gaze is drifting toward Angel's house, where a light comes on in his bedroom. I think of him there, skin gilded with lamplight, and I realize I'm going to sleep with him.

Soon.

26

Shannelle

TO: naomiredding@rtsv.org

FROM: chanelpacheco@hotmail.com

SUBJECT: how few pages

Dear Naomi,

No, I haven't had much time to write the past few weeks. The whole Thanksgiving fiasco with my parents is just going on and on—she shows up every other day for sympathy, and how can I not give it to her? She doesn't have anybody else. It's causing all kinds of tension with Tony, too, because he doesn't want to be involved. My family embarrasses him, and I do understand. They embarrass me, which is an awful thing to say, but it's true.

The good news is, my neighbor across the street, Jade, is a social worker with all kinds of contacts and she found me a dentist who is going to do the work on my mouth for nothing, as long as I let him take pictures and document the "reconstruction." I saw him last week and he did some stuff to the root of the bad tooth, which made it stop hurting, anyway. He's really nice, pretty young, and I guess he can use me to write a paper and get some more credentials. So, I'm seeing him every other week until it's all done. Even Tony didn't make any noises this time about being charity cases. I think the last two toothaches really scared him.

I'm also feeling really guilty because we are still struggling with money so much. I know I'm smart enough to get a job in an office somewhere, and I'm good at organizing things. It seems crazy to be chasing this idea of writing books when I could get real work at $9 an hour and build a nice, ordinary life. Tony is always coming home and telling me about jobs at State Hospital, where he works, and it's so stable and so reliable, he'd really like me to do it. It's hard to stick with my five-year plan, to believe I can really do this. It's getting kind of close now—I only have a year left, Naomi, and then I told him I would go to work for real.

Am I crazy? Give me some words of wisdom if you have any. I'm feeling pretty depressed.

Shannelle

~

TO: chanelpacheco@hotmail.com

FROM: naomiredding@rtsv.org

SUBJECT: oh, sure, work for the state

hey, sweetie—so happy about dentist & teeth troubles getting fixed. did you fill out the form for the writer's retreat? the deadline is next week. you must do this!

so sorry to hear of all the things in your weigh (weighing you down). first of all, recognize that all writers and painters and creative people have times when they are not as productive as they'd like to be. don't beat yourself up for not getting as much done as you'd like. it'll come.

oh, and yeah, i think you should go be a secretary and dress up for work every day and do things you'll hate from 8 a.m. to 4 p.m. c'mon, shannelle, you know better. there's nothing wrong with being a secretary or wanting stability or anything else, but you are a writer, and you know it. if you give this up, what are you going to say to yourself when you're 80? do you really want to be one of those people who tells me at parties, "i used to want to write, but i just got too busy. maybe i could tell you my idea and you could write it for me and we'll split the money."

you are a talented writer with a lot to say, and you ****must not give up****!!! the world needs your stories. you need to write them. the universe NEEDS you to write them, because if you don't do your work, it might not ever get done. there is no other writer in the world like you. no one else can tell the stories you will, in the way you'll tell them.

i can't give you any guarantees about it, though, you know that. if you want stability and health insurance, this is not the road to follow. it's unpredictable and you have to learn to be a juggling artist and most of us don't have big retirement plans. but babe, it's worth it. it's so worth it. it's worth it to get up every morning and be doing what you really want to be doing. it's worth it to write. it's worth it to publish. it's worth all the struggles.

homework for the day: write a letter from a reader to you. tell yourself all the things you most want to hear about your work. date it two years in the future, sign it, and put it up on your writing board, where you can see it all the time.

FILL OUT THAT FORM FOR THE WRITER'S RETREAT AND SEND IT IN!

i'm always here, listening. you can count on me always. i promise.

love,
naomi

~

TO: naomiredding@rtsv.org

FROM: chanelpacheco@hotmail.com

SUBJECT: Homework

I sent in the retreat form yesterday. Cross your fingers. I'm not thinking right now about how I'd work it out. Cross that bridge if/when it comes to that.

Wrote the letter, too. Felt silly at first, then it was fun. And afterward, I ended up writing three pages on the book, I was so inspired! Thank you thank you thank you!

Love,
Shannelle, who has gone three whole days with no family crises

CHRISTMAS

Yemaya

The goddess of the sea and the moon. She is the mother archetype and the provider of wealth. As the one who gives life and sustains the Earth, she is extremely generous and giving. She is the nurturing energy that soothes anyone. But like the ocean, when she is angry, she can be implacable. Therefore, she represents the mother who gives love, but does not give her power away. Yemaya is also the owner of the collective subconscious and ancient wisdom, since she holds the secrets that are hidden in the sea. She is often invoked in fertility rituals for women and in any ritual concerning women's issues.

—www.goddess.com.au

27

Roberta

December 7, 20—

Pearl Harbor Day

Dear Harriet,
So sorry to hear about Mary's cancer. You tell her from
me that she's on my prayer list. The Lord can work
miracles, as we all have seen. And don't you worry
at all about being able to come for Christmas. You're
needed there, and I understand. There'll be a pack of
folks here anyway, you know it.

I'm doing just fine, thank you. The weather is
making the old arthritis kick up, as always, and there
are days I don't want to get out of my warm bed at
all, so I don't. Jade gets ticked with me, but I tell her
I'm an old woman and have earned the right to stay in
bed and sleep if I feels like it. I read my study guides
and Bible and sleep a lot and after a day or two, I'm
ready to go again.

What that granddaughter of mine does not
understand is that the reason that got me out of bed
is gone, and at least when I'm sleeping I can forget it

for a while. She says it's depression, but I just told her to go get busy, because natural grief ain't the same as modern DE-Pression (ha!).

I'm getting sleepy again and am going to slip off and take a nap whiles she's still at work so she won't nag me (ha-ha!).

Love,

Your sister,

Berta

28

Jade

It starts to snow like crazy one early December afternoon. I'm sitting in my tiny office at DSS with a seventeen-year-old mother who already has three children and one on the way. The first three have been removed from her care. She's making the pitch that she's ready to have them back.

I have a headache at the base of my skull from the falling barometric pressure. Likely some of it comes from all the caffeine I've been gulping on the sly. There's a small ache in my upper right arm from a muscle I pulled yesterday—threw a punch and missed, which didn't do my case for getting in the ring any good. Rueben laughed at me.

It may sound like I'm heartless, thinking all those things while this young girl is pitching her story to me, but let me tell you, she's so skinny her stomach sticks out like a basketball. Her hair hasn't been washed in about six weeks. It's gummy and sticky, hanging like snakes on her shoulders.

And still she's trying to play me. Tossing her snake hair over her shoulder, blinking those big blue eyes at me. Once, she was probably pretty, but a drug addict loses her sheen in no time.

I see so many girls like this now. More and more. And if it's not crack, it's booze or weed, and it's always about one more man. One more. The one that's for real this time. The one who might stay. The one who will love his babies.

One more boy. A boy like my cousin Malik, always playing, always braggin', always talking about their bitches. To get them, the girls give away their hearts, their bodies, their kindness, even their children, until they're all used up. Hollowed-out shells of themselves, ancient at thirty, living in public housing for the rest of their lives because they don't know anything else. And they have babies. Boys who grow up to call women bitch and girls who start giving themselves away at twelve and thirteen.

In the early days, when I still had some idealism left in me, I tried to do something about the girls. I taught birth control classes. Parenting classes. Gave assessment tests to find out skills and interests, so they could get jobs or maybe even get into college. Some of those girls were so damned smart, it would break your heart, but there's no place for them to rule in their world. In the ghettos and barrios of America, a girl can't even rule in the crime world, as her brother could.

Only thing she's got is her body. Makes me sick.

Anyway, I made so little progress with those girls, it felt like draining the ocean with an eyedropper. I moved on to the babies. Least there you get a chance, once in a while, to break the cycle. And so, no, I don't have much sympathy for this lost girl in front of me. I'm wondering, instead, how to save her baby so he or she won't be sitting in my office fifteen years from now.

The snow catches my attention. Big, mesmerizing flakes like I haven't seen in ten years. I missed snow in California. These float down and cover up the ugly parking lot.

When the phone rings, I'm hoping it's going to be a way to distract myself. "This is Jade Kingman."

"Hi, Jade." I know the satin-smooth voice immediately. "This is Eileen Robideaux." The mother of the second set of Dante's children. "Am I disturbing you?"

"Give me one minute, Eileen." I cover the mouthpiece. "Bonnie, I can't help you until you're clean. Capisce?"

"I am, Ms. Kingman! I swear!"

"Willing to take a drug test?"

Her eyes slither away. With a defeated slump, she gets up and shuffles out. As she exits, she mutters, "Cunt," without any pretense of hiding it from me.

I uncover the phone. "Okay, Eileen. Sorry about that. How are you?" And it isn't until that very second that my gut knots up. I haven't heard from Dante in weeks. "Is Dante okay?"

"Oh, girl, you know Dante. Always lands on his feet." But there's a depth to her pause that doesn't give me any comfort. "I am calling about him, though."

"All right."

"Look, Jade, we had our differences, I won't lie about that, but I didn't think you ought to be in the dark out there in Colorado, maybe sending him money or whatever."

"I'm—" I halt in my lie. "Yes, I am. What's he done?"

"He got married." For the first time, I hear the soul-deep fury in her voice.

"What?"

"Yeah, that's what I said. It was Portia who told me, and you don't even want to talk to her today, sister, because I mean she'd shoot a man if she had a way—he's been playing her six ways to Sunday, even asked her to marry him. She showed me the letter a couple of weeks ago."

There's an odd fluttery sensation in my chest. Not quite nausea. I press two ice-cold fingers to the place between my eyebrows.

"Jade?"

"I'm here." My voice sounds hollow. I shake the hair off my face. "Who did he marry?"

"Some white woman he met during the trial, just before he went up, a lawyer. Can you believe it?"

The man could charm the panties off the Virgin Mary, so yeah, I can believe it. But I can't even get that much out. "Thanks for telling me, Eileen. I'm going to go now."

"Jade, you know I didn't tell you to hurt you."

"I know. Thanks." I hang up the phone, walk over to my door, and close it. There's a ripping feeling in my chest. It feels like it's taking my breath, maybe all my ribs with it. It spreads upward to the base of my neck.

Married.

A thin little voice winds through my head—But I'm his wife! That's how it was, a comfort to me, that he actually married me even when he didn't marry the mothers of his children. He'd been allergic to marriage until he met me. He said that a thousand times. I took it to mean that I meant more to him than any other woman. That no matter what, I would be his beloved, forever and ever. That what we had was unique. That he would never be able to love anybody else, any more than I would.

I stand there trying to breathe, look at the thick, crazy-beautiful snow falling. I know I'm never going to see this kind of snow without remembering this pain.

Dante, lost to me.

Married. I remember what Eileen said, that it was a white lawyer he met during the trial. I search my memory frantically for who it might be. The main lawyer had a woman assistant, with cropped, shiny dark hair I had admired. She was tiny. Tiny in height, in the shoulders, and had no butt at all. I noticed because her skirts looked so straight. She wore red lipstick and had professionally manicured nails.

I suppose it goes with the territory.

And you might ask yourself what a woman like that would be doing with an imprisoned thief with four children from two different women and an ex-wife. Don't. All of us, all his women, are in that category. Not just good-looking, but especially good to look at in some way. Eileen is one of those cat-eyed, light-skinned island women. Portia's a regal, long-necked African queen with a bustline that captures the attention of any man in sight.

Standing there, I realize that it has not been real, my divorce. I signed the papers. Cut him off financially. Sort of. Moved a thousand miles away. I hadn't even been taking his phone calls.

I'd been telling myself I was over him.

But I have never believed it. Not until this very minute. It hurts so bad, I want to kick something or scream or throw a trash can through the plate glass window, just to hear it shatter.

Instead, I pick up the phone and dial my supervisor's extension. "Shirley," I say when she answers, "I've got to leave early. Taking a couple of personal hours."

There must be something in my voice. "Anything I can do, Jade?"

"Not unless you know any contract killers for ex-husbands."

"Hold on, I have one in my Rolodex."

I chuckle bitterly. She's divorced, too. "See you tomorrow."

I drive blindly home. My grandmother isn't there. She's left me no note or anything like that, but why should she? I kick my toe on one of her boxes, and realize that, slowly, she's filling them up. There are boxes in every room in the house, each with some relative's name on it.

And it strikes me that things are disappearing off the walls, that the house is looking a little threadbare. I wonder what I should do about it. Talk to her pastor? Is this some expression of grief that's common? Is it serious?

As I'm taking off my coat, the phone rings. I pick it up dully.

"Hello."

"Baby, I'm so glad I caught you. Tried to catch you at work, but they said you'd gone home."

I hang up. He calls right back, and I wonder who gave him the phone card. Probably his new wife. I lie there on the couch and let it ring. And ring.

The third time, I pick it up and bark, "I don't want to talk to you!"

"Jade." He says it in that velvet voice. Patient and regretful.

"What?"

"Baby, please don't hang up. Listen."

"You have five seconds."

"I'm just trying to get back to you, baby. You're the only one for me, you know that."

"Dante, how stupid do you think I am? You married her, while you were telling Portia you two were gonna get back together and you're calling me for stamps and money and phone cards and the only one who was seeing you clearly was Eileen, and you're pissed that she told me."

"Baby, wait. Eileen told you what? That I married this bitch?"

I make a noise. "Don't lie, Dante. I'm sick of it. Just try to tell the truth for once in your pathetic life, all right?"

He's silent.

"Too hard?" I say.

"Baby, look. I married her, a'ight? But you saw her. Skinny old thing, not my type at all. But what better way to get out of jail faster than to let this lawyer who has a thing for me do all the work?"

I close my eyes. On my red eyelids, I see a hundred pictures, falling like snowflakes. Me and Dante, laughing over a meal in a nice restaurant, him all dressed up and the waitress fawning on him and me preening to be with a man so many others wanted. Portia, showing up on my doorstep one night like a queen, hair all bound up in a turban, her eyes crazy. Scared the hell out of me, but she just looked at me and said, "Watch your pocketbook, sugar. He'll take you like he's taken us, for everything you got, and make you think you're likin' it." Then she pushed past me into my house, and spit in Dante's face. He didn't do anything. Just picked up a napkin and wiped his cheeks, raising his face to her. There was something hot and dark in that moment of their staring at each other, something I didn't want to see, and I looked away.

I see myself, lying in his arms, nestled close into his shoulder, after we'd made love. It feels like everything inside me is in ribbons.

And I see the new one, so polished and attractive and successful, falling under his spell. Getting ready to be the new sacrifice. "How can you use people like that, Dante?"

"Whatever it takes to get back to you, baby."

"You're a shallow, pathetic man," I say. "You used me, and Portia and Eileen, and you'll use this one until you use her up, then go on to the next. You are," I say distinctly, "one sorry-ass motherfucker."

He hangs up.

The profanity rings in the air of my grandmother's house, as ugly a thing as I've ever said. As I sit there, the echo reproaches me. I can't think of anything to do but go put on my workout clothes. Leave a note for my grandmother. Go to the gym.

There aren't many people there on a snowy Thursday afternoon. The bitch who hates my guts is one of them, unfortunately. Or fortunately. She hisses like a snake when I pass her on the way to the locker room. I just cut her a dark look that says, *Go ahead. Cross me today.*

Rueben doesn't appear to be anywhere around. I'm disappointed, but he's not the reason I'm here. I change and yank my hair into a scrunchie. There's a jumpy tension in my legs, my arms as I go back out. I start with the jump rope to warm up. Bitch is on a punching bag, and she makes little comments as she smashes her gloves into it. "Break that nose." "Crack her pretty-girl jaw." "Half-breed bitch." I ignore her, going through my paces. Rueben will kick my ass if I get in a fight, and I'm mad enough today to do it.

But she keeps on. Louder, uglier. Challenging me, in front of the guys, who are starting to look at me to see if I've had enough. There's a thick rope of lust in the air. They want to see us go at it. My chest starts to burn with pressure, but I stay with my business. Sit-ups, push-ups. Not gonna get into some idiot catfight.

This goes on for half an hour, and the air's thicker and thicker. Tense and tight. Oppressive. The anger at Dante and the bullshit here are mixing up in my body, and I'm aching to hurt somebody. Teach this little bitch a lesson.

To one side is Tony's brother, Gabe. I look at him and he comes over, turning his back to the rest of them so they won't see what he says to me. "You gotta stand up to her, Jade. You're losing all respect here."

"Rueben will kill me."

"He'll get over it. I'll tell him how it was." He narrows his eyes. "You scared?"

I meet his eyes. "No."

"Get in the ring with her. Spar. I'll be in your corner."

And it's what I want anyway, to channel this fury out of me. I step around him. "All right, bitch. Get in the ring."

A little ripple of approval goes through the boxers.

Gabe helps me tie on my gloves. I eye my opponent. She's squat and carries about ten extra pounds through the middle, but I'm not kidding myself. She's got that solid body, powerful through the torso, and if she hits me, I'll know it. But my reach is much longer than hers. I'm faster. She's younger. I'm smarter.

Gabe murmurs warnings. "Watch her uppercut. It's dangerous and could break your jaw. Watch the body blows." He gives me the mouth guard. "Don't hold back, or she'll hurt you."

Adrenaline and anticipation are rushing through me. Rueben is going to kill me, but Gabe's right. No way around this if I want any respect in here.

"Pretty girl," she says, and smiles. It gives me a healthy measure of fear.

We circle and feint, measuring each other. I'm pumped and moving too much and will wear myself out. I slow down, looking for an opening. See how she plants each foot, every time, square and solid.

I can't stand the tension, and throw the first punch, a right that she ducks. But she's quicker than I thought, lands a grazing blow over my shoulder. I hear the murmurs, the catcalls, the conversation as we circle and feint some more.

She lands a right cross to my cheekbone.

Jesus.

For the space of two long seconds I can't see anything, can't hear anything. She hits me again, eye and jaw.

Bam. It feels like my face is going to break in two. Instinct kicks in and I deflect a third blow, hear a little roar from the boxers, grab her. She laughs.

And that's it. There's no anger in me. A cold power surges through my body, into my limbs, and I fling her away. There's nothing now but me and her. No Dante. No death. No sorrow. Just this. The cold strength in my arms. The sharpness of my attention. The fierce, icy focus that makes me see she has a hitch in her gait, every time. I wait for it. Deflect a cross, then an uppercut that would have knocked me down. It just kisses the edge of my jaw.

She wants my eye again. It's closing. It's impossible that we haven't reached the end of one round yet. In a split second, I see my opening. Plant my feet, swing from the left into her hitched gait.

It lands at the joint of her jaw. It's solid, with my weight behind it. The shock rockets up my arm, and she doesn't so much as stumble backward, but sails up and lands flat on her back.

My heart is pumping and there's dizziness in my head and now my eye is starting to really swell, but I wait for Miss Thing to get up.

She just lies there.

A couple of the guys are in the ring now, yelling at her. I'm blinking and panting. Waiting. And it starts to scare me when she doesn't get up after the count, that she hasn't moved.

God, what if I killed her? I send a terrified gaze to Gabe. He shakes his head, lifts his chin toward her. I turn back, and she's spitting and fighting, shouting curses, but they won't let her fight any more today. It takes two of them to drag her out of the ring.

"Fuck you, bitch! That was a lucky punch."

I smile. "Yeah, right."

It's only then that I see Rueben, standing to one side with his big arms crossed. His face has no expression. He stares at me hard for a long minute, then points—first to me, then with a thumb over his shoulder toward the office. He heads down the hall without waiting to see if I'll do it.

"Shit," I say to Gabe. "Help me off with the gloves, then you gotta tell him what was goin' on."

"It'll be all right. You did good, babe."

"Don't call me babe," I snap.

He chuckles. "Damn, girl, you hit like a man."

I pull out of the gloves. "Go. Tell him."

With a wink, he crawls between the ropes and I stand there for a minute, giving him some time to get ahead of me. I catch the eye of one older Spanish guy. He lifts his chin in respect. Not like a man looking at a hot woman. Like a man to a man.

It feels good.

As I make my way to the office, I can tell I'm going to have a massive headache by nightfall. I'm a little queasy, whether from the rush of chemicals in my system or the blow itself, I don't know. Or maybe I'm just afraid of what Rueben is going to say.

He's standing in the office, a whistle around his neck like a gym teacher. "Thanks, Gabe," he says as I come in. "This is between Jade and me."

Gabe gives me a shrug as he scurries out.

"Shut the door," Rueben says. "Sit down."

I do. He hands me an ice bag and I put it on my face.

He sits in the off-kilter office chair. Folds his hands in his lap. Looks at me. "Hurt enough to suit you?"

I peer at him through my good eye. Raise my eyebrows.

"What were you thinkin', Jade? Got a death wish?"

"No! You heard Gabe. I had to fight her."

"You're not ready." His voice is low and furious.

"Fuck that! I knocked her out!" I lower the bag and glare at him. "You're babying me."

"You got lucky. I'm not saying you can't do it, eventually. I'm saying that you getting in the ring with her was like a pup thinking she can take on a seven-year-old pit bull."

Sullenly, I slump. My feelings are hurt. I wanted him to tell me how well I'd done. Tell me I can get in the ring.

All at once, he lets go of a breath and leans forward to put his head in his hands. "Damn, woman, when I came in there and saw you in the ring, it took ten years off my life."

"Rueben—"

"Stop." He lifts his head and stares at me. "You don't know what you're talking about. If you want me to coach you, you've gotta follow my rules, you got it? You don't get in that ring unless I set up the fight and tell you you can. Got it?"

I swallow. Nod.

"Let's go take a look at your eye." He stands up and leads me through a narrow hallway to a staff bathroom where the first-aid supplies are kept. It's dark and gloomy in there. He flips on the light, a harsh fluorescent.

It's the first chance I've had to see the wound and look in the mirror. "Oh, wow." My eye is dark reddish purple across the eyelid and all the way up to the eyebrow. A glove-size red mark surrounds that. By morning, it's gonna be something to see.

"Turn around," Rueben says.

I put my butt on the sink and lift my face toward him. With gentle fingers, he probes the edges, lifts the eyelid to look at my eye. "Close your right eye," he says. "Now what can you see?"

"It's kind of blurry."

"Any red tint?"

"No." I'm looking at his face with my wounded eye, feeling the size and tenderness of him. I look at his mouth and wish that he seemed to feel the slightest attraction to me. Instead it's all business, all the time, with Rueben Perry.

I bow my head. "I'll be all right."

His other hand falls on my neck, then my shoulder. "You're tense as hell."

"It was a bad day."

"Yeah? Want to talk about it?" His strong fingers knead the place between my shoulder and neck, and it makes me irritable. I shrug it off.

"No."

But all of a sudden, it's agonizing, the recognition of how I let myself be used, how foolish I was, how much I loved Dante in spite of all the things I must have known about him. I put my hand over my eye and grit my teeth to keep from crying.

"Come here, Jade," he says in his low, kind voice. I fall forward into the safety of his big arms, putting my face against his chest. He holds me tight. Not one of those wimpy brother-sister hugs. It's real. Solid. I can smell the laundry soap he uses in his shirt. His belt buckle is cold against my belly and his thighs are hard. And I grip him back, feeling a shaky tremble moving through my arms. His hand is gentle on my hair. "You're a strong woman, inside and out. Don't let anybody take you down."

I raise my head. "Thank you."

And for one long second, I think he's going to kiss me. We haven't let go, and I'm looking up at just the right angle. He's looking at me for the first time like he'd like it, like he's hungry, too.

Then he swallows and puts me away from him. "It would be a mistake, Jade," he says quietly.

"Why?"

He steps back, turns half away. "Just would."

But that means it wasn't my imagination. I put my hand on his shoulder. "Rueben?"

He doesn't look at me. "Go home, Jade. Rest up. We'll talk tomorrow."

I take my hand back. Nod. Feel a sting of rejection that is really not what I needed today. It makes me feel stupid and—

"Jade."

I stop and look at him. "Don't worry about it," I say with a bitter smile. "I'll be all right. I'm a strong woman, remember?"

29

Trudy

The afternoon of the first real snow, I go downstairs to my massage room for the first time in five months. It's cold in here, and I know it needs to be dusted, but the smell of aromatherapy oils envelops me immediately, and I pause, closing my eyes at the sudden wave of images that flood through me.

Driving up to Boulder the first weekend of my classes, feeling so sick with nerves that I nearly turned around twice . . . coming home, each time, from the earthy people I'd spent my hours with, to the squareness of the house, Rick pretending to take an interest, but listening for only five minutes before he launched into long explanations of his weekends.

Lies, as it turned out. A familiar brittleness invades me.

I push it away, push into the room as if there is a force holding me back. Deliberately, I stride to the CD player and click it on. Enya glides into the room on a liquid harp, a CD I haven't heard in too long. The sound unknots the tension in my neck, and I'm able to strip the linens from the table, throw them on the floor. My wrist twinges the slightest bit, but I ignore it, open the closet to get some cleaning supplies down.

Methodically, I oil away the dust in the room, off the surfaces of the unnamed goddess statue in one corner, off the small tables and the window ledges and the rainbow array of glass bottles catching the light. There is a yawning sense of pain through it, and my head is blistered with visual and auditory memories—"Marino, huh?" said my client, a new one with long dark hair and red acrylic nails. "A friend of mine has a boyfriend named Marino. Rick? Is he your brother or something?"

I squeeze my eyes closed, wipe down the table itself, remember that resistance is the sure way to see something echo through you forever, but dwelling is equally damaging. So I let it all flow, through me and out of me into the scrubbing this room has needed and is only getting because someone needs me more than I need to resist it.

Jade needs me.

So I get the mop and bucket and let the disaster of that hot July day come through me. Hearing the words, and feeling again the disbelief. Holding my cool until I finish the massage, mind racing with possibilities, then going straight to the phone to cancel my other appointments for the day. Disbelief mixing with knowledge, with dreams of warning, with strange little things that had been bothering me, with shaking recognition as I used Windows Explorer to search the computer for the woman's name: Carolyn Sears. And read the files that came up, dozens of them, chronicling the entire absurdity of an extramarital affair.

I remake the table, and begin wiping down the small bottles of essential oils, one at a time. I'd driven to the Harley shop, and before he even knew I was there, had shattered most of the windows in his truck with the only thing I could find, a tire jack from my own trunk. The sound of the first windows breaking brought a spectator, and his shout brought more, and I ignored them all, swinging the jack with all my might, crash crash crash, methodically. The windshield was on the seat inside the truck, and both door windows were cracked very nicely, but even when I climbed up in the bed and swung hard, the back glass resisted. I gave up and jumped out, aware that my wrist was tired and sore, but not done yet, so I swung it at the body, putting dents in the shiny red doors by the time Rick grabbed the jack out of my hand, and he was bewildered, yelling, "What the hell are you doing, Trudy?"

"Fuck you, Rick, and fuck your girlfriend, Carolyn." I rushed to the car, avoiding him, because he was trying to talk, to get a word in edgewise, to convince me of something, and I reached in, took the emails I'd printed, and threw them in the air.

I got in the car and drove away. Shock or rage protected me long enough that I got to Roberta's house, where I broke down and sobbed hysterically for two hours. My wrist was aching and red, but I didn't really feel the extreme pain until I was getting ready for bed. Without Rick.

I shake it a little now, easing the tenseness. Massage will be good for it.

The mystery is when, exactly, I broke it. I remember, vaguely, hitting the brace of the windshield at one point, but I barely felt it. It wasn't a hairline fracture, either. A clean, visible break on the X-ray, with a broken edge where a piece of bone had been knocked free by the force. Three months in that blasted cast.

Jade shows up at seven, sans makeup, and looks even worse than her voice sounded on the phone. To my amazement, when I touch her shoulder, she starts to cry. "It's not helping to say fuck you," she says, collapsing on the couch, her knees akimbo as they'd been when she was younger.

"Sometimes it doesn't. C'mon, honey. Let me show you where I do this."

She doesn't move right away. "Is it going to be weird, giving a massage to someone you know?"

"Not for me. Are you uncomfortable?"

"I don't know. I've never done this before."

"Never?"

"Well, not outside sexual situations."

I smile. "Remember how it felt when your mother brushed your hair? This is more like that."

She gets up and follows me downstairs, through the family room, into a back bedroom, the room that used to be Richard and Colin's. I have already warmed it up, turned on the lights. I've chosen some Nakai for the music, because it's melancholy and beautiful, and I suspect Jade needs a good cry. "Just get undressed, and get up on the table and cover yourself with that blanket."

"All the way?"

"You can leave on your underwear if you feel more comfortable, but everything else needs to go."

She shifts, tosses her hair. "What do most people do?"

"Take everything off." I find myself using my healer's voice, the soft low one, nonthreatening. "It just makes it easier for the therapist to do the work. But do whatever makes you comfortable."

She nods.

"I'll be back in a few minutes."

And this is my ritual for a new client. I go upstairs, into the greenhouse, to the altar of the goddess I have set up. Tonight it is Yemaya, the African goddess of the rivers and oceans, and a great mother. I'm pleased that it worked out this way—Yemaya can help with the flow of a woman's tears. I light the fat round blue candle in front of her. Her incense is a powdery blue, and I put some in the abalone shell and light it. There is a bottle of an aromatherapy oil called "rain" and I open it, touch small drops to my temples and forehead and throat, opening to whatever Yemaya can give me for Jade. Then I hold in my hand the egg-shaped labradorite I found in Manitou Springs for this altar. It's cold when I pick it up, but warms quickly in my hands, and I close my eyes and take a long, slow, deep breath, blowing out my own negativity, allowing all the healing spirits to come into me.

It's the first time I have done this ritual since that awful day, and as the feeling of peace rushes through me, the sense of heat comes into my hands, I am almost overcome with gratitude that I have a chance to do this for my friend, that I have been trained in ways that will help heal her sorrowing heart tonight, that I can do something so useful. Leaving the candle burning, I return to the kitchen, thoroughly wash and dry my hands, and go back downstairs, knocking lightly on the door. Jade says, "I'm ready."

First-time clients are often a little nervous, and they try to talk. Usually, I dissuade them gently by giving short, quiet answers to encourage them to drift away into the healing world of music and touch and scent, but as I position myself at Jade's head, pulling her hair gently away from her shoulders and neck, I simply tell her, "You can give me direction, but just let go of talking other than that, okay?"

"Okay."

"Close your eyes," I say, and brush my hands with long strokes through her hair and scalp. "You might cry, but that's okay. Don't worry about it."

She's already relaxing. Her voice is a little farther away. "Okay."

And then I let Nakai, with his melancholy, beautiful flute, fill the room, let my hands do their work. Her body is strong and hard, some of it with muscle, but mostly with tension. It lives in her face because she tries to keep from showing anything, and in her shoulders and neck, which are like granite when I first begin, because she's carrying too much with her. I work there for a long time, smoothing and easing, feeling her wince when I find the pockets of painful knots. I ease back a little, smooth and smooth and ease, and she makes a soft sound. I smile.

As I work, something eases in me, too. I feel something buzzy flowing down my spine, through my legs, to the floor, all the poison I've been carrying with me, or at least some of it. The more I work, the more ease I feel through my scalp, through my arms. My wrist twinges slightly now and then, but it's not a dangerous kind of twinging, just a long-unused joint coming back to life.

Ah, I have missed this. Missed the gentleness of this room, the peacefulness of the practice, the great benefit there is in giving. How did I survive these months without it? Why didn't I just come down here sometimes and lie down and just give myself up to my grief and let the healing spirits of the goddesses and all the mothers and ancestors come in and take care of me?

Grieve, as Jade is grieving. Tears appear and disappear, and when I'm finished, I touch her back gently. "Take your time, sweetie. Don't get up too fast. I'll make us some herbal tea. Just come up when you're ready."

I pour her a huge glass of water and put it on the table, and put the kettle on, finding the big ceramic cups I got at the Renaissance Festival a few years ago. I missed it this year, and it's one of my favorite places to go mess around. As I ready the cups, filling two tea balls with a mixture I have made for me at the herb store for things like this, I realize Rick never once went with me.

And for that matter, he always hibernated when I had evening clients come in. It made him acutely uncomfortable that I wanted to do this—it took two years to convince him that I really wanted it, that it wasn't some fleeting interest, but a genuine offshoot of my interest in yoga and natural healing.

Why in the world did I let him bully me that way?

Jade comes up, looking dazed, her hair captured in a scrunchie at the top of her head, and she throws her arms around me in a fierce hug. "Thank you," she breathes in my ear. "I needed that so much."

I hug her back. "I know." What she doesn't know is how badly I needed it myself.

For the first time in months, I feel like myself.

For a while, she's quiet, drinking water, staring at a spot in the middle of the table. I think fancifully that she could be Yemaya, except for the yellow shadows under her eyes. Her eyelids are puffy.

"What I don't understand, Trudy," she says at last, "is why I even care. He's a liar and a thief and a cheat. Why does even one cell of my body still want him?"

She doesn't really want an answer. I raise my eyebrows, nudge the cookies in her direction.

"I mean, I sit there every day in my office, passing judgment on those girls. I'm pissed at them. They make terrible choices. Throw themselves away on those loser men." She spreads her hands. "And how am I any different?"

"Jade, don't be so hard on yourself."

Her red-rimmed eyes look lashless. "Look at me in this minute. I'm crying over a man who married someone else, and I still want to write him a letter and tell him how much I loved him." She puts her head down on her hands and lets go of a deep, pained sigh. Her hair scatters in coppery corkscrews over the table and I reach for a lock of it, rub it between my fingers.

"I hate," she says, "that I know what he's saying to her. That he's saying exactly the same things in exactly the same words and voice. Not just the ideas, you know? The exact same words. And she's thinking, just like I did, that he made them up just for her. Like, he propositioned her in the same way, and he got her into his arms the same way . . ." She lowers her voice, slurs it a little bit. "Come here, baby, let me hold you." She makes a noise, a growl, and covers her ears like that will shut out the sound. "And after sex, he will say, 'Damn, baby, I can't even move.'"

It's only then that she looks up at me and sees my face, which I feel must be gray with recognition. "Oh, Trudy, God, I'm sorry." She loops her hand around my wrist. "Don't think about it. Start singing 'The Star-Spangled Banner,' right now." And she starts it, "O-oh, say can you see . . ."

But I say, "When I read his emails to Carolyn, that was the thing that slayed me. He called her some of the same pet names. Like, I always thought they belonged to me. And I know that he suggested some of the same things sexually. I don't want to say them, but it was very obvious."

"How can they do that? Are they just that cold?"

"I don't know." Maybe it's the fact that my hands are still buzzing from giving a massage, that all that energy is still humming in me, but I put my palms over my chest and I feel the calm pressing through. "Maybe we do it, too, and just don't realize it. Maybe that's why we get jealous, men and women, because we know so much about our lovers and how they do things that it's way too easy to picture them doing and saying the same things with someone else."

Putting his hands low on my/her belly, kissing my/her neck, making that soft, low sound of anticipation . . .

I start to sing, "O-oh, say can you see . . ."

Jade joins in. We sing it all the way through. "America" is next, and then we measure each other for a minute. She narrows her eyes, takes a breath, and starts, "You're a Grand Old Flag," which makes us laugh, and I raise my cup and click it against hers and it's better.

At least for the moment.

～

The next day, I pick up some photographs from Safeway and I'm excited to discover that a couple of the ones I shot of Angel at the park are pretty good, as well as a few others. In my excitement, I carry them over to his little cottage before I even go home.

"I got some pictures back," I say when he opens the door, afraid suddenly that he's going to see through my ruse. Ever since Thanksgiving night, I've wanted to come see him.

He doesn't say anything at first, just stands there looking at me, dressed only in his Ecuadorean pajama bottoms and no shirt.

"Were you sleeping?"

"No." His expression is so serious, and I haven't seen this before. I'm not sure what to do. Stay? Go?

It occurs to me that there might be a woman in his rooms, and I flush. "Sorry. I'll come back when it's a better time."

"This is a good time." He reaches for my arm, pulls me inside, looks out on the street before he closes the door. "Come, drink coffee with me."

"Is there something wrong? If this is a bad time, I can come back."

"No, no." He turns, and I admire his long, smooth back as he leads me to the kitchen, where there are papers scattered over the table.

Letters, maybe. He gathers them into a pile, clearing a space for us. "Please, will you sit down?" A little spark comes into his face, tilting up his eyes. "You have not had coffee so good as mine, I promise."

I settle in my chair uneasily, placing the three envelopes of pictures primly before me. For the first time, I see he is a real man, with a real life that has nothing to do with my fantasies of him, nothing at all to do with me or magic or releasing me from my pain, and I am slightly ashamed for using him, even mentally. When he puts the coffee down in front of me, I smell the fragrance of cinnamon and smile up at him. "Everything about you smells good, you know that?"

He pauses, puts one palm on the table. His ribs, covered by skin as smooth as toffee, are even with my nose. I could kiss them.

I hold my hands on my lap. He waits for a minute, looking down at me with his head at an angle.

All I have to do is give him a single sign. I feel them crowding around my body, a twitch in the neck I could bend, a shiver in the arm I could raise, a tingle in the fingertips that know his skin would be smooth as butter. As if there is something baking, I smell yeast and sugar and something dark.

But I can't even raise my eyes, lift a finger. Instead, I turn my head away, look at the table.

A little *hmmph* comes out of his mouth, but he moves away, gives me the space I am asking for. He sits down again across from me at the table, and I see his fingers land, then move away from the letter in a very thin envelope.

"Is something the matter, Angel?" I ask.

He makes a little noise, a half sigh through nearly closed lips. Again his hand gives him away, strays across the space to the letter on top. A colorful stamp with *ESPAÑA* on it decorates one corner, and it's the spidery, elegant hand of a vigorous young woman who wrote the address.

There is directness and something haunted in his eyes when he looks at me. "Roberta tells me you are in love with the husband who is not living with you, yes?"

I lift a shoulder.

He leans over the table, puts his beautiful brown hands around mine. "Here is my secret. I have been wandering the world shooting photographs of women because this one"—he inclines his head toward the letter, both angrily and with resignation—"broke my heart. She wants a man with money, and I do not have any."

I turn my palms upward to his. "Tell me."

"She lived nearby, since we were very small. Our mothers were great friends, and they were happy that we loved each other. They dreamed they could be *abuelas* together, to the same children. Never was there anybody in my eyes or heart but Juliana, nor anyone in hers."

"What happened?"

"Her father died. And her mother was fortunate to find a wealthy man to love her, and take her to a big house, and my Juliana, she became accustomed to those things." His thumb moves on mine, and he looks there, as if it is too hard to look in my face and speak the rest aloud. "Still, we planned to be married, and I am a photographer with my pictures in the magazines, and I think it will make her happy enough." He tsks, nods to himself. Raises his eyes. "Do you know what she did, Trudy?"

I shake my head.

"She did not come to the church the day of the wedding. Shamed me in front of my family and all our friends and all the people I saw every day at my work, because she decided she did not want to do it, after we planned for a year." His cheekbones redden with remembered humiliation. "She did not come."

"I'm so sorry."

"So, here I am. I could not stay there, face them. I left the next day, came to America, where no one knows me."

"And she writes to you?"

"She is sorry." One eyebrow cocks. "It makes me angry every time."

"Mine says he's sorry, too." I pull my hand free, raise my arm. "I took a tire iron to his truck windows and broke my arm when I found out he had another woman."

He laughs, richly, his brilliant white teeth showing, and I think, How could someone have left this man at the altar? For a moment, I am tempted to stand up and put my hands on his face and kiss him, but it seems too bold, too obvious, and then he's picking up my photographs. "You brought me your pictures, eh?"

"Remember, I'm just a beginner."

He smiles. Opens the envelope.

Light from the north window in the kitchen softly glides over his shoulder, illuminating the sleekness of his skin. He doesn't look at me as he opens an envelope, shakes out the photos, takes his time looking through them. He pauses now and then to drop one on the table, and I realize my hands are working together in my lap. I want him to like them. There's a small pile in a stack when he opens the last envelope, the ones I shot that first day in the park, and the first one is of Angel himself, close in on his face, and he's looking directly into the camera.

"I liked that one," I say. "The light on your nose."

He nods, drops it in the pile, does not smile as I had anticipated. There are two others he drops, too, from this set, and then he puts them away. "You have done well," he says, and smiles. "This one, especially," he says, showing me one of the pond and the Victorian iron fence. "You see? There is good light, good combinations of shape."

There he is, sitting next to me, shirtless, and he offered his body, and I'm smelling his skin, and he's so close that there's a rippling awareness burning in my ears, my thighs. I can't even hear what he's saying because I'm trying to think how to fix this. What would Lucille tell me?

"Angel," I say.

He raises his head, shows me those green-and-gold eyes, and I reach out and touch his cheek. "You surprised me, that's all."

"It is not necessary to our friendship," he says quietly.

"I know." I stand up and bend down to kiss his mouth. My hair falls around us. He makes a soft, rich sound, and puts his hands on my waist, then one in my hair, pulling me down onto his lap. The taste of him makes my skin ripple.

I have not kissed anyone but Rick Marino in over two decades. Angel's lips are lush and firm, and he kisses with genuine pleasure, exploring, letting me lead as long as I need to. There's a wild pulse in my throat, shakiness in my body, and I'm afraid I'm going to look very foolish, but I touch his chest, rub my palm over the sleek flesh, feel his heart thundering beneath my hand, and raise my head. "I have wanted you since the first time I saw you," I whisper, and touch his mouth with my fingers. "I've never seen a man so beautiful. Ever."

Then his hands are on my face, hard, and his mouth takes mine. My hands are in his hair, on his shoulders, stroking the skin I've so wanted to touch. And he's pulling me into his lap so that I straddle him right on the chair, our chests brushing, sex pressed together, hard, and his hands are on my hips, squeezing my buttocks, then on my breasts, and—

Oh, God.

I have not had sex in so long that my entire body ignites at his touch, his kisses, the feeling of his skin and his hair, and he's skimming off my shirt and I'm raising my hands to help him, and his mouth is on my breasts through my bra before I even lower my hands, and then I'm getting out of that as fast as I can so I can feel that rich mouth on my naked—oh—breasts and my neck, and then I need to taste him, and I drink of his flesh, his neck, his face, his mouth again, my hands on those angles of chin and cheekbone. He's breathing so hard, I'm flattered when I notice, and there's a sheen of moisture on me, on him, that is our sweat, our desire steaming out of us in the cinnamon-and-coffee-scented kitchen.

Then he's up and leading me away from the chair and into his bedroom, where it is dark and smells of soap and aftershave and I'm lying on the bed with only my jeans on, while he skims away his loose trousers to show me his whole, lean, long, beautiful body. My voice is throaty, soft when I say, "I think I would like to take your picture like this."

"And I," he says, falling on me, kissing my torso, pulling my hair around me, smoothing it over my breasts and waist like a gossamer garment, "cannot think of anything but this." He touches my sex through my jeans, "and this." He kisses my belly, suckles hard, and makes a mark as he unfastens, unzips, and I lift my hips and let him take that, too. "Red here, too. So beautiful," he says, combing his fingers between my legs, and then I'm spilling over, spilling into him, into this moment, and I hold it at the same time I feel it, the wilderness that is Angel, the exotica of having sex with a man I barely know, in the middle of the day. He thinks of the condom because he is more practiced, and I find I don't mind it, because there is so much else to enjoy—the spill of his wavy hair around my face as he kisses me, enters me, lifts my hips and legs and—

Oh, it's so decadent and so good and I hear Lucille laughing somewhere on the other side as an orgasm splits me in two—taking me to the other side of my life, dividing me into the Trudy who was and the Trudy who will be, and I hold him tightly, rock him close as he follows me, and we shiver into the collapse, but we're still kissing and I'm tasting his neck and his jaw and we're rolling together, slick with our sweat, into a cocoon of release and pleasure.

He lifts up on his elbows, shoves his hair out of his face, looks at me closely and seriously. So close, his eyes are extraordinarily beautiful, the gold and green and flecks of blue. "Are you all right?" he asks softly, touches my cheek.

I start to laugh, slide closer, run my hands over his hips. "Sí."

The catlike sultriness comes back into his eyes. "That's good, Trudee. Very good." And he begins to make love to me all over again, this time slowly and with great skill, and it leaves me absolutely boneless, which is when he takes me to his kitchen and feeds me, and kisses me, and feeds me some more, and I can only imagine how I must look when he says, at last, "Now, sweet lady, I would like to take your picture. Would that be all right?"

"Clothes on or off?"

He smiles, stands, and holds out his hand. I take it and allow myself to be led, wearing only his shirt, into his bedroom. He takes the green-and-purple serape from the chair and tosses it over the bed and pulls open the drapes, which makes light fall in gold bars over the floor and the bed, and there's a quickening in my chest as I begin to understand. Without waiting for his instruction, I shrug out of the shirt and lie down on top of the serape on my stomach. Warm sunlight falls in thick swaths over my bottom and across one arm, and Angel makes a soft sound, bending with camera in hand to spread my hair over my back and shoulder, then he steps back and says, "Look at me, *mi embruja*," and when I do, I feel a shiver wash over me as the camera clicks, knowing it was all for these photographs, that somewhere in his future another woman will lean in and look at my eyes, my hair in this captured moment, and say, "She is so luminous."

Thinking this, I smile very slightly and he makes a sound and his shutter whirs, then he is bending and kissing me and his hands are on my body and I know I will never, ever forget this day.

As the light begins to wan, late, I wander back home, dazed as a creature let free from a fairy kingdom. It feels that my skin must shine, that my eyes will reflect all that I have done this afternoon, and I'm glad when Annie isn't there. I float upstairs and shower, wash my hair, and comb it out.

There's a note on the table from Annie, along with the mail. Her note says: *Mom, I will be late. Going out after work with Travis. See you then. (Where were you??) Love, Annie.*

I smile to myself and flip through the piles of Christmas cards, finding a tuition bill for next semester, a water bill, and a thick packet from a travel agency that catches my interest.

At the very bottom is a letter from Rick. It sends an odd pain through me, and I am tempted to just leave it there until morning.

First I open the travel agency packet and it's the brochures I sent for on Seville. I laugh at the timing—maybe I didn't need to go to Seville. I just needed a lover from Seville, and that makes me chuckle because I think of *The Barber of Seville*, and I realize that I'm as giddy as a girl, which is a very good feeling and one I haven't had in a long time. The pictures of the city make me think of Angel walking there, and I wonder again if I have the courage to do something like travel completely alone.

I put it aside and pick up the letter from Rick. I should just leave it. But the truth is, I'm curious. A single page of notebook paper, written in blue ink in his tiny, hurried way:

December 8 (?)

Dear Trudy,

Just been sitting here, thinking, wondering how I got here. I'm not too good with words, but I'm thinking of that song, the Pink Floyd song, "Wish You Were Here." I don't know how things got all fucked up, babe. I know it's me and there's something wrong with me. Remember how my grandpa Tom used to never eat a strange woman's food because he said they could curse you? That's what I've been thinking about. Like some bad mojo got in my food and made me stop thinking like myself and made me crazy.

Jesus, this is hard and I don't know what I'm trying to say, just that maybe I wish we could figure out a way to get back to where we were, and have this all over and forgotten, and be living a regular old life. I miss the kids so bad I can't stand it. I miss sitting in the backyard.

I guess it's not fair to do this when I'm still out here, all fucked up. Maybe I just wanted you to know I'm really thinking about it. About you. About us. I just don't know what means anything anymore. Mostly I'm afraid this screwed it up so bad we can never get back that old good thing, that you won't ever forgive me.

Anyway, there's the line from the song. Maybe sometime we could just sit down and talk, like normal, huh? I wouldn't mind going to have a beer w/you or something, if you wanted.

Love,
Rick

For one long second, I'm tempted to cry. I hate the timing. It's not fair. Then I think of myself lying with Angel, his hand brushing over my belly lazily, and I pick up Rick's letter and throw it in the trash.

30

Jade

What I don't expect is all the shit I get over the black eye. My grand-mother, yeah, I expected her to fuss. She makes me put some stinky ointment on it every day. That's what grandfolks do. If my mama saw it, I'd never hear the end of it.

But they're older women, you hear what I'm saying? They're strong, but not in the way I want to be. They want me to be pretty and helpful and female. They're ladies. And I don't want them any other way. I don't expect them to understand this.

It's everybody else who pisses me off. The women at work who shake their heads like I've been brawling with a man. They oughta know me better than that. Shannelle, who is straight-up horrified that I could have "ruined my looks." She actually said that. What I didn't say was, *Honey, what if your mama could box?* It just would have hurt her feelings.

Even if it's true.

My supervisor calls me on the carpet for providing a bad exam-ple for the clients. "You can tell them whatever you like, Jade," she says. "But they're all going to think it's okay for somebody to hit them because you've been hit." And she sends me home until the bruises fade.

I drive away from the office with a burn in my chest. For a long time, I just drive. Drive and drive. Up to Liberty Point to look at the valley between two mesas, where the reservoir now lies. Drive down to the south side and by the house of a friend of mine from college, but she's not around anymore and I know it and don't stop. I drive through the seedy part of Bessemer, a proud, poor neighborhood where a lot of my clients eke out their lives. Get out of the car at Walmart and stomp around inside, looking at the women in there. What would their lives be like if they were as strong as men? What if we just stop being pretty and get strong? How does that change us? How does it change society?

I'm so angry. It pulses through me in sparks and waves and ripples, winding through my intestines and lungs. I see a young girl with ribbons in her hair and want to yank them out. Stop! I want to yell at the teenagers trying on lipstick. It's not gonna get you a goddamned thing.

I look at the cashiers with their worn faces, their bad haircuts, and I judge them. I do. I judge their softness, their wornness. They're like rag rugs washed too many times. What if they turned all that bitterness into something sharp and hard and fought back for once?

When I find myself nearly in tears of fury, I stomp back out and stand on the sidewalk in the bright, cold day, breathing hard.

As I'm standing there, a man passes and whistles low under his breath. Another one gives me a wincing look, touches his head. A woman in a nice dress and high heels averts her gaze.

I'm still playing the game myself. Everybody is still measuring me by my physical attractiveness because I'm still in the game. Playing it to the hilt. I think of Rueben laughing when I protested that I didn't want to be beautiful, just strong.

Next door is a MasterCuts, and before I know I'm going to do it, I stomp over there and push open the door and stand there feeling ten feet tall. I feel every muscle in my body, primed and strong. I take off my coat to show that my arms aren't soft, but very hard, and not because I want to be a hard body for the gaze of men.

"Can I help you?" says a young girl with red lips and long lines of eyeliner, and hair that takes an hour to curl, if not more.

"Yeah," I say. "I need a haircut."

~

It takes forever to convince her I really mean cut it all off. She starts with snips here and there, chattering about what good condition it's in, and how everybody spends so much money to get a perm that makes their hair look like this. Even when she starts to cut big hunks of it off, she's sure I mean some cute little cut that shows off my long neck.

"More," I say when she hesitates. And, "More," again.

I stare at my emerging head in the mirror, and I'm scared of what I see. A hard woman's face is coming out from beneath that softness of hair. Her eyes are level and steady. Her chin is high. And she is not as pretty.

I let the girl stop cutting when it's an inch and a half long. There are copper-and-brown piles of curls all over the floor, and I kick it with a grin. "Yeah," I say, running my hand over my head. I give her a twenty-dollar tip and a wink.

And before I can chicken out, I drive straight down Northern to the gym. That's where it will matter. I don't even say it to myself, but it's Rueben's eyes I want to see. I let him down the other day.

There aren't many people around, but they do stare. Rueben is across the gym and he stops jumping rope when he sees me. I stop and meet his eyes across that space. My heart is beating harder than I wish as he just looks at me for a long, long minute.

Then he smiles. A big, knowing smile. I want him so bad, my ribs ache, and in that single second, I see that he wants me, too. The haircut wasn't for him, it was for me, but his getting it matters. "You want to go have some coffee, Rueben? No bullshit."

One side of his mouth lifts. "All right. Let me change."

~

We go in my car to a diner not far away. I realize I haven't eaten all day and am starving, and order a cheeseburger and fries and a shake. "You want something?"

"Nah. I had a big lunch."

When the waitress leaves, I meet his dark eyes and say, "Tell me your story, Rueben Perry."

He bows his head, settles his big hands around the coffee cup, and considers it. "What do you want to know?"

"Start with the tattoos."

"What do you think? They're gang tattoos. Thought I was one badass man. Went to jail, did my time, got my ass out of that town, and started over. Clean," he adds.

"Did you ever have a wife?"

"Yeah. No kids."

"Kill anybody?"

The half beat of silence before he speaks tells the story for him. "Yeah."

"Was it self-defense?"

His jaw goes tight, then relaxes. "No."

Something in me presses on. "How old were you?"

"Seventeen."

I nod. "I'm sorry."

"For what, Jade? For asking, because now you'll have to deal with it? For knowing? What are you sorry for?"

I glare at him across the table. "I'm sorry," I say fiercely, "that you had to go there. People don't end up in that life because they want it. You think I don't know that? I don't know about your mama or your neighborhood or anything like that, but I know that a man as good as you must've had some bad times for that to happen."

"Don't social work me, all right?"

We stare at each other across the space. His irises are as smooth as a river stone, but there's heat in them. He gives himself away in a thousand ways that I haven't noticed before because I was so damned sure I didn't deserve a man like this. He strokes his thumbs. He looks at my mouth. He narrows his eyes. "What?"

I smile. "Tough guy."

He wipes a hand over his face. Closes his eyes for a second. Then he looks directly at me. "I'm not gonna sleep with you, Jade, you understand that?"

I blink. "Oh." Heat touches my face. "Is it me, women in general? I know you don't like boys."

His chuckle eases things. He takes my hand across the table, turns it over. Strokes his fingers across the heart of my palm. "I don't sleep with anybody."

"Why?"

He pulls his lower lip into his mouth. "Because that's not my way anymore."

"You mean you're celibate?"

"That's right."

"Completely?"

His grin is slow and unbelievably sexy. "Yes."

"How can you stand it?"

He gives me a look like, *Please.*

"Oh."

"That's why I don't want to be alone with you."

I smile. "So sometimes you're tempted?"

"You have no idea."

"Like when?"

His fingers slide over my life line, over the heart line. "When you knocked Chantall down. When you're all sweaty and slick-looking and I know you're in the shower in the other room."

At least that much was good. Maybe I could spend a lot of time sweaty. The thought must have crossed my face because he says, "I'm asking you not to tempt me, all right? If you do, I can't be your coach anymore."

"Okay." I say it seriously, but he's touching me and I'm wanting nothing more than to throw myself across the table and convince him, right now, that he's wrong. "Don't you ever want a woman again?"

"Sure."

"Well, how do you get one if you can't touch her ever?"

He grins. "The old-fashioned way, Jade. The way our grandfolks did it—just don't spend too much time alone."

I yank my hand away, make a noise. "I'm getting mixed signals here, Rueben. I don't know if you're saying you want to see me or not see me."

He stands up, holds out his hand. "Come on. Leave your coat." He says to the waitress, "We'll be right back."

He takes my hand, which is not something he's done before, and we go outside into the windy, dark day. I don't have any hair to blow around and it makes me feel free somehow. "What are we doing?"

"This," he says, and he hides me from the world with his giant self and bends down his big old bear head and puts his beautiful, sensual mouth on mine. His hand goes up around my cheek, slides around my neck, and it's not a simple, light kind of kiss. His head is angled just right and our lips fit exactly, and he tastes like a long Saturday night. His tongue invites mine to play. And we kiss like that for a minute. Two. I would keep doing it for ten, twenty, thirty.

He raises his head. "Okay?" he rumbles.

"How can you kiss me like that and not want to have sex right now?"

His thumb goes over my lower lip. "Who said I didn't want to?" And for the first time ever, he lets me see, looks at my face and my body, and shakes his head a little bit. "You're the sexiest woman I've ever laid eyes on, Jade. But you're about more than that."

Something inside me goes still. I put my hand on his face, because I've wanted to for so long, and I say, "How do we do it?"

"Just like the old folks did," he says again. "Be careful about being alone too much."

"You really think that'll work?"

"If it doesn't, then maybe I'll only meet you in church or the gym."

"Okay." I laugh. "I'm willing to give it a try."

"Let's go back inside. Chantall is on my case to let you guys spar again."

"Are you going to let me?"

He takes my hand. "Yeah. Maybe in a couple of weeks. Let's do some more work first."

I can't help a little bounce. "Yippee!"

"You got heart," he says. "I'll give you that."

31

Trudy

At least Thanksgiving is only one day. Christmas lasts for weeks.

The mall gives me a headache. It's overheated and crowded and the design seems more and more dated every time I shop there. I hate the Christmas cheer—snow falling outside, Santa in his chair ho-ho-hoing to the little kids. Christmas carols piping in over the speakers, all my favorites: "Joy to the World," "O Come, All Ye Faithful," "What Child Is This."

I grit my teeth and steer around the choir of fifth graders singing "O Holy Night," trying not to remember when Rick and I had sometimes as many as ten—count them—Christmas events to attend with the children. Recitals, plays, programs, parties.

This year, all I have to do is shop, and the lists are straightforward. Colin needs a new phone, Annie a new television for her room, since the old one is on the fritz. I've already taken care of those big things, plus the gifts for Richard and his family, so all I need to do today is buy some smaller things. Stocking stuffers. Computer games for Colin. Socks and underwear for Annie, because in this I can still please her. It cheers me marginally to pick out the prettiest panties. Aquamarine bikinis with purple sparkles, leopard-print thong, and matching bra.

Socks in purple, her favorite color, ten pairs. Some with multicolored toes, some with furry texture, some sturdy wool to keep her feet warm.

I buy chocolates and peppermints for the stockings. Life Saver books, which have been a tradition since I was little. Wrapped butterscotch, a small box of pralines for Annie, another of toffee for Colin, chocolate-covered cherries for Richard, caramels for his wife. No Jelly Bellies this year for Rick, who isn't a big chocolate fan.

Don't think about it.

At the big box stores, I buy gift certificates for a new CD for everyone, also always a tradition. Three, not four. While I'm there, I can't help stopping by the new twenty-five disk CD player on sale for fifty dollars less than I saw it for in June, when I picked it out for Rick's Christmas present this year.

Standing there, it seems I am surrounded by couples. Young couples. Old couples. Middle-aged couples shopping for children. One guy says to me, "Oh, God. It's got a remote?"

"Yeah." The whole reason I picked this particular model. I hand it to him and walk away. I hate not buying Rick anything this year. I mean, I really, really, really hate it. He was raised in a large family, one of the middle ones, and there wasn't a lot of money for fussy birthdays and Christmases. He pretended to be embarrassed by the way I staged Christmas so extravagantly, but you've never seen a man's face glow like that in your life, trust me. He gets as excited as the kids.

Don't think about it.

As I'm paying for the gift certificates, "Little Drummer Boy" comes on over the store speakers. First time I've heard it this year, and it slams me . . .

I'm sitting at Mass with Rick, pregnant with Richard. The air smells of evergreen and spice and perfume. Rick is holding my hand, and the choir is doing a beautiful rendition of "Little Drummer Boy," complete with drums and bells. Rick sings along, eyes shining. When he notices that I'm gazing at him with adoration, he actually blushes, squeezes my hand, leans over to kiss me. "I love you so much."

At the counter at Circuit City, with a youngster so dewy ringing up my purchases he looks like an elf, I am suddenly overcome. Tears, not the kind I can blink away, are streaming down my face, and I'm humiliated and put on my sunglasses, attempting to take control. They keep coming, streaming down my cheeks. The boy is horrified. A woman behind me takes out a tissue from her purse and nudges me with it.

I flee. In my car, I spend ten minutes trying to get ahold of myself, but grief floods through me, leaks out of my nose and mouth and eyes. I tell myself that it will be better next year, that I'll have gone through the rituals once without him and it won't be so hard, but then I remember that Annie won't even be around next year, and what the hell am I going to do with myself? And it just keeps pouring, snot and tears, and there's nothing I can do but put my head on the steering wheel, hiding my face behind my hair, and let it come.

When it's finally spent, I find some fast-food napkins in the glove box and blow my nose. But that's enough for today. I'll finish another day.

Annie has been bugging me for days about the Christmas tree. We usually buy it somewhere in the first weeks of December, making a big ritual out of the whole thing—breakfast at Patti's Restaurant, a homey diner downtown. Big breakfast—steak and eggs or huevos rancheros or biscuits and gravy. Then we'd make the round of tree lots on Santa Fe, then out to Blende, and circle around to the south side for the lots on Prairie. Annie had not participated in the ritual much the past couple of years, but she wants the tree, and as the days roll by, and the packages start piling up in the corner where I usually put it, she grows more and more antsy. "Mom," she says one night after coming in from her work Christmas party, her nose red from the cold, "can I go get a tree with Travis? He said he could borrow his dad's truck. Then all you have to do is help me get it up and I'll do all the decorating."

Which makes me feel like the very worst mother on the planet. I tell her I'll take care of it this weekend.

She must have called Rick, because he shows up the Saturday before Colin is due to arrive from Berkeley. I am eating a bowl of granola, reading the paper, and quite happily listening to non-Christmas music on the college radio station when the doorbell rings. It's a sunny, crisp morning, and he is wearing a flannel shirt. His hair needs cutting and the long strands brush his collar, the cap of it shining like a child's.

I scowl at him. "I told you to call before you come over."

He nods. "But you don't answer the phone."

"I answer it. Just not if it's you."

He spreads a hand. "You see the problem here."

"You could leave a message."

"Jesus, Trudy, I've been leaving messages. I wrote you a letter. I've talked to Annie twelve times the past two weeks. We haven't been face-to-face since Thanksgiving."

My arms have somehow crossed themselves over my middle. "Did Annie put you up to this?"

"Up to what? Trying to talk to my wife about the fact that my kid, who I haven't seen in damned near six months, is gonna be here in four days and I might want to spend a little time with him?"

I step back from the door. "Come on in. Want some coffee?"

"Nah." He shakes his head, his mouth still hard. I see the effort it takes for him to take a deep breath, blow it out. "Why don't we go get some breakfast, Trudy? Go get the damned tree."

"That's too much, Rick." Unexpectedly, I feel winded and sink down on the couch. "I hate this, all of it," I admit, my hands loose in front of me. "The whole Christmas game is depressing the heck out of me."

He sits down next to me. "Me, too."

We sit there in silence. I notice that he looks tired. "You never look rested anymore."

"Yeah, well. Such a quiet apartment and all."

Athena has heard his voice and comes running to whip madly around his legs. Her purr sounds like a Harley engine. Rick picks her up and tucks her under his chin, rubbing his goatee over her forehead. She swoons in delirium. "That cat misses you desperately."

"I miss her, too."

It's quiet for a minute, the air thick with unsaid things. He looks at me. His eyes are as blue as marbles, eyes I have gazed into so many times it seems impossible that I will go the rest of my life without doing it again. "C'mon, Gertrude, let's go get a tree. You know you need my truck to do it."

I nod. "Let me wolf down my cereal and I'll get my shoes."

"Just go get your shoes. I'll buy your breakfast. I know you're not eating. Biscuits and gravy will stick to your ribs."

"Gravy," I say, fishing my clogs from beneath the couch, "will ruin your arteries."

But he's already picked up the bowl and carries it to the sink, Athena balancing on his shoulder, to pour the uneaten cereal down the garbage disposal. I step into my shoes, wait for him to come back, tear a sheet off the calendar, and see that it's December 17. "Oh, damn, Rick, I just realized that it's Joe's birthday today."

He comes out of the kitchen, his mouth working. Athena curls around his legs, her tail trailing around his jeaned knees. He smooths his goatee, flips open the newspaper to the obituaries, and stabs the page.

I hadn't made it that far and look over his shoulder at the right-hand column, nearly every inch filled with tributes to Joseph Zamora, all with a different picture. A biker photo, with his beard wild and making him look like an old-time Cheech Marin, has a list of all his cousin's names. His parents have used a smiling photo from a picnic. The photo at the bottom is one I've seen a thousand times, it pierces me straight through. It's Rick and Joe at about twenty-two, arms around each other's necks. Below the photo, it says, "Miss ya, buddy."

I blink. Touch Rick's arm.

"Pretty fuckin' corny, huh?" But his forefinger lingers on the beloved face.

"C'mon, tough guy. Let's go get some breakfast, and a tree so your daughter will stop nagging me."

Angel is outside raking leaves, and I wave to him in what I hope is an innocent and casual way. He straightens in his lithe luxuriousness and smiles. Very slowly. Very knowingly.

Or so it seems to me. I hope I am not blushing as I climb into Rick's big red truck.

"Who is that guy?"

"New neighbor. He's been there a couple of months now. This is the first time you've seen him?"

"Yep." He starts the truck.

I fasten my seat belt, trying not to look around for evidence of anything. Do I think he keeps love letters in his truck? The thought annoys me, and I realize as my throat tightens that I haven't ridden in the truck since five months ago, the day I shattered the windshield. Fighting the panicky feeling in my chest, I drum my fingers on the seat.

"So, what's his story?" Rick asks.

"Who?"

"The neighbor."

"Oh. His name is Angel."

"Shouldn't that be Ann-hell?"

I look at him, surprised by the edge in his tone. "I guess. He says it with the right accent, but somehow we all end up calling him Angel."

"Who calls him that?"

"The usuals. Me, Roberta, Jade, Shannelle."

"What, are you guys all cozy with this stranger?"

"Rick, what's this about? You don't get to play this game anymore."

"Are you seeing him?"

"None of your business." The words are out before I realize they're the right ones to use.

There's a grimness around his jaw, and he works his way forward, peering over the wheel. "Well, he looks kinda sleazy to me. Might want to just be careful, that's all."

I give him a suppressed smile, lifting my right eyebrow. Clear my throat.

He shoots a glance my way, the Siamese-cat blue of his eyes so bright in the sunny day that I'm willing to forget everything. "Touché."

As we're getting out of the truck at Patti's, I touch the windshield. "They did a pretty good job on this, huh?" I grin ruefully.

He touches my back. "You're famous now, you know."

"Famous?"

"Yeah. You're like a proverb with the guys at the shop. If somebody's screwing up, they'll say, 'Careful, remember Trudy, dude.'"

"Oh, God. That's so embarrassing." I cover my cheeks with my hands. "I've never been that mad in my whole life."

He lifts a shoulder, guides me into the restaurant. "You had reason, I reckon."

The hostess is the same woman it always is, and she smiles brightly. She's an attractive, slim brunette in her late thirties, her hair fashionably cut in slightly messy layers. "Hey, I'd about given up on you two! It's been ages. How you been?"

I shoot Rick a glance as she leads us into the nonsmoking section without being told. "Must be getting your tree today, huh?"

"Thanks, Vicki," Rick says. "Who has the best ones this year?"

"I got a ten-footer down in Blende. Ponderosa. Real fresh. Coffee?"

"Please."

When she's gone, I look at Rick. "Thank you for not bringing Carolyn here."

"I'd never do that." He glares. "I'd appreciate it if you keep Ann-hell away from our usual haunts. And anybody else you get hooked up with."

I tsk. "God knows they're lining up at the door."

"You're a beautiful woman, Trudy."

Not beautiful enough, obviously. Instead of saying that aloud, how-ever, I just look at the menu. If we are to develop a true friendship, post divorce, this is how it will begin.

And once I make up my mind, it's surprisingly easy to be with him. In a familiar place, doing a familiar thing. I can forget about anything that isn't connected to this. He's wearing a shirt I bought, a crosshatched blue-and-yellow flannel, with a T-shirt underneath, which says HARLEY RIDERS DO IT ON THE ROAD. There are no new nicks on his hands, no strange bits of paper sticking out of his pocket. We're just having breakfast, as we've done so many times over the past twenty-odd years.

There is one difference. His eyes are weary. Dead weary, and he keeps wandering back to Joe in his conversation. "Remember when he . . . ?" and "On his eleventh birthday . . ." and a thousand other things like that.

I have heard all the stories before. I know about the time they got stopped on their way to Las Vegas, carrying fake IDs as Rick Blaine and James T. Kirk. They were taken in for some trumped-up thing—this was in the days when *Easy Rider* was still showing in mainline cinemas, remember. When they got to headquarters in the little Arizona town, the sergeant was so annoyed with his deputy for not realizing the IDs were fake that he confiscated the counterfeits and sent them on their way.

I have heard the stories so many times that I sometimes feel like I was there, too. Often, I was, later on. I finish my biscuits and gravy and take a sip of fresh coffee. "I miss him, too. Not like you do, obviously, but there are so many little things that get me. I found that little trike he gave Colin for his birthday—remember?"

A half smile.

"And that bottle of wine he got at whatever auction it was—he was so proud of himself for bringing it to me. I never have drunk it. I keep thinking I'll just open it in his honor some night, and—" I shake my head. "If I do, then I won't have it in there waiting, from Joe."

Rick blinks. "You are the only thing he ever envied me, Tru, you know that?"

I snort. One thing for sure is that Joe was never attracted to me. He liked hot, blonde, and buxom. Mainly buxom.

Like Carolyn.

I almost forget my resolve not to say anything divisive, because I am suddenly, completely aware of the obvious, that Joe knew her, that he might even have been her lover in the past. And you'd think I'd be used to these humiliating recognitions by now, but this one stings just as much as any of the others, not the least of which is the fact that I am an idiot for not realizing.

Before I can work myself up to a full snit, Rick says, "He envied the way we got along."

It hangs there so stark, black-and-white. "He was a smart guy," I say dryly.

"Yeah." He fiddles with his spoon.

To get to more comfortable ground, I say, "Remember when his cat Loki died? He cried so hard over that cat, I was worried about him."

It's enough. He nods in acceptance. "I forgot about that."

The conversation sticks with me as we drive out to Blende, a farming community attached to Pueblo on the south side of the Arkansas River, the part that would have been Mexico, long ago. Seeing all the new shops with Spanish signs and Mexican goods now cropping up in the strip malls and storefronts, it seems oddly prophetic. At the Christmas tree lot, there is a family walking together, father, mother, two scrubbed girls with their hair in ribbons and braids, the son and father dressed exactly the same in matching jeans, boots, crisp striped shirts, and white straw cowboy hats. I smile as the little boy gives an explanation to his sisters in Spanish and it tickles me as it always does— wow! What a smart kid!

The tree I choose—Rick is quite notably silent on the choice except to make sure the needles aren't dried out—is a seven-foot Ponderosa. I pull the seventy dollars out of my wallet, and Rick waves it away. "I got it."

I can see that something about this is hurting, and say, simply, "Thanks."

We wait by the truck for the owner and his son to bring the tree over. "Did you get one for your apartment?"

"A tree? Nah."

"Maybe you should."

He raises his head. "For what, Trudy? The only presents I'm buying are for you guys." He shakes his head once. "I just don't have much Christmas spirit."

"I bet you just need some tamales."

A slow, gentle Rick-grin spreads over his face, lighting his eyes, erasing the weariness around his jaw. "We should get some."

"Ugh! I couldn't. I'm stuffed." Then, without thinking, I hold up my hand to stave off the ribald comment that's sure to bring. "Don't say it."

The grin broadens and he almost sways toward me, almost in a kiss, before he stops himself. For an instant, our eyes meet, in memory and surprise and maybe even longing. I shift away suddenly, thinking guiltily of Angel's mouth, and then I think that he must kiss Carolyn every day, and before I can stop it, my throat opens and spills out the words I know will ruin the day utterly for both of us. "Did Joe know Carolyn?"

He straightens. Sighs. "What do you think?"

Which is enough. And I'm right—it has ruined the day, because all of it comes rushing back, the fury and the sense of humiliation, and those are the ones I grab out of the mix of emotions because they protect me from sorrow.

As we get back in the truck, Rick pauses with his hand on the ignition. "You know, Trudy, we could have just had a day where it wasn't about anything else but us seeing each other."

"Not as long as you're seeing somebody else, we can't."

"Like you and Ann-hell?"

"It's not like that."

"Yeah." He starts the truck. "You've never given me a chance to even try to make it right, Trudy. You threw me out, just like that."

I suck in my breath. "So this is my fault?"

"No. I fucked up. I know that. But you were pretty damned fast to get rid of me, like you'd just been waiting for an excuse."

I look at him. That's all.

"You never listen, you know that? You never hear anything but what you want to hear."

"You want a different outcome, stop sitting on the fence."

"I'm not on the fence. You threw me over it!"

"Take me home, Rick."

We drive in seething silence. He unloads the tree and starts to take it in the house, but I say, "Leave it."

He starts to protest, and I take a deep breath. "This is too hard for me, babe. I can't be just your friend. I wish I could." I look right into his eyes, and let myself show through. I want, more than I want breath, to reach up, one more time, and touch his lean jaw, smooth away the haggard places, touch his glossy mustache. "I'm doing all right as long as I don't see you, as long as I don't have to think about everything that's been lost here."

He looks down, toes the ground with his boot, makes little waffle patterns in the damp ground. "Sorry."

"I know this is a bad day for you, and I'm sorry, but I can't fix it. All the things that are tearing you up are things only you can fix."

With a piercingly broken expression, he asks, "How, Trudy? How do I fix it? Fix me?"

And despite myself, I chuckle. In the land of therapy for everything, only a biker dude would ask that question. "You could see somebody."

"You mean like a counselor?" He doesn't sound horrified, just surprised. The idea has never occurred to him. I laugh.

"Yeah. A priest, a counselor. You never know. It could help. You've had a lot of losses the past few years."

"I'll think about it." He clears his throat. "I guess you want to stick to the original plan of bringing Colin home by yourself, huh?"

"It would be like today, Rick, so much the same and yet so different. I can't stand it. But you can go up to the airport to pick him up if you like."

"Nah. He'll want to see his mom first. You go. He can call me when he gets in."

"Okay." I turn away, turn back. "Thanks for all your help today."

"No problem." He lifts a hand in farewell. Climbs in his truck as he's done a thousand times. I look at his hands on the steering wheel, the grim look around his mouth. And for one minute, I think, *How in the world did we come to this? How is it possible?*

32

Shannelle

TO: naomiredding@rtsv.org

FROM: chanelpacheco@hotmail.com

SUBJECT: Harley Blue Trailer

Dear Naomi,

Tony has a friend who is a Lakota Sioux, and he was over for dinner tonight. (I have had so many people over lately! It just seems like Tony always knows somebody who needs a meal. And if I'm honest, I have to say I really like it, setting the table very nicely, with the good dishes Tony's mom gave up when we got married, and putting out lots of food for somebody who is hungry. I like having the boys learning their manners and remembering to do some little thing, like remember to put their napkins on their little laps. Mostly they forget a lot still, but they're just little boys. They'll get it.)

ANYWAY, I was thinking tonight while Harry was here that he has a great name. Harold Runs With Colts. Is that great? And then during dinner, my idiot brother called to yell at me over something or another, and I just told him I couldn't talk because it was dinnertime, and I hung up while he was still calling me names. And I was thinking that where I come from, it could be bad to get named like that. For who you are or where you live or what you do. John Collects Junk Cars. Hank Never Changes His Shirt and his wife, Dana No Teeth. Micky Lives in Turquoise Double-Wide.

Now I'm cracking myself up. They are awful, awful people. It's an awful world. I hate it. I hate them. I wish I could move to Pluto.

That's not fair, really. They're not all awful. They're just poor, that's all. Poor and ignorant. Not everybody is even ignorant or slimy. There was Mr. Tesla, who built a porch all around his trailer and had roses growing up the redwood and as much of a lawn as he could fit in the rest of his yard, which was about six square feet, and it was always so green. His grandkids came over to see him and he cooked outside for them on Labor Day and whatever, cooked on a red tabletop grill he told me his daughter gave him. He raised four kids in that trailer and every single one of them lives in a good neighborhood now.

But I was thinking some more about names. Why is everyone in a trailer park named Ruby or Misty? Even me, my stupid name, which could have been cool, being named for a perfume, but my mother got the spelling wrong. (!) Why are all the boys named Darryl? (Even my brother is named Darryl.) Why do girls who see everybody else get pregnant and old too fast go out and do it themselves? Just to see what weird thing they can name their kids? No kidding, I know two boys named Harley and Lightning. They're actually very nice. Their mother worked construction and she didn't drink. She was just a tattooed biker babe who cooked Hamburger Helper every night and grew two giant boys. I think she moved, finally. They haven't talked about her lately.

Now I'm getting depressed. I have to remember that I don't live there anymore. I wish my mother didn't have to. Wish I could get her to see she could leave my loser father and loser brother to drink themselves to death in the pigsty they'd make it by the end of a week, and they'd be dead for a month before anyone noticed.

I've had a couple of dreams about my sister the past few weeks. Would she still be alive if she'd been born to some other family? Would someone, somewhere have seen that she wasn't just a little blue, but suicidally depressed? Would she have had more of what she needed somewhere else? If her bedroom had been spacious and airy, instead of a shoe box she had to share with me, would it have made a difference? If she could have walked outside and seen a few trees and had a place to sit on a little grass, would she have been able to hang on?

Always the same questions. Always the worst one at the last: Why didn't she come to me? Why did she just DO that? I wonder if it will ever make sense to me, if I'll ever put the pieces together.

S.

〜

TO: chanelpacheco@hotmail.com

FROM: naomiredding@rtsv.org

SUBJECT: re: Harley Blue Trailer

dear shannelle,

that is wonderfully evocative material. why don't you write about the trailer court?

〜

TO: naomiredding@rtsv.org

FROM: chanelpacheco@hotmail.com

SUBJECT: re: re: Harley Blue Trailer

Naomi—

Ugh!

Shannelle

~

TO: chanelpacheco@hotmail.com

FROM: naomiredding@rtsv.org

SUBJECT: re: re: re: Harley Blue Trailer

shannelle: meet me online, 4 p.m. it's bronco sunday, right?

Transcript:

CHANEL: Hi, Naomi. What's up?

NAOMI: i am on a quest. <g>

CHANEL: What quest? Am I gonna like this?

NAOMI: i need some character sketches from you.

CHANEL: Let me guess: the Trailer Court Gang, right?

NAOMI: what a smart young woman you are!

CHANEL: Oh, Naomi, I've never said no to one of your exercises, but I can't do this. I don't even want to. YUCK!

NAOMI: do you trust me, shanelle?

CHANEL: Yes.

NAOMI: i want four sketches—john collects junk cars. mother of harley. lightning. and one more: darryl.

CHANEL: I'm not writing about my brother.

NAOMI: scared?

CHANEL: No! I just hate his guts, that's all.

NAOMI: good. it'll make a good sketch.

CHANEL: Naomi!

NAOMI: you can always refuse, sweetie.

CHANEL: No. I know you must have a reason. But please don't make me write a book about them, okay? I don't want to be like that woman who wrote about the backwoods and ended up getting stuck there forever.

NAOMI: that's not going to happen to you. i promise.

CHANEL: Naomi, I do trust you, but this is going to depress me to no end.

NAOMI: you might be surprised.

CHANEL: But I only have an hour a day to do my writing as it is! Wouldn't it be smarter to spend it on the new book?

NAOMI: your call, sweetie, but i'm gonna ask you to trust me to take you on a little journey, all right?

CHANEL: Heavy sigh.

NAOMI: go write the first one, then.

CHANEL: Right now?

NAOMI: how long until tony gets home?

CHANEL: Nearly two hours.

NAOMI: better get cracking, then. when it's done, send it to me raw. don't rewrite, and don't keep a copy.

CHANEL: This is the weirdest thing yet.

NAOMI: heheheh.

CHANEL: Bye!

33

Trudy

At the Springs airport, I wait with the other families gathering missing pieces for the holidays. It's hard to keep my eyes away from the husband-wife pairs waiting for their children or parents.

Don't think about it.

It's too hot, but that's how it always seems to me lately. I wonder, fanning myself with a newspaper, if this is perimenopause, if I'm going to start having hot flashes. There's a thrilling thought.

I spot Colin over the heads of the others—he's the one who looks most like my family, his thick black hair freshly cut to show his good cheekbones, his full lips. He's wearing a greeny-blue sweater I would bet money his girlfriend picked out for him. His khaki pants have a crease ironed into them. He has his laptop slung over his slim shoulder. For the first time, I see he's grown into a young man, one who has left provincial Pueblo behind. I see young women eyeing him, the aura of success he carries, the genial, almost Continental carriage.

He spies me, this elegant, gorgeous young man, and breaks into a grin. Lifting a hand, he hurries past the older couple ahead of him and throws his arms around me in a bear hug. "Hi!" he says. "Man, I missed you! You look good, Mom," he adds, holding me at arm's length. "What have you changed?"

"Do I? Nothing I can think of. You look terrific. It's so good to see you."

It's only as we head toward the stairs to the baggage claim that it seems to dawn on him that Rick is not here. "Dad didn't come?"

"No, but he's hoping you'll come see him tonight. He'd love to cook for you."

"I was expecting both of you." Thunder boils in his Celtic eyes. "It's always been that way." He halts, scowling, at the stairs. "Couldn't you guys have done that much for me?"

"We're in the way." People are staring.

"Mom." He moves, but not mentally.

"Colin," I say. "We're divorcing. We won't be doing things as a pair anymore."

"Divorce? I thought—"

I put my hand on his arm. "Let's go get your bags, then we can find a place to eat before we drive back, okay? We can talk about it over a hamburger or something."

He nods. The polite young man reemerges, but there are two bright patches of color in his cheeks. It makes him look even more handsome, and a girl of about twenty trips over her suitcase staring at him. She bumps right into him, and he kindly steadies her, smiles, picks up her dropped purse, and settles it over her shoulder. The whole thing replays in my mind as we walk to the car, and I laugh. "The same thing used to happen to your dad all the time."

"Really?"

"Constantly. You don't really look a lot like him, but you have a lot of his charm."

"Mrs. Guiterrez used to say we were cut from the same cloth."

Mrs. Guiterrez was our next-door neighbor, the one who lived in Angel's house.

Angel. Wickedness swirls under my skin at the thought of him, anything connected to him. I've been trying not to let my thoughts stray in that direction, and there's been no time to spend with him, though he's been by to invite me. I think I hurt his feelings last night, and have been worrying about it.

But maybe I'm a little embarrassed or ashamed of myself. How foolish is it of me to even think of a liaison with someone so much younger than myself? Someone who will be off on his travels sooner or later? Someone who is in love with another woman? Maybe all those things make it all right. I really don't know. There are no markers to tell me what to do.

"Mom?" Colin says.

"Sorry. Woolgathering." I bend down and unlock the trunk, and we settle the bags. I pause in the bright winter sunshine. Pikes Peak rises behind him, dusted with snow, burly against the sky. "Colin, I don't want you to think your dad didn't want to be here. He did."

"Then why didn't he come?"

"Because I asked him not to." I take a breath. "We are connected, all of us. That won't change. The way we are connected is changing, and I know how much you hate it. But I'm also going to tell you that the sooner you try to see the new way, the smoother it's going to feel for you. Does that make any sense?"

He bows his head. Nods. "I just hate it. I can't help it."

"I know. But let's try to have a great Christmas this new way, huh?"

"That's a good idea."

So that's what we do. We make butter cookies and sit around the table frosting them. Minna comes over to help, and Colin laughs and jokes with her. I play my Christmas CDs, the same ones I always use to get in the mood, and hum along as I stick candy flowers on the snowmen's fronts. We eat as many as we frost. We wrap presents and drink gallons of eggnog. Annie and Colin scuffle over the bathroom, as always, but she's as happy as I am to have someone else in the house to break up the monotony of the two of us.

One night, Colin and I rent movies to watch, a ritual we have not missed since he started college three years ago. He and I share a taste in movies and books that no one else in the family likes, and we long ago realized we could curl up and eat odd things and watch French subtitles and everybody would leave us alone. His toleration for noise is about on par with a nervous cat, which is fairly unusual in a second child. As a baby, we had to play lullabies quietly in his room to buffer any outside distractions, and even in the womb, he used to startle violently if someone slammed a door.

In many ways, he's the one most like me. Richard is clever and ambitious, sturdy and stalwart, most like his grandpa Marino in character than anyone else. My Richard is Italian to his core, an old-fashioned, salt-of-the-earth man who will always take care of his family and do the right thing. Annie is the one cut from her father's heart—charming and outgoing and charismatic, an extrovert and dazzler.

Colin is like me. Cerebral and thoughtful, too serious and often irritatingly idiosyncratic. When he comes home, I enjoy the chance to sit around and just talk for hours at a time—talk ideas and politics, art and music, and current events. He was born to take a doctoral degree in some esoteric specialty and spend his life in academia, taking sabbaticals to foreign shores. It drives his father insane. What kind of life is that for a man? he's grumbled to me more than once. Rick is painfully proud of Colin, brags about the prizes and scholarships he's won, his perfect sixteen hundred on the SAT, his accomplishments. But he doesn't understand him.

Tonight, Annie is working, and rolled her eyes over the stack of movies we picked out, anyway—a French historical drama I've wanted Colin to see; *Quills*, which he's wanted me to see; and two of the year's indie films that are highly favored by critics as next year's possible Best Picture. On Oscar night, we'll be in touch by phone, after sending off in email (by three p.m. MST, no fair cheating) our entire ballot for the evening.

God, I hope he never gets tired of sharing such things with me! Realistically, I know he will. That he'll have a wife one day, and children of his own, and friends to have Oscar parties with. It makes this little space of luxurious time even more precious.

We get a pile of finger foods ready—baby Gouda cheeses, crackers, three kinds of apples, some Bosc pears, and my favorite Vermont Cabot cheddar, little cold shrimps for Colin—and carry them into the newly arranged television room. Colin says, "Wow! It looks like the *Arabian Nights* in here!"

"Mmm." It's a theme that seems to be spreading through the house these days, I'm afraid. Splashes of scarlet and fringes of gold and tendrils of velvet.

"It looks like you."

"Thanks." We settle in, prop our feet up on ottomans, and nestle elbows into pillows. Zorro wanders in and spreads himself royally along the back of the couch, his extravagant tail twitching. Athena follows shortly thereafter, nudging Colin happily for tidbits of shrimp. "How's she doing without Dad?" he asks.

"All right." I chuckle. "But she faints with pleasure when he comes over."

We put in *Quills* and I sip cold wine. "Do you drink yet, Colin?"

He raises an eyebrow. "I'll take the Fifth on that."

I laugh. "D'you think I don't know everyone drinks wine in Italy?"

"Well, that's there." But he lifts one side of his mouth in a rueful smile. "Yeah, sometimes I drink a little."

"What do you drink?"

"Mom, I'm twenty years old. I'm not legal yet. I drink what's available."

"Not hard liquor, I hope."

"Fifth."

I laugh at the pun. "Just be careful."

He puts a slice of cheese on a cracker. "I got this lecture about seventeen times the summer before I went to school, remember? I heard you." He enumerates the points on his fingers. "No shots. No shotgunning beers. No sweet drinks, like rum and Coke, unless I want a massive hangover the next day."

"Did you test the truth of my injunctions, my sweet?"

"I did, Mother dear, and discovered you to be correct on all counts." He picks up the remote. "Can we watch the movie now?"

"Sure."

He hesitates before pushing the "Start" button. "If I ask you an honest question, do you promise to give me an honest answer?"

"I'll try."

"Was my trip to Italy one of the things that led to you and Dad splitting?"

I dodge a direct answer. "What gave you that idea?"

"I know you guys fought about it. Dad didn't think I should go. He wanted to use the money for something else."

"A new bay on our garage." When we already had two and he works in the garage at Harley-Davidson. "But that was my money. Lucille left it to me, and it wasn't to be used for things like houses and garages."

"What was it for?"

I take a breath, pluck a sliver of apple from the plate beside me. "Travel and education."

"So why haven't you used it?"

"I haven't really had a chance. I've been busy raising you guys. I might go to Seville, though, did I tell you? I've been exploring the idea pretty seriously."

"You're sidestepping my question, Mom."

I look him straight in the eye. "No, Colin, the trip had nothing to do with the problems between your father and me."

"Promise?"

What could he possibly do to change the past, even if I told the truth? "Promise."

But it's hard, as the movie begins, not to think of this again, think of the money Lucille had left and the way it had become so immovable and gigantic between us. The first time he wanted to use it was when I was pregnant with Colin, to put a down payment on a house. It had never occurred to him that I would not agree, that I would see anything wrong with it, and it honestly shocked him when I steadfastly and simply said no. I was equally astonished that he had even expected it. It had been a very specific inheritance—a substantial sum of money which, thanks to the big boom in the stock market, had nearly tripled over the past decade. I'd only recently moved it to less risky investments.

It represented the sum total of Lucille's life savings, and she'd left it to me with the knowledge that I would understand what she meant it for. A woman needs money of her own in case of emergencies, or in case she needs to go somewhere, make an escape. She did not mean for it to buy a house, which she thought an overrated practice. She did not mean for it to go for cars or boats or down payments on anything material. It was for travel, I knew, or education, or anything else both ephemeral and enduring.

Only twice in two decades had I dipped into the nest egg. The first time was to pay for the natural healing course in Boulder. Rick had been hoping to talk me into a new truck. The second time was for Colin's trip to Italy.

And the shit, as they say, hit the fan. Rick was furious, didn't think it was fair to pay for Colin to go to Italy when neither of the other kids were getting a trip like that. I argued that I would happily pay for any one of them to do something similar. Annie has talked to me about a six-week stay in Hawaii when she graduates, and I fully intend to give it to her. Richard had turned down the chance to go to Venice for his honeymoon, choosing in his Richard-like way to drive to the Grand Canyon instead.

Do I feel guilty?

If not, what's this lump in my throat?

If it had tipped the scales toward losing Rick, this one thing I'd kept to myself, what did that mean? Am I selfish, or is he? Are both of us?

But the movie captures me, carts me away from the buzzards of thought, and by the end, I'm sobbing into my hands with acute satisfaction. Colin hands me a napkin and smiles gently. "Told you. Just your kind of tragedy."

"I'm shattered." I wipe my face. "It was perfect. Love and art."

The doorbell rings, just once, so I know it has to be someone other than Rick. Stopping by the bathroom on my way, I blow my nose, and Colin beats me to the door. It's Shannelle standing there, hair flying in the wind, arms crossed tight against her chest. "Hi, Shannelle," I say, surprised. "Come on in."

She comes in, nods at Colin. "I hope I'm not interrupting anything."

"Not at all. What's up? Want some tea?"

"We also have coffee," Colin says.

"Oh, that sounds good."

He holds out his hand. "I'm Colin."

"I forgot you two haven't met. Shannelle, this is my middle son, Colin, as I'm sure you've figured out. Colin, this is Shannelle Pacheco, who moved in across the street."

She smiles and I see her blush a little. "Nice to meet you. How's school?"

"Going well, thank you." He is still holding her hand, and lets go quickly, tucking it into his hip pocket. "Sorry."

I smile, bemused. They are, after all, only four years apart, though Shannelle seems much older because of the way her life has gone. "Sit down, Shannelle." I gesture toward the table. "Coffee or tea?"

"Whichever one is less trouble. Is it all right if I take off my coat?"

"Sure." I get the coffee and come back and see her through my son's eyes for a moment. Her tumble of glossy blonde hair, the bright-blue eyes, long silver earrings dangling beneath her hair. She has taken off her coat, which shows the slightly threadbare sweater beneath it and the small, roundedness of her body. He appreciates it.

Shannelle spreads a piece of paper flat on the table. The hand that smooths it is shaking a little. "I got this in the mail today," she says, and pushes it across the table as if it has poison on it.

I pick it up. It reads:

> Dear Ms. Pacheco,
> We are delighted to inform you that you have been selected to participate in the Orcas Island Writer's Retreat, February 18–28, 20—. All fees, lodging, and board are included in the scholarship. Participants will be expected to—

I raise my eyes and reach over the table to grab her hand. "Shannelle, this is fantastic! You must be over the moon!"

Her eyes fill with tears. "How can I possibly go? Tony will have a cow, I don't have the money for the flight, I don't know if I can leave my boys for ten days." She puts her free hand on her chest. "I just don't know what to do, where to even start!"

"May I see it?" Colin asks.

She nods. Blinks hard. "I can't believe they picked me," she says in a near-whisper. "This woman who has been sort of teaching me gave me the homework assignment of applying and I just did it. I never thought they'd take me."

Colin whistles. "This is a very prestigious workshop. You must be really good."

"I'm okay." She plants her hands on her thighs, stares at the letter with some fierceness. She raises her eyes to him. "I love it, though." Her hand touches her heart again. "Really love it."

"You have to go," Colin says. "No matter who gets mad. This is the program that gave Allen Naranja and Naomi Redding their starts. You know that, right?"

Animation floods Shannelle's face. "Naomi is my teacher! The one who gave me my assignment."

His mouth drops. "Naomi Redding is your teacher?"

"Yeah! We met online, at a character workshop she led, and we hit it off. Right away."

I'm looking at them. I don't know the name, but I haven't kept up with the world of letters. Colin's envy is almost palpable. He's a poet and a student and one day may very well be a writer, but it's plain that Shannelle has captured his entire interest.

"You must be very good," Colin says, and puts the paper down in front of her. "You have to go. Life doesn't give you opportunities like this every day."

The excitement drains away from her once again. "I know that. I just don't know how to make it work."

"Mom," Colin says. "Tell her."

I smile. "He's right, Shannelle. This is a big break, a chance to get what you want, and your teacher believes in you enough to have given you the homework assignment to apply. She probably knew you'd make it. And imagine what you can do with ten uninterrupted days to write, in the company of other writers like you."

"Oh, and you should see this place," she says. "It's in a forest and everybody has a little cabin of their own, and they bring you meals all day. You don't have to do anything."

"So what we have to figure out is what the blocks are, one at a time, and see if we can come up with solutions. What's number one?"

"There are three and they're all important. Tony, airfare, the boys."

"Okay. Tony—let's come back to him. The boys. I can understand how it would be hard to leave them, but the angle to think about is that you might have a chance here to give them a better life, and a happier mother. If you're doing what you love and believe in, you give them permission to pursue their own goals."

"Oh! I never thought of it that way." She nods. "And I might be able to sell something to get the airfare. I looked online—it's three hundred dollars."

"You can go through Priceline and get it for about half that," Colin says.

"Really?"

"I'll show you later."

"Thank you." She looks at me, sighs. "Tony."

"All right." I can see that he will not be happy about this. He's a good man, but old-fashioned and blue collar. "He'll say all kinds of things, but the big fear at the heart of it will be that he's going to lose you if he lets you do something like this."

She nods. "That's part of it, but he won't like taking care of the kids by himself and he doesn't cook too good."

"Maybe your mother-in-law would help."

"I'm sure." She looks at me, then at Colin. "The other thing is . . . oh, I don't know."

I give my son a look and he gets up. "I'll let you guys talk. I have to call some people." But he stops and squeezes her shoulder. "I know about fifteen people who would kill to have that letter."

"Thanks." She waits until he goes, then raises her head. Her mouth is working and I see that the tears are right there beneath the surface again. "What if they all laugh at me, Trudy? All those people Colin is talking about, they're from a different world than me. They'll have the right clothes, say the right things, know things about life that I just haven't ever had a chance to figure out yet. I'm sure they've all been to college and stuff. I'll never fit in."

"Oh, sweetie!" I grab her hand, and suddenly I feel the presence of Lucille in the room, around me. The air smells of a loamy garden on a hot summer day. "The first day I went to college, I was about to turn around and leave because I was so afraid of those same things. Everybody seemed so much more polished and together. Nobody in my family had ever gone to college, and in fact a lot of them thought it was stupid. But I got there and found out nobody cared about my background. They cared about my future, who I would become."

"I'm scared to death. Scared to take it, scared not to."

"All I can tell you is that when you get to be my age, it will haunt you every single day if you don't do it. You owe it to yourself to claim it."

"Was there anything like that in your life that you think about now?"

The smell of earth rises more thickly, the scent of tequila and overgrown roses. I close my eyes, dizzy with it. "Yes. I never finished my education. I got pregnant and I came back to Pueblo and I've been happy, but I would have been happier if I'd kept going."

"Are you going to do it now?"

On the wind, I can hear Angel's wind chimes. "I'm going to Spain in February. To see where Lorca lived and wrote. That's where I'm starting, anyway." And I know, saying it aloud, that I'm really going to do it. That it's almost a sacred promise now.

Somehow, I also have to help Shannelle take the chance in front of her. I look at her hands, working together, with their worn flesh and the chipped nails. I see the faint stain on the front of her sweater. I see myself at that age, and Lucille telling me a woman needs money of her own. I know what I'm going to do, but it has to be done right. "I have a feeling that if you just open yourself up to all of this, it's going to work out just fine, Shannelle. If you like, I'll go shopping with you. We can find some inexpensive sweaters and things to make you feel more confident."

A little light of hope is glowing there in her blue eyes now. "Okay."

"Promise you will call and accept first thing in the morning."

"I promise."

I give her my best grin. "Wow. I might be sitting here with a someday acclaimed writer."

She laughs, then gets up and hugs me. "Thank you, Trudy. I mean it. This helped a lot."

"No problem, kiddo."

After she leaves, I get online and go to Priceline and book a flight to Seville on the eighteenth of February, returning on the first of March. I have no idea what I will do there. I don't know if I'm insane, if I will regret it, if this is the craziest thing I've ever done.

I know that it scares me and that it is my promise to Shannelle. If she can be that brave, so can I.

34

Jade

The week before Christmas, Rueben calls me to come to the gym on a Tuesday night. It's practically empty when I get there, except for Rueben, who crosses the gym as I emerge from the stairs. "Where is everybody?"

"Exhibition in Colorado Springs. Pablo's fighting."

I open my mouth. "Why didn't anybody tell me?"

"Not important. Get changed and we're gonna warm you up. Chantall will be here in forty-five minutes."

My grin blazes over my face, too big to contain. "I get to spar with her?"

He nods.

I'm back out on the floor in five minutes flat, loving the fact that my hair isn't getting in my way. Rueben is waiting with a jump rope and we go through my paces. I love the part where he rubs my shoulders. We've been very good since that kiss at the diner. Truth is, I haven't had a lot of extra time, and he's been working with the boys at the home nonstop. Christmas is a bad time for those kids.

Chantall shows up with her trainer at exactly 6:45. There's a fierceness about her, and Rueben leans in to give me some pointers. "Watch for the uppercut." I nod, and he laces my gloves. I'm ready.

It's different this time. Without the chatter of onlookers, it's quiet enough I can hear the shuffle of our feet as we circle. I have time to be scared, thinking of my just-barely healed eye. I know it's a mistake to favor it, but I do find myself angling my body so that she'll hit the other side. She notices. Swings from the right, catches me lightly below the jaw. I dance back, watch for that hitch in her step, swing, and catch her, but not as hard as I'd like. She nods to herself, lifts her chin, comes back at me.

It goes like that. Back and forth. Taking each other's measure, throwing some punches. A few do a little damage, both mine and hers. She knows now to watch for my right and I realize it's the strongest punch I've got, so I have to struggle a little.

I'm frustrated. In the rise of emotion, she lands a sharp jab to my mouth. I taste blood. Adrenaline cracks through my body. I catch her with a flurry of softer, faster jabs, and she grabs me. We struggle for a minute. I can smell her sweat.

We're locked together and she lands a body blow. Lower-back ribs. Better than the kidney. "Bitch," I hiss, and shove her away.

From there, it's grim. She's hurting and so am I. She's ducking my cross and I'm ducking hers. The hitch in her gait is more pronounced and I know that's the secret to knocking her down this time, but my arms feel like they weigh 940 pounds.

She rallies and lands a one-two punch to my face and the just-healed eye, and I think, fuck.

I'm slow recovering.

The uppercut slams my jaw hard. Sends me staggering backward, but not quite down. I'm quick with defense, hold her off, shake my head.

It's what I needed. The cold kicks in. Silver all through my veins. I plant myself, wait for her to come to me.

Hit her.

And down she goes. I'm panting, and can feel the sweat dripping in my eyes. She's struggling to her feet, but her trainer waves his hand. It's over.

"Fuck you!" she cries out at me. "I'm gonna kill you."

I'm walking away. Back to Rueben. I meet his eyes, let him see that it took everything I had.

"Good job, Jade." He gives me water, helps me off with the gloves. "Let her get changed first." He gives a signal to the trainer, and we go in back.

Behind the doors, he says, "How's the jaw?"

Tomorrow, I won't be able to talk, but it moves up and down okay. I put my hand to it. "That's a bad punch."

"You only caught part of it because you were going backward when she landed it."

I whistle.

"Yeah." He says gruffly, "Get on the table," and I lie down on the massage table on my stomach. There's a feeling like soda pop has replaced the marrow in my bones. He's rubbing my shoulders. I make myself think of the fight. "Did you see that she has that hitch in her step? That's how I got her the last time."

"Used it again this time, too. Good work." His thumbs burn into my sore shoulder and I groan. "She hurt you a little bit, though, huh?"

"Some," I admit. "I was favoring my right side. Didn't want her to hit my eye again so soon, and she knew it."

"I saw that."

"But it was still good. I learned a lot." The buzzing in my bones is growing. I feel powerful and alive. Like there's light burning up through me. "God, I love that feeling when my glove connects."

He chuckles. "I know what you mean."

"I wish I could give that to every woman in the world. All those young girls who sit in my office with no friggin' power—I mean, Chantall could be one of them, but she made herself strong. Oh!" I scramble over to my back, sit on my butt, grab his hands in my excitement. "Oh, God, Rueben! Why couldn't there be boxing for girls. I mean, for real? Why couldn't we do that? Maybe not all of them. But some of them." I look up at him, my mind swirling with the possibilities. "It could be so good!"

"Lord have mercy," he says, and then his giant hands are around my head, and he's kissing me. It hurts a little and I pull back the slightest bit. He says, "Sorry," but doesn't stop, just goes easier.

There's so much in me already that everything just explodes, and I'm kissing him with all I've got. It's impossible not to let it just flow out right this minute. I don't care where it leads, where it goes, if we stop or start. It's just right to be devoured and devouring, our mouths so hungry we're practically biting each other. I move so that my legs go around him, and I pull him into me.

And this is a man who is over the line. I can feel it. His hands are on my back, on my neck, my face, my ass, pulling me into his very hard self. There is almost a sound of humming between us. I don't know if it's the sounds we're making or the sound of our hunger spilling out of us. "Touch me, Rueben," I whisper.

His hands skim off my sweaty T-shirt and then the sturdy, unsexy sports bra beneath. He's bending into my flesh, kissing my neck, the upper rise of my breasts, back to my mouth as his hands stroke me. "I should take a shower," I breathe.

And he says only, "No," as he curls me into the crook of his big arm and turns me sideways and kisses me. My mouth and my face, his hand running over my arm, my breasts, my side. "Let me taste you like this one time."

That's what he does. Then we're skimming out of our pants, me out of my shorts and him out of his sweats, and we're joined, hard, my arms around his neck, his strength all that we need, and it's not pretty or sweet but it's really good.

And there has never been a man, ever, who felt like this. Just right. His body fits my big one. His height is right for mine. I hold him inside me, my drained arms looped around his neck, and breathe into his chest. He kisses my head and rubs my back and we're swirling back to earth.

"I wasn't trying to tempt you," I say quietly. Afraid now that he'll be angry with me.

"No. I know." He moves against me. I feel him smile. "I'm weak."

"No." I laugh. "You are very, very strong."

We simply lean against each other like that for a long time. "Are you mad?" I ask finally, raising my head.

"No," he says gently. "Do you want to come to my house?"

"Yes."

"Just for tonight, though. We'll go back on the wagon tomorrow."

I smile at him. "Aren't you supposed to stop when you realize you've had a drink?"

He swallows. "Yeah. But I'm already drunk."

"Me, too," I whisper.

It is a night I will not forget. By the end of it, my skin no longer belongs to me. Every inch has been tattooed by Rueben's breath. He is not, when he lets himself go, a sober or serious lover at all. He tickles me. He plies me with food. He kisses the aching places. He's frank. Wicked, even. Earthy.

He leaves me at my car near dawn, damp and sated, with a long, long, long kiss. "Once the sun rises, we start fresh."

I nod. Not believing.

35

Trudy

Rick comes to get Colin the next morning, a day they can spend together. It's a little awkward arranging it, and then watching the two of them try to decide what to do, but I stay out of it. They finally settle on a drive down to Trinidad, just to pick up some tools and have lunch. In the quiet, I finish wrapping presents, clean up the house, and think some more about Christmas Eve, which is looming in two days. It will be the worst for me, and I need to find some way to celebrate that will be fun and have meaning and be a little different from what I've done for the past twenty-something years.

As I'm mopping the kitchen, it comes to me: I'll have a caroling party. Make the chocolate fondue the kids have loved all their lives, and invite the neighbors. Leaving the floor half done, I prop the mop against the sink and call Roberta, who is delighted at the idea, and talk to Jade, telling her she can invite Rueben if she likes. Shannelle can't come, because she's going to Mass with her in-laws, but promises to stop in for a few minutes anyway. She tells me in a whisper that she made the call and accepted the scholarship, but that she hasn't told Tony yet. Last is Angel. I realize I don't have a phone number for him, and I put on my coat and walk next door to invite him personally.

I have seen him only a few times, very briefly, since our encounter. He stopped by one evening, hoping to be invited in, but Annie was home, glowering in the corner, and he stayed only a few minutes, winking at me on the way out. And I've been so busy with Christmas preparations, I haven't gone over there.

Standing on his porch, I pause for a second, suddenly aware of a rush of tangled emotions. I want him and I don't. It was decadent and unlike me, but it was also quite wonderful. He's too young. He's too wild. I'm not looking for anything.

But neither is he. As I raise my hand to knock, he opens the door. "Trudee!" he says with genuine warmth and a big smile. "I have been hoping to see you. Come in. I have something wonderful to show you."

"Really?" I step inside and smell the cinnamon that always hangs in the air here, and it makes my hip joints weak. He closes the door behind me and I step aside to give him room, but he halts directly in front of me.

"How are you?" he says, looking directly at my face.

"Good," I say. "How are you?"

His smile is slow and wicked. "Very hungry."

I blush, and it's ridiculous. Lowering my eyes, I make a sound like hmmm. He laughs, takes my hand, draws me into his dangerous kitchen. There is a pile of fresh vegetables on the table, red peppers and green ones, and even an orange one. They cost so much, I never buy them, but it's beautiful there with a scattering of yellow onions and the long shape of a zucchini. "What are you cooking?"

He laughs again. "Nothing yet. I was playing with my camera. Would you like to try?"

"Sure." He gives me his heavy Minolta, lightly touches the small of my back to nudge me toward the inviting still life. I look at it all through the lens, the way the light plays over the red and yellow and green skins, swooping here, disappearing there. I snap a photo, close in, of the curve of the orange one, lift the camera, touch it. "You should make stew."

"Maybe I will. I'm going to kiss you now, Trudy, all right?" And before I can say no, not that I would have, he's doing it, just leaning in and touching my mouth with his own. A brush of lips, of tongue, of his palm on my cheek, then away. "Is that all right?"

"Yes."

"Now I have to show you what has me so cheerful this morning." He takes an envelope from the counter and opens it. He's always lively, but this is more than usual, and he takes out a sheaf of photographs. "You are going to make me famous, *mi embruja*. Look."

He gives them all to me, a thick stack of eight-by-tens. They're all of me. "Oh, my God," I breathe, both appalled and enchanted. There is the series on the bed, with the light falling in bars over my naked flesh, and I have never seen myself this way, through these eyes. My hair and the curves of my back and hips, the length of my legs, the smoothness of white, white skin. There are several others, too, the ones he took the morning of Thanksgiving, standing in his kitchen, and a couple in the white shirt I wore after we had sex, photos I wasn't aware of him taking. In one, the curve of a breast brushes the edge of the open fabric.

Looking at them, though, the woman in the photos somehow becomes not me, but a subject of light and glitter and color. They are so exquisite that I nearly want to weep.

I raise my eyes to him, stricken.

"Do you not like them?" he asks, touching my face. "Say only a word, and I will burn them all forever."

"No! No, don't burn them. They're wonderful. Beautiful. I want to see the whole world through your eyes." And this time, I touch him, touch his beautiful face. Lean in and kiss him very gently. "What a surprise you are."

He takes the photos from my hands and comes close, touching my back, my hips, lifting my blouse to stroke my skin, just looking at me. "And you, such a creature of light. It is darkness that sets free the duende. How does all your light bring it to my heart?"

One day, this will all be a memory. Right now, it's real. It's happening. "Can I kiss you, Angel?"

"Please," he whispers, and meets me halfway. He talks as we kiss. "Light me up. Set me free."

And I laugh softly, because they are the things he's done for me. "I'm going to Seville in February," I say.

"That's very good." His hands are in my hair, hips pressing close. "To study your Lorca. To see that world. They will love you, they will fall in love with your light."

Not love, I want to say. He doesn't mean fall in love that way, and I know it, and it's very fine.

And when we are finished kissing, and touching, and setting each other afire again, he takes his camera and settles me in the chair in the kitchen and puts the vegetables in my lap and shoots rolls and rolls of film. I feel beautiful and alive. He takes my picture and I take his.

I forget, until the very end, to tell him that I am having the caroling party. He smiles wickedly. "Your daughter will not chase me with a broom if I come?"

I laugh. "No. I won't let her."

"Then I will be happy to come and eat chocolate. I will bring wine and something sweet, yes?"

"Yes."

And I leave him as bemused and light-footed as I always do, crossing the grass between our houses with a silly smile on my face, one that is reflective of all that has transpired today. In my hand are the photos, copies he's given me for myself. I'll have to hide them somewhere safe, but I couldn't bear not to have them. I wish I could frame them and hang them in my living room. Perhaps my bedroom.

When the kids are grown up.

In the meantime, they are my own luscious secret.

It isn't until I round the trees that I see Rick's truck parked in the driveway. The envelope of photos suddenly burns my fingers, and I look around for a place to hide it. There is nowhere, and I have to carry it inside, pulsing a red light from within. The red of my passion, the red of my hair.

Rick and Colin are sitting on the couch when I come in. No music is on. The television has been moved to the other room, of course. Neither of them looks particularly happy. "Hi, guys," I say. "What's up? How come you're home so early?"

Colin's face has a ruddy stripe of color on each cheekbone. "We just finished sooner than we thought. Can I go now?"

I send a questioning look toward Rick. He shrugs, defeated. "I'm making supper in a little while," I say.

Colin stands, bends over to hug his dad. Neither of them looks in the other's eyes. My son goes upstairs. We hear the door slam, the music come on. I look at Rick. "What happened?"

He rubs his face. "I don't know. He just started busting my balls about everything and I yelled at him."

I take a breath, sit in the chair. The envelope is still in my hands, burning my fingertips, and I put it aside in what I hope is a casual way. Then I pick it up again, afraid I'll leave it and Annie or Colin will be curious, pick it up . . .

"Where you been?" Rick asks.

"Next door."

He narrows his eyes. "I don't think Roberta put that look on your face."

I only lift my eyebrows.

"Jesus, Trudy. He's like twelve years old."

"Don't go there, Rick," I warn. "It's none of your business."

"Right." He stands up. "None of this is my business anymore, right? Not you, not my kids, who I never see, who—" He flings up a hand. "Never mind." He stalks toward the door and I'm telling myself not to feel sorry for him, that he made his bed and has to sleep in it, that—

But he was the center of my universe for a long, long time, and I see the agony and sorrow in the bend of his neck, the frustration in his balled fist. "Rick, you just have to give it some time. The kids will come around."

He halts by the door, chin raised. "Will they?"

There are a thousand things in my mind. His eyes are so familiar. I know every shadow and smile that can come over that mouth. I see that his mustache needs trimming, that there are circles of weariness under his eyes. I stand, put the photos on the couch, and say, "Come here."

He collapses into my embrace, his long strong arms fierce around me. "How did I get here, Trudy? What day can I find to go back to and fix?" His breath is warm on my neck and his body is so achingly familiar and so distant at once that I almost can't bear it.

As I stand there, holding my husband, I feel the difference in myself. With Angel, there is light and relief. With Rick, it goes down through the soles of my feet, through the marrow of my bones. It's a love so deep and wild and fierce that it sucks away my breath, and I am ashamed to want to weep into his shoulder. My arms tighten, and we simply stand there like that for a long, long time, holding each other, giving each other relief from everything else that might be out there. He presses a kiss, very lightly, to my ear, and lets me go. "I'll see ya," he says.

I nod.

~

Christmas Eve, Roberta and Jade are the first to arrive. Colin and Annie have helped me clean the house and I'm pleased at the joy they're showing. We've spread out the lace tablecloth, and the red glasses Rick's mother gave me three years ago.

Colin holds one. "I miss Granny."

Annie says, "Me, too. A lot."

"Let's set a plate for her," I say. "What do you think?"

"Wrong holiday, Mom."

"I think it's a good idea," Colin says. "I'll get it."

Annie raises her eyebrows. "Can we put one for Dad, too, then?"

"Are you missing him tonight?"

A shrug. "Kinda. It just doesn't feel like Christmas without him. I mean, we can pretend all we want, but aren't we all thinking about how hollow it feels?"

"You talking about Dad?" Colin has brought a plate and silver, which he settles to the right of the head of the table, where he always sat.

"Yes." I fold a napkin. "Are you missing him, too?"

His face closes; then he flicks a glance toward Annie. My little tough girl is near tears. Colin relents. Nods. "It's not the same."

"I know." I take a breath. "But that's why we're doing something different tonight, something we can celebrate on our own."

"Do you miss him at all, Mom?" Annie asks.

Every second, I want to say. *Every millisecond. There is not an instant of any day that isn't filled with some thought of him, some memory, some hunger.* Aloud, I say, "Of course I do. But sometimes things change and you have to make the best of them."

Roberta's arrival halts the conversation, thank God. She looks frail and tired tonight, and she leans on Jade's arm. In her other hand, Jade has a cake. I gesture for Annie to take it, and Jade settles Roberta at the table. Bending down to hug her, I smell a hint of L'Origan perfume and the oil she uses in her hair. "How are you, sweetie?"

"I'm all right." She points. "That cake is for your husband. You'll be seeing him, I expect?"

I shoot an amused glance at Jade. "We'll see him. Even if I have to make a special trip, I will, okay?"

Angel arrives next, and with him comes a glorious smell of chocolate and cinnamon. "Hello, beautiful lady," he says to Roberta, and kisses her cheek. He puts a tiny wrapped package in front of her. He hands Jade one that's slightly larger, and a matching one to Annie, who blushes the slightest bit.

In front of Colin, he halts and extends his hand. "I am Angel Santiago. You must be Colin, yes?"

"That's right," Colin says, ice in his voice.

He has another package, slim and flat, which I'm afraid might be a photograph. He's also got a pot of something, and I say, "Bring that into the kitchen."

There's a rustle of arousal on the back of my neck as he follows me, as if he is touching me. Which of course he cannot. In the kitchen, he stands very close, keeps up the chatter, cheerful and upbeat about the ingredients in the stew he's brought, and he looks over his shoulder, then puts his hand on my bottom and squeezes lightly. "Beautiful ass," he whispers. "Sneak away from your children tonight, Trudy. Come to visit me."

"I don't know if I can."

His eyes up close are like the bodies of dragonflies, iridescent. "Try. I have a surprise for you."

I nod, and slip back into the other room. Colin gives me a speculative look. The doorbell rings and I dash for it gratefully. "That must be Shannelle."

It's Rick. For one long second, I'm frozen dead as a statue, staring at him, his hair, his eyes, the gray creeping around his mouth. He's holding a box of presents, and he notices my hesitation. "Can I come in?"

"Sure. Yes. As a matter of fact, Roberta made a cake just for you."

"Sleigh Ride" is on the radio, ring-ring-ringing into the suddenly still room. Jade and Roberta, Annie and Colin, and Angel, looking distinctly mischievous—and God, so young!—all turn to see who I let in.

Annie leaps up. "Daddy!" she cries, and throws her arms around his neck. "What're you doing? I'm so happy to see you!"

Rick has an abashed and grateful expression on his face that breaks my heart. "Bringing you presents, silly girl."

Colin comes over, too, and gives his father a hug. "Sorry about the other day," he says quietly.

Rick squeezes his arm. "It's all right, son."

The phone rings and I pick it up. There's an immediate click, and I growl at it. "That's about the tenth hang-up I've had in three days." Even though I know the caller ID box will not show a number I recognize, I punch it anyway. It's a 970 area code. Nobody I know.

Rick is looking at me with an odd expression. "What?" I ask.

"Nothing."

From across the room, Roberta says, "Come sit down, son. We're fixin' to sing Christmas carols."

"I . . . uh . . ." He touches his mustache, looks at Roberta, the kids, me. Angel, who is perched at the end of the table in Rick's old spot, licking a crumb off one finger. There's a bright, feral look in Angel's eyes as he plucks a strawberry, dips it in the fondue, and eats it, and it is meant to make us—me—think of other things. Which it does. He winks.

Rick catches it. "I'm Rick Marino," he says, sticking out his hand.

"Ah, yes," Angel says. "The old husband." He wipes his hand on a napkin, and I have to press my lips together to keep from laughing. "I am Angel Santiago."

Jade covers her mouth with her hand. I take a long sip of water as the two men shake hands. Rick drawls, "Ann-hell."

"Sit down, Rick," Roberta says.

"We're going to sing Christmas carols, Dad," Annie says, and she shoots an urgent look at Colin.

"I don't think so, kids. Your mom's got her party going." He looks at me. "Merry Christmas."

My discomfort and amusement suddenly explode and all I feel is an agonizing wish to make him feel better. It's a sickness in me, I swear to God. My weakness makes me angry and I hold up my chin. "Merry Christmas to you, too."

"C'mon, Dad," Annie pleads. "Just sing a couple of songs with us. We'll sing your favorites first."

A flash of a Christmas Eve Mass and "Little Drummer Boy" comes over my imagination. "I'm sure your dad has things to do. We'll see him tomorrow."

But Annie starts to sing "O Come, All Ye Faithful," and Roberta, her partner in crime, starts to sing, too, and Rick stands there with his hands at his sides, looking winded. I give in and start to sing, too, and the other three, Angel included, chime in. Colin's voice is deep and true, Annie's light and high, Roberta's has the robustness of Aretha.

Rick simply stands there, looking at the children, then at me. I see he is very close to tears, and I go over to him, take his hand, sit him down at the table. Still singing, I pour a cup of wassail for him, put it in front of him, and when we reach the end of the song, I let the pause grow the smallest bit. Then I start to sing, "Come, they told me . . ."

In our family, we sang this song every year, practicing the rhythms as a group, learning to weave our voices together sweetly. My reedy alto, Richard's deep bass, Annie's sweet soprano, Colin's steady midrange. And Rick, there at the center, with his low, strong, sweet voice, adding a stabilizing weight to the soft melody.

I put a hand on his shoulder because he is still not singing, and look at Angel. His eyes are bright and warm, and he gives me the slightest of nods.

But Rick does not sing. He doesn't lift his cup of wassail. He doesn't even look at his kids. In the middle of the song, he stands up and lifts a hand and walks out.

"He forgot his cake," Roberta says.

Annie jumps up. "I'll take it."

I stop her, giving Rick the chance to get out before his tears spill. "We'll take it over there tomorrow."

The evening goes well after that, at least for the purpose I had intended—to give all of us, on this difficult Christmas, a place to go and be with others. Roberta is fairly cheerful, which I find heartening after the lull the past week. Jade sings vigorously if not well, and at one point, Angel and I sing "Fum, Fum, Fum" together in Spanish.

After they leave, the kids disappear into their rooms and I warn them to stay there until morning. In the stillness, I clean up the party mess, get out my favorite Christmas CD, the one with "Angels We Have Heard on High," then get out the stockings and all the hidden candy.

Rick and I always did this together. I think of those times now, all the years we stayed up late getting out presents and labeling them for each child, writing notes from Santa to them, eating the cookies and milk the children left out.

And it strikes me that I won't be doing this much longer. This part of my life, the mommy part, is over. It has been for a while. For the first time, it doesn't grieve me. I wonder, instead, what my life will be like next Christmas. If I will spend it here or somewhere else. If I will still be living in this house. If I will be far away, studying Spanish. As I get ready for bed, showering, then sitting on the edge of the bed to brush out my hair, I'm bemused by the sense of release, mixed with a kind of hollowness I can't quite name.

It won't let me sleep. I'll need to be rested to get through the day tomorrow, but after an hour, I get up in the dark and pull open the curtains. There is a light in Angel's kitchen window, and I can see his shoulder in a white shirt. He's sitting at his table. I wonder if I can call him to the window, to look up and see me.

It shames me a little, and I go downstairs in the dark, surprised that neither Annie's nor Colin's light is on. I smile. Some things never change. They'll be up early, my two vampires, eager as when they were eight to find out what Santa brought them.

It's one a.m. The moon is bright and the wind is still. Through the window, I see bare branches outlined against the sky, and they look beautiful. Dragging a velveteen throw around my shoulders, I wander outside.

All I can think of is Rick's haggard face, the threat of tears in his eyes. I am still furious with him, furious over his betrayal, furious that he could not just come to me and say, "I'm really unhappy and I don't know why. Help me figure it out."

But it comes to me, standing on my porch in the middle of the night, under a full moon, that I had not been happy, either. I'd begun to resent all that I'd given up to be with him. There were times during my stint at the natural healing school that I'd talk all afternoon with a man and think, *Why can't Rick hear me this way? Why doesn't he ever want to talk about what I want to talk about?*

There were times—a lot of them, I realize now with a thrum of guilt—that I shut him out during that long, dark stretch. I was grieving, too, after all. Joe was not my best friend, but I loved him. My mother-in-law had been more of a mother to me than my own, and I missed her desperately sometimes. If she were still alive, I sometimes thought none of this would have happened.

In the chair on the porch, Lucille says, "Getting there, sweetheart."

"Are you real?"

She gazes at me with her cornflower blue eyes. "What's real?"

And then there is a step on the porch, the heavy foot of a real man, and for one long moment, I'm hoping it's Rick, letting go of his pride to come to me and ask for his place back in this house.

Instead, it's Angel, who says nothing at all, just comes close and puts his arms around me and kisses my forehead. I lean against him, my head in the hollow of the wrong shoulder, and the tears come. He strokes my hair and presses his cheek against my head and makes a low, soft noise of comfort.

"You love him very much," he says at last, his strong young hands rubbing my back.

"Yes."

He takes my hand and we sit on the step. "Listen," he says, quiet and earnest, his voice as lovely as a song. "Tonight I saw him. His love is for you, not his other woman. What will you do about that?"

"What can I do?"

He chuckles, brushes hair away from my mouth. "Americans have forgotten the passion," he says. "Let the duende help you. Fight for him."

I raise my head. "And you, Angel, are you going to fight for your woman?"

"Pssh." He pulls away, shakes his head. "She is not worth it."

"Is anyone?"

He bows his head, and I want to kiss the vulnerable bend of his neck. "She shamed me in front of my whole town."

"Bring her to America, then."

"She does not love me. I say you should love a man back who loves you."

"She doesn't love you?"

He shakes his head.

"But she writes you letters? How often does she write her letters?"

"Every week. And every week, the same thing. She is so sorry. So sorry. So sorry."

"Maybe she really is, Angel."

He says nothing, only stares with his shattered heart into the night. I lean over and kiss his cheek. He picks up my hand and kisses the palm. "Perhaps, this night, we can soothe the sorrows of the other, eh?"

"I think, love, that part is over for us."

He looks at me, a half smile on his face. "I will not forget you, my Trudy."

"I won't forget you, either, my sweet."

And he kisses me, a dark rich kiss that tastes of cinnamon. His breath rustles over my hair, and then he's gone.

36

Trudy

The children drag me out of bed at eight, their eyes shining with mischief. "Come see what Santa left you," they say. "C'mon!"

"What?"

It takes me a minute, but I brush my teeth and come down the stairs to the smell of coffee brewing. Beneath the tree is a package wrapped in red foil paper. Annie puts it in my hands. "Where did it come from?" I ask.

"Santa," Colin says.

I grin. They've obviously cooked up something between the two of them, and I feel the heft of the package curiously. It feels like a book. I give them a quizzical look.

"Open it!"

I tear away the paper, and halt. It is a book. An old one, in Spanish. A first edition of *Libro de Poemas*, Federico García Lorca's first book of poetry.

Signed.

I cover my mouth with my hand. Whisper, "Oh, my God!"

Rick has enclosed a card, and my hands are shaking as I open it. It says only, "I hope you like it, kid. Love, Rick."

I'm blinking away tears as I look at the expectant faces of the children. "I wonder how in the world he found it."

"We helped," Annie said. "Me and Colin. He called Colin to ask him how to find it, and then one night when you were gone, me and Dad got online and tracked down a copy and ordered it. He sent it to Colin at school."

"Thank you."

"Thank Dad. He's the one who did it."

"I will," I say, and tuck the book close to my chest.

"You should call him now, Mom," Annie says.

I want to, but what if he has someone there. Or isn't home? The familiar burn kicks up. And it brings with it an edge of despair. Last night, with Angel, I had felt hope. This morning, it feels as bleak as ever. But they are looking at me so earnestly and I can't let them down, so I get up and pick up the phone and carry it into the kitchen. While I dial the number, I pour a cup of coffee. Stir in some sugar, listen to it ring on the other end, my bones thinning with each ring . . . two, three . . . four, and I'm going to hang up when I hear a rushed, "Hello?"

"Hi, Rick," I say. "I hope I'm not disturbing you."

"Of course not. I just couldn't find the damned phone."

"I called to thank you." There are tears in my eyes again. "This is the most thoughtful gift I've ever received, and I know you paid a fortune. I love it."

"Really? You like it?"

"I cried when I opened it."

"Colin said you would."

"I didn't get you anything, Rick. I didn't think we were doing that. I'm sorry."

"Trudy, that's not why I gave it to you. I didn't expect anything."

"I know. I just feel bad. All year, I planned to get you that supercalifragilistic CD player, and it bummed me out not to get it."

"The one with the remote?"

"Yep." I grin.

"Ah, man." A reverent pause. "But I wouldn't have wanted you to get it."

"Still. Thanks." In the silence between our voices, I hear the gurgle of the coffeemaker, the soft clank of a heavy iron pan on the stove. He's cooking breakfast. "Well," I say, "Merry Christmas, Rick."

"You, too, kid."

"Bye."

~

After lunch, Colin says, "I told Dad I'd come over and visit this afternoon. Is it okay if I call him now?"

"Sure."

A few minutes later, he comes back. "He sounds really depressed. We should take Christmas to him, Mom."

"What do you mean?"

Annie says, "Let's take him some turkey and the cake Roberta made for him and his presents and a stocking and everything." She gives me a pleading look. "Will you come with us?"

"I don't know." I sigh. "I think you two are trying to put things back together, and it's sweet, but it's not your job."

"We just think Dad is really lonely and we'd like to see him have a decent Christmas, that's all," Colin says.

"I'll drive you over there, but I don't think I'll come in."

We pack food and cookies into a basket. Colin even brings a half gallon of eggnog, in case Rick doesn't have any. I pack a Tupperware container with his favorite cookies—angel bars and chocolate chip and pizzelles—and dig his traditional stocking out of the box of Christmas things I have stashed in the back room. I used all the candy in the kids' stockings, so they each ante up a portion of the Hershey's Kisses, candy bars, and Life Savers. "There aren't Jelly Bellies," Annie says. "We have to get some." She's so tragic, I stop at Safeway, the only thing open, and pick up a box on the way.

It's a bright, clear Christmas Day. Quiet as all holidays are. I have butterflies in my stomach as we drive through town. Little kids are outside in their shirtsleeves, riding new trikes and Big Wheels. Families sit out on front porches, drinking beer and tea in the mildness. The air smells of baked turkey.

Even in Rick's grim neighborhood, things look festive. A kindly looking uncle or grandpa waves at us as we park behind Rick's truck and get out, all of our arms full. As we walk over the grass, I feel a wave of unsteadiness, warning, something, and just shake it off. It's Christmas. Everything can go on hold for one day.

We go into the hallway to his apartment and Colin starts to sing "God Rest Ye Merry Gentleman," and Annie joins in cheerfully, her arms filled with packages, her cheeks ruddy with good cheer. Neither of them has a hand empty, so I knock.

Disaster opens the door. It's Carolyn, who stares at all of us with tear-reddened eyes.

Colin says with chilly fury, "Is my father here?"

Rick pulls the door out of her hand. "I'm here, son. Carolyn was just leaving."

He looks furious. He's dressed up, in a pair of nice slacks and his turquoise corduroy shirt, even a necklace I gave him years ago, a Saint Joseph medallion, which I thought would be sexy against his dark chest. I see again that it is.

Carolyn resists, but Rick shoves her very lightly, and she lets go of the door, pushes between the kids and me. Rick puts his hand on my arm. "This is not what it seems," he says, looking right at me. "Don't go, okay?"

Carolyn starts to say something, and Rick says in that no-nonsense tone, "Not right now." To us, he says, "Go on in, I'll be right with you."

Annie and Colin look at me for direction. I waver, feeling sick and nervous. Their hopeful eyes give me the answer. It's Christmas. I'll go in. One hour, then home.

I nod.

The sound of his low voice countering her hysteria comes to us as we stand in the middle of the living room, waiting for him to come back. It's very silent and we're trying to figure out what to do. Sit down? Remain standing? "Put everything in the kitchen, Annie," I say. "Colin, the packages can go right there on the coffee table."

"Mom," Annie says, "I'm sure he didn't mean for us to see her."

"I know, honey." I touch her shoulder. "Don't worry about it."

Rick comes back in a moment, his cheeks bright red. "I am so, so sorry, you guys. She just showed up without an invitation and—"

I catch his eye and give him the parent look, waving my hand discreetly—*Let it go.* He nods, sighs, pushes a hand through his hair. "We brought you some goodies," I say, and sit down. "Presents and cookies and even—"

Annie pulls out the stocking. "Ta-da! Jelly Bellies."

He hugs her, looks at me over her shoulder. His eyes say how thankful he is.

~

We feast on the food we've brought, eating turkey and dressing and gravy all over again. Rick puts a CD in the stereo, and we tell stories about Christmases past, and talk about Colin's plans and Annie's hopes for college admission.

After a couple of hours, I'm thinking it's probably time to go. Soon the conversation will wane and there will be nothing for us to talk about except the dark things. The sun is going down. Maybe I want to be home when it gets dark. I'm about to say that, when Colin says, "We need to play Monopoly."

"I'm not playing Monopoly with you," I say. "No way, Mr. Real Estate."

"Aw, c'mon, Mom. Nobody ever plays with me."

"I'll play," Annie says.

Rick and I look at her in astonishment at the same instant. She hates losing to her big brother, and she does lose, every time. "What?" she says. "Is it okay if I want to play a game with my family?"

"I was honestly thinking it's probably time to go."

"No!" Annie protests. "We haven't even had dessert yet."

"I don't have Monopoly," Rick says.

"Will you play if I go get ours?" Colin asks, directly to his dad. Something shimmers there between them and it makes me feel nostalgic or sad or maybe touched.

"Sure." Rick's voice is a little rough.

"C'mon, Annie. You can ride with me. Mom and Dad can talk or something."

"No," I say, standing. "You two sit and visit and I'll go get the game. It'll only take a few minutes."

But Annie already has her coat on and they're moving toward the door. "I need to check my messages," she says, and pushes on her brother's back the slightest bit. "We'll be right back."

They're gone. I sink down on the chair and look over at Rick, who is grinning. "They're plotting, you know."

He chuckles. "You think?"

Against the turquoise shirt, his skin looks dark and smooth. There's a twinkle in his eye that makes him look like a pirate. I think of Carolyn suddenly, red-eyed, and I almost say, *Woman trouble?* Instead, I let it all go and lean back in the chair. "Do you have any wine around here?"

"How about a beer?" He stands to head for the kitchen, and I'm remembering the man I met so many years ago, the lean, irreverent man who stole my heart.

"Heineken?"

It takes him a second; then he turns slowly. "Skunk piss." His eyes are sleepy and slow, and my entire body goes on alert. "How about a Bud?"

"Buffalo piss." I cross my arms, incline my head. Give him a slight, pained sigh. "Guess it'll have to do."

He gets two and brings one to me. Standing in front of me, his hips slightly thrust forward in that bad-boy way, he screws off the top and hands it over. Our fingers brush as he gives it to me. "God, you were a snot."

I laugh. "Yes, I was." I take a good swallow, toss my hair back. He sits on the couch, but forward, on the edge. "And you thought I was the hottest thing you'd ever seen."

He raises his eyebrows, ducks his head, abashed a little. "That's the truth. Jesus, it was awful."

"Awful!"

His face is sober. "What'd I have to give a woman like you?"

"Ended up being quite a bit, didn't it?"

"I guess."

I say, "No dark stuff allowed, okay? Let's just not. Think of something good."

He takes a breath, falls backward, kicks up his feet on the battered coffee table. "You know what I was thinking about the other day?"

"Something good?"

"How big your breasts got when you nursed the kids."

I laugh. "That was great. So much power. I loved it."

"It was pretty sexy, all right. But then I always missed the regular ones and was glad."

A ripple goes over my back, and it feels so sensitive that a brush of his hand could give me an orgasm. A single, tiny brush. I try not to look at the length of his thighs, the darkness of his throat. My voice sounds a little husky when I say, "You never told me that."

The phone rings and Rick scowls, doesn't move.

"Better answer it," I say. "It might be the kids."

"Right." He punches the button, and growls, "Hello?"

The glitter lights up his eyes as he listens, making his eyes look like a lake on a sunny day. "Okay," he says. "I'll get her home after a while."

I start to laugh. "Those schemers."

He hangs up, purses his lips. "You know, you didn't get me a Christmas present."

I take a sip of beer. "That's true."

"Open to suggestions?"

I lean back. "What'd you have in mind?"

He stands up and walks around the coffee table, kneels down in front of me, and takes my beer out of my hand. He tugs me forward, and I'm already breathing hard, I want him so badly. My hands are even shaking as they circle his shoulders, and we look at each other, close, like new lovers anticipating a first kiss.

His hands go through my hair, touch my scalp, my ears. I touch his mustache. His mouth.

He says, "Jesus," and then we're kissing for the first time in five months. It feels like a miracle, like rain and sun, like morning. His hands are on the back of my head, and it's a fierce, hungry kind of kiss, deep and long, and I put my hands on his face, kissing him back, touching those lean cheeks and the edge of his goatee.

Then I bury my face in his neck, that place where he smells most like himself. I inhale it deeply into my body, letting the fragrance permeate every part of me. His hands are roaming over my back, then tentatively sliding around, edging toward my front. I pull back a little, meet his eyes, take his hands, and put them on my skimpy breasts.

"Oh, God, Trudy. God." He kisses me again, wildly, and I'm tugging his shirt out of his slacks.

His voice is raw when he lifts his head. "Is that a yes?"

I stand up and take his hand, turning to go into his bedroom, where I've never been. It's dark in there, and cold, and very spare, but it doesn't matter. I take my shirt off and let it fall on the floor, and I'm reaching back for the clasp of my bra, but he's there with his big hands. "Let me."

He bends his head and kisses the hollow of my throat, oh, so gently, and it makes me want to cry. His hands lift my breasts and his fingers know exactly what I like, the gentle circles, the slow glide. His chest feels hot against me when we lie down on the bed.

And what it feels like is that light is entering us as we make love, that it's filling all my cells and his, that it's healing the ripped and broken places. I tell myself that this is common, divorcing couples who have sex with each other. It happens all the time.

But do they feel this way? The way I feel right now, touching him, my husband, the only one I ever really wanted from the first time he kissed me?

Do those women want to weep with the bone-deep honor of their husband kissing their throat like he means it? Do they breathe him in, touch every inch they can reach, and caress his back like it's a sacred object?

Does it feel holy when he kisses their chin slowly, their eyes, their lips?

Traitorous tears leak out of my eyes as his hands cover my body, leaving no inch of it untouched. I weep as I worship his body, too. Weep as we make love, as we join together one more time. I think he's weeping, too. I feel a splash on my wet cheek, taste salt on his lips. We kiss and move, as we have a thousand times before, and I know the tiniest signals, the sound of his breath, the smell of his skin. I have missed him every single second of this separation and this is as close to heaven as I can be. Back in his arms, loving him.

It isn't until we are spent, collapsed against each other, that I see the print on his wall. It's a Waterhouse, a lady and a knight. He's kneeling in front of her, and the lady's hair is long and wavy and red, and I know that he loves this print because he thinks the woman looks like me. I close my eyes and hold him close, not saying a word.

Lying there, I know there is a difference between me and Lucille. I do have a sense of adventure and passion for new things and new places, but Rick Marino taught me that I am also a woman of deep and abiding passion. I have been so shaken these past months because I had no idea I loved him like this. That I even had the capacity.

But I cannot speak any of that aloud, not now. Maybe not ever. What I do instead is turn and give him a coy smile. "Well," I say. "You haven't lost your touch."

A shadow crosses his eyes, but then he's purring a little, pulling me closer. "You, either."

In the other room, the phone rings, and I feel Rick tense next to me. He doesn't move to answer it.

"What if it's the kids?" I ask.

"It isn't." He says it with great certainty, and starts to kiss me again. The ringing stops. Then it starts again. Stops. Starts again. His face goes hard. "Sorry, Trudy."

I blink at him guilelessly. "Woman trouble?"

"You have no idea." There is great weariness in his words, and as he starts kissing me again, I laugh.

The phone starts to ring again, and I laugh a little more.

He pulls up and looks at me. "What's so funny?"

I tuck my tongue over my teeth. "Not a thing."

When the phone stops this time, he says, "Just a minute," goes to get the phone, and turns it off.

Then he comes back, throws the covers over us, and we make love a second time. He takes me home an hour later at my insistence, and I'm glad to find the children are both gone somewhere. I go upstairs and climb into my own bed with the scent of Rick Marino all over me. In the night, I waken and remember and lift my hands to my nose and smell him there, and I fall asleep again with a softness in me that's been missing for a long time.

37

Jade

Christmas is a strain. All the cooking falls to me, though the relatives bring potluck. They also bring their noise and their children and ten thousand presents, and the house is demolished. By evening, I'm sprawled out on the couch staring at the TV, every bone in my body just dead tired. There's a kids' Christmas show on, and I watch it with half an eye, but my brain's buzzing and jumping, zapping. Here. There. Here. There.

Little blips of the day show up. Grandmama lying on her bed in the dark, crying and crying. Mama finally showing up to help me get her up and moving. Then the whole swarm of Denver folks down to try to cheer up Roberta. She didn't take any cheering. She put on her lipstick and sat there pretending to be happy.

Mama hugged me on the way out. "Baby, I'm so glad you can be here for her. She needs somebody real bad."

"I'm worried about her, Mama. She won't get up some days at all. Just wants to lie there. Or she's putting all her stuff in boxes to give away. It's creepy."

She rubbed my arm. "Day by day. Keep getting her up, whatever you have to do."

"I think she needs drugs, Mama. Antidepressants to get her through."

Mama took a breath. "Sit down a minute with me, baby." She led me over to the couch and took my hand. "I hear what you're saying, that you're worried that she's going to fade away, but it hasn't been but a couple of months. Pretty quick here, she'll start having good days once in a while."

"What if she doesn't?"

"Let's give her another month, and then we'll see, all right?" She brushed the top of my short curls, smiled a little. "She tells me you've been keeping company with a real nice young man. That true?"

"He's a very nice man," I said, and stopped, frowning. Not sure I wanted to say any more. But that's how I got in trouble with Dante, not talking about him to anybody. Probably because I knew what they'd say: *Be careful.* "It's hard to know where I stand with him sometimes."

"How's that?"

"He's my coach, my boxing coach."

She started to say something about the boxing, but didn't. "All right."

"He's . . . um . . . very straight. Like he'll only see me right now at church or when we can be 'chaperoned.'" I hung my fingers in the air around the word, widened my eyes. "He had a bad time when he was younger, and straightened himself out. Doesn't drink or smoke or—"

"Sleep around?" Mama laughed. Patted my hand. "He sounds wonderful, Jade! Just right. And your grandmama cannot say enough about his manners and how good-looking he is."

"Oh, you should see him." I shook my head, thinking of his fine rear end and that twinkle in his eye. "He is the most gorgeous man I have ever seen."

"Will I get to meet him?"

I shrugged. "I don't know. He's always so reserved. I mean, I hardly know what he feels. I'm probably making it all up in my head."

Her smile was gentle. "He sounds old-fashioned, that's all. Is that such a bad thing?"

"No," I said in a near-whisper. "What's scaring me, Mama, is that I keep thinking about babies when I'm with him. Babies and supper and all that. I don't want to be so serious about somebody. It seems too fast after Dante."

"It's not fast, Jade. You only left California a couple of months ago, that's true, but you'd done your work of leaving him already, all through his trial and all the betrayals. I know you loved him, and I think he loved you, too, baby, but some men just don't know how to grow up, and he's one."

I lowered my eyes, trying to hide the piercing sensation that gave me. But Mama, being Mama, saw through it. "Trust your heart," she said.

"I'll try."

She hugged me again. "Remember what I said about Grandmama. Call me if you want to talk about it anymore, or if she seems worse, all right? Maybe you could take her out to get her hair done."

"Okay. I love you, Mama," I said.

Now I'm sitting with my feet sprawled out in front of me, watching a television program, wishing I had babies to put to bed, all scrubbed and clean. A baby and a toddler and a kindergartner, bathed and worn out from a long, happy Christmas. I wish they were slumped against me in sleepy contentment. I can feel the empty spot at my side where they should be by now.

The phone rings and I leap on it, hoping for Rueben. "Hey, baby," says the snake-smooth voice of Dante Kingman. "Merry Christmas."

"Dante," I say wearily. "Do not call me ever again." I hang up. When it rings again, I ignore it, and not with any effort. I'm not interested in his games, his player ways, his bullshit. When it rings a third time, I'm afraid it's going to wake Roberta, and I grab it savagely. "I said never, and I meant it."

"Jade?"

"Oh, Rueben!" I sit up straight. "Sorry. I thought it was my ex. He's been calling tonight."

There's humor in his rich, deep voice as he says, "Want me to go beat him up for you?"

"Sure. Would you?"

He chuckles. Then, "Listen, I was wondering if it might be okay if I came by for a few minutes. I worked all day, but I have a couple of small things for you and your grandma."

"I would love it, Rueben. You have no idea." Then I realize that I have to tell him the truth. "My grandmama's already sleeping, though. It'd just be me and you."

"Is that right." I'm not sure if it's wishful thinking that makes me hear the promise in his tone. "Well, I think it'll be all right, just this once." A pause. "To tell you the truth, Jade, I been thinking about kissing you all day. Would that be all right?"

I close my eyes, a shiver running down my neck. "It's very okay."

"All right, then. I'll be there in just a little while."

My weariness evaporates, just like that. I rush into the bathroom to wash my face, put on some fresh lipstick. Change out of the sweater I've been wearing all day, into one that's a little more flattering. I put some perfume behind my ears, alongside my mouth, between my breasts.

By the time I open the door to him a few minutes later, every cell in my body is primed to touch him. They all shout, *Yes!* when he comes inside, carrying packages, and puts them down on the couch.

"Come here," he says in a growl. Without even taking off his coat, he pulls me close to his big body. I wrap my arms around his neck, and we're kissing like lovers who've been parted through a war. Deep and hard. Then we're just hugging again. "Damn," he whispers, his hands rubbing up and down my back, "you just don't know how bad I wanted to do that all day."

"Me, too, Rueben." I could stand here like this for a hundred years, just holding him. Smelling him. Feeling the solidness of his body, his strong arms.

But pretty soon, we're rubbing almost helplessly against each other. Out of deference to his vow of celibacy, which even though we broke he wants to keep, I pull away a little. "Can I make you a plate? Got everything in there."

"Now, that sounds real good."

"Let me hang up your coat, and we'll go in the kitchen."

He grabs the wrapped packages and follows me. I make him a plate piled high with turkey and dressing, greens and macaroni and cheese, and some of my aunt Ti-Ti's tender rolls. "It's a wonder any of these are left," I say. "She's the best cook I've ever known."

He digs into the food like he's starving. "It's so good, Jade," he says after tasting a bite of everything. "I been away from good cooking for too long. You really miss it on the holidays."

"I bet."

When he's filled up, he picks up the smaller of the two packages. "I hope it was all right to bring you something. Merry Christmas."

It's jewelry-size. He leans forward to put his elbows on his knees, tucking his lower lip under his front teeth as I open it. It's a necklace, a fine gold chain with a charm. I laugh in delight, because the charm is a nicely cast set of boxing gloves. "Golden gloves! Rueben, it's perfect! Thank you." I lean over to kiss him.

"You like it?"

"Yes."

"Good." We fall into some serious kissing, with his hand on the back of my neck, brushing and stroking, and this time he's the one who pulls back. For a minute, he looks into my eyes with a serious expression. Touches my lips. "You are some woman, you know that?"

"Thank you."

He straightens. "I'd better go. Give your grandma a kiss for me."

"You won't stay for some coffee and pie? There's pecan."

"Don't think I'd better."

I'm going to be adult about this. "All right. How about if I send you home with a piece to eat later?"

"That'd be really nice."

So that's what I do. Put him a big slice of pie in some Tupperware, and kiss him goodbye at the door. It starts to get out of hand, or maybe it's our hands getting out of hand. Mine on his beautiful ass, his on mine, then our hips pushing together.

"Okay," he says. "Good night, Jade."

"Thank you, Rueben. Merry Christmas."

And when he leaves, I lean against the door, reliving it all one more time. What a man.

What. A. Man.

38

Shannelle

TO: naomiredding@rtsv.org

FROM: chanelpacheco@hotmail.com

SUBJECT: money for airline ticket!!!

I got a $350 voucher in the mail today for an airline ticket.

Anonymously. I burst into tears.

I know it had to be you, and I don't deserve it, but I thank you anyway. Someday I hope I can repay you for the friend you've been to me.

Love and kisses and many tears, Shannelle

∾

TO: chanelpacheco@hotmail.com

FROM: naomiredding@rtsv.org

SUBJECT: not me

shannelle, i am so thrilled for you about the airline
voucher, but much as i wish i could do such a thing,
i'm not exactly rolling in dough. somebody loves
you a lot. and you deserve it, girl. you really do.
book your flight right now.

naomi

~

TO: naomiredding@rtsv.org

FROM: chanelpacheco@hotmail.com

SUBJECT: DISASTER!

Dear Naomi,

I'm sorry if this ends up sounding hysterical. I've
been fighting with Tony for hours and he will not
budge on the writing retreat. He's making it into I
either choose the writing or I choose him and I don't
know what to do.

This is why I was so scared to bring it up with him,
because I knew he'd take it like this, like some threat
against the Pope or something. God, I'm so mad! And
I'm crying and can't even see the screen half the
time while I write this, but I am not going to sleep in

the same bed with him tonight no matter what. He can be as mad as he wants about me being on this computer. I'm going to stay on it until I can't keep my eyes open anymore.

I planned it out so carefully, Naomi! We had this great Christmas, everybody all happy and eating. I baked like twelve thousand cookies and fixed all his favorite things, including, I might add, tamales, which take an entire day if you do them by yourself, which I did because I wanted him to be happy and proud of me. The kids were thrilled with the presents we got for them, and I've been saving all year to get Tony a really nice television with a remote and a screen within a screen. He was so happy!

And then the kids went to bed, and I decided this was the best possible time to talk to him, so I put on something a little more comfortable, if you know what I mean, and we made love, and it was really very sweet, and I do love him, damn it! Then I got us both a Dr Pepper and we sat in the candlelight in our room, just talking, and I told him about the scholarship and everything. I told him how honored I was, and how happy, and about the airline voucher, and my whole plan for the cooking, and that I'd arrange everything so it's as easy as pie for him.

You know what he said, Naomi? "No." Just "No." Not, "I'm so happy for you," or "I know you've wanted to be a writer since you were ten and I'm proud of you," or anything. Just flat, plain "No."

I argued with him, tried to present it in a new way. My neighbor across the street told me that whatever he said, he would be afraid that he would lose me if I went, so I was trying to be compassionate, and I told him how much I loved him, and how I would think of him every day, but I really want this chance, that it was rare and special, and I even told him he should be proud of me.

And what he said then was, "No." Again.

And in that minute, I was so mad I couldn't even see straight. I thought about my mom, turning into this gray person, trying to please my dad. I thought about my sister killing herself over some stupid boy who used her and broke her heart. I thought about how hard I work to make this family comfortable and real and good. (I'm crying again, damn it!)

That's when I told him I didn't need his permission. I wanted his blessing, but not his permission. I told him that I was going whether he liked it or not. He said, "If you do, our marriage is over."

The one thing in this life that terrifies me is being a single mother, Naomi. It scares the hell out of me. But turning into my mother scares me more, and I have to do this. I have to see if I have what it takes to be a writer. If I give this up, I won't be me anymore. I won't be me. And he'll just be married to a ghost anyway.

I'm hoping he'll come to his senses in the morning, but if he doesn't, that's his problem. My neighbors will help me, I know they will. And my mother-in-law will help, too. Watch and see. I am just so furious with him!!! If he had some big chance to do anything, I would stand on my head to make sure he could do it.

Love,
Shannelle

~

TO: chanelpacheco@hotmail.com

FROM: naomiredding@rtsv.org

SUBJECT: hang in there

ah, shannelle, i'm sorry you're getting so much resistance from tony. do you think it would help if i wrote him a letter?

he will come around. he loves you and your children and your life. you have to keep on your own path and be true to your goals and your life, and he will come around.

if you're tempted to give in, i want you to think about your boys and the example that you are providing for them. you're showing them that it's worth fighting anyone, everyone, for a chance to really be yourself.

and i haven't said it before, shannelle, but i'm deeply honored to know you. you are brave and strong and beautiful. i know where you come from, because i'm from there, too. my world was the reservation, but it's not all that different. poor is poor.

you have my phone number. if you feel scared or lost or lonely, call me. anytime, day or night. i mean it.

love,
naomi

39

Trudy

The day after Christmas, my airline ticket for Seville arrives.

As I stand on the porch in the very cold sunshine, the envelope seems to burn my fingers with light and promise. My heart pings. I've become enamored with myself again, planning this trip, loving the vision of myself as a woman who can set out on her own, see what she wants to see.

I bring it in and sit down on the couch, open the envelope, and look at the itinerary. For a moment, I can see myself settling in on the plane, buckling my seat belt over my yoga pants, which I've worn to be comfortable on the long flight. I booked a window seat so that I can see when we land in London and again in Seville.

Then the vision of me in that seat wavers and I see Rick, kissing my neck, and a filmstrip kaleidoscope of memories, more than twenty years of them. If I want my marriage, this stretch of time is critical, and with a pang of regret, I realize I can't go. Not now. I'll do it later, when things are stabilized between us, when this dark time is behind us. Maybe Rick will even go with me.

No.

My body protests that idea so vehemently that I'm amused. Okay, so I'll go alone. Yeah, that's good. I notice when the tenseness flows out of me. I'll go alone, maybe next fall.

For now, though, I can't go. All day, I've been alight with possibilities. Hope. I keep thinking of the painting of the woman on Rick's wall, and what that means. I think of my tears, of his. For the first time in months, I feel there is a chance for us, and I'm not going to let it pass.

I prop the ticket by my computer monitor to remind me to cancel it and my reservations in the Old Jewish Quarter in Seville. Time enough. If I can't cancel the ticket, maybe I'll give it to Angel.

As I'm standing there, the phone rings. Without stopping to check caller ID, I answer it. There is silence on the other end of the line. After a minute, I hang up, shrugging it off.

But it happens six times over the course of the day. Again the next day. And the next. The numbers are different, but all are local, and after the twelfth one, I sit down with the internet and do a reverse lookup. Two of them are cell phone numbers and return a "no information available" response. The third is Maggie's Place.

The bar where Carolyn works.

I sit there for long moments, mulling over my options. I haven't talked to Rick since yesterday, and I want to keep it that way for a while longer. The ball is in his court.

The phone rings again, and I look at the caller ID. It's the one for Maggie's Place, and I let it ring through to voice mail, wondering if there will be any message. Maybe if she doesn't have to talk directly to me, she'll be able to speak her mind.

But when I retrieve the message, there is only a little sound of distant traffic, then the connection is ended.

I hear Angel's voice say, *What are you going to do about that?*

In sudden decision, I put on my boots and grab my purse before I can change my mind. The air is bitterly cold and I have to pull a scarf around my face to keep from freezing the little hairs in my lungs. I start the car and let it warm up while I scrape the ice from the windshield. It's a quiet holiday afternoon, too bright with that cold sun and cloudless turquoise sky, and there aren't many children out in the bitterness. I drive through town without feeling the slightest bit nervous until I park in front of the bar on Santa Fe.

I stand by the car for a minute, doing some yoga breathing to steady myself. When my heart has stopped racing, I cross the sidewalk, hearing the heels of my boots hit the sidewalk with a sound of purpose, and take a breath before I enter the bar.

In the light of day, it's a grim setting. The bottles look cold, and the air smells of old nights. There are only a few aging men dotted along the length of the bar, and a pair of businessmen in a booth, eating hamburgers. The jukebox is mute. The television is broadcasting a talk show. Carolyn is washing glasses and looks up as I come in. Her face goes still.

As calmly as I am able—which feels about as steady as an earthquake—I cross the brown-and-white linoleum and settle on a stool at one end. "Hi," I say, taking my wallet out of my purse. "I'll have a soda and lime, please."

For a moment, she only looks at me. Nothing shows on her well-schooled bartender face. No speculation, no fear, nothing. She dries her hands on the sparkling white bar towel and takes a tall glass from the counter, fills it with ice, then soda, squeezes a lime wedge into it. As she does it, I'm observing her in a way I've never had an opportunity to before. There are things I've seen before—her hair is painfully overprocessed and dry, but today it's pulled back in a French braid. Her pants are too tight, but the body is still good enough that she can get away with it.

There are things I haven't noticed before, too. Her hands are long and graceful, with very long, very attractive nails. She's wearing turquoise-and-silver rings on three fingers. One is on her left ring finger and I wonder with a little pinch in my chest if Rick gave it to her. As she carries the drink to me, the daylight coming in through the windows is not kind to her face. She looks good for forty-nine, but it won't be long before she'll have to give up the tight jeans and long hair. And what will she do then?

I feel a sudden pity for her. If Rick and I divorce, I still have a lot of good in my life. I have my education, the money Lucille left me, a sense of possibilities, children, a home. She has a rented house, two children who are going nowhere, a job as a bartender. She needs him more than I do.

Carefully, she puts down a square white cocktail napkin and settles the glass on it exactly in the middle. "A dollar twenty-five," she says. Her voice is resonant and lilting, very appealing in some way I can't name. She puts her beautiful hands on the five I've laid on the bar. "Take it out of this?"

I nod. Sip the soda while she makes change and brings it back. She fans the three bills out neatly and puts the quarters down on top. I push one dollar toward her. She picks it up, loops it around her finger. Looks at me.

"I came to talk to you," I say.

"I figured that out."

I find I have to clear my throat. "I still love him, Carolyn. I think he still loves me, too."

"No, Trudy." She lifts an overplucked eyebrow. "He loves me. I've given him something you couldn't."

"I'm sure you have. I'm not here to argue. I don't blame you or want to hurt you. I just came to tell you that I've spent twenty-five years loving that man and I'm not going to roll over and play dead. I'm going to fight for him."

Her eyes narrow. "That's pathetic. He's been cheating on you for over a year. He hasn't lived with you for six months. He loves me." She touches her earrings, brings them out of her hair. They're pretty silver-and-turquoise. "These are what he gave me for Christmas."

And this does hurt. Like a punch to the solar plexus. But what did I think? That they wouldn't exchange Christmas presents? Tacky.

"You could be right," I finally manage. "I'm not saying he doesn't have feelings for you. I'm saying that I'm not giving up." I stand up, put my purse on my shoulder. "May the best woman win."

~

As I pull into the driveway at home, the sun is going down. The air is so cold that the sky takes on a layering like a parfait, a smoky dusky blue on top, with a wide swath of pink below. I run inside and get the camera, even though I know it won't be as beautiful as it is to my eye. It frustrates me a little, trying to get the perspective just right, and I suddenly remember a tree down the street, on the corner. Carrying the camera, I hurry down there, afraid the light will fade before I can capture it.

And there it is. A Chinese elm with black bark, reaching into the luscious layers of color, showing by contrast how bright the tones are. Through the breaks in the street, I can see all the way to the mesas in the west, and the sun is lying between them, gold and promising.

I think of Angel and lower the camera. This is a moment I would like to share with him. The color, the light. Maybe he would speak to me in Spanish about it, teaching me new words. What is the Spanish for parfait sky? As I walk by his house on my way back, I am very tempted to stop, go in. Smell the cinnamon-and-brown-sugar scent of his rooms.

But I keep walking. His car is in the driveway, his magic pumpkin, and a light is burning in the window against the encroaching dusk. I focus on the fading pink in the sky, do not look through the window.

As I climb the steps to my porch, Shannelle arrives, her two boys in tow. "Hi, Trudy," she says. "Do you have a minute? I need to talk to you."

She sounds so weary that I glance at her sharply. Her eyes are red-rimmed. "What is it, honey? Another toothache? Come in and let me get you some tea."

"Not a toothache," she says. "Boys, go play in the back for a little while, okay?"

I touch her shoulder, flick on a light. Her cheeks are bled pale. "Let's go in the kitchen. Boys, hold on and I'll let you have some cookies." They're solemn, big-eyed, as they accept them. Always so perfectly

brushed and groomed, these two. Without a word, they carry the cookies out to the back porch and take toy cars from their pockets. "What's
going on, Shannelle?"

She slumps in the chair without even taking off her coat, and pours
out her story in a weary voice. I put the kettle on, take out big mugs,
three boxes of tea, and a new box of Pepperidge Farm cookies. "So this
morning," she says, "he packed a suitcase and went to his mother's."

"Damn."

She leans forward and combs her hair out of her face with sharp,
strong strokes. "Yeah, well, he's not going to bully me. He's not. I'm sick
of everybody telling me what I am and should do and be." The kettle
whistles and I pull it off the burner, pour hot water into our cups. "The
reason I'm really here is to ask you a favor."

"Shoot."

Dipping her tea bag up and down through the water, she says,
"Tony's mom will let the boys stay with her during the day, even though
he's pissed about it. Roberta is going to keep them weekday nights,
which made me feel guilty, but"—she shrugs one shoulder—"I think,
and Jade agrees with me, that it's good for her to stay busy and have
something meaningful to do."

"Yeah. So you need weekend nights? I'd be happy to do it. When
are the dates?"

"February eighteen through twenty-eighth. It starts on a Friday, so
that night."

The dates overlap the Seville trip. It feels like a sign—this young
woman needs my assistance more than I need to go to Spain. But I'd
already made up my mind to give it up.

Hadn't I?

"Okay, not a problem."

She lets go of a sigh, reaches over the table. "Thank you, Trudy. So
much. You're the one who gave me enough courage to do it."

"My pleasure, sweetie." I squeeze her fingers. "I'm sorry Tony is so
upset. I'm sure he'll come around."

"Either he will or he won't." But a betraying glaze of tears makes her eyes brighter blue. She blinks hard. "It breaks my heart, though, Trudy. It really does. Why do I have to choose one or the other?"

I shake my head. "I don't know."

~

After she's gone, I'm restless, roaming the house looking for something to do. Annie is working, Colin is out with some high school friends. There's a creeping sense of doom closing around me and I'm not sure what it's about. I go to the greenhouse, with Zorro happily following behind.

Spider Woman is the goddess of the month, a mother image beloved by the Navajo, among others. The statue I have of her is a Native American woman with long black hair and angel wings, her arms outstretched to indicate bounty, openness, giving. I light a smudge stick of sweetgrass and sage for her, and the earth-colored candles, and I sit in my little corner with her, among my plants. It is very quiet. The grow lights I use to supplement the darker corners provide a soft rosy glow. The smell of sweetgrass and earth and damp growing things eases some of that creeping doom.

This is my sanctuary, this narrow room. It's always been the place I retreated to, where I felt I could come and just be myself, putter in the dirt, and grow flowers that are only for beauty and pleasure, nothing else. It was in here that I began to seriously consider the natural healing classes that I saw advertised on a university bulletin board, where I felt free to erect my altars to the goddess figures who started to appeal to me. Against the dark glass, the angel-wing begonia's spotted leaves glow, flowers hanging down in giant, sensual clusters, and I think of the photographs of the hotel courtyard in Seville.

Aloud, I begin to chant poetry in Spanish. Lorca, of course, but Neruda, too, and fragments of some others I only vaguely remember. I close my eyes to hear my voice roll through the Spanish syllables. My accent was always excellent, they told me, a point of pride, though I had nothing to do with it. I grew up where the lilt of Spanish influenced English so much that it was easy. And then Lucille spoke to me, gave me words, so passionate, so rolling on her tongue when she read to me the poems of her beloved Neruda. Those words, the words now falling from my lips in my own voice, promised adventure and courage and passion. I hear them and there are tears rolling down my cheeks because I've spoken this language only to Angel in all these years.

It will be sad when he leaves, goes on to his adventures.

And still I sit and recite poetry in Spanish. I think of the colors of Lorca, his green moons and silver grasses and water flowing through it all. It gives me goose bumps of pleasure, and I open my eyes to see the green of my world, the yellow glow of the candle, the softness of that rosy light. I see my hands in my lap, long and white, and wonder what they will do a year from now. Five. Twenty.

Zorro curls around my ankles, his tail a bushy softness. "How can I be so old and not know anything about myself?" I ask him. He meows quietly, blinking yellow-green eyes at me seductively. My long white hand moves to his head, fingers rub his ears. It's like something that belongs to someone else, that hand, and I'm suddenly burning to see the photographs Angel took of me. I blow out the candle, scoop up the cat, and hurry upstairs to the closet in my bedroom, where I've hidden them away beneath a quilt we never use.

I pull them out, spread them over the bed, look at them. At myself, but not me, a being of light and shadow, luminous promise. He is such a genius with light, I think again, seeing the way the bars of sunlight caught in my hair, making small bursts of stars seem to glitter there. In another, the half-moon shape of my small breast is the only curve of light in heavier shadows, echoed by the curve of a cheekbone.

Who is this woman?

I'm drawn to my window, lift the curtain to Angel's kitchen window. The light is on. I press my forehead against the cold glass, and my breath condenses in a circle. It draws my attention, and I draw in it as

I have not done in many many years. I draw a heart. I don't know what initials to put in there, so I just put my own, GOM, Gertrude O'Neal Marino.

Angel moves into the window. He stands there, looking up at me, then leans into the glass and presses his lips against it. I laugh, and put my palm against my own window. He is so beautiful. I loved his making love to me. But I don't feel any rush to go down there and throw myself at him. This creeping sadness has nothing to do with ending a brief love affair with a man who healed a lot of fissures in my soul, my psyche, my ego.

I look back to the photographs and wonder what Rick would see in them. I can't imagine hiding them forever, but what man would like such sensual pictures of his wife taken in postcoital glow by another man? I laugh to myself. But I have given Angel permission to sell them, display them, whatever he wants. They're artful and not at all lewd, and truth be told, I'm fairly delighted to look so hot at forty-six.

The door slams below and Colin calls out, "Mom?"

"Damn." I dive for the pictures, gather them up, a dozen eight-by-tens, trying to do it carefully and quickly. "Up here!" I say when I've got them safely in a stack. There isn't time to get them in the envelope, so I dash to my dresser, put them down, and pull the scarf over them.

He shows up at the door with a Mountain Dew in his hand. "Whatcha doing?"

"Just straightening up. How was your night?"

He plops down in the chair where Lucille sat that first night I broke my arm. "Kinda weird, to tell you the truth. We don't really have a lot in common anymore."

"That happens, I'm afraid." I settle on the bed, prop my head on my elbow. "There might be one or two of them that you'll want to know twenty years from now, but not many."

"Do you know anyone from high school?"

I snort. "Not hardly. I couldn't get out of there fast enough. Like you and Pueblo."

"I don't see how Pueblo is that much better than Clovis, frankly."

"It is, though. A lot different."

He leans on his knees. "But, Mom, this wasn't exactly what you had in mind when you left, was it?"

"No," I say honestly. "Sometimes life can turn out okay anyway, though."

"Why haven't you ever gone back to finish your master's?"

"Haven't really had time. Kids, you know." I smile.

He meets my eyes. "It's time, Mom."

I sit up. "Is it? Three days ago, you and your sister plotted to get me and your dad back together. Tonight you're telling me to go back and get my master's, even though—" I cut it off. Clamp my mouth down. Inappropriate.

"Even though going back to school caused trouble between you and him?"

"I don't want to talk about this, Colin. A marriage is a very personal thing."

Stung, he leans back. "Sorry. I was just trying to help." Mutinously, he raises those extraordinary eyes. "Where there's a will, there's a way, you know. I think it's sad that you left all that behind."

The easy tears of earlier come back before I can stop them, and it's aggravating. It must be PMS or something. I lower my eyes, but Colin sees.

"You really want to, don't you?"

I nod. I think of my ticket to Seville, propped up by the computer, waiting for me to cancel it. Quietly, I recite, "'*Chove en Santiago, na noite escura. Herbas de prata e de sono cobren a valeira lúa.*'"

"That's beautiful. What does it mean?"

"'It rains in Santiago in the dark night. Grasses of silver and of sleep cover the empty moon.'" I open my eyes. "Isn't it beautiful?"

"Mom, you always told us to do what we love. You told us, so many times, that you have to spend so much of your life working that it's the one big thing you can do for yourself." He leans forward, so young and idealistic. "Why aren't you doing it?"

I blink. "I don't know."

JANUARY

Spider Woman

According to mythology, Spider Woman spun two silver strands, one connecting east to west, the other north to south. This connected the four corners of the earth, with Spider Woman as the centre. (The strands created the Road of Life in the Hopi tradition, which has as its symbol the equal-armed cross.)

In her aspect as Creator and Mother, Spider Woman affirms that women are essential and central to the life process. She reminds us that people of all races were created from the same source, with equal rights and responsibilities.

—www.goddess.com.au

40

Roberta

January 2, 20—

Dear Harriet,
Just a quick note this morning to thank you properly for the beautiful scarf and gloves you sent me for
Christmas. They're beautiful, and I'll enjoy wearing
them.

    Love, Berta

41

Jade

Sunday morning after New Year's, Rueben calls very early. "Good morning," he says in a hearty voice. "Y'all going to church?"

"Yes." I make the word short as my temper. I have not seen him or talked to him in a week.

"Mind if I come along?"

"I guess not." I glance over my shoulder at my grandmother, and her weary face gives me pause. "Why don't you come to lunch here afterward, too." I lower the receiver a little, so Rueben can hear why I'm asking him. Grandmama needs this man to cook for. "G'mama, that be okay? Rueben can come to lunch?"

"I ain't got nothing to cook right," she says.

"I'll cook. You can just sit back and relax."

"That'd be okay, I reckon."

On the other end of the line, Rueben says, "Not doing too good, huh?"

"No."

"I'm ready. I'll come over and we can get her cheered up."

My exasperation comes back. "Rueben, what do . . ."

"What?"

"Nothing. Never mind."

"You want to know where I been."

"Bingo."

A small quiet. "Trying to be good."

"Whatever."

"We'll talk later, Jade. I do have a surprise for you. I'll be there in a little while."

I was going to wear a plain Sunday school dress, but now I rush back to my room and change into a long black sweaterdress. It has a turtleneck and comes to the middle of my calves, but with a silver belt, it looks hot. I put on some swinging silver earrings to go with it, and a big African bracelet. When I go back to the living room, Grandmama is still just sitting there, doing nothing, not even drinking her coffee. She's dressed except for her shoes and hair, which is sticking up nine ways to Sunday.

"C'mon, Gram, let me do your hair." I have to put my hands on her shoulders and nudge her to a standing position. She comes along, limping because her knee is swollen. "Here you go. Sit down on the toilet and let me do this pretty for you."

I plug in the hot comb and the curling iron she likes. While they heat, I use the long-bristle brush that feels so good on the scalp. She hasn't had a perm in a while, and the new growth at her scalp is tight and silvered. I put a small bit of oil in my hands and rub it in—really rubbing her scalp to help her wake up and feel tended. She smells like soap and tea, and I can remember ten thousand times I've brushed her hair or she's brushed mine. We were so tight when I was a little girl. "You know how much I love you, Grandma?" I say now, rubbing away.

"That's sweet, baby."

Real easy, I hot-comb the nap into gentle waves. "You know what?"

"What, baby?"

"When I was a little girl, I used to think that if you were a hundred when you died, I'd be into my fifties and might be able to stand it."

"Did you?" There's a hint of a smile in her voice.

I keep combing, slowly and gently. Her hair starts to shine. "I sure did."

There's a knock at the door. "That's Rueben. Don't move. I'll go let him in."

I dash to the door, pull it open. I'm about to let him just follow me in, but he opens the screen and he looks and smells so good that I stop, every cell in my body swelling up. He's so damned tall and solid-looking, and his face is freshly shaved, his mustache trimmed and combed, the suit sitting just right on his shoulders. He's carrying a bouquet of sunflowers.

Very quietly, I say, "Am I allowed to kiss you, just once?"

He bends in and does it, and in the hurry, I can tell it's taking everything he's got to do just that much. His tongue touches mine.

We pull back. "C'mon in. I have to finish doing her hair." He follows me into the alcove outside the bathroom door.

"Good morning, Rueben!" she says in her sweet voice.

"Morning, Ms. Williams. I brought you some Texas sunflowers."

"Oh, now, that was a nice thing to do. Look how pretty they are!"

Already she sounds better. I smile over her head at him, so grateful. "This won't take long. You can find a vase in the cupboard next to the sink."

He meets my eyes as I twist a lock of her hair around the curling iron, and there's an expression of breathlessness there that I don't get.

He holds my hand through church. I can see the old folks eyeing us with approval, can feel the waves of heat from some of the women. I am achingly proud to be seen with him. In church. This beautiful, strong, healthy, good man who is holding my hand. It makes me feel emotional, and I start daydreaming.

First I see us saying our vows, me in a white dress because it's for real this time. I see us sitting in these pews, year after year. We bring our babies with us and they go to the nursery. Oh, they would be such beautiful babies! We'd have monster-size babies, little girls who can stand up to anybody, sturdy boys.

I look up at him, and he's looking back at me. There's a soberness in his eyes, so sober that I think he might be thinking the same thing. Not hot sex. Long love. I can see my children in his eyes, our children. Babies that I've been wanting for so long, babies to love and take care of and continue the lines.

His hand tightens around mine.

Foolish fantasies, I think suddenly. I bend my head, away from his gaze. He tugs my hand and I look up. He mouths, *I love you.*

And I don't know what to do, except pick up his hand and kiss it.

Outside in the brutally cold sunshine, we're waiting for my grandmother to finish talking to one of her friends. I say, "You said you had a surprise for me."

"So I did." He gets a secret smile on his face. "I got you a fight."

My heart leaps so hard, it bangs on my ribs. "Oh, Rueben, really?"

"Yep. It's right here in town, three weeks. Think you're ready?"

"You know I do."

He clears his throat. "You're boxing Chantall."

I widen my eyes. "Ah!"

"That's the reason you got it. She's on the ticket and she wants you."

"Cool." I raise my eyebrows. "I can handle her."

"I know you can."

"Thank you, Rueben. It means a lot to me."

He nods.

42

Trudy

One of the pleasures of a university position is the long breaks, and the week after New Year's, I'm enjoying the process of a little winter cleaning and rearranging. I've divided the plants from the greenhouse into two groups, and have moved half of them into the house. Once a week, I'll trade them—putting the houseplants back in the greenhouse and vice versa.

I'm painting the kitchen on a Thursday afternoon when Rick calls. "Hi," I say into the receiver.

"Hi. I can't believe you answered the phone."

"Feeling chipper, I guess. How are you?"

"Not bad. How come you're chipper?"

"Because," I say, dipping the roller into the tray, "I am finally painting this kitchen."

"Hmmm. What is it? Turquoise? Red?"

I chuckle. "It's somewhere between butter and ocher."

"And that's what?"

"Kind of a warm, deep yellow."

"That sounds nice."

"It is."

"Well, um, I was just going to leave you a message, and this is a little harder to do in person, but um . . ."

I'm smiling in curiosity and put down the roller to listen. "What?"

"I was wondering if you, um, would want to go on a date with me. Out to dinner or something. Whatever you'd like."

"A date?"

"If you don't want to or whatever, it's okay, I understand."

I start laughing. "Okay, who is this and what did you do with Rick Marino?"

He laughs, too, a little shyly. Then he says, "So will you go out with me, Trudy?"

"I think I might enjoy that, Rick. When did you have in mind?"

"Well, as soon as possible. Tonight?"

"I don't know," I say. "A man who calls a woman at the last minute probably had some plans fall through. And a woman who says yes just looks desperate."

"Oh."

"Rick," I say, laughing again. "It's a joke. Tonight would be fine. What should I wear?"

"A jean skirt with nothing under it?"

"Ah, now there's the man I know."

"Worth a try. How about if we go over to the Pub and have some of their good ales and some supper, maybe listen to the open mike for a while?"

It's my favorite bar and he knows it. "That would be great, Rick. I'll look forward to it."

"I'll pick you up about seven."

"I'll be ready."

~

Annie says, suspiciously, when I come out wearing my wild red sweater and a jean skirt that comes to midthigh and my best knee-high boots,

"Where are you going? Out with Jade again? That skirt is too young for you."

I lean into the mirror in the living room to put on my lipstick. "I have good legs and my generation invented miniskirts, so we get to wear them as long as we want."

"Sorry. You're right." She inclines her head, comes over, and brushes my hair smooth. "You really are very pretty. It's nice to see you seeing that. You were just such a mom for so long."

I turn. "Was I? Have I changed?"

"Uh . . . duh!" She rolls her eyes. "You always had those dowdy skirts and put your hair up in a bun and never wore much makeup. I mean," she hastens to add, "not that you were ugly or anything. You just looked like a mom. It's better this way."

"Thank you."

The doorbell rings once and Annie is flying across the room to open it when Rick steps in the door. He's wearing a red corduroy shirt that makes his hair look black as wings, and his goatee is freshly trimmed, and there's a look of excitement or expectancy on his face that goes right through me. He sees me and lifts one eyebrow. "Jean skirt," he says.

"Mmm-hmmm." I meet his eyes wickedly.

He takes a breath, puts a hand on his heart. Then he looks at Annie. "Hey, kiddo. You don't mind if I steal your mom for the evening, do you?"

"You guys are going out?"

I drop my lipstick in my purse. "You don't mind, do you?"

"None of my business," she says, shaking her head. Then she pauses. "I have very weird parents."

Rick laughs. "How'd you think you got to be so weird?"

"Very funny." But she's smiling. "Don't be too late!"

Outside, he pauses to look back at the house. When it's clear there are no observers, he puts a hand up my skirt. I've worn a thong, so he gets the rush of a little bare flesh. He says in a raw voice, "Jesus, Trudy. How am I supposed to think?"

I smile. "You'd rather think?"

"Good point."

Settled into the bar, with its agreeable atmosphere of an old Irish pub, we order ales and shepherd's pie. I take a sip of my ale and sigh. "This is nice, Rick. Did you have something you wanted to talk about, or is this just for fun?"

"I wanted to see you," he says, and reaches across the table for my hands. "I miss you and I wanted to be with you. And," he rubs his thumbs over my knuckles, "it seemed to me that we have to start over in a way, don't we? See where it will go?"

"Okay, that's fair."

He bows his head, and I can tell by the way his mouth is working that it's hard to say the rest. "I don't want to spend the evening on the past, Trudy, but I'd like to tell you a couple of things, if that would be all right."

"Sure."

"I've been an asshole. I don't know why it all happened. I've been seeing a shrink, and she's pretty good. She thinks—well, it doesn't matter." He raises his eyes, that same beloved neon blue. "I was wondering if you'd come to counseling, too. I'll keep doing mine by myself, but maybe we can work on the other stuff together, figure out how and why and what."

I pull my hands away gently. "What I'd like to know, Rick, is where you are with Carolyn right now."

He looks surprised. "I broke up with her a couple weeks before Christmas. I thought you knew that."

I think of the phone calls, of my visit to her. "She was at your apartment on Christmas."

"Yeah." He winces. "It's been a little bit . . . uh . . ." He sighs. "She's pretty broken up. Kinda wacko."

"What a surprise," I say with a smile in my throat. "Joe's girls, right?" This is a reference to the kind of women Joe Zamora always mixed himself up with. There was always trouble at the end. Once, a tough girl from Mexico tried to shoot him.

He laughs, even as the color shows in his cheeks. "Look, I don't want to talk about her, not ever again, unless we do it in counseling. Can we do that?"

"I can try." I reach across the table, touch his beloved hand. "I'd really like to try."

"Good." He squeezes my fingers. And again, "Good."

After we eat, we carry our ales into the other room and grab a table, sitting side by side to listen to the music. It's oddly electric feeling his arm brush against mine, leaning in to tell him something, and seeing him admire something about me. His hand keeps straying to my bare thigh, pushing at the hem of the skirt the slightest bit. I keep pushing it away with a secret smile.

It's wildly erotic in some way I can't name, then he leans over and says, very quietly, "You know what I want to do to you?"

I laugh. It's an old game. One we invented to survive PTA meetings and boring recitals and long events we didn't particularly want to attend. "What?"

"I want to make your nipples hard so I can see them right now."

"How are you going to do that?"

His hand moves lightly on my knee, circles around the inner thigh. "When we get out of here, I'm going to push up that sweater and unfasten that bra and stare at your beautiful breasts without touching them until they're cold. Then," he says slowly, moving his hand a little higher, "I'm going to put my hot mouth right on there and flick my tongue over it."

"Hmmm," I say, and catch his hand creeping up my inner thigh. "Touching isn't fair."

"In real life, my hand is still, but in my imagination," he says, "it's moving very, very slowly up your leg and my fingers are touching your hot middle, and I'm pushing away those little bitty panties, while everyone around us thinks we're just talking, and I'm stroking you and teasing you until you are ready to explode." He laughs. "Ah, there we go." He sighs a little, meets my eyes. "I'm ready to go whenever you are."

"I think it's my turn."

"Your turn to make my nipples hard?"

"No, big man. Something else."

"Already there."

"Not like it's going to be." And I start to talk, in great graphic detail, about taking him into the boy's room and doing luscious things to his body.

So by the time we leave, we're both weak-kneed, and when we climb into the truck in the dark corner of the parking lot, I tug him over and start kissing him, straddling his body until he's groaning. And then we drive to his apartment and we're having sex within three seconds of shutting the door, most of our clothes still on, fiercely joined in the hottest sex we've had in a long time.

"God," he breathes at the end. "We always did have this part right, huh?"

"Stop talking," I say.

He laughs, wraps his hands in my hair, and we make love again.

The next morning, I sit down to read my email for the first time in a week and there is my airline ticket, propped against the computer. I need to get this taken care of, and it's bugging me that I haven't done it yet. In sudden decision, I grab it, put on my coat, and walk with purpose next door. Angel's orange car is in the driveway, and it gives me a pang to see it, a nostalgia that sweeps through me for that magical time.

"Trudee!" he says with surprise, and gestures me inside. "Come in."

"It'll only take a minute." I keep my coat tight around me, like armor. "I have this ticket to Seville and I'm not going to use it. It's too late to cancel, and I want you to have it. Go see your woman."

He holds up both hands, palms out. "No, I will not take it. It is for you."

"I can't go. Not right now. I need to work on my marriage. This is a pretty crucial time."

"Trudy," he says. Only my name. It sounds so sad.

I bow my head, fling away. Plop down on the couch, ticket still in my hand.

Softly, he says to me in Spanish, "Will you give up all you are for love?"

I reply, brokenly, in the same language, "But what is life without love?"

"A true love lets the lovers bloom." Swiftly, he moves and sits beside me, takes my hand. "You must go, Trudy. You must."

I can't even look at him. It's as if Angel himself has become Seville, that my desire for Spain has become embodied in him. If I look at his face, I'll hear flamenco. I'll see myself walking those ancient cobbled streets. On his mouth, I'll see the promise of green courtyards. It swells in me, the desire, something wicked and just out of reach. In his house, I smell the multitude of spices he uses. "I can't."

He makes a sound of annoyance, a tsk that is peculiarly Spanish. He stands up and tugs my hand. "Trudy," he says, a command. "Come." I follow him less out of a desire to see what he wants than out of inertia. He drags me across the room, into his bedroom. I halt, pulling back, suddenly afraid this is about sex. He doesn't let me stop, drags me around the corner, and takes my chin and lifts it up. "There you live, *mi embruja*." There is anger in his voice. "Look."

And there is one of the photographs he took of me, blown up to eleven by fourteen, or maybe even bigger. It is a high-quality print, cropped a little from the one I saw. I am lying in sleepy splendor across the green-and-purple serape, my hair scattered over my back and arms. One hand trails off the bed, and in my eyes is a smile, an invitation.

He stands behind me, his hands on my chin, and the only thing I can do is close my eyes to shut it out. I can't shut out his voice, so close to my ear, though. "Here is the woman you are, inside, the one who has been hiding. He loves her, too, your husband. Let her free, Trudy."

I am weeping, suddenly, my shoulders shaking. He puts his arms around my shoulders, kisses my hair. "She is beautiful," he says quietly. "Do not send her away. Not for any man."

Loss overwhelms me. Not loss of love or loss of my marriage. It is Lucille in my mind as I stand there in Angel's bedroom weeping, Lucille standing so brazenly in her yard on a summer day, strong and sturdy and as sexual as her poppies. I know, in that minute, that she is the reason Angel is here, that he's a messenger from her. In fierce gratitude, I kiss his hand. "Thank you," I whisper.

"No," he says softly. "Thank you. This picture, it will make me famous."

I start to laugh, cover my face. "I never thought I'd be a muse."

He lets me go, tugs a handful of tissues from a box by the bed, touches them to my tears. He suddenly seems the older, I the younger. An old soul with golden eyes. "You are so many things," he says seriously. "Fling open your heart and your arms and let it all live with you. He is a good man, your husband. He will love you if you are yourself."

I kiss his cheek. And go, my ticket still in my hand.

I've set the table with a batik cloth and candles and orchids. I've used the mismatched china and beautiful goblets, but I've cooked pork chops and mashed potatoes and gravy, which is one of his favorite meals. Annie is at work.

When Rick arrives, hair damp at the neck from a shower after work, I'm nervous. My hands feel too big. "Let me take your coat."

He gives me a puzzled look. "Everything okay?"

"Yeah. I just wanted to talk to you a little bit."

"Okay."

I bring out the dinner, serve our plates, get him a beer. He tells me about a customer at work, about a letter he got from Colin. Athena, hearing his voice, runs down the steps and trills at him. Idly, he strokes her back and he remembers aloud when we found her—a starving street cat, pregnant and with a BB in her side. The first cat he ever wanted to keep.

When we're finished eating, I get him another beer, pour myself some coffee. Take a breath. "I'm going to Spain next month."

His eyes darken. "With Ann-hell?"

"No. By myself. He's helped me arrange it, he has a lot of family there. But I'm going alone, in the middle of February for eleven days."

"I don't get any say in this?"

"No. I'm sorry."

He looks away, scowls. "We can't do it together, maybe next summer or something?"

"I thought about that, but I think I have to do it alone."

"Is this some kind of payback, Trudy? Tit for tat?"

I sigh. "No. Not even a little bit. It's just that while you've been away, I've had a lot of time to think about what I want and where I want my life to go. This is part of it. Travel, and studying Spanish."

For a long moment, he's silent, his hands working around each other. Then he looks at me. "Okay. I get it. I don't have to be happy about it, do I?"

"Well, if you're not, then it takes a lot of the joy out of it for me."

"Oh." He looks surprised, then breaks into a grin. "I see your point."

"It's not about men, or sex. It's about my mind, you know?"

He reaches for my hand, scoots his chair a little closer. "I do know," he says, and his voice is a little raw. "But you're so goddamned beautiful I know you'll have offers."

"Rick, I have never wanted another man. Not since the minute we met." I touch his thick black hair, going so silver in beautiful streaks. "I love you, only you."

His eyes are vulnerable. "Me, too, kid. Only you."

We kiss, and it's magical, like light bursting out of us. "Hold on," he says, and goes to his coat, takes something out of the pocket. "I know it's a little soon, but I wanted you to have this."

It's a jeweler's box, blue velvet. I look at him. "What's this?"

"Open it and see." He sits down and puts his hands on my knees.

My heart feels off-center, trembly, as I open the box. It's an engagement ring, something I never had before because we were too broke. It's a beautiful, table-cut diamond, medieval in spirit. "Oh, Rick, it's beautiful!"

"You don't have to say anything yet, but I wanted you to know where my heart is, Trudy. I want to renew our vows and be with you for the rest of my life. You're the only woman I've ever loved."

A part of me knows he wants me to say yes right now, and a part of me wants to do it—take the ring out and put it on my finger and be safe again. "I'm going to try it on, okay? I'm not going to wear it yet, but I do want to look at it."

He swallows. Nods.

"You have such beautiful hands," he says when I slide the ring on my finger. "I looked all over for the right one. Do you like it?"

"It's perfect." I take it off my finger, but before I put it in the box, I press a kiss to it.

He sighs with pleasure, puts his hand around the back of my neck, leans in to kiss me. "I love you," he says. "I've missed you every minute, this whole time."

"I know," I whisper. "Me, too."

"How long is Annie going to be gone?"

I smile. "Hours and hours."

"Good."

We go upstairs to my room, to the bed we've shared a thousand nights, and make love. It isn't wild sex. It isn't fancy. It's the joining of two people who know every inch of each other. It's very good, and I've learned to appreciate it. Afterward, we lie in each other's arms and talk.

He asks me about Seville and what I want to see there, listens quietly. He tells me that he's been thinking a lot about how much freer our lives will be when Annie goes to college next year, and that he's been looking at ways we could travel.

It's simple. It's quiet. It's good.

I click on the lamp by the bed when it's time for him to go, and lie there watching him get dressed. He flung his watch on the dresser as he always did, and reaches for it.

And I suddenly remember the photographs I tucked under the scarf, and in the instant before he sees them sticking out, a hundred possibilities run through my mind, how to stop it, how to change it, how to make it seem different.

Instead, I lie there as he sees them peeking out beneath the scarf, reaches for them. I see his long, smooth back, the curve of his arms, the fall of his tousled hair. My body is still.

"God," he says. Blinks as if to make them go away. "I guess Ann-hell is good for something besides tips on travel, huh?"

I know the emotion he's experiencing right now. I know it intimately. The burn of sexual jealousy, the acid of knowing you are not the only one. "Rick—"

"Don't, okay?" He puts the photographs down very carefully, slips his watch over his wrist.

I sit up in bed, blanket tucked around my nakedness. "I wanted to tell you before you saw them. They're art photos, Rick. He's an artist."

"Yeah, I bet."

And suddenly, I'm furious. "Don't you dare take that tone with me. Did you think I would pine away for you forever? Sit here in my lonely house and cry while you were out with another woman, getting laid whenever you felt like it?"

His jaw is hard. "No."

"I was devastated by what happened, Rick. Devastated that you betrayed me and our family. That you could be so cold-blooded about it! I was furious with myself for giving up so much to be with you, and thinking it was enough to keep you happy. Angel made me feel like somebody again."

"Yeah?" He's furious now, too, standing there shirtless, barefoot, wearing only his jeans. "Well, it goes both ways. God, you got so damned stuck-up when you went to that school in Boulder. Started talking to me like I had the brains of a maggot. You were always so much better than me, weren't you? Slumming with old Rick, passing time with me until you got to your real life."

I stare at him, feeling the truth of it through my whole body. "Rick, I . . ."

He meets my eyes. "From the first minute I laid eyes on you, I was in love, Trudy. That never changed for one second. I always knew I wasn't good enough for you, but I couldn't stop trying. I kept thinking, over and over, that maybe one of these days you'd really see me."

"Rick, that's not fair! I was a snobby girl, I know I was. But I loved you. I have always loved you. And I did give up a lot of my dreams, which I didn't regret until you pulled the rug out from under me."

"You think you're the only one who gave things up, Trud? You think there weren't days when I was working my ass off to make sure we had what we needed that I didn't wish I could still take my trips with Joe once in a while? Just go hang out and be on the road, the wind in our hair?"

I lower my eyes. "You're right."

"Shit." He sits down and tugs on his socks. "I don't know why I keep—"

"Rick, let's stop this, okay? You're upset about the photos and I understand. This is a stupid fight. I don't want to fight with you."

"It's not a stupid fight. It's real. I fucked up, I know I did, but the thing I keep asking myself is, why? I love you. Why go with another woman?"

"Are you going to blame it on me, Rick?"

"No." He shakes his head sadly. "It's not your fault."

I look at him, waiting. "Why?"

"Maybe I just wanted you to see me, Trudy." He sighs, picks up his shirt. "I'll talk to you later."

"Not even a kiss goodbye?"

"Not tonight."

When I hear the door slam downstairs, I fall back on the pillows and stare at the ceiling. Which came first, the chicken or the egg? Who got lost, who stopped seeing whom?

I don't have any answers. Not a single one.

43

Trudy

There's something stirring in me this January Monday. I have to go back to work Wednesday and I'm not looking forward to it. Not to mention I usually hate this month. If we're going to get below-zero temps, that's when they'll show up, and we've had some this year. They come in stretches of five or six days, when the air is so cold and dry, the grass crackles underfoot, and you don't dare take a deep breath. January is so bright, it burns my eyes.

This morning, a thick layer of agreeable clouds have raised the temperature, and there is a threat of snow in the pinkish light, and I find I'm in the mood for cooking. There's a Celtic program on NPR, and I turn it on loud in the living room so it will lilt all through the house. I've decided I need zucchini bread and have grated squash into a big, wet pile in a stainless steel bowl. It's my own recipe, adapted over the years into a food that is truly one of my favorites in the world—half white flour and half wheat flour, for nutrition and heft. As I stir the ingredients together, I think with a little shock that it's been years since I made it. I soak the raisins in vanilla and egg, a trick my mother taught me, and the walnuts are many sizes, for the pleasure of getting a big chunk once in a while—the zucchini with the skins still on, for that rich color. The music floats through the house, the Celtic drum and the delicate sopranos, and I think with pleasure of going to Denver to see *Lord of the Dance*, and how it had stirred my heart that day.

My wild Celtic heart.

The whatever it is keeps growing inside of me. It's a taste, a glimpse of something just out of the corner of my eye, and when the bread is in the oven, I think a quiche would be the perfect accompaniment, so I grate cheese, taking some pleasure in the fact that I have all my favorite kinds in the fridge—some havarti and hard Dubliner and fresh parmesan. They won't suit one another particularly in the quiche, so I stick with the hard Irish cheese and mix it with a leftover piece of ham steak in the freezer, and roll out the piecrust.

Sometimes the drum makes me tap my feet, and I think of the Celtic war drum I saw in a shop in Manitou Springs and wonder if I might love having something like that. It makes me feel silly, but why not? I know women who spend two hundred dollars on earrings without a blink. Jewels have never captured my attention, but a drum or a flute, something simple to learn to play—why not? I am allowed a hobby that does nothing but amuse me.

The lunch is going to be too good to eat alone, so I call Jade to see if she wants to come share it with me. She's going to the gym for her boxing lesson, but promises to come by after. Roberta is on a shopping trip to Colorado Springs. I call Shannelle, but she has found a babysitter for the afternoon and wants to work on her writing, which is wonderful. I think about going to get Angel, but things are too tense between me and Rick as it is. He's not called me since that night he found the photos, and I'm determined I will not call him.

But I don't want to cause any more trouble, either.

And for a moment, a little of the sheen goes off my pleasure. The cinnamon smell of the bread, and the mingling cheesy scent of the quiche fill the house, weave around the music, making the atmosphere rich and warm.

I suddenly think that it's all for me.

Me cooking for me. Giving myself what I want.

So I set the table with my favorite plate, the black and fuchsia, and brew a huge mug of spicy tea, and find my latest Oprah magazine, which came in the mail and I haven't read, and put out a napkin. The cats, drawn by the scents, arrange themselves in spots where they can be seen, in case I have an urge to share my leftovers.

Through it all, the sometimes melancholy, sometimes joyous music lilts through the cloudy day. I don't even need the magazine for company when it comes down to it. The view through the window, toward the fields and Angel's house, are enough to accompany my thoughts. I'm pondering an advanced natural healing class in Taos, one I saw on the web. Next summer, four weeks long.

Or I could go to Ireland. After Spain. That money, Lucille's gift.

When I'm finished with my delectable lunch, I realize that I have not baked a quiche in years, either. No muffins, no whole wheat bread kneaded with my own hands, no baked cheese casseroles or cheesecakes or—

God! How could that have happened?

In a sudden burst of energy, I throw open the greenhouse door and grab Brigid—how appropriate that it is she on the altar this cloudy, Celtic afternoon—and carry her into the living room. There is a small table by the door that ordinarily collects keys and odd mail, and I put Brigid down carefully on the floor, and sweep all the junk into a pile, return to the greenhouse, and bring out the altar cloth and materials.

And as if Brigid herself is approving, a pounding, celebrating piece comes on the radio, and in my own house, my belly warm with food, I begin to dance. Spin in circles, my hair flying around me, my feet tapping and leaping, my heart taking flight, and the emotion in my heart coalesces.

Joy.

The recognition brings a wild sense of freedom with it. I can't remember how long it's been since I felt this, felt myself all around me, my heart and soul inside of me, leaping as it did when I was a girl, once upon a time, a girl filled with dreams and hopes.

As the woman is now.

When I spin one last time, sweating and breathing hard, I nearly screech, because there is Lucille, dancing with me. She's wearing a white peasant blouse with full sleeves, and three silver bracelets on both tanned wrists, and she dances close, and takes my hand. I laugh and start to dance with her, the two of us alone in my living room. Her hand is not ghostly or cold. It's solid and warm, and I'd forgotten the suppleness of her fingers, and how the first joint of her first finger has a knot from an old injury. I laugh as she spins me around.

I smell her perfume, mixing with the cinnamon of my bread, and the taste of possibility, and think I must remember to grow some poppies, and—

"Mom!"

The mood shatters, and I whirl, feeling as guilty as if she'd caught me dancing naked. There is an ashen color around her mouth, and I'm about to tell her she doesn't need to be afraid of the ghost, that it's only Lucille, but Annie says, "Dad's been in an accident."

My hand flies to my throat. "What? What kind of accident? Is he hurt?"

"Carolyn called me. He was on his motorcycle. He lost control and ran off the road." She says it by rote, the words drained of color. "He's at Parkview, in the ER. She said she'll leave as soon as we get there."

"Annie," I say harshly. "How bad is it?"

She shakes her head. "Not dead, conscious, that's what she said. Not hurt too bad."

My body softens, warms after it was flash-frozen in terror that he might have died. "Okay." I grab my purse. "Let's go."

When we get to the ER waiting room, Carolyn stands up. She looks like the morning after. Her hair is ragged and too dry. Her jeans are a little grimy. She's not wearing a bra and the look is not flattering. I don't think she has a drop of makeup on.

"He's okay," she says in a hoarse voice. I can tell when we get up close that she's been crying hard. "His leg is broken, that's all." She pauses, looks at me. "The bike is totaled."

"Ah, damn. Poor Rick." But suddenly this doesn't make sense. "How did you avoid getting hurt?"

"I wasn't on the bike. I wasn't even there." She brushes a lock of hair out of her eyes and I see she's still wearing the earrings he gave her. "They, um, just called me as an emergency number. He had a card with my name. I'm sorry." She hikes her purse on her shoulder.

Annie rushes forward, eyes narrowed. "You fucked up my life, you slut."

"Annie!" I grab her arm.

She flings it off. "You want a man, try finding one that doesn't have a wife."

Carolyn's eyes are full of misery. "I'm sorry for any pain I caused you. I won't bother you anymore."

She heads toward the door, and I shove my daughter in a chair. "Don't move. I'll be right back."

And it's weird, I know it is, but this woman has lived in my head so much the past six months that she's almost a sister. I run after her. In the parking lot, she's taking out her keys with her long-fingernailed hands, and I see her wipe away a tear. "Carolyn!"

She turns, waits for me to catch up.

"I just wanted," I say, "to tell you I don't have any bad feelings toward you. I hope you find what you're looking for."

She swallows. "I was looking for Joe," she says. "He really loved me, you know, Joe did. I made him laugh. I didn't take all his bullshit. And I just missed him so much after he died, and so did Rick, and one thing just led to another."

Broken hearts, I think, and for the first time I see how Joe might really have loved this one. Her tough facade and soft insides. "I'm sure he did love you."

"Rick never did, you know."

"I know."

"I'm really sorry. It's been over for more than a month. It wasn't that great before, to tell you the truth."

"Thank you." I hold out my hand, but she just shakes her head. I let it go.

~

The leg is broken badly enough that he can't walk on it for six weeks. Crutches only. And although it makes me feel oddly trapped by circumstance, he really can't be alone for a couple of days, and we bring him back to the house. After Annie has gone to work, I wander into the television room, where I've settled him, and bring a new pain pill. "How are you?"

"Lousy. Thanks for coming to get me."

"No problem. How's the leg?" I smile, raise my wrist. "I've had recent experience, you know."

He manages a choppy laugh. "Then you know how it feels." He takes my hand, kisses the wrist. "I wish I'd been there to take care of you that night."

"Lucille visited me instead."

"Lucille?"

"Yeah. She was a ghost. Kept me company." I tuck the afghan around him more securely, kiss his forehead. "Maybe Joe will do the same for you."

~

I'm up and down through the night, worried about Rick, who does suffer quite a bit, unfortunately. So it's late when I finally get up. He's sleeping hard in the dark room, and I start some coffee, then go outside to get the newspaper.

Sitting by the door is a backpack. It's Angel's. I know from the times I've seen it on his shoulder. Battered, but strong. I pick it up and it smells of him. Pinned to the outside is a note in his continental handwriting: "Fly, my friend."

Inside are some notes. A page of contact information for Spain. "They know you are coming. You must not be shy."

There is also a photocopy of a letter in Spanish from a gallery in Barcelona. I can't make out every word, but I get the gist of it—they're accepting a showing of his work for the gallery. My heart jumps a little—and I'm glad the showing won't be in the United States, or in Seville before I go there. I think I can handle being a mysterious nude. Much more alarming to be one with a face people would recognize.

Finally, there is just a phone number. Maybe it's the next place he will be. I don't know, but I carefully tuck it into my Rolodex.

As I'm pouring my coffee, a knock comes at the front door, and I hurry to answer so Rick won't be disturbed. It's Shannelle and her two boys, everyone dressed and shiny. There's a wild look in her eyes. "Oh, I'm sorry," she says, seeing me in my robe. "I'll come back. I just didn't realize—"

"No, no, no. Come in. What is it?"

She starts to laugh, puts her hands over her mouth, blinks. "I just got a phone call," she says. "It was from an editor who read my ghost story." Tears fill her eyes, and she has to stop to blink.

I take her hands. "What?"

"I sold it, Trudy. They bought it. They liked it and they want to publish it, and—" Tears are streaming down her face, and she's laughing at the same time, and I start to laugh with her, grab her into a giant hug, and whoop, forgetting for a minute that Rick is asleep. "I can't believe it!"

"Oh, God, Shannelle! I'm so proud of you. Sit down, and tell me all about it. Every single word."

"I want to call Tony so much. I know he never really believed it would happen. He thought I was crazy." She sniffs. "I miss him, Trudy. So much."

I pick up the phone, hand it to her. "He needs to know."

"Is it okay if I tell him to come here?"

"Sure."

"I just want to see his face."

I grin. "I can understand that." To the boys, I say, "Want some breakfast?"

"We had breakfast a long time ago."

"Of course you did. I'm the only lazy one around here. C'mon, I'll get you a snack. Let's give your mom some privacy."

44

Shannelle

TO: naomiredding@rtsv.org

FROM: chanelpacheco@hotmail.com

SUBJECT: Tony

Dear Naomi,

I'm still as giddy as can be, can't believe it, am afraid I will wake up in the morning and find out I dreamed all this—the contract and the reunion. As long as I live, I will never forget this day.

Tony was the best part, though. I called him from my friend Trudy's house and he came over and we went out on the front porch. He looked tired, and almost weepy when he saw me, and he said, "Baby, I'm sorry, I don't—"

But I held up my hand. "Me first." And by then, I was smiling so much that I know there had to be sparks flying out of my eyes. I told him the story, that an editor had called, that she liked my book, and then I said, "And they're going to give me $5,000 for this book, and $5,000 for the next one, which means I don't have to work at the bowling alley, at least for a while."

He didn't get it. He said, "What do you mean?"

I said, "Someone bought my book, Tony. And they gave me a contract for two books, this one and another one, and they're going to send me money."

And it's so completely impossible to him that it could actually have happened, he says, "So you're going to have a book at, like, Kmart?"

I started to laugh. "Yes. Kmart and Walmart and Barnes and Noble. Next year, right about this time. With my name on it."

"Wow," he said, and then he did start to cry. And he hugged me and told me he was proud of me and that he would do whatever he could to make my life easier with the boys so I could do my work. Which are words I never, ever thought he would say.

Later, after he moved his things back from his mother's house (And, oh, my goodness, the whooping there was so much fun! I feel bruised from all the hugs!) we cuddled on the couch again after all these days apart, and I felt so perfectly fulfilled. My man and my children and my work and my house, all of it, all those corners have to be there for me to totally love my life. He said, "Just don't leave me behind, okay?" And I told him the truth, that without him believing in me, without his love, I would never have had the courage to try.

I'm running on and on. Thank you for listening. I'm going to float off to bed now. (Oh—my father said, "Guess you'll be one of those snotty bitches now, huh?" Typical.)

Love, Shannelle

~

TO: chanelpacheco@hotmail.com

FROM: naomiredding@rtsv.org

SUBJECT: savor it

dear shannelle,

although i gave you my most heartfelt scream over the phone, i am still thinking about you this evening, vibrating in my pleasure for you.

there is no other day in your life when you will feel just this way. mark it well, remember the date, and revisit it in your imagination every year. you have done what so many dream of and never accomplish—you have sold your first novel. you've leapt the river and forevermore, you will be a published writer.

Your life is going to change now, in ways you cannot imagine, and most of them will be for the better. don't let anyone take that sheen of accomplishment from you, shannelle, and there will be those who will try. they will tell you that your struggles are only beginning, that the life of a writer is not an easy one, that there will be things that happen to your books that will break your heart. cynics who thought to make the writing serve them, make them rich, or make them famous and were disappointed will tell you with a roll of their eyes that it's not all it's cracked up to be.

i'm writing to you tonight to tell you that not only is it everything you imagine, but it's more. It's not about riches, but the payment from publishers means you get to keep working on the thing you love.

you began the journey with your writing the day you first committed a story to paper, and your heart flamed with the joy and curiosity of it. it will continue now through your life, your constant companion, your joy, and your outlet. it will be a source of frustration and despair, but not because of things that happen outside, as often happens, but because you will sometimes need to go to the marrow of your bones for the truth of a story, and it is not easy.

i chose you as my student out of the hundreds who ask me—and you did not even ask—because i saw in you the fire, shannelle. not your talent, which is vast and mature for one so young. the fire i speak of is the passion and courage you have. the joy in the process. the willingness to serve the work.

you will have a million questions over the next few weeks and months. i am here to answer whatever i can, and if i don't know the answer, i'll see what i can find out. i hope we can still work together on the new work, the one you are resisting, but of course your editor will now have some say in what she'd like to see next from you.

welcome, my sister, to a new life. i am so proud of you.

love,
naomi

p.s. i am so glad tony finally came around. i've never doubted that he loved you.

45

Jade

The night of the fight, I'm as tense as a cat on a wire. Rueben's with me, trying to loosen me up, talk me up and down. There's been a change in the slate. I'm not boxing Chantall after all, but a woman by the name of Tiger O'Gara out of Denver. The decision was made by the promoters without much reason. Rueben is not happy—we had only two days' notice. He wanted me to give up the fight.

I dug in my heels. No way. For two solid days, between training, I've been looking up stats. Found clips of one fight in Omaha that put the fear of God in me, though I'm not telling Rueben that.

"Tiger," I say dismissively, pacing. "That's ego, calling yourself that."

"Come on," he says. "Let's go around and see who's here."

I love wrapping up in my robe, with my taped hands, to go out in the crowd. I feel a roll in my walk, feel them eyeing me. It feels good.

The neighborhood contingent are sitting together at one table. Trudy is there with Rick, which makes me a little suspicious—he broke his leg and can't live in his apartment, but he's getting around well enough to come out to a fight? Still, looking at him I remember why I always liked the two of them together. He has—has always had—that look in his eye for his wife that'll melt stone. Shannelle is there with Tony, who is holding her hand so tight, it seems like it would break her fingers. I stop. "Girl, I am so proud of you! I heard the news about your book."

Her glow is something to see. "Thank you." She holds out her hand. "You have to be Rueben. It's nice to meet you."

Tony stands up to shake my hand. "Have a good fight, you hear me?"

"Do my best."

Which leaves Mama and Grandmama. I don't see them right away, and I'm sick with nerves that they might have made good on not coming because they purely hate it that I'm boxing in the ring, where I could get killed. Then I see them, two older Black women dressed up and out of place, and I rush over and hug them. My stepfather is there, too, beaming at me. "Knew you had it in you, baby. I been bragging about you all over Denver."

"All right! Thank you."

I've forgotten that they haven't met Rueben until my mother nudges me. "Oh! I'm sorry!" I draw him forward. "This is Rueben Perry. My coach."

His deep voice and courtliness nearly put her in a swoon. "How do you do, ma'am."

I look back at her when we're walking away, and she gives me a big thumbs-up sign. I grin.

As we're crossing the room, I see my opponent. She's standing at the edge of the crowd, one foot propped up behind her against the wall. Her pictures don't do her justice. She's not quite my height, but not far off, solidly built. The hair is strawberry blonde, French-braided tightly away from a face dominated by very high, prominent cheekbones. A white girl. Big tits. Very good-looking.

Also not stupid. Her mouth twists and she shakes her head. Fuck, the expression says. Now I know why they changed the fight. So does she.

But while the promoters might have discounted anything but the babe factor in selecting the boxers, I see her straighten as she takes my measure. As I take hers. She has the lats of a swimmer, the biceps of a professional bodybuilder, and strong, square, powerful shoulders.

Like a tiger.

I know from the video clips that she's known for her power. Which is my strong point, too, but she won't know that looking at me. She'll think I have speed or dancing on my side, and I have a little of both.

A bolt of challenge rushes through me. "This'll be a good fight," I say to Rueben.

"You'll know you've been in the ring tomorrow."

"So will she," I promise.

It's still a long time till my fight and we pass the minutes walking up and down, trying to stay loose without getting tired. I watch part of the first fight, welterweights who are mediocre boxers at best. It means the fight goes on and on, with nothing of much interest happening. But I skip the second, discovering it's making me nervous to watch them. My whole body feels zingy, ready, pulsing with the wish to get out there, but my mind is worried sick she's gonna kick my ass and I'll look like an idiot. I wish I were boxing Chantall. I had a feeling for her in the ring.

I'm not going to watch the third one, either, but we start hearing the crowd go nuts in the first round, and I'm curious. It's a good fight. Well-trained boxers in top condition, both of them with some talent. They trade some good hits, and dance away, and I'm impressed. "He's good, the one in red."

Rueben nods, his arms crossed over his chest. "They both are."

In the fourth round, Sanchez, he's the one in red, goes down, but he gets back up and keeps fighting. He lands a flurry of cross-punches that leaves his opponent dazed, dances backward.

Sanchez goes down. The crowd murmurs, not sure what's going on.

"Damn," Rueben says beside me.

The boxer is still lying there, and my heart squeezes. His hands are flung to his sides in a loose way. "He's out cold."

"Yeah."

The medic leaps up there, and then there's a crowd gathered around the boxer. The other guy looks stunned, rubbing his face with his glove every so often. It seems preternaturally quiet, then a serious roaring starts in the crowd as everybody asks everybody else what's going on.

The downed boxer still has not moved, and now his family is rushing the ring, trying to find out what's going on. A stretcher is brought, and an announcement is made. I see one paramedic lift his head to the other, and there's a grimness to his face that makes me feel sick. "Rueben, is he dead?"

"I don't know." He nudges my arm. "Let's go. You don't need to be watching all this."

In the back, he settles me on the table and rubs my shoulders hard. "You okay?"

"Yeah." But I'm scared. I really am. I knew, intellectually, that people could get killed boxing. My stomach heaves and I break away from Rueben to rush for the toilet, where I throw up mostly nothing. I ate early today, but will save the big meal for after. Too nervous.

"Jade," Rueben says behind me. "You don't have to fight. I can call it right now."

I rinse my mouth, spit. "I'm fighting, Rueben. You see how they set this up, two pretty girls, but she's a real fighter and so am I. It'll be a good match, and I'm not giving that up."

"You're a thousand things more than a boxer, Jade."

"I know that." I narrow my eyes. "That shook you, didn't it?"

"I've seen it before," he says, his jaw hard. "But it made me think. You're both powerful fighters. It might not be you. It might be her. What then?"

"Some coach you are!" I back off. "You're supposed to be pumping me up, not bringing me down."

"I should have quit coaching you a month ago. I knew it then, but I wanted to see it through."

"Then see it through. Stop being my lover tonight and be my coach."

For a long minute, we square off. Both of us have our hands on our hips, scowls on our brows.

"Jade," he says gruffly.

"What?"

He purses his lips, narrows his eyes. "I'm with you, baby."

I heave a sigh of relief. "It matters to me, Rueben."

"I know." It's time to get ready, and he starts checking my taped hands.

"Rueben," I say then, realizing I want it out there before I go to maybe get knocked senseless or dead. "I love you."

He smooths some tape with the pad of his thumb. Smiles. "I know." He gestures for my other hand. "I'm gonna marry you, you know."

I smile at him. "Oh, really?"

"Give you twenty babies and go to church every Sunday. Think you could do that?"

"Do we get to have sex every night?"

Those big sleepy eyes blink. "Every morning, too, if you want."

"How about three babies?"

"Three's good." He picks up my glove. "I knew you were my wife the minute you walked in that gym."

"It's weird to be having this conversation without even touching, but you know I can't waste that energy."

He grins. "I'm doing it this way on purpose."

"Surely we can have sex if we're engaged."

"Nope."

"Wedding night?" I say in some despair.

"That's right." He ties my glove. "Better be soon, huh?"

A knock comes at the door. "Five minutes."

I look at him, touch my glove to my diaphragm. "Whoo. I'm scared and thrilled and nervous and pumped. Is that normal?"

"Yeah." He smacks my butt. "Let's go kick some ass, girl."

It feels unreal, walking out there when they announce my name. Out into the brightly lit room, toward the ring. I'm wearing yellow trunks. She's in red. I climb into the ring and see all those people looking up at us. I want to faint.

What if I lose?

Then I look across the ring to my opponent. To another woman who wants to be strong. I see her muscles, the lift of her chin. I feel my gaze level, feel the power in my shoulders. Shifting my head, I feel the bareness of it.

I think of Dante, how proud he would be of me right now. I think of how my anger led me here, to a strong and mighty place, and I'm glad he was in my life. I'm also glad he's out.

The bell rings.

I dance forward.

46

Trudy

My heart stops when the bell rings for Jade's fight. Without realizing it, I grab Rick's hand and hold my breath for the first few seconds. "Look at her," I breathe.

"I'm looking, I'm looking," Rick says with a chuckle, then sits straight up as Jade throws a punch, and her opponent, Tiger, counters. "Whoa."

I can't breathe the whole time. My heart is in my throat, out of both fear and admiration. By the end of the first round, the crowd is on its feet, cheering wildly. Both fighters go to their corners, breathing hard, and I hear the murmurs around me.

Damn, this is gonna be the best fight of the night.

Shee! You see that Black girl hit?

What about the other one?

And my favorite: *Either one of them could fight a man, I bet.*

Round two gets a little darker. Jade takes a hit to her left eye, the same one that got hurt at the gym, and I see her stagger, but she counters and Tiger jumps back. There's blood on Jade's face and I put my hand to my eye, wondering if I could do that. Take a punch like that.

Near the end of the second round, there's an instant when I see something come over Jade. Suddenly, she shimmers through a cloak of stillness. The other woman sees it, too, and brings up her gloves, narrows her eyes. She keeps her distance for a moment, but Jade advances, throws a series of little punches that mostly miss, then when Tiger is off-center, she swings her right hand up—I almost see it in slow motion—and it hits the other woman right at the corner of her jaw.

"Holy shit!" Rick says, and he whoops.

Tiger drops to the ropes, clinging, and I'm holding my breath. It's scary because of what happened earlier, with the other boxer, and I don't want Jade to—

The crowd roars as Tiger shoves herself up, throws her arms around Jade for a second; then the referee is breaking them up. The bell rings.

Shannelle says, "Oh, my God!" She holds out her arm. "I have goose bumps. This is so exciting!"

"Me, too!"

I look toward Roberta, who is sitting with her daughter, and I nudge Rick. "Look at her!" I say, laughing.

Because mild-mannered, sweet-voiced Roberta, in her black dress and neat stockings, is on her feet, hollering along with the rest of the crowd. When the bell dings again for the third round, she throws a fist in the air and yells something. Probably like, *Go, baby!*

Rick laughs.

But the rounds follow each other excruciatingly. The women are well matched and fierce. They swing and hit and rally, duck and roll and connect and embrace. This minute, that one's down. The next, it's the other. It's six rounds long, and by the end of the fifth, I'm not sure I can stand another minute. Rueben's talking hard to Jade, who is covered with sweat dripping from every pore in her body. Her shirt is soaked. Her eye is swollen, but not closed, which I gather is the way they decide whether to call the fight. She's nodding at Rueben, listening intently, wipes sweat off her face. He pours water on her head, wipes it down, talking, talking, talking.

Across the ring, I see the other woman spit blood into a bucket, see them squirt water into her mouth, and she spits out more blood. She has a black mark along one side of her face, and her lip is split, but she's scowling fiercely at the obvious pleadings of her coach. When the bell dings, she stands up, shakes out her arms.

And what I notice is that the crowd is absolutely enthralled. Not by their beauty. By their heart, their strength, their power. It feels like the round lasts ten thousand years, and it has to feel like twenty thousand to the two of them, but they're still throwing punches. The crowd is whooping and yelling and pounding their feet.

At the very end, the bell dings. And I don't know if everybody sees it, but I know Jade. She stands still, holds out her glove. The woman across taps it. They go to their corners.

It's a split decision. A draw. And the crowd is thrilled.

~

Rick is truly exhausted by the fight. He needs help getting back up the porch steps, leaning on me hard, and his face is gray with pain. I get him settled on the couch and get some pain pills. "Are you okay?"

He does a man toss with his head. "I'll be all right. It's only been a couple of days."

"My arm didn't hurt after the first day or two. It's worrying me that this is still obviously excruciating."

"Excruciating." He gives a dull nod. "Yeah, that's a good word."

I sit down next to him. "Maybe I should call the doctor."

"Nah. He told me it might be pretty bad for a couple of weeks, even."

"You didn't tell me that!"

"You can't make it stop, can you?" he says with a shrug. "I'll get out of your way tomorrow. You don't have to keep putting me up."

I meet his eyes. "It's too soon for us to live together, Rick. I think it would hurt us in the long run."

It's not the answer he wanted. He lowers his lids. "You're probably right."

I take his hand. "There's a lot to work out, my love."

"I know." He tightens his fingers around mine. "I just . . ." He sighs, meets my eyes. "I guess I'm a little depressed tonight. It's sinking in that I lost my bike. I rode that baby for more than thirty years."

"I know. I'm so sorry." I rub his hand with my free one. "Maybe it's not as bad as it sounds."

"No, I saw it." He shakes his head. "Don't worry about it. I'll take my little happy pills and go to sleep and it'll all look better tomorrow."

"Maybe," I say, "what you really need is a good cry."

"Or a big bottle of whiskey."

I remember the night I bought the bottle of wine to mourn our marriage after Edgar's funeral. I lift my eyebrow. "Or both."

"Maybe." He falls back on the couch. "For now, I'm going to sleep."

"Call me if you need me."

≈

Somewhere in the middle of the night, I get up to check on him. He's fallen asleep with the television on, and the light drifts over his face, flickering on his white forehead. The mask of pain has fallen away. I tiptoe in and pick up the remote to turn off the television. His voice, rough with sleep, stops me. "Leave it on, if you don't mind. Keeps me company."

"Of course I don't mind." I put the remote down and come around the coffee table to kneel by the couch, touch his face. "How you doing?"

"All right." He moves his hips sideways, groans a little, pats the space he's cleared. "Sit with me?"

The smell of him is rich in the air, the mingled scents of his skin and hair, a fragrance so heady that it's always made me dizzy. I breathe it in as I settle next to him, put my hand on his arm. "Is there anything I can get for you?"

He shakes his head, picks up my left hand, the one I broke, presses a kiss to it. "That was the worst day of my life."

344

"Mine, too," I say quietly.

"I've been doing a lot of thinking since the other night, Miss Gertrude."

I brush my fingers over his face, touch the new lines at the corners of his eyes. "Yeah? About what?"

He clears his throat. "I don't know what it'll take to put this all behind us, Trudy, I really don't. The counselor says it's hard to tell who'll get through an infidelity and who won't, but it's gonna take a lot of work from both of us."

"I guess I can see that's true." A question boils up from my heart, the one that's been burning me from the first discovery. "I wish I could . . ."

"What?"

"I was going to say understand why, but I think I've worked that out." In the soft dark, with the quiet of our home all around us, I feel free, and put my palm against his beloved cheek. "I think we both just got lost in the losses. Your mother, and then the boys were leaving home, and then Joe died."

His fingers curl in mine, warm and tender. "It was a lot."

"It all made me start looking at my life, Rick. At all of it—what choices I made, what I wanted. I don't want to be a secretary. I want to teach and study and travel."

"Yeah." His free hand takes a tendril of my hair. "That's what scared me. It seemed like maybe you were regretting . . ." A shrug. "Marrying me, I guess."

"No." My heart is aching. "Never that. I regretted not being brave enough to follow through on the rest of it. I could have taken my master's at UCCS in the Springs. I didn't."

"You gave a lot to these kids, though, Trudy. You didn't have time."

I nod. "I know."

"I started thinking, especially after Joe died like that, that I was nothing but an old five-and-dimer." He smiles in the dark. "From the song?"

It's a Waylon Jennings song about a man who only aspires to be a friendly old drunk. "You've always been so much more than that."

In the soft blue light, he stares up at me, touches my face. His eyes are suspiciously bright. "God, Trudy, I've missed you so bad. Every day. All night, every night. I just didn't know how to make it right again. How I could even ask you, after all you did give up, to forgive me."

"All you ever had to do was ask, Rick. That's all I was waiting for."

Now there is no doubt there are tears in his eyes. One falls from the corner of his left eye, and I bend down, catch the silver and salt against my lips. He pulls me hard against him, into his chest, his arms around me so tight, I can barely take a breath. "I am so fucking sorry, Trudy. I don't know how to make it right, make you believe that there is no other woman in my world but you, but I hope you'll let me try. I hope you can forgive me someday."

"I forgive you now, my love." I breathe it into his neck. "I'm not saying we don't have things to talk out, but I know why, and it's okay."

We're weeping together, kissing, hugging. "Is this all going to go away in the morning?" he asks.

"Not for me. Will it for you?"

"No way."

I sit up again. "Rick, this wasn't all your fault, either. I was pulling away from you. I was feeling distance and loss and I didn't know how to get back to you. I wasn't a very good wife to you for a while there, and maybe it was the time you most needed for me to be one."

"No, Trudy—"

Putting my hands on his mouth, I say, "I'm trying to say I'm sorry, too."

He nods. "Thank you."

I am bone-weary and fall on his chest again. "Do you need anything? Water, painkillers, anything?"

"No," he says, stroking my hair. "Just this."

We lie there, and he says, "Those pictures he took are beautiful, Trudy. They really are. Don't take this wrong—you're a gorgeous woman—but he made something more out of them."

"Do you really feel that way?"

"God, I was pissed at first, and I can't say I'll ever want to look at them every day, but I couldn't stop thinking about the one. It just hit me in the gut, kind of hung there for two days. That's art."

I nod. "Good." We can talk about the fact of that art going out into the world some other time. Maybe in counseling, I think with a smile.

I lie against his chest, dizzy with love and connection and relief. "I love you, Rick Marino."

He presses his lips against my hair. "You can't help it."

FEBRUARY

Ishtar

Ishtar represents the fullness of womanhood and dares us to dream. Her power is strongest at the full moon, when the essence of womanhood heightens in response to the moon energy that is all-encompassing.

Ishtar's energy represents love, fertility, passion, and sexuality.

She is descended from the goddess of romance, Venus, and her energy encompasses all that is "woman"—nurturing mother, inspired companion, playful bed partner, wise advisor, insightful leader. She is revered especially on days of the full moon, when it is right to engage in joyful acts of love-making to celebrate being "woman."

—www.goddess.com.au

47

Roberta

February 7, 20—

Dear Harriet,

I'm ashamed of myself that I didn't write for so long that you had to waste good money on long distance, and then I wasn't even here to take the call! So, I'm sitting down right this minute, before things get all crazy again, to write you a good letter and let you know you don't have to be fretting about me no more.

Sister, we're about to have a wedding around here!! Valentine's Day, which has taken some doing, I'll tell you what. Jade is so excited, I can't hardly get her to do much of anything, so it falls to me and her mama, and both of us are so happy she's found herself the right man now that we sure don't mind. I'm having a ball, to tell you the truth. Been so long since there was a real wedding, with flowers and food and in the church where it means something, I'm having the time of my life.

It's happened a little bit fast, but Harriet, you know how it was when you met your Elmus, and when I met my Edgar. You just know, don't you? He is a very good man, and he's got that look in his eye like he's just died and gone to heaven when he looks at my granddaughter, which is enough for me. He's a clean-living man, and he'll be a fine father. It gives a body faith in the world again to see a wedding like this.

And faith in them, too. They're trying to work out details for a program for girls—underprivileged girls, mainly, I guess—to get strong. They both have all that social services background, so they're working out the red tape, and both of them are such athletes, I'm sure they'll help a lot of young women. Rueben told me there's a lot in place for troubled boys, trying to save them, but not much for girls.

Listen to me! Ha! I guess you can tell I'm proud of my grandbaby, can't you? Just bragging away!

I've also been watching some children, and it's funny how it brings back the laughter in you, just being with little ones. I always have loved them. And did I tell you about the young woman across the street? She's a writer, Harriet, and she sold a book to a big-time New York publisher! Isn't that something? I never thought I'd know a writer! Ha!

Hoping you can come and visit sometime soon, or maybe I'll rouse these old bones and come down and see y'all sometime in the spring. It could be an adventure, I reckon.

Love,

Berta

48

Trudy

It is a smoky purple dusk. The air is as soft as feathers on my face. It smells of orange blossoms and jasmine, flowers that tumble in profusion from baskets and pots and balconies, their pale colors ghostly against the deep reds and golds of evening brick.

Beneath my feet are ancient stones, worn smooth by unimaginable numbers of feet, and now mine are among them. My own feet, alone, carrying me down this narrow street in Seville. Above me is the sound of supper being cooked, and I smell the exotic spices, cinnamon and something darker. There is no wind.

All around me—in the soft conversation of two youths just ahead, and in the shopkeepers calling out to one another, and in the music of a broken ballad being sung by a woman sweeping her step—is Spanish. I pause for a moment, swept with wonder and a fierce joy, and I close my eyes to listen to it lilting and flowering all around me, seeping into my soul.

"Nothing like it, is there?" says Lucille. "Stepping out by yourself?"

Nothing. All I have brought with me is the backpack Angel gave me. Inside are three pairs of underwear and my camera and spare socks and the first edition of Lorca's poems.

This, right now, this evening in Spain, walking on my own feet, by myself, is all I have ever wanted. Life showed me there were other riches—children and a husband and a greenhouse—and I'm grateful. But without this cornerstone, too, my life was unbalanced.

I look at Lucille, but she's gone.

The lane onto which I turn is narrow. Light, golden from the last rays of the setting sun, pours through it like a river of magic, and I tug a slip of paper from my pocket. Angel's mother, a glorious redhead with flashing eyes, has written an address on it. Together, we had come up with a plan, and I am here to begin the first steps.

The door I've been looking for is set into an ancient Moorish building, shaped in an arch. A young woman with hair the color of butter and a face as smooth as the moon opens the door. There are shadows of sorrow and longing around her eyes, and I smile at her gently. "Juliana?"

She spies the pack over my shoulder and her nostrils flare in annoyance. I hold out my left hand, where I am wearing only a plain gold band, the diamond Rick gave me hidden beneath my shirt. "I have come," I say, "to speak with you about a young man."

"Angel?" she breathes with hope.

I smile. "*Sí*. He loves you very much, you know."

She begins to weep. "I have broken it."

Now I am the elder, the wise woman. "Nothing is ever broken completely as long as there is love. May I come in?"

Juliana gestures me inside.

ACKNOWLEDGMENTS

Every book has its midwives. For this book, they include Sharon Lynn High Williams, for twenty years of solid friendship that's seen us both through the darkest and brightest times; her mother, Roberta, who was an inspiration in life and death; Katherine Gomez, wise woman and healer; and Jenny Crusie for support and cheer and the best weekend in a long time.

I would also like to acknowledge Anita Ryan, who has a beautiful website devoted to goddesses; and the Women Boxing Archive Network, www.womenboxing.com. Thanks!

ABOUT THE AUTHOR

Photo © 2009 Blue Fox Photography

Barbara O'Neal is the *Washington Post, Wall Street Journal, USA Today,* and Amazon Charts bestselling author of more than a dozen novels of women's fiction, including the #1 Amazon Charts bestseller *When We Believed in Mermaids* as well as *The Starfish Sisters, This Place of Wonder, The Lost Girls of Devon, Write My Name Across the Sky,* and *The Art of Inheriting Secrets.* Her award-winning books have been published in over two dozen countries. She lives on the Oregon coast with her husband, a British endurance athlete who vows he'll never lose his accent. For more information, visit barbaraoneal.com.